Biblioasis International Translation Series
General Editor: Stephen Henighan

Since 2007, the Biblioasis International Translation Series has been publishing exciting literature from Europe, Latin America, Africa and the minority languages of Canada. Committed to the idea that translations must come from the margins of linguistic cultures as well as from the power centres, the Biblioasis International Translation Series is dedicated to publishing world literature in English in Canada. The editors believe that translation is the lifeblood of literature, that a language that is not in touch with other linguistic traditions loses its creative vitality, and that the worldwide spread of English makes literary translation more urgent now than ever before.

BLACK BREAD

EMILI TEIXIDOR

BLACK BREAD

TRANSLATED FROM THE CATALAN BY
PETER BUSH

BIBLIOASIS
WINDSOR, ONTARIO

Originally published as *Pa Negre*, Columna Edicions, Barcelona, Catalonia, Spain, 2003. This translation incorporates revisions made by the author for the Spanish translation, *Pan negro*, published by Seix Barral, Barcelona, 2004.

FIRST EDITION

Library and Archives Canada Cataloguing in Publication

Teixidor, Emili
[Pa negre. English]
    Black bread / Emili Teixidor ; translated from the Catalan by Peter Bush.

(Biblioasis international translation series)
Translation of: Pa negre.

Issued in print and electronic formats.

ISBN 978-1-77196-090-8 (paperback).--ISBN 978-1-77196-091-5 (ebook)

    I. Bush, Peter R., 1946-, translator II. Title. III. Title: Pa negre.
English. IV. Series: Biblioasis international translation series.

PC3942.3.E35P3213 2016   849'.9354   C2016-901176-3
                                               C2016-901177-1

Biblioasis acknowledges funding from Institut Ramon Llull and the Ministerio de Educación, Cultura y Deporte of Spain.

Edited by Stephen Henighan
Copy-edited by Cat London
Cover designed by Zoe Norvell
Typeset by Chris Andrechek

PRINTED AND BOUND IN CANADA

For Pep and Marina.

For Joan Rosaura and Anna M. Camprubí, friends.

"The deceit of History is the deceit Reality introduces.

There are endless vagaries that slip through the fissures in Reality. When people write History, they do so by fixing boundaries around names, even dates, thus attempting to squeeze what brims with infinity into a real, finite form. A time comes when you recall an event from your own world and don't feel happy with the explanation, with the way Reality has been categorized and quantified. You feel that wasn't true; it aspired to the truth, but didn't make it."

—Agustín García Calvo

"It would be hypocritical to look back to the years 1940–1945, and say they were terrible times. I think we are still fully within that era."

—W.G. Sebald

1

From Easter to early autumn, when the weather was fine and the woods changed colour, we lived on the branches of trees.

We climbed all the trees in the fruit orchard strong enough to take the three of us and low enough to shimmy up without a ladder, and once we'd tested them out we decided on the old plum tree as our permanent base. The old plum tree's branches were dark and welcoming like the bottom of a cauldron and the fork of its broad trunk with its three branches allowed us to lean back in comfort and divide the space fairly: one apiece.

The tree fork was the place where we met. The branches, on the other hand, were private territory, where we hoarded the things we wanted, and we treated the smaller branches as we felt fit, hung ribbons or paper from the leaves, picked plums to eat, which we weren't duty-bound to share with our cousins, and we didn't even have to reply to questions that shot out from neighbouring branches, as if we lived in a sealed chamber with walls of leaves that kept words out.

The other trees, next to the old plum, were mostly apples, with a few pears, and young plums or sloes with branches too slender to bear our movements, dwarf trees, as Grandmother called them, with thick foliage and stunted. Past the orchard were a couple of half-worm-eaten elms and the cherry tree by the bend in the track, the grove of oaks in the meadow, level with the spinney, and the huge elder tree at the back of the farmhouse that was so tall we'd never been able to count all the branches that spread out to infinity like a net cast over the roof. The elder tree was Grandmother Mercè's favourite because apparently the flowers had medicinal properties, and whenever we could, we left the back windows open to allow the scent from the flowers to waft in—Grandmother called it "fragrance"—and the mere smell drove away all sickness, what she called "sickerliness," and also tribulations when she imitated Father Tafalla's words.

Only the old plum tree's branches were long and strong enough to accommodate us. A natural house made of rough, dark, age-old timber as if from a log cabin in the middle of the woods or a sooty kitchen wall.

The apple trees were undersize and when the apples ripened, all their tops ballooned over, like bellies of pregnant women. And when they blossomed, the scent was too strong and sickly sweet and the blossom too white and dense. The pears were much the same. I was disgusted or frightened by the elms; their trunks were too old, scabby and perforated, as if they were rotten, and their branches were too small for their size, like the village blacksmith and the brawny men with big chests and small heads who took him their horses to shoe. The cherry was more welcoming, but its foliage was too thick and its branches too fragile for our aerial games, and the cherries stained clothes, hands and legs and that would give us away. Besides, its location, by the track that ran to the farmhouse on the side of the kitchen and meadow and then to Mother's town, the factory town, made them all too visible to adult eyes. The oaks were too far from the house, even though they could have coped with our onslaught. And the elder, Grandmother's tree, was beyond reach, a life-restoring medicinal wonder we thought was sacred.

The old plum tree was the ideal haven. Right opposite the farmhouse, sufficiently far away for us to hide yet visible enough to make it hard for anyone to accuse us of shirking, and its dense foliage spread out to make a kind of curtain that allowed us to see without being seen when we were up above, almost on a level with the house's front gallery.

We kept an eye on everything from up there: the entrance, the galleries, the stables... On the left, we could see the meadow and oak trees by the track with the cherry tree that went to Can Tona and other neighbouring farms and through the spinney to Mother's town, and a second broader track that went right round the house, past the well, animal troughs and lumps of rock salt, and on the right, surrounded by a barbed-wire fence, we could see the stables, chicken coop, pigsties and threshing-ground with haystacks, stooks and barns—Grandmother said city people couldn't tell a stack from a stook; such a slip was enough for her to tell whether someone was a countryman or what she called a flat-footed city slicker—the pond at the top of the hillock made by the dip in the land and the small hazelnut spinney that skirted the stone wall round the monastery orchard. The second track re-emerged on the other side of the farmhouse to become the track to the school and neighbouring town—the other factory town was much bigger, Father Tafalla sometimes called it a village, but Grandmother never adopted that word, perhaps because it wounded her local pride—level with the huge forest that filled the whole distant landscape except on the side of the main road to Vic, with its double row of plane trees, arable land and the dark mass of the Saint Camillus of Llellis monastery, a place for sick young men who had been abandoned.

We'd stretch out along the branches at the top of the plum tree and spread our hands or arms over the smaller branches, Quirze on the highest, me in the middle, and Núria, tiny goldilocks, just under me, her head and back facing away from the farmhouse, while we boys had the house full in our sights and didn't have to move our heads one inch to get a full view: visitors coming along the track, women in the top gallery mending clothes or separating the kernels of sweetcorn, men in the stables, animals penned in the threshing-ground or dipping their snouts in the pond, the dogs on the gravel in the entranceway, and the horses tied up to metal rings in the corner.

Núria always complained she couldn't see a thing. We called her Cry-Baby.

"What's going on? What's going on? What can you see?" she asked when Quirze and I commented knowingly on what we'd spotted from our vantage points.

"We can't see a thing," Quirze retorted, not even bothering to look at her, as if he was speaking to himself. "At this time of day when people are having a siesta, nobody's here, there's nothing to see."

Cry-Baby started to whimper it wasn't right, you couldn't see what was happening from her branch. But we paid no attention, and acted as if we couldn't hear her. When she stopped, distracted by a small animal or to straighten messy fair hair that she never plaited properly, as if relenting, Quirze added, still acting as if he was talking to himself, but loud enough for us all to hear, in a tone that aped Grandmother's voice and expressions when she told us horror stories, her scary ones, we'd call them: "This hour is like the depths of the night, when the only sound is what the shadows in the woods make. When a wind blows, a miserable night owl hoots ominously, the cries of the dying echo, the monastery bells toll, fearful whether the friars will arrive in time to give confession and the last rites, and the lamentations of the deceased who died in mortal sin…"

Cry-Baby covered her ears and implored him: "Shush!"

Just as she did when Grandmother came to the exciting moment we'd all been waiting for, when the executioner's axe was poised to cut through the delicate ivory-white skin of the princess's neck, or the thief drew his sharp knife from his belt and demanded the heart of the youngest, prettiest maiden.

And Quirze and I burst out laughing.

2

It was different in winter.

Life in winter was lived around the fireside, in the downstairs kitchen we all called more sparingly kitchen, and only very occasionally downstairs kitchen or winter kitchen. The upstairs kitchen, on the first floor, was the summer kitchen or the masters', next to a small dining room which looked over the first gallery, with two corner cupboards full of glasses and crockery and walls decorated with hand-painted, gilt-edged plates, high-class china, people said, that hung off wire hooks. The upstairs kitchen had another door that led to a lumber room and pantry, a dark, windowless place, with a door to the large sitting room.

Nobody could tell us why a farm-tenants' house had such a wonderful display of china in the upstairs dining room. One day, Grandmother Mercè told us they were the remnants of the life of luxury led years ago by the owners, Mr. and Mrs. Manubens, when they set up in the top of the building, and their hands and tenants struggled to survive downstairs bundled together with the animals and the fug from the stables. So we had to take care never to touch any of the plates or run our fingers over their golden edges, because any day now the masters might reclaim their property and take those jewels off to one of the houses they owned in Vic, where they lived now, or to their much newer houses in other areas, like the one in Igualada, or even the flat in Barcelona, or wherever, in a word, those people weren't short of a house or two! However, the masters must have forgotten those plates, or perhaps they weren't as valuable as people said, because when they did pay the odd visit to take their cut from the harvest and the livestock, they never remembered to reclaim them, and we never heard them mentioned once.

The downstairs kitchen was also the dining room where a long table rested against the back of a bench—that Father Tafalla and Grandmother dubbed the pew that looked onto the big fireplace. That way nobody's back felt the flames or heat. Another smaller bench against the back wall was set at right angles to the longer bench, Grandmother's pew, and a lot of small chairs with cushions to hide the worn seats, on the other side of the hearth.

"That fire is half our life," Grandfather Hand would say on the few occasions he came into the kitchen to warm up. We rarely saw him, he spent almost half the year in the mountains and woods, from the Virgin of the Rosary's Day to All Saints' Day, and when he did return he stayed with his flocks that grazed on the lower slopes and spent the harshest days of winter in the woods, deep in Les Guilleries; he rarely brought his flock to the pen on the farm, it couldn't take that amount of sheep, he'd say. He brought them to shear, when it was clipping time, as he called it, before it got really hot, and to stamp or brand them with hot black pitch: an M on one flank and sometimes an incision in the right ear and a circle on the left, the symbol of the Manubens' ownership. After singing the fire's praises, Grandfather Hand followed up with a racy remark: "Fire in front and fire behind, for a life time, and much besides!"

Grandmother shook her head disapprovingly and groused: "Why do you carry that cloth pouch over your shoulder the whole damned day, that you keep hold of even when you're asleep? I bet it's full of tobacco and rubbish. It's about time you threw it on the fire and made a clean start."

Grandfather always carried a huge bag which he called his "baggy," slung round his neck and he never allowed us see what it contained. It was a hide pouch, like a hunter's but bigger, filthier and more worn, and he never let go of it.

"What the hell do you think I carry in it? It's got my grub, or do you think there are bakeries selling bread in the mountains?"

If Grandmother scowled, he'd add: "If you'd rather, I'll say I'm carrying the rosary and saints Father Tafalla, from Saint Camillus, gave me, so me and my flock don't meet a bad end, so now you know."

Whenever the name of Father Tafalla, the Superior in the Saint Camillus monastery, cropped up, Grandmother kept a respectful silence and left her husband, Grandfather Hand, in peace.

The winter kitchen's walls were soot-black and only had one big window looking over the side of the house, the track with the cherry tree to the left and the track to the well and drinking-troughs to the right. Its panes were grimy and steamed up, and when the dogs barked, we'd rub them so we could look out and see if someone was coming, but all we ever could see were the lumps of rock salt in the meadow, the salt vat next to the well and the zigzagging track by the cherry tree that disappeared round the first bend among the oak trees, undergrowth, fields and first trees of the spinney, until the black shape of a visitor shivering with cold did finally emerge, treading on air, as if reluctantly taking flight, because he strode out of a sea of dense mist that had enveloped him, kicking his legs out violently to avoid drowning in the bluish-grey haze that was flooding over everything.

"So where are you nesting these days?" Grandfather Hand asked whenever he saw me, two or three times a year, almost always in winter, when he unexpectedly put his head round the kitchen door, feeling the chill and exuding a fierce, acrid smell, a mixture of fodder and livestock, like a ghost that comes and goes without warning, never saying where he's from or where he's heading. "Are you still here? What's your mother up to? What news have you had of your father? Has that rapscallion returned?"

I said nothing. I had learned it was pointless answering because Grandfather Hand never listened to anyone or took any notice. He went about his business without waiting for replies. Only Grandmother, from her corner of the pew, would grumble, without raising her voice or making any effort so Grandfather heard: "Let him be, for goodness sake! He's here with us and will be as long as needs be. You never catch on. As if you didn't know only too well that Andreu is one of ours now."

She'd pause for a moment, like when you're feeding a baby, and waiting between one spoonful of broth and the next, or pausing with a chunk of bread dunked in wine and sugar, so the tot didn't choke and had time to swallow, before adding: "Don't go upsetting the lad because he's got enough headaches, as it is. If you didn't spend your time up in those damned pasture lands, you'd not need to ask what is common knowledge. Or do you think Lluís can come back when he feels like it, as if he was in charge of his own life? And what do you think Florència, his poor mother, can do but work every hour God sends to keep her head above water? You'd be better off bringing her a sack of potatoes or a piece of pork belly when you decide to grace us with your presence, rather than saying stupid things to a lad who's already got enough on his plate."

Cry-Baby would stand behind her, stick out her tongue and make silly gestures and then she'd look at me, as if supporting me and getting her own back on Grandfather's forgetfulness, what she felt to be a mark of rejection.

Grandfather Hand gave his wife an odd look, said nothing, and nodded high-and-mightily as if he'd forgiven her, then turned round and mumbled: "Then they say…, it's not as if I knew already… as if I was spoiling his pitch…, as if I wasn't…"

They called him Grandfather Hand or Old Hand because he'd worked there as a farmhand before marrying

Grandmother Mercè. When Grandmother became a widow, the farmhand married her, even though he was much younger. As he came from a family of ten or twelve children and had spent all his life among mares, cows and sheep, by the age of eight or nine he'd started working with livestock and when he wasn't being a shepherd boy he worked as a farmhand round-and-about or sheared sheep when the flocks were down for winter. After the first years of their marriage, as soon he could, he persuaded the masters to buy more sheep and a good ram and became their stockman, the main shepherd, spending half the year in the mountains with the other shepherds who organized it so they could take turns in the pasture land, doing shifts, as he called it. Dad Quirze, Grandmother Mercè's son with her first husband, I mean Ció's husband, and Bernat, the second-born, could manage the farm without him. Better that way, he'd say, because the young'uns—Grandfather Hand always called them the young'uns—had known him as a farmhand and couldn't get used to thinking of him as their stepfather. That's why they called him Old Hand, rather than Grandfather Hand, as we did.

At some point in the day the whole household paraded past Grandmother Mercè, who by early morning was already perched on her fireside throne, with her sewing and knitting basket on the floor, her long skirts down to her feet, her black headscarf—Father Tafalla called it her comforter—in place and glasses sitting on the end of her nose. She didn't budge even for meals. We put her plates on a stool she pulled out from under the pew, while the others sat around the table and ate in a bad temper, staring into the fire. Ció, and often Enriqueta, if she arrived early from her work in Vic, set and waited on table. The men didn't do a thing, didn't even fetch a glass of water or go down to the wine cellar of Saint Ferriol, the patron saint of wine, to fill their wine-jars. Everything had to be ready when the men came in from the fields or stables. Some meals were eaten in complete silence, the logs crackling on the fire the only sound. It was as if the men were ground down by their worries. Or perhaps it was the winter, fog, ice, frost, snow or rain that was preoccupying them as if they were a plague that might infect the animals or crops. Perhaps it was being forced to live together day in, day out that made them hate each other. Ció often made us three eat before or after the men. She called us the kids or nippers, even though by then Quirze was a big lad, as well as a rogue, or so Grandmother reckoned, and also a rapscallion, a word she borrowed from Father Tafalla.

Mid-afternoon, if it didn't come earlier, Aunt Enriqueta took Grandmother Mercè her newspaper from Barcelona. We all knew her reading time was sacred. We had to keep completely silent in the kitchen until she'd finished reading *La Vanguardia*. Even Ció and Aunt Enriqueta, if they were washing the dishes or preparing an afternoon snack, depending on when Enriqueta arrived, tried to leave the noisiest chores until after she'd read her daily paper.

When Grandmother put the newspaper down on her skirt, she'd sigh long and wearily, as if she'd just travelled around the world, and comment: "For Christ's sake, the allies are never going to get here in time! If Churchill and Roosevelt really knew what's happening here, it would be a different kettle of fish."

At night, before going up to bed, when the men were milking and the women were putting hot embers in the "donkey" bed-warmers—they called them "monks" as well, though sometimes they used huge, hot stones in a pillowcase—we three and Aunt Enriqueta, and often Uncle Bernat and the occasional hand asked Grandmother Mercè to tell us a story about the woods, and better still if it could be a scary one.

"First we must say our rosary prayers," she'd say, extracting a string of black beads from her pocket.

"No, later, later…" we protested.

"No, not later, because you'll fall asleep with my first mystery," she grumbled.

"You just see, we won't fall asleep today."

Grandmother Mercè gave a knowing smile, and started on the story we'd specially requested. We knew them all, she'd told them time and again. The best were the ones about the girl who was beheaded in the middle of the woods when she was coming back with her friends from the factory in Mother's town, or the one about the heroes of the battle of Stalingrad, who didn't leave a single German standing, or the one about the old woman from the farmhouse in Cós who was left all alone one night and the devil appeared and carried her off live to hell, or Josephine Baker and the dress made from bananas that covered her privates who was so beautiful—even though she was as black as Arumí chocolate—and all the men wanted to marry her, or about the day Death didn't come in time to take away the sick man who had mocked it and never made the rendezvous they'd agreed, or the French *maréchal* under sentence of death who on the night before his execution asked to play a game of chess with the Grim Reaper to see who would win, or the one about the world stuffed into a bucket of dirty clothing because it was so disgusted by mankind… Every single one authentic, Grandmother Mercè assured us. *Authentic*, she said. There were words like that, which she alone used, and we suspected that many of the words she now liked to use, like allies, armistice, treaty, resistance, allegations, fascism, legality, exile… she'd collected from the pages of her daily newspaper.

"Once upon a time there was, and you must believe that this is truly authentic…"

3

We lived up the plum tree until autumn came.

When the days began to shorten, nighttime sometimes caught us in the tree and Ció had to shout to us to climb down.

"Blessed kids!" she'd gripe after she'd stopped bawling, when we were standing in front of her. "You spend too much time playing for the age you are. One of these days a branch will break and you'll crack your skulls open."

"They're all up to no good, they run riot," said Grandmother, keeping her eyes glued to the knitting needles her fingers moved over her ample bosom, while she kept her arms still.

The Novíssima didn't start until early October, and for the early weeks of school when we three chased back to the farmhouse, the first thing we did was put our cardboard satchels on the stone bench in the entrance, go into the kitchen and grab the slices of bread spread with oil and sugar or wine and sugar Ció or Grandmother had prepared for us on a dish in the middle of the table, then we'd run with our snacks to the plum tree so we could climb up and eat them lounging back on our branches.

Now and then, when a colder breeze blew and the reddish sun didn't linger as it did in summer, when evenings were like the inside walls of a bread oven that retained the heat from the flames of logs burnt moments before, we took blankets up the tree to wrap around us and fought off as best we could the cold and early nighttime damp coming out of the woods. The damp, stifling heat, treacherous cold or gusting wind all emerged from the forest that was like an immense belly or huge pantry full of small compartments that hoarded all the good and bad luck that existed in the world. Up in our plum tree we often thought we'd be able to catch the moment when the leaves changed colour, but the change in the leaves, like moulting feathers, always happened from one day to the next; overnight an area of wood turned a dazzling saffron yellow, and a few days later the beech trees had turned wine-red, soon to be followed by the silvery white of the poplars, the dark brown of the chestnut trees, the humid greens... We looked at each other in dismay, as if someone was making fun of our wait and one year Cry-Baby suggested we stay there the whole night to catch the precise moment of change.

"You're such an idiot!" laughed Quirze. "How would we ever see anything? It's pitch black at night and we won't see the new colours until the following morning, when it will all be over and done with!"

However, Cry-Baby was stubborn and ignored him. She'd say nothing and I could tell from her determination, from her staring eyes, firm lips and jutting chin that she wouldn't give up until she got a proper answer.

From the tree we used to gaze at the mysterious little lights in the cells in the Saint Camillus monastery as they lit up one after another, indicating that the friars, brothers and novices were getting ready to go out to care for the moribund souls in the neighbouring farmhouses or village.

Until someone howled from the gallery: "Where have those little blighters got to?"

"I want to see them here breaking up the sweetcorn. Or fetching buckets of water for the troughs or the sink."

Cry-Baby was such a ninny nobody ever included her in their summons.

"They're back up the plum tree!" shouted an astonished Dad Quirze or a farmhand, usually Jan, the oldest hand, who was like a piece of the furniture.

"Where did you get those blankets?" raged Ció, as she watched us walking towards her, shamefaced, with our blankets. "No corner of this house is safe with you drones buzzing around. I've told you a thousand times not to touch the things I keep in the two big baskets in the doorway, whatever they might be. These blankets don't belong to us! Put them back where you found them right away."

And when we were just about to return them to the big basket, before removing the lid, Ció snatched them from us, looking alarmed: "Leave them on the floor! Don't ever touch them again. Nobody must touch them. They are all infected. Go and wash your hands at once, you naughty devils! You're disgusting!"

We three didn't know what to do next. We knew Ció was contradicting herself and we put that down to her being so upset by our mischief-making. We didn't understand why the easygoing Ció was getting worked up by what we thought was a worthless pile of cloth no doubt destined to be used by the livestock, the mule, the mares, the horses or the colt, that was small and frisky like a toy and the one we liked best.

"They are the blankets the Saint Camillus friars threw out because they stank to high heaven. Ugh! They used them to cover their ill patients until they breathed their last. Most were draped over the ones with TB who sun themselves in the heartsease garden. Ugh! I wasn't very keen to take them, and I only did so as a favour, and I didn't touch a single one with my hands, I stuffed them in the big basket using tongs and a pitchfork."

However, whenever we spied on the heartsease garden from the top of the plum tree, or, especially when we'd stood by the wall separating the land around the farmhouse near the pond and hazelnut spinney from the monastery gardens and orchards, we were horrified to see a row of naked, skeletal bodies stretched out, all young men, sunning themselves in a meadow full of yellow daisies, pale pink carnations, bright red poppies and purple, almost lilac or mauve heartsease, the colour of the habits the Saint Camillus order reserved for Holy Week. All those boys, or rather, young men, lay on the whitest of sheets, some clutching a corner to cover their nether parts, the area that most drew our attention, the bit that fascinated us infinitely more than their emaciated faces, sunken eyes, the small beads of sweat on their temples, their chests striped by protruding ribs, bellies, collapsed in some cases, swollen in others, and their off-white or yellow rancid butter skin…, those blackened, shrunken genitals and a crop of lank hair like an obscene black bloodstain…, monsters in our eyes, phantoms from a forbidden world, sickly, worn down and consumed by a horrible microbe, victims of a contagious, suppurating disease like the rabies dogs spread or sheep's foot-and-mouth, that can be caught simply by breathing the air or drinking from the same glass a TB sufferer has used, an accursed disease, contracted as a result of an errant life of vice, sick men condemned in life, proof of the deity's pitiless punishment of sin, swaddled in white sheets like premature cadavers in dazzling white shrouds… Yet we'd never seen one under a blanket.

A black umbrella was planted next to the sheets of just three or four TB sufferers, so the shade protected their heads. The presence of those faceless bodies, some shamelessly displaying their sexes, were shocking in our eyes and beyond words. A mystery and a secret no one could fathom. And a friar sat next to the little gate from the vegetable plots to the monastery garden, reading his breviary and never looking up, as if to have sight of the infirm was to behold evil, physical evil, a palpable sign of invisible spiritual evil, a repugnant manifestation of sin.

We didn't touch another blanket that autumn. But the two baskets, especially the big one, were inexplicably marked out as things only adults could handle. Why did they keep those dangerous blankets in that place of transit, within everyone's reach and what should the movers and shakers in the house—Dad Quirze and Aunt Ció—the delegates of our invisible masters, do about them? Why didn't the friars destroy them in the monastery if they were worthless? What deal had they done over those ignominious bits of cloth?

"They should be washed back and front, boiled, scrubbed, scraped, dusted and dried and then we'll see if they are any use," said Ció on that occasion, after she'd calmed down. "On Saturday when we go to the market in Vic, we'll leave them with the wenches who launder the lovely linen from the Poor Hospital, and let's see what they can do. The Town Hall allows those nuns to use the communal wash-house all night, when nobody else washes and the water is filthy from all the daytime washing. On Sunday, when the sisters have finished, they change the water. And even then the wretched Saint Camillus folk won't make anything from them."

However, one day, surely another autumn, when we were looking for clothes to keep us warm, when the weather drove us from our tree, when we'd all forgotten her little rant, Aunt Ció mentioned those blankets again.

"Don't touch the blankets!" she said this time. "God knows where those damned friars found them! I expect they collected them up after the war, when they returned to the monastery the lice-ridden militia had occupied like a barracks, and the church was full of shit, with hens running round the altar and sheep penned up in the Chapel of the Most Holy Spirit as if it were a stable... I bet they found them on the floor abandoned by the Republican soldiers who'd had to beat it hell-for-leather when the fascist troops, led by the Moors, entered Vic. And now they don't know what to do with them, they can't use them, not even to wrap up the sick, and they want us to sell them in the market: I wonder what we'll get for rags that are so

27

old and filthy not even the novices in the monastery want them, ugh, and so full of bugs they need washing at least ten times."

We never saw anyone take the blankets to Vic market on that Saturday or any other.

Adults think children have the same poor powers of recall they have. They forget we children have no memories of anything, that words and acts are all new to us and every little detail remains automatically etched on our brains.

4

The colours of autumn brought all kinds of other transformations.

Many trees started to shed leaves; the green grass of the meadow faded; flocks of swallows and finches spread across the sky like nets in flight and waited a whole evening or a couple of days for stragglers to join them and when they were all gathered, they'd be gone in a flash until next year; the elder tree behind the house rained down tufts of white that bathed the ground in warm, round flakes of snow and the entire meadow was filled with that strong, sharp, medicinal smell, the one that shot up your nose to your brain, leaving a taste of mint and aniseed.

In our refuge at the top of the plum tree, we'd keep quiet while the front of the house became a distant hub-bub that might focus on us at any moment. We watched darkness advance through the woods, until Cry-Baby said: "We'll never be able to see how the colours are born. Grandmother told me. So now I know."

"And what fairy story did Grandmother tell you?" retorted Quirze nastily.

"That it's like dreaming, we only remember dreams when they come to an end, if we wake up in time, but never how they began or how long they lasted. And if we don't wake up in time, we only remember for a few seconds when we get up before it's gone forever."

Quirze said nothing, landed a gob of spit on the ground and went on: "It's not the same at all! You must sleep to dream, and if you want to see a leaf change colour, you must be wide awake and keep your eyes on the same spot.

It's completely different. That's what *she* reckons. Anyhow I never dream."

We knew the wood's changing colours were the signal for us to leave the plum tree and seek shelter in the winter house, the stone and plaster house, the hard, shut-up house, the opposite to our cool, airy, open, rustling home among the trees. We abandoned the fruit orchard like refugees making their way to an unknown land. The world of adults, grown-ups, or rogues, rascals and rapscallions, as Grandmother and Father Tafalla called them, and their obligations, squabbles and disagreements, particularly of the men who lorded it over everything with their coarseness, their filth, their clogs and their sullenness. The world of women was more fun, but it wasn't independent, it always revolved around men: their meals, drinks, clothes, mending, changes of clothes and mind, moods, orders, guests, friends, cleanliness and silences… Women never had time for themselves, they couldn't stop whirling in the orbit of men the whole day long, preparing for when they arrived, left, were absent or needed something… For the odd moment, on the odd day, a space opened up when two or three women came together to rest, a few minutes mid-morning, a short break mid-afternoon, or at night, when the men went out after supper or went upstairs to bed and left the women and children alone, and then you heard sighs, giggles, intimate exchanges, secrets, lamentations, desires, advice…all whispered or murmured, almost always in someone's ear, all said with a wary eye on the stairs, on the crack in the door, on the light in the window for fear the men might come and catch them in those brief, almost obscene moments when they let off steam, in that brief opportunity to relax, a short respite they didn't deserve because men worked hard from dawn to dusk and women only did chores, men used up every bit of their energy outside the house and were drained and exhausted while women only had any skill and guile with respect to their domestic duties and the effort they expended on housework never went beyond their skirts or the length of the kitchen sink. Nevertheless in those scant blissful moments, in those unexpected parentheses, in those interludes of truce in the war men waged on them simply by their presence, we runts, kids or snot-noses had the chance to catch new, mysterious words that sparkled in their strangeness, that we lapped up, though the women never noticed. In fact, adults spoke completely freely in front of the children, said what they needed to say and kept to themselves what they needed to silence. However, barren, desert terrain did straddle a frontier between total freedom and absolute secrecy, where innuendo, gripes, curses, phrases or comments fell now and then, and travelled from one side to the other, from the zone of freedom to the zone of secrecy, before disappearing into the darkness, or dissolving in the light from one of the two extremes, and thanks to those moments and words that rescued us from our world of ignorance and dependency, we glimpsed the breadth, substance and intriguing complications of the adult world from which we were excluded, distanced or even protected. We fished out those frontier words, momentarily dismissed them, lodged them in a corner of our brains, and sometimes they came back when it was time to go to sleep, before we dozed off, or in conversations whose meaning we had to probe to clear up the riddles, like the mania we had for collecting all sorts of rubbish that we kept in secret hiding places—the hollow in the plum tree's worm-eaten trunk, under a loose tile in the granary, a hole in the meadow covered by a stone—where the three of us hid our little treasure troves of grapeshot found on the field where the Moors had camped out during the war, photo-cards of footballers or film stars we swapped at school with village friends, that we got from chocolate bars the women brought from the market, comics Aunt Enriqueta brought us from the seamstress's, that she called *Smurfs*, pages of magazines from the same source, eggs that had been blown, dead crickets, matchboxes and packets of cigarette paper made in Olot, spinning tops and marbles, prints from the Saint Camillus monastery like those of Saint Tarscisis with the martyr's palm, Saint Lucia, her eyes gouged out and displayed on a tray, Saint Luis Gonzaga holding the lily of purity and lifting his eyes up to heaven, Saint Andrew crucified head down on a cross like an X, and above all Saint Camillus de Llellis, in white with a red cross on his chest, surrounded by lepers, the blind and the maimed, the poor and ragamuffin children waiting to be cured and saved. From time to time, when nobody could see us, when we remembered, we revisited our hoards and enjoyed the pleasure of touching, moving and holding those objects, in the knowledge that they were ours and we could treat them with the authority ownership confers. As we could with the words we found on that frontier: repeating them, thinking about them, wrestling with them, interrogating them, elaborating them, letting them sail around our heads until they found a port that might link them to a continent of terra firma, of known experience and things.

"A bugger," they said and we'd repeat later, "He's just a downright bugger."

Who were they talking about? However, the impressions made by those words—"bastard," "bugger"—were too strong to indicate the individual in question. You bet, we thought, you bet it's someone outside the family, the house, even the locality. The individual besmirched by such a vile insult was like a chimney sweep too begrimed by chimney soot and filth to have any individuality worthy of respect; a chimney sweep had to wash and comb his hair and remove all the grime before he was allowed to come and eat in the kitchen or upstairs room, and even then we all stared at him rather apprehensively, as if it really wasn't him, as if his true self belonged to that hidden realm of smoke and shadows, of dirt and ashes.

"Is it one of those nasty diseases? Ay, poor fellow! A nasty disease that has no cure. What bad luck!"

What *were* nasty diseases? Were there diseases that were pleasant and nice? A feeling of disgust mixed up with eternal condemnation like the one coming to miscreants on Judgment Day. An incurable disease that is repugnant. Were they talking about an acquaintance? Or was it just gossip picked up in the factory, at the seamstress's, in the shops, in town?

The bundle. Another of those words that meant everything yet told us nothing. The bundle. The bundle had arrived. They'd taken the bundle away. Are there more of them? What was in the bundle? It's a very complicated bundle. And most puzzling of all: have they buried the bundle? For ages I imagined it referred to the burial of a newborn baby, one of those children who die very small, just after they're born, and are buried in a small white box with minimal mourning because they've gone straight to limbo, so the burial was more like a party—Father Tafalla called them little princelings and Grandmother little angels—that's why you had to baptize the newly born the moment they came into this world because anything might happen and if the stain of original sin wasn't removed they could go straight to hell and it would be the parents' fault for not splashing water over their heads; if necessary, they or anyone could do that, even a complete stranger, with a wash bowl; they shouldn't give evil time to sink its roots into the soul. The bundle. But they seemed to be talking about a burial nearby, and we weren't aware of any in the neighbourhood or in the village, until Quirze suggested something that really upset us. He said: "It must be a baby that died before it was born."

Neither Cry-Baby nor I reacted; the idea of meeting death before you've tasted life was too outrageous and Quirze was in the habit of saying gross things about childbirth: he said it was like cows, sheep, rabbits or pigs giving birth—which we'd all seen—but we couldn't understand or accept that childbirth was the same. Quirze must have been right, right in a simple, brutal, basic way, as usual. That was the only explanation for a secret burial; it was a baby who'd not breathed even a second of life. However, Cry-Baby and I lived in the hope that things weren't as Quirze said and we trusted that the world would suddenly change for us, like the holidays or Sunday clothes that broke weekday routines and showed us that life could be different.

"Our folk" were other words they repeated. Our folk, pronounced in a special way, our folk, not like when they said our plates or our glasses, but as if it were a more prized, more private possession, like private property only the owner knows about. The outside world was divided up between our folk and the others we guessed were enemies. We gradually discovered that the others were also the fascists. Initially we didn't know what this word referred to. But it didn't take us long to understand that the others and the fascists were one and the same: the enemy. They sometimes used different names, particularly Grandmother, who spoke of the "four bigwigs" and other such, but Grandmother's language was so idiosyncratic that soon we only had the others or the fascists against us. For example, Grandmother never referred to the pairs of civil guards who poked their noses into the house now and then, as anything but "scoopers," because of the three-cornered helmets they wore, which from behind looked like the implement we used to collect up grain or straw in the barn: the scoop. Scoopers.

Each proper name the adults uttered immediately fell into one of the two categories: our folk, or the others, the fascists. And one thing we worried about was allotting each new name we got to know to the right side. With each name, we had to listen carefully and try to catch every detail so we could decide on its moral location, whether that person was good or bad, our folk or alien, upstanding or fascist. All kinds emerged from that dark bevy of strangers, and each word or insinuation added a trait to their personality, until one day, as if miraculously, the names showed up at home in flesh and blood and then we'd stand and stare, in a state of shock, comparing the ideal image we'd invented with the real presence and making the necessary amendments, in favour or against.

The names that most cropped up in conversation, apart from family and friends, were Filthy-Face, Mad Antònia from Can Tona, Freckly Fair or Canary and Curly Lettuce, a pair of civil guards who always went together, "in tandem" said Grandmother, "those two always go in tandem," Father Tafalla, the Superior at the Saint Camillus monastery and his companion, the novice from Navarra, Mr. and Mrs. Manubens, the masters, naturally, and Brunet Who Never Stops because he was the local head of the *Movimiento* in the village and that's why Grandmother had given him that nickname, Mr. Madern, the schoolmaster and Miss Pepita, Miss Silly, the ex-nun at the Novíssima, and Pere Màrtir, who was a big surprise...to mention but a few.

From one day to the next they would put in an appearance on the track that went round the house; they all had another air about them, different to the one inside the house, and as far as we kids were concerned, they opened doors to strange and terrible worlds we had never imagined until their visits lit them up in a searing, sulphurous light from hell.

In winter we went to school well wrapped up with scarves and caps, our toes, hands and ears covered in chilblains. Quirze always wore fewer over-garments than us and called us wimps. He also said chilblains could be cured by a good dose of piss in the morning and evening.

"Yuck!" Cry-Baby and I screamed in horror.

"That's right," he mocked, "what an idea, right! As if you two have never pissed on yourselves!"

The track from home to the Novíssima was short and full of bends. We had to skirt round the house, walk past the lumps of rock salt, the well and elder tree and then head up the track to the woods and the monastery.

It was a cart track that crossed a clearing in the woods, pitted by big wheel marks, that snaked towards the main road across a mixed terrain of arable land and animal pastures. The monastery was on the left, on the Vic side, and the Novíssima on the right, near the village. The Novíssima was a modernist mansion straight out of a fairytale, in fin-de-siècle style, with lots of Valencia tiling, lots of pointy doors and windows with stained glass, elaborate patterns, exposed brick, friezes and designs embossed on white walls, lots of twisted, wrought-iron grilles in the shape of vegetables… Before the war, when the village filled up with summer residents who came to take the sulphurous, medicinal waters in a spa that has since closed, it was the newest, most modern mansion—La Novísima. It was now a school, we said "classes," and brought together all the kids from local farms who didn't want to go to the village school. Farming folk had a different town hall to the village and a right to their own national school.

During the war it had been used as a hospital or convalescent home, when the monastery was emptied out and requisitioned, like all the factories and estates of the rich. After the war a defrocked nun established herself there and reopened the primary school. During the war young kids were forced to go to the village school, much to the disgust of the farming folk who refused to accept the amalgamating of the two town halls. The authorities had allowed the ex-nun to set up while they were preparing the competition to appoint national schoolmasters, because they weren't mere schoolmasters any longer, they were *national,* with a job for life. There were two classes, the one with the youngest, taught by Miss Pepita, nicknamed Miss Silly or the Ditherer, because she gave the impression she wasn't quite right in the head, had a screw loose, as people said, and the class for big kids, taught by a man also reputed to have a murky past, who'd made the most of the confusion of the post-war situation to get appointed to the job without sitting any competitive exams, Mr. Madern, a middle-aged, sprightly, tense man, with a shock of white hair, bright eyes and white skin covered in horrible blotches, reddish patches that sometimes turned purple, depending on the weather, and caused by heaven knows what. He was a pleasant, if rather absent-minded, man who always seemed to have his mind on his own inner demons, but not like the schoolmistress—she made you laugh because when people spoke to her, she'd stand still for a while as if she were searching for a pot of ready-made answers from a shelf in her mind and didn't know what to say or do until she'd found it, unlike Mr. Madern the schoolmaster, who, when spoken to, seemed to descend from another world, though he soon came to and found an answer to whatever he'd been asked; he was very fond of chess and his voice sounded hoarse, weary and rough.

When we walked along the track round the woods, we looked warily up at the mass of trees, a dark enigma confronting us, the light, majestic movements of foliage, the changing shapes and colours that faded and died in the heart of winter, and if we weren't in a big rush, we stopped in the places we had made our own: the clearing among the wild climbing plants with little flowers like green and white candles where we threw stones, the hollow in the middle where we hunted for mushrooms and medicinal herbs that we took to Grandmother, like rustyback fern that cured stomachache, watercress or parsnip for salads, rockrose to light the fire in the bread oven, galingale to decorate altars and balconies in Corpus Christi, cattails with small white flowers, honeysuckle with yellow and red flowers and a lovely scent, sheep sorrel that was a kind of spinach Grandmother cooked with haricot beans or that could also be eaten raw…or the start of the shortcut along the stream to look for traces of animals or people who'd forded the water to go straight to the village or the other side of the woods, as far as the crags overlooking the river. It would take something extraordinary to waylay us in the morning—"Careful with the brambles," Grandmother would say when we left, "they're enchanted and if you stop to look at them, they'll turn you into stone," but on our return in the afternoon, after Christmas, when the days were slowly lengthening, we sometimes plucked up courage and dared head deeper into the woods, and enjoy feeling surrounded by the greenness and marooned between a circle of tree trunks and a sky of branches, a kind of compensation for the plum tree house we so missed. We'd sit in silence for a while in the place we'd chosen, whichever seemed the most mysterious or gloomy, and let time pass us by, listening to the sounds surging from the depths of the forest. It was like entering into Grandmother's fantastic stories, as if horror, any sort of horror—the murderous axe, the beast on the rampage, the wild man or the apparition from the grave—might appear at any moment, from anywhere, proving with their presence that it was a scenario as *authentic* as her stories.

"A greenfinch!" Cry-Baby suddenly shouted when she heard a bird sing nearby.

"Idiot!" laughed Quirze. "Greenfinches trill like canaries. That's a tawny owl."

A friend from school, Oak-Leaf, nearly always accompanied us on these forays. She was Quirze's age, a year or two older than me, the daughter of the tenant farmers in Can Rovira, a farmhouse on the edge of the forest, in the direction of the crags. She only came with us occasionally because she often played truant, if there was a lot of work on at home or somebody was ill or she had to take things to the village shops or even Vic, a whole day's walk there and back, when she would miss school. She had to walk the farthest and couldn't stop with us for long; she said she was afraid to cross the woods in the pitch dark.

"What are you frightened of?" laughed Quirze sarcastically.

"Salamanders," Oak-Leaf confessed, shutting her eyes as if she could see one in front of her. "They disgust me. And the little brook from the spring by the stream is full of them. When I walk close by, I run like mad so I don't see them."

Whenever her fear of salamanders came up, I wanted to add that Mother had been scared of them when she was a child, and even now, as a grownup, they still scared and disgusted her. But I didn't because whenever I mentioned Mother, Quirze laughed, and said I was a mollycoddled softie, a little piece of shit...

"So what else frightens you?" persisted Quirze. "Salamanders are no big deal."

"I'm afraid of Mad Antònia," Oak-Leaf answered timidly, as if the revelation of the wood's secrets might scare us or spark evil-doing.

These were the best bits of our little meetings with Oak-Leaf in the woods. They always ended the same way. First we went into the thickets to play, on the excuse that we were looking for birds, mushrooms or herbs, but we always ended up in some arbour asking Oak-Leaf to tell us what she'd seen at the bottom of woods. Then, when the time for secrets was over, we'd start a special game, the one about a peeping tom Quirze had got from somewhere, which was as exciting as the revelations about the secrets of the woods, with a number of big differences.

"What does Mad Antònia do when she runs through the woods?" enquired Quirze.

"She runs stark naked…" said Oak-Leaf, lowering her eyes, her cheeks red with embarrassment, "she wears no clothes at all…"

We'd all heard fragments of the story of the mad woman of Can Tona, who'd lost her senses at the end of the war, when they murdered her boyfriend in front of her, executed him by the fence round the pen that belonged to Antònia's farmhouse, when neither her parents nor any-body else did anything to stop it.

"She went crazy," Quirze reminded us, "because they found them in the barn coupled together like a dog and a bitch. They couldn't separate them, just like dogs when they catch them at it. Sometimes, they have to cut off the male's prick to pull them apart."

Cry-Baby put her hands over her face. Oak-Leaf smiled obliquely, mischievously. I admired Quirze because he was so bold, nothing scared him, not even the strongest language.

"He was a lad on the run who'd worked at Can Tona during the war. A deserter from Aragon. The family didn't want Antònia and the lad to keep seeing each other. He was too young, they said. And when the war was over, he'd be gone like all the refugees and they'd never see him again…"

"So when you see her running through the woods, is she really stark naked or does she wear something?" kept on Quirze. "Could I see her?"

"I've seen her run through the thickest part of the woods three or four times, in nettles and bracken, wallowing on the edges of fields in the sunlight, getting dirty on the ash and charcoal left by the burners…without a stitch on her, stark naked, her legs scratched and streaming with blood."

Quirze kept on: "Tell me when I can see her, or the place where you can get an eyeful…"

Oak-Leaf nodded but didn't commit herself.

The three of us were astounded by the girl's lunacy—a young lass, said Grandmother, a young lass who was unfortunately fated to be a spinster—and the terrible things her madness made her do. And, in a way, we also understood the profound mercy shown by the woods that hid and protected her secret madness with an indifference that was more dignified than Oak-Leaf's brutal interference, her vision that sullied everything and was an insult to the gentle discretion of the trees.

6

Oak-Leaf told us more stories. We didn't have to lean on her to persuade her to come out with everything she'd discovered in the woods. The moment evening shadows began to darken the tops of the trees, she'd become agitated and say she must be going, she couldn't stay and play or chat with us any longer: she was scared. That was the agreed prompt for us to persuade her to spill the beans about what she'd recently seen that she found so disturbing.

"A soldier's bag…" she said. "The kind they call a kit-bag. Abandoned on a brambly path."

"What was inside?" chirped Quirze right away.

"I didn't dare touch it. It looked empty. I walked round it and started running in case a soldier or somebody was hiding in the bushes…"

"How could there be any soldiers if the war ended years ago?"

"You know, the ones that cross the border and kill people in their farms…"

"*Maquis*, you mean the *maquis*. But they don't wear soldiers' uniforms, they dress like smugglers or country people, with a blanket over their shoulder, and a revolver and hunter's pouch to carry their grub. That's how the shepherds and farming folk say they dress. They've met quite a few, higher up in the mountains. And Grandfather Hand says the same, but he refuses to talk about them, and it puts him in a bad mood if he ever hears us mentioning them."

"And what did you see next, I mean the next morning when you walked past that spot?" asked Cry-Baby.

"The morning after, it had gone, nothing was there. Someone had taken the khaki bag."

There was a moment's silence until Quirze came out with one of his outlandish comments: "A passing thief or charcoal burner had hidden it so he could squat down and have a shit; that's why you didn't see him. Kit-bags don't walk by themselves."

"A thief," said Oak-Leaf, trying to ignore what Quirze had just said, like a card player who suddenly flings an ace or a high trump on the table to try and forget a previous bad play. "One day I did see a thief."

"Hey!" I chimed in. "How did you know it was a thief? Perhaps he let on to you?"

"It was Charcoal Pete."

"The one who comes to the woods to make charcoal?" we chorused incredulously.

What a discovery! Charcoal Pete was a thin, short, insignificant little guy, with sunken cheeks and an aubergine nose; the back of his pants were always torn, and he wore a collarless blue shirt, a waistcoat and cap too big for his bonce; a cigarette butt always hung from the corner of his lips; he was as poor as a church-mouse, with stacks of children and a wife as crazy as he was, who could never work because by the time her last child was starting to crawl, she already had another bun in the oven. Charcoal Pete took advantage of the early evenings his job in the textile factory left him free to come to the woods and make charcoal and slack he then sacked and sold in the village for stoves and braziers. When Charcoal Pete had covered the wood pile with earth, he'd light the bonfire and sit down a while to wait until it was all embers, plaiting reeds and herbs he found on the river bank to make round fans with a handle that he hawked around the houses alongside his small sacks of charcoal.

"That scavenger thinks nobody owns the woods," groused Dad Quirze when the name of Charcoal Pete cropped up in conversations in the house; his son always mentioned his name when he wanted to rile his father. "One of these days we'll give him a fright and teach him a thing or two. Or hasn't he heard about poaching?"

"And why should you get hot under the collar about what that poor man does or doesn't do? Do the woods belong to you? What harm is he doing you?" retorted Grandmother Mercè, pleasantly enough, and we were shocked that Dad Quirze acquiesced to her scolding without saying a word, because he was a man who couldn't stand anyone contradicting him or raising their voices above his. "Don't you see what poverty-stricken lives they lead? Better forget him for now. The masters are in Vic where they don't see a thing."

When Grandmother talked about poverty, I'd think about the women, alone or with a female friend or neighbour, who came along the cherry tree track to the house to beg for fresh bread, a few potatoes to fill their baskets, oil and fruit, even the maize we gave to the hens. The odd one, according to Mother who knew them from the factory, brought Scotch thread or Egyptian cotton, I don't remember which, that they hid in their lunch baskets and when they had a bundle, they would barter it for food. Mother never used the word "steal" when she spoke about their actions, she'd say "took with them," or "put in their lunch basket," or "they were quick with their fingers," as if they acted naturally enough like a farm worker who picks a peach or a plum or takes a few lettuce leaves from the orchard at the end of a day's work. But the fact the textile worker had to hide the thread she was taking away rang alarm bells, warned us something wasn't quite right in her story. So, of course, discovering the identity of a genuine, downright thief sparked our curiosity.

A year or two later, I saw that thief's identity confirmed, one he assumed in public as a fate that merited a double-edged reaction of respect and disapproval. I felt silent disapproval was always a kind of respect triggered by a mixture of reproach and envy when Charcoal Pete was caught early one morning snaffling potatoes—the refugees who stayed on after the war called them spuds—from a farmer's field and was forced to parade at the end of the General Communion procession as an act of penitence. This was one of the most solemn processions in the year, when the entire factory town, led by the ecclesiastical and political powers-that-be, brought communion—that in some cases was also the Eucharist—to the village's chronic sick who couldn't leave their beds to go to church and do their Easter duty: confession and Holy Week communion, at least that one time in the year. The skinny, benighted charcoal burner was forced to process carrying a sack of potatoes over his shoulder in full view of all his neighbours who knew only too well how that sad, bluish runt of a man, with his stubbly cheeks and weary eyes scraped a meagre living; he was now forced to trail behind the incense-burning, chanting, ritualistic retinue in an unnecessary, humiliating, offensive spectacle.

It was on a day I happened to be in Mother's small town. The authorities in the factory town were very fond of these exemplary displays, processions like the General Communion, Remembrance parades, Mission and Penitence weeks and the like because, or so they said, the town served a number of factories and the workers—male and female—lived a life far from the eternal verities, and were in huge danger of neglecting the virtuous straight and narrow. As for Charcoal Pete's penitence, I thought what was shocking was not so much his humiliation but the public declaration of his new persona as the town's official thief that from now he'd never be able to cast off, a stigma they'd branded him with forever. The suspicion, doubt, gossip about his stealing was one thing and quite another the imposition he meekly accepted of an activity and skill that would tar him for life—Charcoal Pete, the thief, the potato thief, the town thief. How could he live with that slur that would always remind him of a part of his life he'd have preferred to hide, that indelible mark on his forehead that made him the butt of everyone's barbs, scorn and banter? It was as if they had the power to take possession of your dreams, your nighttime acts, your darkest secrets, your innermost self, the hidden kernel that set you apart from everyone else. Something deep down told me that this kind of justice wasn't right, that the desire to destroy an individual deserved no respect at all, and I could tell from the shamefaced expressions of the townsfolk accompanying the procession on the roadside with their tallow or Easter candles, that they were vaguely of the same mind: the punishment was too harsh and simply highlighted the lack of mercy and the arrogance of the contemptible pillars of that society. The wretched, stunted figure of Charcoal Pete, half-swathed in the low morning mist, assumed a luminous sanctity, a yellow and blue aura from the Easter candles, an extraordinary illumination that transformed him into something transparent, beyond punishment, an invisible energy ensuring the thief would necessarily emerge from that test fortified and transfigured like a martyr destined for the lions who at the last moment is protected by an archangel who welcomes him under his wing and vanishes into the low rain clouds.

"Right," said Oak-Leaf. "While the pile of charcoal is burning, he goes off somewhere or other and comes back carrying all kinds of things in his sack: eggs, rabbits, hens, small bags of grain and flour…"

"Where does he get that all from?"

"Ah!" exclaimed Oak-Leaf, opening her eyes wider and lifting her hands up as if to ward off a punch. "I don't know. When it's not eggs, it's mushrooms or flour. He always hides the stuff by wrapping it in pieces of cloth or paper at the bottom of the sack of charcoal he takes away."

"I thought you said that while he was waiting for the charcoal to burn, he amused himself by making small fans…"

"The charcoal has to smoulder for ages. Sometimes he lights a pile in the evening, goes back to the village, lets the night go by and separates out the charcoal the following morning. He's got time to do all kinds of things. That's a lot of hours."

"Have you told anyone at home?"

"No, though they sometimes gossip about things going missing from the farmhouses roundabout, from La Coromina, La Passarella or La Bruguera. They say it might be a fox, farmhands or a thief on the loose in the woods."

We all had a good laugh, delighted to share that secret that seemed significant and to listen to the innuendo Oak-Leaf used to insinuate things, just like grownups did.

Oak-Leaf craved being the centre of attention and seeing us hanging on her every word. Perhaps that was why she always rounded off her revelations with a sentence full of promise that left our mouths watering; it was her way of retaining her power over us: "And lots of other things I can't tell…"

That was her parting shot to wind us up further; the woods were still and Oak-Leaf stood up to leave. Protest was futile: "Hey, come on!" we implored.

"You always do that. Tell us what else you've seen."

"Tomorrow, you must start off with that."

"I promise you I will."

"Swear on it. If you don't swear by God or the death of your mother, we won't believe you."

"No, it's a sin to swear an oath."

"All right then, promise you will by making a pledge to Baby Jesus, turn your fingers into a cross and kiss it with your lips."

Oak-Leaf crossed two fingers and lifted them to her mouth to kiss the middle of the cross.

"That's not enough," protested Quirze. "You didn't say anything. We've all got to hear you."

"I said it to myself, and that will do," she replied. "Ugh! I can't say that!"

"If you can't, it means you don't know anything else, and haven't seen a thing," Quirze now changed tack and went on the offensive. "You're a liar. That's what our teacher told me, you're always telling lies."

Oak-Leaf turned a bright red and her eyes glistened. And that was the cue for Quirze to sing and mock her:

> The master who teaches me,
> fol-de-rol, fol-de-ree,
> the master who teaches me,
> has fallen in love with me.

Oak-Leaf burst into tears and often threw stones or whatever she could lay her hands on at Quirze. But Quirze never relented and sang the chorus louder than ever:

> Has fallen in love with me!
> Has fallen in love with me!

Sometimes it became a real catfight, and they'd kick and punch one another, and Cry-Baby and I watched them on edge, not daring to separate them. Of course, Quirze always came out on top, and when he'd beaten her and had her flat on the ground, he kept her still by sitting astride her waist and then sang into her face:

> He says, "Don't you be a nun,"
> fol-de-rol, fol-de-rum.
> He says, "Don't you be a nun,
> 'cos you're goin' to marry me."

When he let her go, Oak-Leaf ran off sobbing, while at the same time she'd threaten us:

"I'll never ever play with you lousy lot from Can Tupí, never ever, 'cos everybody knows you're lice-ridden rats. I'll never tell you anything again. You won't find out any more of the wood's secrets. Not even its biggest secret that I'll tell everyone the day I really want to hurt you and that will serve you right, and everyone will laugh at you and you'll be the laughingstock of the village."

While she walked off, Quirze shouted even louder, as if he was chasing her with his voice:

"Cos you're goin' to marry me!
Marry me!
Marry me!"

Quirze and Oak-Leaf were the ones who squabbled, and Cry-Baby and I kept well out of it, just spectated, but one day, when Oak-Leaf was fleeing Quirze's taunts, she turned round all of a sudden and attacked us, accusing us of not defending her, of always siding with the strongest; perhaps she couldn't think of anything else to bawl at Quirze:

"And you two are a couple of waifs and strays. That's what everyone says, your house is full of waifs and strays, and nobody knows where your mother and father are, and they were reds, worse than reds, and that's why they had to scarper. They should take you to the Sisters of Charity because you're nobody's children. They keep you on the farm because they took pity on you, they took you in like stray dogs, you don't have anyone, you are tramps and gypsies, and more pathetic than those degenerates with TB in the Saint Camillus monastery! Waifs and strays, reds and tramps…!"

Quirze clammed up, taken aback. Oak-Leaf ran off. Cry-Baby's face and mine had gone scarlet, as if our bodies were in the throes of a hot flush. My eyes sank into their sockets and for the first time in my life I realized how poisonous words could be, how they got under your skin even though you didn't want them to, words other people uttered shamelessly, that made no odds to them, and I understood how we'd never forget that litany of labels and any day they could turn into a flurry of cruel insults we threw into someone else's face, like a mirror where we were forced to contemplate the ugliness we'd hoped we had concealed. I bit my lip as I stood in that clearing in the woods with no strength to move my limbs, and pledged never to say anything, never to do anything others could store in their heads and throw back in my face the day they felt like it. Never again did I want to be stunned or buried under a load of words that fashioned a portrait of myself drawn by others, one I couldn't erase.

"Let's be off!" Quirze snapped, walking off in the direction of the farmhouse. "One of these days that lunatic will get a nasty surprise. Bastard witch!"

Cry-Baby and I followed Quirze, didn't exchange a glance, and walked tight-lipped along the path.

For two or three days after these squabbles we went home separately, each of us on our own. Oak-Leaf didn't wait for us after class or took a different route, but by the end of a week or so some excuse or other made us the best of friends again and we'd giggle and play in the woods, and tell more racy stories.

7

Our stories weren't always about the secrets of the wood Oak-Leaf had discovered: sometimes a glimpse of animal life diverted our conversations down other paths, the surprising lives of animals that occasionally revealed habits that were almost human.

Dogs were closest to us. Birds as well. And horses and cows, though the former inspired mainly respect and grownups treated them with extreme caution, as if they were special, very prized, and rarely let us near them; cows, on the other hand, were contemptible, like pigs, dirty brutes that let you grab their teats without complaining and nobody valued them at all. As far as we were concerned, the only good thing about pigs were the days when a couple were killed, a real party, when the slaughterer arrived with his tools and the offal expert and her helpers who extracted the bloody guts they turned into sausages, raw, and black puddings, cooked. The slaughterer, the offal expert and her helpers arrived in the early morning and laboured all day; Grandmother pitched in cleaning the entrails and the men were splattered in warm, red blood and the stench of flesh rose, singed by burning thistles. They sang:

> Six things were ate at Pep's wedding:
> pig and chitterling,
> hog and suckling,
> swine and scratching.

They shocked us with revelations that demonstrated the cruelty and whims of nature, and worried us no end because they cast doubts over the whole of creation, so much praised by priests and teachers, above all by Father Tafalla, as when they pointed out that sows have eight tits and that was why they nearly always farrow eight piglets, the eighth of the litter being the runt; though they sometimes produce nine or more, and then those surplus sucklers, damned at birth, are fated to die, and are called no-hope piglets, no-hope sucklers. Cry-Baby and I shuddered when we heard those curious details, as if nature had also got it wrong with us, who through lack of tit and lack of parents were also destined to be abandoned and forgotten. No-hope children.

We also talked about the animals in the woods, lords and masters of that whole universe of vegetation, in particular the ones living in the depths of the forest that only showed themselves when they attacked or hunted, like badgers, foxes or wild boars.

When dogs barked at night, whether on our farm or Oak-Leaf's, Can Rovira, we felt uneasy because we suspected that, while we slept, the lives of adults smouldered silently in the darkness, like the wood pile turning into charcoal beneath a blanket of soil, the dark, silent, opaque lives of adults only revealed by the barks of Mustela and Moro, the farmhouse's two guard dogs, always in the doorway or stretched out across the entrance.

"Everything happens at night," Oak-Leaf confessed, leaning forward and lowering her voice, as if about to disclose something earth-shattering, but she left us in suspense, as usual, tailing off with a "You'll find out soon enough. Our dogs guess everything, I only have to look them in the eye to know what…"

Dogs could hitch up and give birth anywhere and Grandfather Hand recounted incredible cases of canine loyalty. A dog he once owned pursued him through the woods for two or three weeks with a broken leg until it found him; that was after Grandfather Hand had left him at home to convalesce. These were shepherd dogs that looked after the flock better than any shepherd.

"A shepherd can do without almost anything," he'd say, "even food, but not his dogs."

Unlike dogs, stallions and mares coupled more spectacularly and nobody could remain oblivious. It was almost the same as when they brought a cow to the bull, something they wouldn't let us watch or did when we were in class. They occasionally brought in a stud from outside, along with a vet and a couple of hands to ensure the male didn't hurt the female; they said he could rip her if he didn't take care. Quirze had been present at one of these mountings, as they called them, and later when he told us all about it, he used his forearm to describe the animal's thrusting. He said they forced the bull to cover the cow.

Grandfather Hand had told us that the rebec, an ancient, single-stringed wooden instrument, was made from hair from a stallion's tail and never a mare's, the mare's was no use, and we'd put that riddle to Oak-Leaf: "Why the stallion's and not the mare's? Because the mare's hair goes rotten from piss, you fool! They wouldn't withstand the bow's movements, they're as rotten as the TB boys in the monastery. Stallions piss straight and clean!"

And then she'd tell us, to show she was better informed than we were, why in the old days the boys played the *zambomba* drum in fiestas and the girls the mortar, and never the other way round.

Quirze waved his hand and laughed: "It's the same story as the hair from the stallion's tail, the drum is further away than the mortar. Only boys can handle the *zambomba!*"

The worst of the birds was the night owl. When it shrieked it brought on the shivers and meant someone was dying and the friars staggered out of the monastery in trepidation to go and give a dying individual the last rites. There were also sparrows, nightingales, swallows, finches, greenfinches, goldfinches…that a lot of villagers hunted in the woods with all kinds of wires, traps and pincers, and then they burnt their eyes out so they'd sing more sweetly and win prizes and cups in the competitions organized in local villages.

"Bugger me, if it isn't time for the quails to sing," said Uncle Bernat, when he prepared the fine green netting in early June that he put over the corn before he hid himself and blew through a hollow bone in a woollen sleeve to imitate the female's cry, and when the male flew down, he pounced, the net fell and it was trapped. He also hunted with a coat hanger.

The salamanders that came out by the spring were the little beasties in the forest that most frightened us with their lurid black and yellow skins; they were wetter and stickier than lizards, and people said they came from hell and that was why they could walk over flames or embers without burning themselves. They were creatures of fire, like dragons. Snakes scared us too, and foxes and toads, all reptiles, in fact, though not Quirze, he'd pick them up as cool as anything and kill the snakes with a blow from a stick.

We played with crickets, and when we found a nest, Quirze peed in the hole so it flooded and the panicking crickets crawled out or drowned. Quirze stood with his back to us to pee and the girls would walk away or turn their heads, embarrassed to see Quirze with his fly open. He would summon me to his side: "Andreu! Come here, so we can make more water! The girls would have to crouch down and they'd never hit the hole, they'd spray it around like hens."

We cut the tails off lizards and waited to see if it was true that they grew back straight away. We hunted flies and insects and put them in the middle of the cobwebs spiders had spun between leaves and branches and watched the weaver shoot out of his hideout, wrap them in a white gauze of saliva and down them there and then or take them away and hang them by a thread. We'd block the entrances to anthills to see how frantic the line of ants got that didn't know where it should go, as if they'd been driven crazy. We caught butterflies with our fingers, by waiting for them to close their wings when they settled on a flower or a leaf in the meadow, and afterwards, if we liked their colours or patterns, we'd press them hard between the pages of a book, and announce we had embalmed them forever, as we shook off the powder their bright, dusty wings had left on our fingertips…

One day, when I'd been staying on and off for almost two years on the grandparents' farm, or at Granny's, as Mother sometimes said, we found a dead horse in a small field on a bend in the track round the woods, mid-point between the farmhouse and the Novíssima school. That obstacle by side of the track was a peculiar sight from afar, like a heap of dung.

It was one of those autumn mornings when the countryside was a misty blue as if the sun hadn't the strength to disperse the nighttime dampness. As we drew nearer to the bend, we got a whiff of a dung-like smell that gradually became unbearable, and heard a cloud of flies and other insects buzzing that was unusual for the time of year.

From closer up, we thought it was a mound of red earth swarming with ants. Then we saw four legs dwarfed by a bulging belly and liquid and guts sluicing out. We only spotted the head, the gaping, foaming mouth, the huge, magnolia-white teeth, and the only eye we could see, like an open flower, when we got closer to the carcass, because it was half-buried under clumps of dead grass, separated from its body by a long, narrow neck. The size of its swollen body also helped to conceal its head.

The three of us observed the carcass in respectful silence. It wasn't one of ours, for sure, because we know all our animals by name, just as the dogs did.

We decided that if the people on the farm knew nothing about it, we should rush to school in case they could shed some light. Perhaps it came from a stable on a neighbouring farm.

"There's a dead horse with its guts hanging out on the track," Quirze told Mr. Madern the teacher, when he'd finished the ritual prayers, called the register and everyone was thinking about opening their desks and starting on handwriting exercises. Apparently nobody was aware of the dead horse.

The teacher only said: "I expect you mean injured. Animals sometimes suffer attacks of exhaustion or congestion, like human beings. Horses have strong hearts, but they can also give up on them when they've had enough. Its owners will call the vet, if needs be."

Quirze looked at me and at Oak-Leaf—we didn't know whether she'd seen the horse or not—as if he was wondering whether we felt like adding anything, but we didn't. Girls and boys were in the same class, it was a deal Miss Pepita and Mr. Madern had reached, because the dopey ex-nun only wanted the little ones, as she was frightened by the bigger children she couldn't handle. Of course, they'd warned us that if an inspector ever called, we'd have to separate out, boys with boys and girls with girls, because mixed education was banned. But there weren't many of us at the Novíssima, we all knew and trusted each other, and there was no need for precautions. Cry-Baby was still one of Miss Silly's little'uns.

The teacher decided to start the day off with a dictation and while he was walking between our desks, holding the book he was reading in one hand, we heard voices, people running and cars driving up and down the road that went past the front of the Novíssima. Mr. Madern stuck his head out of the window, then gave the book to Gamundi, the brightest boy in the class, so he could continue the dictation, while he went and spoke to the infant teacher in the classroom next door.

Gamundi was a boy from the Basque country who'd come to the district as a refugee during the war and stayed on after being adopted by a farming family, and he did his best to keep order but our eyes were all riveted to the window and the busy road. The schoolteacher and mistress had gone to the small garden by the entrance and were talking to a couple of civil guards. When Mr. Madern came back, he stared at Quirze and rasped: "You should've said it was a horse that had been disembowelled and abandoned. Heaven knows who it belongs to. I expect it was gypsies who ran for it, or animal thieves who'd ridden it into the ground…"

He didn't complete his sentence as if there might have been other explanations.

The to-and-fro-ing gradually slowed down, and at lunchtime, when we walked home, the horse was on the edge of a ploughed field close to the meadow where we'd found it, with three well-dressed men, one being the mayor, Filthy-face, as Dad Quirze called him, and other people, with a couple of civil guards in close attendance. They were discussing whether the field's owner would give permission to bury the horse there or if it would be better to do it elsewhere.

Those in the farmhouse were now aware of what had happened.

"It's not a horse from these parts," said Grandmother Mercè. "The men would have recognized it if it was."

Aunt Ció and Enriqueta, who'd just arrived from her dress-making, said nothing; their minds were more focused on what they were cooking. That day the men didn't come home for lunch.

"There are animals," Grandmother went on as if to distract us from something that seemingly preoccupied Ció and Enriqueta that we couldn't fathom—just like when she was storytelling by the fireside—"who can scent death, I mean they can guess which day they are going to die. They know their end is nigh. The Red Farmhouse had a mare who'd been born in La Bruguera that the tenants bought when she was a foal to mate with a young purebred they had. Well, after years at the Red Farmhouse, after giving birth to a host of colts that were scattered around the district, Pack-of-hounds, which is what we called her, because she always brought the hunting hounds behind her, when she was very old and knew she was about to die, one night, when we were all asleep, she escaped from the farm—she was so old they didn't keep her tied up inside—and slowly made her way to La Bruguera, that's not very far, as you know, and the next morning, when the new day dawned, the hands found her dead by the door of the stable where she had been born. How mysterious, it's hard to warrant how clever these animals are!"

"Do you mean the dead horse we found had escaped and was running away from death?" asked Quirze, as if he didn't believe a word.

"Pack-of-hounds wasn't running away from death, quite the contrary, she was rushing to find it," laughed Grandmother Mercè and we thought it was odd of her to laugh when talking about such sad things.

"I thought that when they saw the end was round the corner, they fled to see if there was any way they could escape," persisted Quirze. None of us could get our heads round the idea that anyone, let alone an animal, could go out to welcome death like a revered guest.

"Ay!" exclaimed Grandmother Mercè as if she was about to teach us a lesson that was way beyond us. "Animals have a special instinct for finding remedies for their ailments: when they are injured they know to select burning bush or gas plant, and when a scorpion bites they immediately look for oregano. But when they realize that death is nigh, they aren't alarmed and don't try to flee in terror like us, they submit and greet it with resignation, as we do when we can't go out because it's pouring down, though we hope the rain will be a boon and bring buckets of water, a good harvest and blossoming fields. And if they can, if they have any strength left, like Pack-of-hounds, they go out in search of death, preferring to meet it in a pretty spot. If it weren't like that, where would the horses that used to die in battle have found their valour? Knights fought for a cause, their personal gain and honour, but the horses accompanying them wanted to encounter a worthy end outside the stable, on a field of flowers where death was master."

"Mother," whispered Aunt Ció, "don't say such things."

"Why do you keep putting fear into the children's heads?" nodded Aunty Enriqueta.

"Fear? What fear?" retorted Grandmother. "Animals don't fear death. And there are a lot of things we should learn from them and try to imitate."

"When Mother holds up a rabbit to break its neck with a stick," riposted Quirze obstinately, looking at Aunty Ció, his mother, out of the corner of his eye, "it wriggles as if it would like to escape. And roosters and hens cackle and run when they are going to cut their necks and put them in the pot."

Ció turned her head and stared at Quirze.

"Because rabbits and roosters don't want to die," chuckled Grandmother. "I'm talking about old or sick animals who've lived their lives and are looking for a change."

The loud, angry voices of men arguing reached us from the kitchen. The three women exchanged worried looks. Initially we could only make out the voices of Dad Quirze, Uncle Bernat and Jan the hand who was with them, and then the voices of the village mayor, Filthy-face, a plump, stunted man with a puffy face and no neck, and a civil guard talking in clipped Andalusian Spanish, Corporal Martínez; the other guard was silent and we didn't recognize him.

"I'm under no obligation to bury that animal!" shouted Dad Quirze in his most hostile tone of voice.

The voices of the mayor and the civil guard were quieter, more relaxed, and wafted our way like a whisper and it was impossible to make out what they were saying: neighbourhood, community, authority, owner..., and in Andalusian Spanish, *rezponsabilidá, órdenez, gobie'no civí, comandanzia...*

"It's one thing for Mr. Manubens the master to agree and quite another for us to have to do the work!" countered Dad Quirze.

The municipal officials spoke up again, now considerably more irritated, files, investigations, patrols... and in Castilian Spanish, *cuarta región militar*, *consecuencias desagradables*, *que cada palo aguante su vela*, we all have our crosses to bear...

The women hastily put our plates on the table and urged us to eat up and not be distracted.

Enriqueta and Ció, the two sisters, shifted plates and pans, creating a racket with ladles and milk jugs to shut out the men's conversation. Grandmother listened silently, head down and worried. Suddenly, we heard the corporal of the Civil Guard: *"Aténgaze a laz consecuenciaz!"*

And immediately after, the mayor's hoarse, strident voice shouting: "For fuck's sake! I don't want to see one hair of that animal on the path tomorrow!"

Silence descended like a gully into the hills. We watched the mayor and a couple of civil guards walk past the window.

Dad Quirze, Bernat and the hand entered the kitchen where we'd just eaten lunch. Grandmother gestured to us to go back to class and not wait around. Ció put apples in our pockets as we went out through the porch.

Dad Quirze stood still in the middle of the kitchen, his face redder than ever, his small, blue eyes flashing angrily like steel blades, his paunch heaving up and down as if he'd been running a race. Bernat planted himself in front of the fire. Jan the hand sat down on the chair with the broken seat, head bowed.

Before walking out the door, we heard Dad Quirze curse: "The bastards! A plague on the bitch that spawned them!"

8

The eviscerated horse was still lying in the same place at the edge of that field, with even more flies buzzing around and a worse stench in the air. We ran past holding our noses.

By evening, when we went home, with Oak-Leaf back in our gang, the horse had gone. A white sandy patch, that Quirze said was lime, covered the place where we'd seen it. Grass had been flattened and plants by the side of the path had been demolished as if they'd been forced to drag the horse along. There was no trace of the carcass.

We went into the woods feeling more excited than ever. In the twilight we all had the death of that unknown horse on our minds and started telling animal stories, as always happened when others ran out of steam or we teetered on the perilous brink of risqué conversations about peeping toms and flashers or Oak-Leaf's secrets.

"Well, I once heard about a shepherd dog"—each of us contributed their best-kept memories and on this occasion it was Oak-Leaf's turn—"that stayed by its master's side when he died of a heart attack in the middle of the woods, felled like a tree that had been axed, angina, and the dog didn't eat or drink for over a week, barking this way and that to attract someone's attention, until passing charcoal burners found them and took the dead man home with the dog trailing in his wake. Dogs never desert their masters."

"When Grandmother was a young woman, they had a goat at home they called Nanny because she acted as her mother's wet nurse, and reared her mother on the milk from her titty," reminisced Quirze. "When her mother shouted to her, Nanny came into the house, went to the cradle and placed her titty so the baby could suck as much as it wanted. That way Grandmother could get on with other chores. Nanny suckled all Grandmother's children: Andreu's father, Núria's father, my mother, Enriqueta, Uncle Bernat... everybody. And when Nanny died of old age, they all cried as if she were family. Grandfather Hand who'd not yet married Grandmother didn't bury her, he skinned her and made three or four bags for drinking wine, milk and water. And even now when we have a drink and press the skin to make the liquid squirt out, the skin bleats, like Nanny's maa-maa."

"My father had a horse," said Oak-Leaf, "that was very old and had worked hard its whole life until it was short of breath, so he let it do nothing but graze all day long in the meadow. Well this horse, when it saw the mares and young horses go by carrying heavy loads, it would go over and stand in front of them as if it wanted to help and followed them to where they had to unload and licked the sweat off their backs. He sensed they were tired and was helping them, even though he was so old he was almost blind. When he died they buried him on the quiet so the other animals didn't see, but when night fell and the other animals returned to their stables and couldn't find him, they started to whinny softly as if they were crying."

At the end of each story we stayed silent as if savouring and digesting the mysteries of these animals who had feelings like ours. We were all in contact with dogs, horses and chickens, and even Quirze appreciated their loyalty and was delighted when they jumped up and gave him a welcoming nuzzle.

Once we'd run out of stories, the ghost of that dead horse returned to fill the gap in our conversation.

"So you say the Civil Guard came to your house, right?" asked Oak-Leaf.

"Yes, they came at midday, at lunchtime..." I replied.

"To see if they could land the burial on us," added Quirze.

"Where can it have come from? Horses don't go off and get lost as easily as that…" Oak-Leaf asserted.

Quirze shrugged his shoulders.

"There's one civil guard who knows every hideout and corner of the woods. He's tall, young, fair, with a moustache."

"We didn't see him," I said. "We only recognized Martínez, the one in charge."

"They call him Canary because he comes from the Canary Islands. And Freckly Fair because he likes larking about. He's a real live wire. He's always with another one they call Curly Lettuce, who's also very handsome. The others are tall and have such huge paunches I don't know how they can walk all day long as they do. They're always panting and hanging out their tongues."

"My father says they're good for nothing," said Quirze, "that they're a load of layabouts who suck money and blood like ticks. You tell me what use they are if they don't do a blind thing all day."

"They keep an eye out," said Oak-Leaf, "so there's no thieving or fighting."

"The other day you said you'd caught Charcoal Pete stealing in the middle of the woods," Quirze whooped. "They're not that eagle-eyed."

Oak-Leaf felt deflated. Cry-Baby and I laughed.

"They're not always keeping an eye out," she protested. "They sometimes relax, have a siesta… Nobody can see them in the middle of the woods, so they do whatever they feel like… I once saw Canary by himself taking his clothes off and swimming in the river…"

"Did you really see him swimming?"

"And what was the other one doing?"

"He was by himself, they must have split up. Or maybe he was keeping a lookout further up so they didn't surprise his mate in the water."

"Was it Canary?" reacted Quirze, intrigued. "Did you see him stark naked?"

Oak-Leaf looked down, as she always did when something embarrassed her or she wanted to ask a favour.

"It wasn't the first time…"

"You're making this up," Quirze retorted. "You're a liar."

"Don't believe me then. I've seen him several times… lying on the ground sunbathing. As he comes from the Canaries, I expect he misses the sun and doesn't want his skin turning white."

"Does he strip off only to sunbathe?" asked Cry-Baby who chimed in now and then.

"And to swim in the river, when it's hot, I just told you."

"If we're going to believe you, everybody runs around these woods stark naked!" said Quirze, turning the screw.

"No, only mad Antònia and him, but it's different. Canary's not mad. Antònia doesn't know what she's doing."

"What's so different, if they're both in their birthday suits?"

"What else? Come on, tell us. What else does Canary do?"

Oak-Leaf sprang to her feet. "I must go. I'll tell you another day."

"You always do this!" I protested. "You're one big tease."

"He's a man and she's a woman, it's hardly the same. I'll tell you some other time."

"How wonderful! How mysterious! He's a man and she's a woman! Men's peckers droop and women have tits and a fanny, that's the big difference."

"You're disgusting, Quirze!"

"And you're a lying cow!"

"There are lots of things I can't tell."

"You're a piss-pot!"

Oak-Leaf ran home while Quirze screamed after her: "That's what the teacher always says: 'Oak-Leaf's a piss-pot!'"

"That's a lie!" She swung round, still running. "Mr. Madern doesn't call me Oak-Leaf. He calls me by my proper name, Elisa. Elisa. My real name."

"Oh, really!" Quirze mocked the fleeing girl's voice. "Elisa! How lovely, Elisa! Call her Elisa, that's so posh. Oak-Leaf, rather than Oak-Leaf, you stink of dung and glue!"

And he began to shout and murder that song:

> "The man who teaches me
> fell in love with me
> fol-de-rum, fol-de-ree!
> Fell in love with Elisa,
> saying, don't you be a nun,
> you're going to marry me,
> fol-de-rum, fol-de-ree!
> The teacher'll marry
> Elisa Oak-Leafie!"

9

Nobody mentioned the horse again, it was as if we had never seen it. Dad Quirze was grumpier than usual. If it was difficult to get a word out of him before, he now acted like a dumb mute after that shouting match with the local dignitaries. As if their visitation had passed on a disease that was silently eating away his insides.

On one of the few days he was on the farm with his flock, Grandfather Hand bumped into him on the porch, just as we three were leaving for class with our satchels, and he talked to him as if he were a stranger.

"Watch out for the scoopers, they're a scheming bunch. They're a stinking lot. And those other bigwigs are nasty too. They all live on cushy handouts."

"Bigwig" in Grandfather's language was any person of authority who didn't deserve the place he occupied, that he'd simply inherited.

"Tell them the horse was mine and let them turn their fire on me. That I brought it down from the mountains. That it was a breed from the Pyrenees I wanted to transplant down here. That I was bringing it with the flock when it wandered off, as lots of animals do…"

Dad Quirze said nothing. When Grandfather Hand noticed we'd come to a halt and were listening, he raised his stick and waved it threateningly at us: "So what are you three doing here? Clear off to class, you don't deserve the crumbs on your plate! Beat it, and quick, or I'll set the dogs on you."

Several days went by before we got back on friendly terms with Oak-Leaf and she walked back with us after school. We'd fallen out over something silly, or she and Quirze had had one of their squabbles. And then she always found excuses not to come with us: one day she left class later, another she had to run an errand in the village, on yet another she dilly-dallied chatting with her girlfriends by the exit. Walking home without her wasn't such fun. If she wasn't there, we didn't fancy going into the woods to hunt crickets, pick herbs or tell stories. It was if something was missing in the woods—her voice perhaps.

One afternoon, when the scent of spring was in the air, though the weather still wasn't fine enough for us to climb our plum tree again, Cry-Baby stayed behind in class because the teacher wanted her to do a test to see if she could change class, leave the tiny tots and join us; she seemed big enough and advanced enough in her schoolwork.

While we were waiting, Quirze and I amused ourselves playing a game of marbles with a couple of friends, Gamundi and someone else. Oak-Leaf was chatting to some girls, and from time to time she looked round and glanced our way out of the corner of her eye, as if waiting for us to leave so she could follow. However, that may just have been a hunch of mine, because we'd not walked home together with Oak-Leaf for days.

When Cry-Baby finally appeared, Quirze and I couldn't leave the game and we told her to wait a moment, we were winning. A minute would do it.

Oak-Leaf left the other girls to go and say hello to Cry-Baby. They sat down on the roadside and chatted while we finished our game.

"Let's go," shouted Quirze, standing up and stuffing the marbles we'd won into his pocket.

Oak-Leaf and Cry-Baby got to their feet as well, and I did too. Pleased with our winnings, Quirze walked on ahead, not aware of Oak-Leaf silently bringing up the rear.

"Got over your tantrum?" he finally asked when he turned his head and saw her.

Oak-Leaf said nothing.

"And what about you?" he asked Cry-Baby. "What did the teacher say?"

"That she'll join our class," replied Oak-Leaf, anticipating her answer. "She may have to stay behind on other days, because the teacher wants to give her extra lessons by herself so she can catch up. She's a big girl now and will be joining us. She'll take her First Communion this year."

"She's big is she, this jenny-wren, this runt?" rasped Quirze, not even bothering to look behind him. "Can't you see how she's stuck for words when she's asked a simple question? Have you swallowed your tongue, or do other people have to speak up for you?"

Cry-Baby said nothing. Oak-Leaf glanced at me as if to say my cousin's tone of voice indicated he was raring for a fight.

We walked silently along the track. After a while, when we were nearing the turning into the woods, the spot where Oak-Leaf went her way, she lowered her voice, as if saying something unimportant: "Núria's tired. She should take a rest before she goes home."

Initially we were surprised to hear Cry-Baby's real name that we never used.

"Tired?" grimaced Quirze, stopping in his tracks. We all followed suit, and waited for her to react.

"The teacher gave her a dictation and a decimal division and she got into a bit of a state," Oak-Leaf continued in the same vein, as if speaking up for the younger girl. "She's upset."

"Upset? What do you mean 'she's upset'?" asked Quirze, apparently more surprised than ever.

"She's a bit scared."

"What's up with the ninny?"

Oak-Leaf hesitated for a second. "She's scared of the teacher of the big class, Mr. Madern... She's worried about changing class and mates... She's scared of joining the class with the big kids. She's afraid they'll give her the evil eye."

"She'll get over that. If she wants to be a big girl, she'll have to learn to handle teething problems."

Quirze turned round to walk off down the path, but Oak-Leaf dropped Cry-Baby's hand and positioned herself in front of him as if to block his way, in a friendly way, not at all aggressively, and she implored him: "Quirze…"

We were astonished to see Quirze look at her calmly, quietly intrigued by the way she continued with that begging tone.

"Quirze… Núria's not feeling well. Let her rest for a bit."

Oak-Leaf's voice sounded eminently reasonable.

"Please, Quirze. I'll tell you everything I've seen in the woods. Whatever you want to know."

Quirze said nothing and took the turning as if he was leading us into the woods and we all followed.

10

Cry-Baby took First Communion in the chapel in the Saint Camillus monastery. The other farm children taking their First Communion that year did so in the parish church, accompanied by their families, as was obligatory, with the other new communicants in the locality.

It was very hard to get the parish priest to permit that special arrangement. However, Dad Quirze was a tough nut and never softened until he got his own way.

Dad Quirze didn't want to step foot inside the church or deal with that devious, two-faced priest—his words—and he called on the Father Superior from the Saint Camillus monastery, a squat, ruddy-cheeked Navarrese, to help him. Father Tafalla and Uncle Quirze were friends, got on well, and were involved in stuff that we didn't understand. The truth, according to Grandmother Mercè, was that Dad Quirze didn't want to show his face. That was all she ever said: "He doesn't want to show his face. Quirze is like that, he doesn't want to be seen and fuel village gossip," she repeated when someone outside the family asked what was behind his surprising decision.

If the strangers' questions began to harass, Grandmother gave her answers a further twist: "We don't know where the girl's parents are," she said, "Quirze, my son-in-law, doesn't want anyone to think he's assuming the role of his in-laws. If the girl's parents, Fonso and Mites, were here, there'd be nothing to worry about, but the idea of organizing a First Communion party when we don't know if her parents are alive or dead upsets him, you must understand that."

And she added, by way of a weaker argument: "Besides, every Sunday Quirze goes to mass at the Saint Camillus monastery, he doesn't go to the parish church. You know, he can't change his habits just like that."

Of necessity she stated loud and clear that he abided by his Sunday duties that were almost compulsory in those days. Nobody could dodge them. At school, we pupils went to mass every Sunday organized and accompanied by our teacher, Miss Pepita, since Mr. Madern spent the weekends in his house in the city. And we saw how the pupils in the national school did likewise, accompanied by their teachers, a few pews in front. That organized attendance declined over time and we were allowed go to mass by ourselves or with our parents, at any time, morning mass or solemn mass, but on Monday, when we reached school, the master made us say which mass we'd been to, with whom, what was the colour of the celebrant's chasuble, what was the sermon about, who'd seen us there…as if he was interrogating us. When somebody couldn't go, for whatever reason, he or she had to bring a note from their parents with an excuse, an illness or a trip, if they didn't want to suffer the requisite punishment. Control of the adult population was more subtle, but no less efficient. Nobody dared be defiant and openly say they didn't go to mass, that they didn't do their duty. Men normally went reluctantly, always to the main, solemn mass, just before aperitifs in the bar on the square, and stood at the back of church and constantly went in and out on the excuse that they were going for a smoke in the entrance or the small square, need a quick drag, they'd say.

We took it that not wanting to show his face meant that Dad Quirze refused to accompany Cry-Baby to her communion. Not because he didn't want to support her, but because the priest and Uncle Quirze couldn't stand the sight of one another. Even though she wasn't a woman overly keen on mass,Ció had no difficulty in supporting the girl and even going to the altar and kneeling to receive the sacred wafer on such a day. However, Dad Quirze was tough as steel and we didn't know why he held that attitude towards the priest, who seemed polite and unassuming enough. With the exception of Ció, everyone on the farm used the slightest excuse to skip mass, Grandmother Mercè because she was too old and could hardly walk, Grandfather Hand because he was away almost the whole year and nobody ever knew where he was, Dad Quirze because he said he went to the monastery chapel with his friend, Father Tafalla, Uncle Bernat because he disappeared with his young friends from the farms round-and-about and nobody was going to keep them on a leash, Aunt Enriqueta because she said she went to the cathedral in Vic, that she preferred all those canons and bishops in their finery…, and the hands did whatever they wanted and nobody asked them what they did or didn't do when they had a free day. Aunt Ció was the only one who ever put in an appearance in the parish church—"put in an appearance" was her way of saying to go to morning mass, or else "drop by," or "it's a good idea to cross the threshold now and then"—and she also attended the occasional big religious ceremony like the Corpus procession, the singing in the month of the Virgin Mary and a few Lenten or Novena sermons, when the preacher was renowned and silver-tongued, or so they claimed.

The heart-searching began the moment the school opened the list to inscribe pupils who were going to take their First Communion that year. Cry-Baby had already missed out one year and couldn't wait another before "putting in an appearance." Grandmother, Ció and Dad Quirze went into a huddle after supper because the date for registering was almost up. Uncle Bernat, Aunt Enriqueta and the hands retired upstairs to bed, to the attic, as Father Tafalla said, making Grandmother split her sides. The decision fell exclusively to Dad Quirze. The school and parish priest had been piling on the pressure. It was compulsory for parents to take their children to communion. But Cry-Baby wasn't

Quirze or Ció's daughter and that had saved her the previous year. They claimed they were expecting the parents to return, in particular her father, because they said her mother had fled to France with her father at the end of the war as easily as they claimed she'd gone into service with a couple in Barcelona, all to avoid reprisals from the nationals.

"We can't go on pretending," Ció implored, "if we don't want to put in an appearance. The excuse that her parents are abroad won't do anymore. Everybody knows her father fled to France, and that her mother followed soon after, leaving the girl with us. It's common knowledge. Up to now we've been able to convince them Núria was staying with us while she waited for her parents to come back, but too much time has now gone by and the parish priest is pursuing us. He says she's too old, that it's our responsibility..."

Dad Quirze listened and said nothing. He leaned his head over his dirty plate and his beady eyes stared at the knife his hand was waving.

"He says the girl's behaviour will help dispel her parents' bad reputation," insisted Ció.

"They didn't hound us over Andreu," whispered Dad Quirze, making no effort to make himself heard.

I was Andreu.

"He's different," noted Ció. "Andreu comes from elsewhere and spends time here and time with his mother. Núria is a local, from our parish. Andreu's town is further away. Florència took him to school with the clergy and to have communion when he was of an age, not so very long ago. She did what she had to. The clergy know that's the case. They mull it over among themselves. They know the state of play. And they're hand-in-glove with the bigwigs in the town hall. Your stubbornness could damage us more than you think. All the efforts we've made will count for nothing if we get on the wrong side of these people just because you've decided to dig your heels in."

Dad Quirze clammed up again. Quirze and I were playing cards at the other end of the table, but I hung on their every word. Cry-Baby had gone to bed. Young Quirze didn't seem to care a fig about what the grownups were whispering about.

"I don't think there's any way around this," insisted Grandmother. "We could do what we did with young Quirze…"

Ció looked fearfully at Grandmother: "The priest wants it to take place in the parish church, and wants her to appear before the whole congregation. We can't repeat with her what we did with Quirze. They want the daughter to atone for the sins of her father; they want to see the rebel's daughter bow her head!"

Dad Quirze mumbled, as if he was talking to himself: "For Christ's sake, that blasted cleric doesn't care a damn about the girl! The bastard wants me and every man-jack of us to lick his boots! And if he could, he'd like to see Fonso drag himself through the church hanging his tongue out, begging him to allow her to take communion!"

The women looked appalled and glanced at us children as if apologizing for the father's oaths.

"You should think it over…" resumed Grandmother warily after a moment. "Fonso says… Fonso would agree… we have no choice, they leave us no other option and we can't delay it any longer."

"I swore I'd never step inside that place while I had a breath of life inside me!" Dad Quirze now raised his voice.

"Times have changed," responded Grandmother. "We can't be tied to what we said or didn't say."

"Perhaps Father Tafalla can find a solution," suggested Ció hesitantly.

When they told us to go up to bed, they were arguing over who should broach the problem with the monastery's Father Superior. Within days Cry-Baby was added to the list of new communicants and began to attend the twice-weekly catechism classes. The little girl's new time-table obliged her to go to the parish church as soon as afternoon school was finished and return home by herself. Grandmother suffered those first few days and made us go out to look for her, until Dad Quirze said: "If she's big enough to take her First Communion, she's big enough to come home by herself. She knows the way by now."

Father Tafalla had promised Dad Quirze he would speak to the parish priest so the girl could take First Communion in the monastery chapel, by herself, in a private ceremony. That was the only way Dad Quirze would assent to her going to catechism classes, or doctrine, as they called it.

The conversations between the priest and the Superior weren't easy. The precedent set by Quirze, who had done just that, namely, a ceremony by himself in the monastery chapel, with only his closest family in attendance, was no help. His case, according to the priest, belonged to the period immediately after the war, when the church hadn't been entirely rebuilt. Everybody else just about avoided taking their First Communion in the monastery chapel, he said, given the way the church had been left, with only its walls and altar left intact, it was a miracle it was still standing. It was different now, the priest continued andCió explained what Father Tafalla had said to her: "He says it is different now, it's the community that matters, the example, showing she belongs to the parish. He tried so many angles! No exceptions could be made. I don't think we can not go through the performance this time."

Dad Quirze listened silently, as if he wasn't listening at all.

"And what if the girl falls ill?" he piped, nodding, a glint in his beady eyes.

"What do you mean?" asked Ció, half fearfully. "You mean…?"

As usual at that time in the evening, after supper, Quirze and I were sitting at the other end of the table a long way from the fire and playing cards. In step with household tradition, Quirze and I were big lads now and nobody would have thought to exclude us from adult conversation. When they didn't want us to hear something, they simply didn't mention it in our presence. They never began a conversation they would have to cut short because of the presence of someone, let alone us. They certainly had their secrets and private conversations, but the first condition to guarantee secrecy was that nobody should even know they existed. A secret exposed to the view of someone was like a tightly closed drawer that had been put on display for everyone to see on top of the chest: it drew every gaze and aroused everyone's curiosity. That's why they talked freely about everything and we acted as if we couldn't hear or understand them, and they did the same.

"That's not a bad idea..." commented Grandmother Mercè, smiling.

When Father Tafalla was consulted, he didn't find it a bad solution either. *In extremis*, they said he said. I thought it was strange for Saint Camillus Father Superior to agree to such a childish ploy, against the rigorous views expressed by the parish priest. It was then I suspected that there must be some secret link, some strange connivance, between my uncle and aunt, Dad Quirze in particular, and the monastery and its Father Superior.

One week before the May Sunday set aside for First Communion, Cry-Baby fell ill.

11

Cry-Baby slept in a small bed next to Grandmother's big bed in a small room they called the alcove that led to a larger room separated off by white curtains gathered up by a thick rope hooked to the wall.

The large room had a wardrobe with a mirror, two chests of drawers, an armchair and an osier rocking chair, and the walls were packed with pictures of saints and Sacred Hearts.

Quirze and I slept on a couple of straw mattresses in the room where the hands and Bernat slept in three or four little beds and bolsters, though you never knew who'd be there because there were hands who could sleep there or go and spend the night in their own homes, depending on the demands of work. It was a room as big as the sitting room. And right opposite the hands' room, or the boys' room, as it was also called, was another door in a small passage that led to the girls' room with two beds, where only Aunt Enriqueta slept. Aunt Ció and Dad Quirze slept in a room at the back of the living room that looked over the elder tree.

All the bedroom doors opened on to the sitting room and at the back were French windows to the gallery. The sitting room looked huge, and was full of chairs lined up against the wall, old paintings, bulging chests of drawers with saints stuffed inside glass domes, like the butterflies fading between the pages of our books, and two or three trunks, what they called crates.

The door to Grandmother's room was old and there were lots of cracks in the ill-fitting timber. The door's rustic roughness contrasted sharply with the relative elegance and cleanliness of the room and the alcove.

The day it was decided the little girl would fall ill,Ció and Enriqueta spring-cleaned the sitting room, bedroom and alcove; they put clean sheets and pillows on the two beds and a pink eiderdown with images of fantastic birds on the bigger bed, one Grandmother said was made of pure silk, a wedding present—it was antique!—as good as new, because, as we know, good things last a life time.

"That eiderdown must be real quality," said Grandmother, "because the village borrowed it every year to decorate the balcony for the Corpus procession. Nothing could beat it. It gleamed like a pink, silken sun."

Quirze and I were charged with the responsibility of telling the priest about Cry-Baby's illness, and her probable non-attendance at catechism classes until her fever abated. The priest scowled and said nothing.

On Friday, Father Tafalla went to see the priest to suggest a solution: if he agreed, he could give the sick child communion on Sunday. However, the priest said under no circumstances, the girl must come to the parish church, ill or not, and that if she couldn't come next Sunday, the one after, or next month, then let it happen as soon as she could get up.

Dad Quirze chuckled whenCió told him the outcome from Father Tafalla's negotiations after supper.

"Any Sunday will do…" he repeated. "It could be in the middle of summer when everybody's forgotten about all this."

"If it's all about not showing your face," Grandmother repeated, "you've got what you wanted."

"One of these mornings, the girl, the lads and I will go to morning mass," Ció proposed, "and we'll end this nonsense."

"I couldn't care less whether it is early morning mass, or solemn mass," added Dad Quirze, "because they won't be organizing any special ceremony for us."

"In any case, people take communion in the Chapel of the Holy Sacrament and parishioners don't take a blind bit of notice," commented Ció.

Every day at school the teacher asked after Núria and Oak-Leaf too. Quirze and I always replied that she had some sort of fever: a horrible cold that could be flu or worse even, scarlet fever, because her neck was a deep red.

Uncle Bernat took the colt and trap to go fetch the village doctor; he was an elegant old man who always wore a hat and cravat and carried a small case as if he was setting out on his travels. That same day, at noon, Ció had given Cry-Baby a potent beverage of water boiled with stinking herbs; it immediately produced a violent sneezing fit and her face and neck flushed red as if she'd had a rush of blood to her head.

The doctor recommended rest, eucalyptus steam baths, a medical ointment from the chemist's and hot towels on the chest. However he never said what in fact was wrong with her.

After First Communion Sunday, the parish priest himself took advantage of a half-holiday to visit the farmhouse accompanied by the Father Superior from Saint Camillus. Both strolled up in the afternoon under an open black umbrella to protect them from the sun. Both clutched a breviary, and Grandmother Mercè, who had spotted them coming along the path through the woods, shouted to us that two characters from the Nativity were on their way. As soon as she heard that, Ció began laying the table with the best napkins so as to invite them to have a bite to eat. Dad Quirze was out hiring the thresher, men to guide the oxen and teams of reapers and hands for the harvest. There was a lot of work to do.

"We just happened to walk past your house deep in our breviary prayers," said the Father Superior, "so we thought we'd look in on the sick child."

First they sat around the table and ate their snacks like two fine gentlemen with white napkins dangling from their necks like bibs, while they discussed the history of the village and neighbouring farmhouses.

They were fascinated by the story behind each house and their nicknames—Shepherd-boy's, Always's, Pretty Girl's, Smocky's and the bigger places like Tona's, Soca's or La Bruguera's, or even the ruder tags like Dry Shit, Twisted Cock, Filthy Face or Dirty Whore—a subject on which Grandmother displayed an encyclopaedic knowledge. Now and then, the priest shamelessly asked about family members or business, like the whereabouts of Dad Quirze, whether he worked even on a Sunday, or whether Aunt Enriqueta was courting someone in Vic, thus making a meal of the fact that she went there every day to sew, or whether we weren't overwhelmed by the constant visits from the women who worked in the factories in the small towns along the river who came to the farmhouse to ask for fresh bread or flour, potatoes or fresh eggs at knockdown prices or, in fact, to beg any food they could get.

Grandmother never gave a straight answer: "Ohh!" she'd say: "Not so many come these days. It was a daily procession after the war. Men as well, to be sure."

They asked about Aunt Enriqueta, but Grandmother acted as if she'd not heard and carried on chatting: "The fact is that nobody can eat the black bread they give out as rations. Once a hapless woman came with a crust of that horrible bread so I could taste for myself what they were forced to eat. I almost wept, it was like a lump of coal or dirty sawdust. I just thought how war can even destroy bread, can even murder bread, because that was no kind of bread, it was bread that had died and been stripped of its soul and goodness. I kept that piece of black bread, I didn't dare throw it away, and put in by the feet of the Virgin Mary on the sitting-room sideboard, to see whether those up above might work a miracle like the one at that wedding when Jesus turned water into wine because his mother asked him to, though he'd not noticed the wine had run out and that the guests were drinking anything they could lay their hands on, but heaven seems to be turning a blind eye, apparently we don't deserve a miracle."

Dressed like a shepherdess and looking like an actress in her hat, enclosed in a bell jar on the sideboard, the Virgin Mary always had something placed at her feet by Grandmother or Aunt Ció, especially unusual stones, smooth pebbles from the stream, withered flowers, bits of tallow candle, tops of Easter candles, religious prints and funeral mementoes, but we'd never noticed the piece of black bread Grandmother had mentioned. What we had all seen was the way Grandmother rushed to pick up any piece of bread that fell on the floor and put it back on the table, or the way she kissed the drawer. And when she collected up the napkins after a meal, she and Aunt Ció were very careful not to let a single crumb fall on the floor; they emptied them all into a bowl and used them to make soup or mixed them into our breakfast milk, to make a milky gruel.

As the clerics again asked after Enriqueta, Grandmother finally had to respond: "Enriqueta seems very frivolous, but in fact she never gets involved with anyone. I don't know why people gossip so much about seamstresses, especially those who work for men. It's all idle talk, you know, all those hours spent with hands at work, and mouths free to…"

"So what about Quirze?" inquired the parish priest.

"Dad Quirze can't keep up with his work. He's run off his feet. However, he does rest a bit on Sundays. He even finds the time to make it to your monastery, isn't that right, Father Tafalla?"

The Father Superior nodded, though he didn't glance at the parish priest and tried to bring the conversation back to the subject of the nicknames for local farmhouses.

"Sundays are sacred," said Grandmother, "but, dearie me, not at harvest time, that will soon be upon us, when people do work on Sundays, you know, they only stop when it's raining, or if it's soaking, when the straw clogs up the machine and the men can't do a thing."

The priest also took an interest in me and Cry-Baby, the refugees, as he called us, and in our parents. He said my mother was reputed to be upstanding and hard-working, that's what he'd heard from the priest in my town, a worker much esteemed in her textile factory who had handled the situation she found herself in with exemplary resignation: God was putting her to the test, perhaps it was a penitence that would allow the whole family to purge the excesses of the past. He barely mentioned Cry-Baby's parents, simply said it was strange we'd had no news of them for so long.

"The two brothers are quite different cases," declared the priest. "And the fact that Fonso and Mites fled attested to their guilt. Let's hope that God can forgive them."

He said "attested" and that was the first time I'd heard that word, which not even Grandmother used, perhaps she wasn't aware it existed, and I was also shocked that God would put people who didn't believe in him through such hard tests. How could he ever expect to convince them of his existence and his acclaimed goodness if he hounded them like that?

These thoughts came to me quite spontaneously, prompted by remarks made by grownups. I myself was quite shocked and never mentioned them because I recognized that they were tiny seeds of evil now sprouting within me, the evil I'd been warned about in catechism classes, against which the priests told us to be on our guard, the evil that sullied everything, the accursed evil that never gave up and even penetrated our brains and burrowed away into our most private selves, into our thoughts, dreams, desires, plans, hopes, memories…anything might harbour the worm of evil that rotted the roots of the deepest, most invisible things.

Such thoughts were proof of the existence of evil and I'd found the way to rid my mind of them. I let them take shape so I knew exactly what they said they were like and were after…, and then I riposted with the formula I had learned in class or from doctrine, as written in the bishopric's catechism they made us learn by heart. When these evil thoughts surfaced, I classified them according to the doctrine I had learned, the commandments of God's Law, the commandments of the Church, and the sins that called out for God's or heaven's vengeance, that I really didn't understand, and all that made me imagine a vengeful, scheming God who was extremely clinical in his punishments, especially those that called for revenge, new sins that had apparently been added to the old traditional ones, because men had found evil ways that went beyond the original ten precepts, and these commandments that aroused God's anger were deliberate murder, impure sinning against nature, not paying workers their proper rate, not paying the church its tithes and quota from the harvest…and one or two others I don't remember, perhaps belonging to a category deemed to be against the Church. If I couldn't find a rule to counter my thoughts, to placate my inner voice, I told myself they were facetious, frivolous and trivial and couldn't be sins. However, I couldn't for the life of me fathom why all-powerful, almighty God wanted men to believe who weren't so inclined. Why did he persecute non-believers like that? Why did he set his priest-hounds on them threatening eternal damnation in hell? Why couldn't God's glory shine equally brightly without requiring the submission of those ignorant simpletons who said they only believed in what they could see and thought priests were a gang of charlatans? Why did God need those incredulous people? Weren't they free to damn themselves? I couldn't find an answer to all that, and told myself I couldn't understand because if I could, I would be as intelligent as God, and that was unthinkable, pride comparable to the devil's, to darkest Satan's, and that was why I might allow myself such thoughts, because they were the clearest proof of my mediocrity, of the superiority of divine intelligence. And all that made me wary, pensive, cautious, ingenuous, in a word: cowardly. God had vanquished in the war by helping those who had fought in his name, and the non-believers who had burnt temples and mocked his laws had lost and were now persecuted, imprisoned, vilified and blacklisted. Could one ask for clearer proof of his omnipotence?

When we accompanied the priest and the Superior up to the alcove, we found Cry-Baby sunk in Grandmother's big bed, the whole room full of the vapours and scents from infusions and every small table and chest of drawers strewn with glasses and jugs of herbal waters and boxes of medicine.

Cry-Baby looked frightened, her face wan and pale, her eyes damp and feverish surrounded by dark bluish circles, her hair a dishevelled mess over the huge pillow, her nose peeping out from beneath the turn of the sheet. Cry-Baby was so timid, so impressionable and susceptible that she believed everything she was told and never doubted for a moment: when we said she'd got very thin, every bit of food began to disgust her, if we said she seemed deaf, she made us repeat what we'd said three or four times, and when people said she was ill, her temperature immediately rocketed as if it had been waiting for the order to do just that.

"We've no news of her parents, I suppose?" the priest asked, staring at the girl hidden under her sheets, keeping well away, as if afraid he might catch something.

"Nothing at all," Ció replied curtly.

"That's another reason not to rush into doing things on a grand scale…" Grandmother Mercè took the opportunity to add. "Without her parents, we don't know what we should do."

"Her parents can't complain," interjected the priest. "If they'd responded as they should, they'd not be able to find the words to thank us."

A very loud noise came from the sitting room, as if something had fallen on the floor or the ceiling had collapsed. We all looked round in the direction of the door, and Ció went off to see what had happened. She came back immediately and said: "It's nothing. A copper pot fell on the floor. A cat must have been getting up to its tricks."

"This house is full of goblins," laughed Grandmother. "Looks like the scattering of hyssop and holy water at Easter didn't rid us of all our evil spirits."

The two clerics exchanged shocked glances, not knowing how to react to what Grandmother had said.

"As we were saying, without her parents and with this illness…" resumed Father Tafalla, leaving the alcove. "We must come to a decision."

"The parents are not a problem," retorted the parish priest. "It's our responsibility."

"I mentioned them because they are important factors that count in the village," persisted the Saint Camillus Superior, "Nobody will be surprised if the ceremony is a quiet affair…"

The priest muttered to himself until, on his way to the door, he retorted: "If they at least came to take the sacraments more often, mass at the very least… Reprobates, they'll end up reprobates or worse if they don't change their ways."

Father Tafalla turned to the women as if to explain or translate a sentence that had been uttered in Latin: "He's referring to Núria's parents. They were vicious priest-baiters. Quite shocking."

"The whole lot of them!" insisted the priest as he walked through the doorway.

"That's precisely why the uncles, aunts and Grandmother want the girl to do her duty," the friar stood next to the priest and took his arm, trying to persuade him. "They are caught in an uncomfortable position, and we must take that into account. And they're doing their best to please everyone."

The priest said nothing. He stood stock still in the middle of the big sitting room and looked around to find the reason for the big din they'd heard a moment ago.

"When the girl recovers a bit, the entire family will accompany her to communion in our chapel," the Saint Camillus friar added, trying to get him to swallow the pill. "And then she can quietly continue convalescing. That will also help to bring us all together a bit. It will be a step forward for the parish."

We went silently downstairs. In the porch, before he left, the priest held out his hand for us two nippers to kiss, andCió and Grandmother followed suit.

"You do what you must do," he finally conceded, as they walked off, "but be aware that we must get the Bishop's permission."

Father Tafalla gave us a knowing look before they disappeared into the distance.

12

Mr. Madern, the master, Clever-Clogs, as Grandmother had nicknamed him, asked after Cry-Baby's health day in day out and seemed the one most worried by the slowness of her recovery. The ex-nun, Pepita, Miss Silly, on the other hand, never inquired about her, as if she'd forgotten her the moment she switched class, as if she meant nothing to her anymore, wasn't even an acquaintance.

The night before First Communion Sunday, the three women in the house summoned us to Grandmother's room to try on the clothes we'd wear to the ceremony on the following day. Aunt Enriqueta had made a new dress for Núria and two sets of trousers for Quirze and me. They were long trousers, the first I had worn since my own First Communion.

They gave us our trousers to go and try on in our bedroom, while they inspected Cry-Baby's dress to see how well it fitted.

Quirze pulled his trousers on in a flash and said nothing. Those long trousers unleashed a stream of thoughts in my head, as I pulled them on, a strange feeling, a bittersweet mix of nostalgia and excitement. I saw myself in that small factory town, next to Mother, on the day they said should be the happiest day in one's life, in the theatre in the Parish Centre that had been changed into a church, because the reds had burnt down the church that was a little farther up the street and hadn't yet been rebuilt, even though the owners of the riverside textile factories had given buckets of money to that end and even had had some to spare to pay for a new building in Vic, a seminary that would be one of the biggest ever built. However, while they finished rebuilding the parish church, they held mass and other ceremonies in the theatre in the Parish Centre, where a huge cross and Sacred Heart had been luridly painted on the wall at the back of the stage, and an altar placed in the middle with candles and clerics distributed around, as if it were a theatrical performance without a curtain or scenery.

I had worn long trousers for the first time on my First Communion day in the small factory town by the river. They were plus-fours made from long trousers they'd found somewhere or other, which the tailor and Aunt Enriqueta had bamboozled my mother into thinking were the latest big fashion: a young boy was only polite and well brought up if he wore plus-fours and they tried to convince us of that by showing us magazines with adults and young men modelling Prince-of-Wales-style check jackets and plus-fours. And as the tailor was Aunt Enriqueta's friend and it was a way to make those old trousers new because they only came down to the calf and people wouldn't see the worn bottoms, Mother acquiesced, I suspect to save money rather than to follow fashion. A few months later the tailor and Aunt Enriqueta realized I couldn't wear those trousers around the village, not even on Sundays, and they cut and converted them into short trousers with bottoms almost at knee level.

"We made them like girls' skirts that can grow, but in reverse," laughed Aunt Enriqueta. "Trousers that can grow, except that rather than having cloth to let down, we've shortened them."

In other words, Aunt Enriqueta's long trousers were the first properly long trousers I ever wore, that is, down to the ankle, not chopped at the calf and tied up with a shirt collar like those golf plus-fours that looked like bloomers worn by Falange girls, dubbed the Daisies, in their gym classes with the nuns and on parade through the town preparing the way for the arrows, the *flechas* in metallic blue shirts and red berets, on Caudillo Day, on Victory Day, on the Day of the Race, on the Day of Unification…days for fortifying the nation, so they said.

On that day in the Parish Centre in the small factory town I sensed there was an invisible presence on everybody's mind: that of my father in prison, who was far away yet somehow present. Mother was wearing a simple, if pretty, dress, with a small blue flower pattern that matched her eyes on a purple background, and her hair combed back, though not at all flirtatiously, in a way I thought really suited her. In my view, Mother was very beautiful; she was so slim, her eyes huge and lilac like two huge olives, her lips unpainted, her head erect and defiant, and her stance silent and stubborn.

"Nobody will force me to bow my head!" she said, as she combed her hair in the small bathroom, and I tried to walk along the corridor in my plus-fours. "They won't be seeing me cower. The person has yet to be born who can make me bow my head."

She went out into the passage and looked at me while I strutted in my new trousers like a preening peacock.

"And the same goes for you," she said. "No sad or sour looks. I've already killed a rabbit and afterwards I'll make rice with peas that will make you lick your lips. You'll have a banquet, like the best of them. Don't let them see us looking sad; your father wouldn't like that. Head held high, because we've never hurt a soul. *They* are the fascists."

Before we left to go the Parish Centre, she cast an eye over me from head to toe: white shirt, trouser belt properly tied, clean shoes, socks to within two centimetres of the bottoms of my bloomers, a handkerchief pointing up from my jacket top pocket, a bow tie, a white missal with ivory covers and mementoes in the form of a print with a ring and a Baby Jesus on one side and my name, the date and a prayer on the other.

"That mending tailor has done a good job, guided by Aunt Enriqueta," Mother nodded approvingly and then tittered to herself: "They'll never guess where I got that new outfit from! That'll be one in the eye for the four bigwigs, as Grandmother calls them. Let it be an end to poverty for one day. The person has yet to be born who can keep me down. If we have to perform, then so be it! Off you go, my lad, and hold your head high."

I could feel the eyes of the whole parish locking on us throughout the ceremony, and Father's invisible presence, like an empty void not even my mother's serene defiance could blot out. A kind of ghost, like the huge cross and heart painted on the wall at the back of the stage.

When I tried on my long trousers in our bedroom alongside Quirze, I thought of myself alone, at a loss, in the town's streets, after mass, because when Mother got home and we had breakfast—a good cup of hot chocolate with the wafer biscuits she'd prepared beforehand—she said she had to get lunch ready, and I should go by myself to pay a visit to friendly families, ones that had helped us or that she reckoned were on her wavelength, together with some who were not so friendly but who now fawned over us as if attempting to apologize for their secret collaboration in our downfall. I should give them all mementoes of my First Communion.

"They know where your father is. They stuck him there," she said as if trying to raise her own spirits, "Don't be afraid! Let them see the situation they've landed us in, and that we're not on our knees."

The other communicants paid these polite visits accompanied by their parents, but I had to call on all my resources and remember my mother's words so I didn't go bright red with embarrassment.

I didn't know what ties my mother had to the families she had me visit: the Querols, with the husband who was a turner at the foundry and always wore his blue overalls and must have been a colleague of my father; the Teco family were pastry-makers in one of the town's bakeries, and so devout they'd lost three brothers in the war, one of whom was a priest; the young women from Can Triadú, two dowdy spinsters who loved me like a son; the Pratsdesalas, from the grocery store where we always shopped; Tuietes and Carolina, Mother's workmates on the same shift at the factory, in the same section, on the nonstop machines, the most gruelling work, like the men's, where you earned the best rates; Ca la Filosa, with Mrs. Dolors whom people nicknamed Napkin Lolita and the kids, Fatibomba, because she was so fat, who always wore black because she was a widow and she owned the town's smallest factory, a mere ten or twelve workers, a close friend of Mother's; the neighbours, obviously, the Boixassas and Ferriols, who lived in the top and bottom in our cheap housing…

They all gave me a kind welcome, stared at me, and some even made me spin round so they could see my outfit from every angle, admiring the daring modernity of my plus-fours, though they couldn't tell whether they were apt or not for a First Communion; they accepted the memento that they stowed away somewhere or other, and most gave me a little something, *cèntims* or sweets I pocketed, and everyone praised my overall appearance, sent their regards to my mother and congratulated her on the way she'd dolled me up. Whenever they gave me *cèntims*, I grasped why Mother was so keen on my paying these visits. Mother had acted as if it were Holy Week when she'd tell me and a couple of my friends from town to learn some ditties which we then sang with a small flute accompaniment outside the houses of small farmers who lived on the outskirts and we carried a well-padded basket decorated with ribbons and bows for the eggs, cold sausage and odd small change they gave us. She warned us off joining the parish choir, saying we'd have a much better time by ourselves, we'd get to the farmhouses before the big choir, and would collect more money, because priests gave their choristers nothing, priests were tight-fisted and only took them on an excursion to the coast at Pentecost. So we spent every evening before Holy Week rehearsing these ditties that she invented:

> This house's master
> is a very kind fellow,
> he'll fill our basket,
> and live for many an Easter.

If the lady of the house came to the door we only had to change master to lady or young man, or son-in-law and the rest didn't change:

> This house's lady
> is a very kind…

In the evening we'd come home with our basket loaded with eggs and sausage and our pockets full of small change. She divided it up and we had a supply of snacks and lunches for a few weeks.

And she did exactly the same on the day of my First Communion, by insisting I call on friends and acquaintances.

"Poor Florència has really made an effort!" they said. "I don't know how she has managed. You're turned out like a little model. Congratulations and many happy returns."

Mrs. Dolors, Napkin Lolita, Fatibomba, was the only one who ignored my clothes and she gave me the most money, a wad, that she told me to put in my pocket, not show anyone, and give to my mother.

Though nobody ever told me, I gathered that the garment the old-fashioned tailor had adapted with Aunt Enriqueta's help, was one Mrs. Dolors had preserved that used to belong to her dead son, and that's why it was on the old side, straight out of *Little Lord Fauntleroy*, said the girls in Can Triadú, a film about a boy they liked a lot and thought very handsome and distinguished, one they'd just shown in the village cinema.

Mother and I had lunch by ourselves, seated at opposite ends of the table.

"It's better without guests," she said. "It's such a lot of work cooking for six or seven! The family can do that; we're not in a fit state for parties. Isn't that so, Andreu?"

And she sat there with a spoonful of rice hanging in mid-air, gazing out beyond the balcony windows, and didn't say another word, as if she'd forgotten she was eating or had lost her appetite.

I imagined the sadness that was overwhelming and paralyzing her but I resisted succumbing. I always thought of the future, of that same afternoon, tomorrow or the day after, when the cheerfulness I associated with cars and mechanics would return, and my father would throw me up in the air like a ball, and catch me with a shout before we collapsed on the bed where we romped, laughed and hugged each other.

Perhaps that was the day when the invisible seed of an idea was planted in my head that grew over the years, though I was quite unaware; namely, that God was about solitude, isolation and silence. God is man's weak spot, I heard the Saint Camillus Superior remark one day to Grandmother, though I hadn't a clue what they were talking about. That was why he appeared to us when we most needed him, in sickness, poverty and moments of suffering. I couldn't remember what Grandmother said, but I was surprised by the friar's response, as if he was saying that God was like the doctor who came as the last resort, or something similar. Those empty streets when families were eating lunch, my mother's vacant stare, those endless boring, lethargic afternoons, all that must be God's way, God's tortured joy that was sadness on the outside and hid unknown joy inside. Sometimes, when I took communion again with my school, when I still lived in Mother's town, I shook with fear when approaching the altar, and experienced the same feeling I'd felt that afternoon after my First Communion, fear of a step leading to a mystery that became more alien with every forward step I took, like someone repeating a piece of mischief, who feels a twinge of repentance that he immediately represses so he can relapse again. Once the host was inside me, I felt nothing. I tried to feel things, to hear voices, to speak to somebody, and was overcome by the absurd sense that I could only recognize my own inner voices that were unfolding in a kind of lunacy. Man's weak spot. The world's silence, Father Tafalla could have added, as he seemed to know all there was to know about such matters.

Quirze had to shove me in the back to stir me out of my daydreams.

"Come on, they're waiting for us!" he said.

Soon after, when Aunt Enriqueta cut my plus-fours and turned them into short trousers, Mother gave a sigh of relief. She had no more time to waste washing and ironing, she said. From that day on I didn't have to wear those long pants, or whatever those ridiculous bloomers were.

Cry-Baby wore a white dress just below the knee, with an ample skirt, a transparent belt round her waist, white gloves, socks and shoes, and a white veil over her face. She looked like an enchanted princess. Sleeping Beauty.

13

The Saint Camillus monastery chapel was small, narrow and dark. It had choir stalls, a small harmonium and side balconies level with the centre of the stalls, that for Sunday mass would be filled by novices in white habits and the infirm wrapped in white sheets lying on chairs or stretchers. From down below that whiteness melded the novices and the infirm into a kind of angelic host or limbo replete with pure spirits, innocent little black or white stillborn babes, who'd never tasted life, phantom penitents.

Dad Quirze accompanied us as far as the door, went into the chapel for a moment, but soon walked out on the excuse that he was going for a smoke. The men did that in every parish, they poked their head inside and then spent mass outside having a drag and exhaling smoke through their noses and mouths.

Cry-Baby walked between Ció and Enriqueta like a sick princess. Her white dress made her resemble the novices and TB patients in the choir balconies, like a blessed soul who'd come down to earth.

Quirze and I sat on the bench at the back behind them. Early that morning my mother had rushed at top speed from town to bring me my all-white missal and rosary beads. Núria didn't have mementoes to give or visits to make to show off her dress or collect presents, because Dad Quirze said that kind of fancy behaviour wasn't for country folk, that such ceremonies were for city dwellers, and he criticized the fact that townsfolk copied everything the nincompoops in Vic and Barcelona did, and the workers too, who were people with their feet on the ground, like farmer labourers, but had been infected by the bad habits of factory owners and shopkeepers who lived far from the land and shamelessly aped the habits of city bosses and phoneys, thinking that was the way to clean off the dung still sprinkling their backs, upstarts, as Father Tafalla called them.

When we got back to the farmhouse, Cry-Baby refused to play with us while we waited for lunch. She said she might get her white dress dirty. The grownups had let her wear it the whole day and she walked through the upstairs and attic galleries scaring off any dog that came near and gripping her missal and rosary beads like a novice.

Quirze and I called to her from the plum tree, but she never deigned to answer. It was as if she had rediscovered herself, as if she'd seen herself in her Sunday best, all la-di-da, to the manner born, as if she now only heeded the inner voices she must have heard that morning for the first time. I imagined she must have experienced those things someone taking First Communion was *supposed* to feel, the kind of spiritual ecstasy the clergy spoke about in catechism classes, celestial voices and a sensation of joyous fulfilment that transformed one into a species of archangel protected against the mire of sin by the goodness of God. I was rather envious of Cry-Baby because of that touch of grace she'd apparently experienced and that I'd never tasted. In contrast, Quirze ignored his cousin's strange behaviour. He remarked in his surliest tone: "That lunatic thinks she's turned into a nun. She's not right in the head. The least thing drives her crazy," and he shouted, "Come here! Climb up the plum tree, you blessed charmer, or we'll take over your branch. If you don't come today, you'll never be able to climb up here again. Even if you stay inside, you'll still dirty your clothes."

But she ignored us and walked through the gallery and sitting room as if in a trance; she said Grandmother Mercè, AuntCió and Aunt Enriqueta wanted her to show off her dress the whole day and they kept making her go to and fro and parade across the sitting room so they could see her properly, like a bride, who would never be as dazzling as she was then, and they wouldn't let her sit down, so her feet were sore, she added.

We had lunch upstairs in the summer dining room, and the array of plates gleamed more brightly than ever, and stood out against the lurid blue of the walls, a bright fairground blue, the most revolting, artificial blue possible that stung your eyes and convinced you they should strip it off that very minute.

"They're a left over from the Carlist war," Grandmother always told visitors, "when the owners still lived here. One day they'll remember all the crockery they left and take it to their house in Vic or flat in Barcelona, and none of this furniture will be left. They're not short of a house or two."

Father Tafalla and the bubbly, bald novice accompanying him were the only people invited.Ció, Aunt Enriqueta and Mother cooked and served lunch, ferrying trays continually from downstairs kitchen to upstairs dining room. Grandmother was head at one end of the table and Father Tafalla at the other, with Dad Quirze, Bernat, Jan the oldest hand and almost one of the family, the young novice and we three, Quirze, Cry-Baby, still dressed up to the nines, and me along the sides.

Grandmother and the Father Superior initially drove the conversation. They talked about the medicinal herbs Grandmother collected and dried out in the attic and compared her way of doing things to the friars' methods and explained the places in the woods where they found— Grandmother said "scavenged"—the different species; then they talked about the old folk in the nearby farmhouses and their ailments and when the cannelloni was finished and they brought up the capons in a couple of earthenware dishes, they exchanged cooking tips, regretting the fact the women labouring over the stove couldn't be there to add a practical touch to their recipes.

101

"Never feel sorry for the cooks," laughed Grandmother. "Just remember how they never bring anything to the table they haven't already tasted. They are the first to enjoy the flavours. They have healthy appetites and always dip into the dishes they're cooking."

Now and then she'd look our way and encourage us: "Hey, you starving kids! What a spread!"

I reckoned Grandmother chose lovely words to enhance the feast, as if they were her present to her granddaughter, because it was the first time I'd heard them.

Sullen as ever, Dad Quirze's eyes glinted and he merely nodded, going along with everything that was said, adding commonplaces like: "You bet!" "God willing!" "They can eat as much as they want. If only people ate as well in towns and cities! That crew, you know…!"

Nevertheless, halfway through the meal, perhaps spurred on by the continuous flow of red wine from bottle to glass they downed with such pleasure, he began to talk to the young novice sitting next to him: "Well…?" he asked. "Isn't this tastier than the reheated hash they serve up in the monastery?"

The youth smiled shyly and nodded. The delicate sky-blue of his eyes was in stark contrast to the loud, garish blue of the walls and ceiling. He had white, fragile skin, an amiable, symmetrically featured face, a straight nose, thin, finely curved eyebrows, cheeks that looked to have endured lots of penitence, small ears, fleshy red lips and a head that was so bald there was no way of telling whether his crown was shaved down the middle of his skull, what friars called a tonsure, or not.

"What did you say your name was, Brother?" asked Dad Quirze.

"Xavier," replied the novice respectfully.

"Is that your real name or the one they gave you when you entered the monastery?"

"*De veritat…*" the young man spoke Catalan with a clipped northern Spanish accent.

"You're from up north, right? Nearly all the friars that join Saint Camillus are northeners. Most are Navarrese, like the Superior."

"Yes, from Tudela, but I lived in Barcelona for a while…"

"How long you got left on the ranch before you finish your studies?" Dad Quirze pursued what seemed like an interrogation.

"Five…"

Dad Quirze pursed his lips as if to whistle. "Crikey!" he exclaimed, "how do you manage the business of living without a family, like a rooster without a coop to bed down in? You know what I mean…"

The novice turned as red as a hot coal and didn't know what to say. His Superior spoke on his behalf and rescued him from his quandary: "We religious folk comprise a family that is as numerous, if not more, than yours, and much larger than most families living in towns and cities. Our family is the whole community, all our brothers and, beyond that, all the faithful in the big family of Christianity."

Dad Quirze's face went bright red and his eyes sparked. He winked at Father Tafalla and continued tongue-in-cheek: "Family, family… Let's be straight about this. A family of men doesn't serve the same ends as a family of couples, of men and women… Is that clear enough?"

"There are many families… and within families, there are families and families…"

"I'd prefer to say that there are couples and couples…" Dad Quirze was unrelenting and his obstinacy dismayed everyone; we'd never known him to be so vociferous. "Every family is more or less the same, but every couple is different, has different problems…"

Aunt Enriqueta, who'd ground to a halt by one of the corner cupboards, holding a tray of nut and dried fruit desserts, chipped in to break the logjam: "Everyone has a right to his opinion and they're all good," her voice sounded strained, as if she was reluctant to intervene or was upset by the subject they were broaching. "They have their problems in the monastery, as we all do."

Dad Quirze was shut up by his sister-in-law's remarks. After a moment's silence, when he'd looked Aunt Enriqueta up and down, as if thinking through his response, he began sarcastically: "And what do *you* know about these things?"

"I know as much as the next…" Now it was Aunt Enriqueta's turn to blush a bright red, while she looked round and opened the corner cupboard door to take out another dish.

"Woe betide the man whose only knowledge is what he's been taught!" Dad Quirze laughed slyly. "That's what you always reckon, don't you, Grandmother?"

Grandmother nodded anxiously, immediately made an effort to get up, and then said, giving the conversation another twist: "Why don't we eat our desserts and drink our coffee in the gallery? There's a delicious sun that's not reached here yet. And while we're about it, we can take photos for the goblins."

Grandmother's suggestion threw everything into the air. All those eating jumped to their feet; we were the first to do so to help the old lady extricate herself from her end of the table, and everybody gradually went into the nearby gallery commenting: "Now that's a real brainwave! A First Communion photo without a photographer!"

"We could have arranged one!" said Bernat. "This only happens once in a blue moon."

"Stuff and nonsense!" growled Dad Quirze. "What's the point of a photograph at her age when her body hasn't yet grown and filled out, when she's still got to grow into a proper woman? It would be like photographing a silk worm before it's changed into a moth."

"But it's a memento…" retorted Aunt Enriqueta who'd started spreading the cloth on the long table in the gallery and setting out the dessert dishes and plates. "When the years have gone by, we all love to see what we looked like when we were little."

Father Tafalla put his arm on Dad Quirze's shoulder, as they sat down together, asking: "How's business going? When will Grandfather Hand be bringing down his flock?"

Dad Quirze settled himself and answered cautiously: "More of the same...we can discuss that later."

Quirze, Cry-Baby and I were the ones who were most excited. We asked: "What should we do, Grandmother?"

"How do you want us to stand?"

"Is it true the goblins can see us?"

"Will we be able to see the photo later?"

Grandmother laughed mischievously. She seemed to be getting more fun from her game than we were.

"Go into the middle of the sitting room. You must stand in the middle, facing the French windows, veer slightly to the left, next to the lumber room, so the light falls on your faces."

While the grownups sat down around the table, we three stood in the rectangle of sun coming through the door between the sitting room and the gallery. Cry-Baby clutched her rosary and missal and stood between Quirze and me. Grandmother sat on the trunk that was squeezed behind the door, an old portmanteau, and directed operations with a stick. Ció and Mother came upstairs and watched from the landing, laughing and digging their elbows in their sides as if these fun and games were a little light relief from their chores. Aunt Enriqueta poured sweet wine into the glasses and smiled cheerfully.

"First the three of you and then Núria by herself," said Grandmother.

We three cousins grinned, held our breath and stood still and silent for a moment like statues, our eyes staring at the luminous rectangle of the door.

"Click!" shouted Grandmother, who was also grinning and knocking the trunk lid with her fist.

"One more! One more!" we shouted, jumping and breaking up the group.

So we stood in three or four different poses until Grandmother said enough was enough.

"Now Núria by herself!" insisted Grandmother, with great determination as if she believed in her game even more than we did.

Quirze and I moved reluctantly aside and observed Cry-Baby as she was left alone, white and almost transparent in the centre of the sunspot.

Ció and my mother applauded from their vantage-point, and as they returned to the kitchen, they said: "You all looked wonderful! You were a real picture together!"

"Especially Núria looking like a bride."

"Every corner of the house will remember you looking so smart. These walls were so proud to see you so pretty."

"Especially Núria, we'll always remember her lovely like today."

Aunt Enriqueta was also laughing in the gallery.

"Where were the goblins watching from?" we chorused. "Do they have a magic camera that can take pictures without light, at any time, even at night?"

"They're all around us," answered Grandmother. "They see everything and hear everything. Especially at night, of course. They move around most at night-time."

"So why can't we see the photos they take?"

"Because if you'd wanted that kind of photo, we'd have contracted the local photographer, or the one from the Estudi Nadar or Casa Napoleón in Vic," continued Grandmother as if it were the most natural thing in the world to say. "These are special photos only we can take here. Professionals only catch what our eyes can see; goblins, on the other hand, din these happy moments into our brains, the whole group around us, when everyone's full of it, the laughter, the sunlight, and the scents of basil, rosemary and azalea and allow us to remember them forever. These photos will never fade."

"We can't see those photos because this is just Grandmother's nonsense, you donkeys," Quirze laughed at us good-temperedly, going along with the game.

"Don't be such a numbskull!" Grandmother retorted. "Silly! You tell me where there's a camera that could capture this yellow lemon-juice sun, the fug in this room, this pleasant afternoon, you jumping and running around, the women's laughter and the men's banter? Only the goblins can catch all that and stick it in our heads so we remember it for evermore—the tiniest detail, the joking around, the anisette aroma of the desserts and the strong wine tickling your noses and your throats... A photo, ugh! All you can do with that is take it to the cemetery and nail it to the door of the niche so everyone knows what the dead man was like. But the people who knew the dead man shut their eyes and don't look at the photo, because that photo tells them nothing. The real friends of the dead man carry him alive inside their heads, with his voice and his smell, his way of walking and his gestures...even his tantrums and his cheerful moods."

Grandmother stopped, closed her eyes and stayed silent.

From the gallery Dad Quirze observed the exchange with a grin. He just said: "Ridiculous nonsense!"

We were surprised that a man as surly as he was, without a scrap of patience or sense of humour accepted that larking about and didn't say a word more.

When we went into the gallery to sit around the table and eat our desserts, Dad Quirze and Xavier, the novice, argued about the rule of three: "Now I'd like to get to the bottom of this mystery," said Dad Quirze intrigued. "This *does* seem like the work of goblins."

So the novice took a piece of paper and wrote down some numbers and examples that we all thought looked like a magic trick. The rule of three, direct, indirect, simple and compound interest...

"That's more like it," said Dad Quirze. "This could be a good enough reason to be closeted inside for a while... without a family."

Later on, Quirze and I persuaded Cry-Baby to change her clothes and climb up the plum tree with us. Dad Quirze and Father Tafalla went out for a stroll and the novice stayed in the gallery helping Aunt Enriqueta to clear the table. When he came back from their stroll, Dad Quirze accompanied them to the door of the monastery, the novice bringing up the rear two or three steps behind, by himself. Ció linked arms with my mother and accompanied her along a stretch of the path back to town. They always followed the same routine: they came out and chatted awhile under the cherry tree, then walked on a bit to the meadow or oak trees always talking, gesturing quietly and nodding as if they were agreed on everything, and then when they decided to walk on because night was falling, they called to me, and I climbed down the tree and walked with them as far as the bend by Can Tona, where Mother stooped down and kissed me on the cheek and I smelled the scented soap smell she always gave off, and then she hugged Ció, her sister-in-law, and walked off by herself, tripping along the path to her small town, her long skirt down past her knees, carrying her bag of supplies—eggs, flour, bacon, milk... that Ció had prepared for her. Her bundle. I turned and watched her blackened, solitary figure disappear round a corner or fade into the darkness and felt a stabbing pain in my heart no fun and games could ever drive away.

14

What mysterious secrets did the two sisters-in-law discuss during those long goodbyes? They kept up their conversation until darkness fell and almost cloaked the path. Mother visited me every fortnight, on a Saturday or Sunday, depending on whether she had permission to visit Father in prison in Vic. She'd arrive at lunchtime or mid-afternoon, because in the morning she had to do the week's household chores, and would leave at dusk because the following morning she'd be up at five to go to the Boixets' factory. She was on the early shift until two p. m., eight hours on the trot not counting the half-hour for breakfast, and as soon as she arrived home, she had to light the charcoal fire, warm up the lunch she'd prepared the day before, gulp it down, clean the house, fetch water from the fountain, wash clothes, mend for a bit and go shopping, by which time it was pitch-black.

Moreover, ever since Father had been imprisoned, she was forced to do all the haggling with those in power in local government, the *Movimiento* (that had seized premises right opposite the Town Hall they'd confiscated from the Left Republican party during the war and that displayed on its balcony a flag that was divided diagonally, half red, half black with the letters CNS, which was why they were also called the *Sindicato* or people in the Falange, the JONS) and in the church, and she often went to Vic to talk to the lawyer to prepare the paperwork, present recourses and help the defence. We'd been waiting a long time for the trial to start and didn't know whether it would be held in Vic or Barcelona.

"I don't know how you manage all by yourself," I'd often heard Ció commiserate.

When I lived in town, before Father went into prison, I'd see Mother run off her feet the whole day, but happy and even singing. In the early morning, when the cold was so sharp it was frightening because you stuck your nose outside the top of the eiderdown and you felt your skin was being lacerated, I'd be woken up by the voices of the girls from nearby farms walking past our house and calling to my mother from the road, two or three times, and they'd wait a couple of minutes for her to rush out with her esparto lunch basket and a large woollen scarf wrapped round her from head to waist like a shawl.

"Florència!" they shouted.

"Come on, Florència, or we'll be late!"

"Better late than never!" they laughed. "No more dilly-dallying!"

As she left the house, Mother replied: "I'm coming. Just wait a second."

She was afraid to go all alone. We lived on the out-skirts of town, in a small two-storey house with a garden, that people called one of President Macià's little houses, because they'd been built in the era when Grandfather Macià implemented his policy of building "the little house with a garden" that every citizen should have.

She'd never been late or overslept, let alone not gone to work because she was sick or exhausted. Mother was never sick. I felt she was indestructible, the kind of woman that defied the laws of nature and didn't feel the same cold or sleepiness, the same tiredness or hunger that we did. I had never heard her complain about toothache. Even when she started stealing, I felt unable to accept fully that what she was doing was wrong. I decided she was the one who laid down the law, so she couldn't possibly break it, and as I gradually saw strange objects appearing round the house that she sold on the side to people we hardly knew—rag-and-bone men, farm women—who came to our house at peculiar hours with big baskets or capacious bags, I put it all down to the business skills of an entrepreneurial woman who knew how to overcome all manner of obstacles and run a household because her husband was having such a hard time.

Shortly after my father was jailed, Grandmother and Ció persuaded Mother to let me spend some time on the farm with my cousins so she'd not have so much housework to do, wouldn't be so stressed and could go more freely to Vic or Barcelona to pick up certificates, endorsements, references and whatever paperwork she required on Father's behalf.

That was how I came to spend almost three years going to and from the factory town and farm, particularly at Christmas, and every two or three months, because, as Grandfather Hand said: "If the lad doesn't get a whiff of his own house now and then, he'll never know how to go back, won't find the path, and won't even know where he has come from."

Mr. Madern, the teacher at the Novíssima, and the priest at the town parish school agreed to let me come and go, because as they said, I was more advanced than pupils of my year in either school, particularly in reading and arithmetic that, they insisted, were the two keystones, "reading, writing and the basics."

My appearances and disappearances added to my prestige in both classes, as did the rumours about my father in prison. Whenever I came to one of the schools, especially over the first few days, my mates observed me with a respect and consideration they didn't feel towards each other, as if I was a disturbing apparition, and should be bringing them news from another planet, or I was enjoying an adventure in freedom that they envied, trapped as they were in a fossilizing routine. That also allowed me to view the world of the farmhouse and my home with fresh eyes every time—as well as the people inhabiting them—it created a distance that made me a stranger in both places, as if another person were living in my shoes. A fragmented life I now observed more carefully than I used to when I didn't live a fractured existence, and each fresh encounter with my cousins, aunts and uncles, grandparents or Mother was like an addition of new knowledge, a discovery of new features that changed my perspective on all of them. This was true in regard to everyone, especially my mother.

She had always deeply admired her friend the factory owner Dolors Cerdà, Napkin Lolita or Fatibomba, who'd been able to save a small factory as tiny as a clenched fist that she now ran by herself, after her husband and son had been killed at the start of the civil war, and she managed that factory her husband had bequeathed her in the teeth of silent opposition from the bigger factory owners who, for some reason, couldn't stand her and put every possible hurdle in her way to try to make her business go bust, so they could take it over. Perhaps because its tiny size had spared it the requisitions other firms had suffered at the hands of the revolutionary factory committees? Mother and Napkin Lolita—whom I had to call Mrs. Dolors—were friends and I think my mother would have liked to own a factory like her. She admired the success and freedom economic well-being brought. That was why I wasn't surprised by their discreet exchanges. I would wonder how she'd managed to find such pretty items of clothing or the boxes of balls of thread that smelt of the garden or metal spare parts, small wheels, little cogs, spanners, hammers, tool boxes and so on. Nevertheless, in a period when a bar of chocolate or fresh white loaf was a surprise treat, when we'd manage to eat something every day at home, even though there was a difficult period when we were forced to ration everything and divide the bread three ways, one chunk per member of the family, eking it out as best we could and asking for more two or three days later when there'd be more rations available or the basket of provisions arrived from the grandparents'. At first the presence of those rare items, that turned up at the bottom of the dirty clothes basket or the most secret drawer in the bedroom wardrobe, seemed like symptoms of Mother's efficient management, products of her absolute power, small miracles of chance like the ones she worked every day so we could keep the pot on the boil, as she'd put it.

I watched those transactions from afar in my bedroom, and their everyday normality granted an air of homely legality, like selling a rabbit or chicken from the coop to the woman next door. A diffuse, unconscious thought attributed those manoeuvres and items to help from Napkin Lolita or one of Mother's other friends. In the end perhaps she was even doing *them* a favour by relieving them of damaged goods they couldn't sell to shops. However, those scenes became etched deep in my brain where I knew I could find them some day. There were episodes I stored away unlabelled, with no judgment passed, though I knew that at some stage, in some measure, they might help protect me against that miracle woman's harshness, a life-buoy to ensure I didn't drown in the sea of the demands made by her feelings.

Father was different. Too good, said Mother. Too handsome, I heard Aunt Ció, his sister say. Too political, said Dad Quirze. Mother adored him. Literally adored him. Mother wouldn't lift a spoon at the meal-table until Father had tried and approved each dish and wouldn't start eating until he'd swallowed his first mouthful. After each meal that she cooked and served him up so lovingly, she'd sit and watch him take out a packet of tobacco and cigarette paper and slowly roll himself a smoke, very aware of the power of attraction he wielded over his wife and son for quite different reasons.

Before he was jailed and fell ill, he looked like a movie actor disguised as a worker. He was conceited and I never saw a single hair on his head out of place. He never used brilliantine or cream, but it was always beautifully combed with a parting on the left, above a smooth, shaven neck. Even when he wore a mechanic's blue overall he retained the elegant details that distinguished him, like his immaculate white scarves, shiny polished shoes and black socks—"Your socks must always be black, my boy," he'd tell me, "you can never go wrong with black, black goes with everything, because other colours stand out a lot and a colour must really match your shoes and suit if you're not going to look like a clown"—and perhaps a dapper little neckerchief.

He worked as a mechanic in a repair workshop in Vic and no factory manager in our town would take him on, least of all the textile factory where nearly all the men worked, because, according to Mother and Grandmother, "he stood out too much" before and after the war. My parents opened a small grocery store years before the war, just after they married and set up in the small factory town, having departed the farmhouse they'd left in the hands of his sister Ció and her husband, Dad Quirze. The character of my paternal grandfather, a man I never knew, had been instrumental in my father's decision to give up life on the farm. It seems my dead Grandfather was a fiendishly difficult man, prickly as a hedgehog, who insisted that his sons do a farmhand's work without pay, on the excuse that they were working for themselves, that they were the masters and that everything they saved today they would reap on the day in the future when they inherited the farm.

Father and son didn't get on at all. Perhaps if my prickly grandfather had died earlier, they'd have got on better with Grandfather Hand, who was an easygoing fellow, and wouldn't have left the land. Mother said my father was dead set on finding other work, on doing something else. Father didn't want to spend his whole life on the land, he wanted to go to night school and learn to repair and drive cars and get involved in the political and social movements that were organizing in the villages around the farm. Father "had ideas," as Mother put it, and joined a left-wing party unbeknown to everyone, though they never said which it was.

Mother was the second of twelve children in a farming family, from the most remote, sparse area of Les Guilleries. By the age of nine or ten she was working in the Boixets' factory, in the small town where she later went to live with Father. They worked a ten-hour day and some of the working girls were so small they had to stand on bobbin boxes so they could tie the threads on the spinning machines. Ten hours labouring until the eight-hour day was imposed and a day of rest on Sunday. And a ban on children under ten working. However, by that time she was fourteen or fifteen and people were dreaming of what they called "the English week"—"*anglesa*" on her lips—so as not to work on Saturdays. It was over an hour to go and come back from the factory, carrying the basket with our supper. She met two other girls more or less her age on the way, one from La Bruguera and the other from El Pradell, at a spot called "the Rock of Light" because the people in the nearby El Pradell farm placed an oil lamp on a boundary stone at night to guide the girls returning home from the night shift. Mother told us about the pranks the three girls got up to on the way there and back, from crossing barefoot the stream that flowed into the River Ter to scrumping in the orchards of the wealthy. When she reminisced about those times, my mother smiled with an inner contentment as if she was describing the happiest days of her life.

"That's how I met Lluís," she said, as if that daily walk was justified by the encounter with her young man.

They'd meet twice a week by the spring that had the salamanders. And her two girlfriends went on ahead, as if they were walking separately or had fallen out. After a few weeks of courting Father began to accompany her to the farm. My mothers' parents were pleased such a handsome lad came with her to their door, or at least to the spot where the dogs started barking threateningly at night. On the other hand, they weren't so pleased he wasn't the heir to a farm, but merely the son of tenant farmers. However, as they had so many children to bring up and feed, or so my mother said, they had no time to be too choosy.

They were married and looked like children, so much so that when they boarded the train in Vic to go to Barcelona and Montserrat for a weekend honeymoon, a civil guard arrested them because people thought they must be under-age kids who'd run away from home.

And they soon fell out with my grandfather and left the farm to try their luck in the factory town. The grocery store was beginning to make money when my father got involved in politics. "Right up to his neck," according to Mother. Even though he was married and ran the store, he went to night classes in the national school where his teacher was far more revolutionary than any turner in a foundry. That was when other shop-owners began to see him in a bad light, spread slander and incite the conservative population to boycott his shop.

"He's another bright spark who wants to organize a consumer co-op among the workers and plunge the lot of us into poverty," they railed, because they'd heard him make the occasional speech calling for fairer ways of trading and distributing foodstuff.

Their shop started to go downhill at a vicious turning point in the war when the FAI had just murdered the parish priest on the side of the road to Vic, and the three brothers from Can Teco—one being a priest who'd said mass not long before—were found early one morning by an out-of-the-way track, shot in the back of the neck at a time when many property owners and church-going folk were going into hiding or fleeing across the mountains into France. Father spent all his time at rallies, meetings and on his political commitments. They were forced to shut their shop and Mother had to go back to working in the Boixets' factory so she could bring home a daily wage.

My memories of that time in the war are very hazy. I was too young and didn't really know what was going on. I have a clear recollection of the ample, welcoming skirts of Beneta, and the backyard of her house, a cool, luminous garden with a large cistern under a fig tree that acted as a roof. Mother left me with Beneta, who was very old, while she went to the factory. She was on the afternoon shift at the time and left me at midday and picked me up, asleep and in nappies, just before midnight.

When the war finished, Mother moved heaven and earth to get into the good books of the victors. In private, at home, she called them "the fascists" and "that handful of bigwigs." They were shopkeepers, *falangistes*, rich Catholics, priests, factory owners, except for Napkin Lolita, who had a foot in both camps. Initially, they enrolled me at the parish school the new priest had opened in the ground floor of the rectory, rather than taking me to the public school—called a national school—where Father had once become acquainted (my mother's word) with that revolutionary red teacher executed in the first days of the new regime.

I don't how long it was from the end of the war to the jailing of my father. All I recall is that one afternoon when I got back from class, I found the stairs full of civil guards blocking my way. I took refuge in the house of neighbours who took me in.

"Don't worry," they said. "It's only a raid. They won't find anything."

By the time I was allowed back into the house, my tearful Mother was trying to put order into the mess from the wardrobes they'd emptied, the open drawers and clothes strewn everywhere and the wool scattered over the floor like curdled streams of white blood.

"We couldn't do anything to stop them…" Mother said. "We won't be able to get him out. He was too prominent. Blasted politics! Why did he have to get involved? So now you know, politics always ends badly. Don't you ever get involved!"

I gathered she was talking about Father. He wasn't there. He'd escaped into the woods, perhaps to Can Tupí or the maternal grandparents' farmhouse. But he'd not escaped to France like his brother, Fonso, Cry-Baby's father, because he said he had never killed anyone, he hadn't even fought at the front, all he'd done was work for the people, and that was exactly why they had let him stay behind, because nobody else wanted to take responsibility for anything.

"Don't say that," Mother gestured, trying to cover his mouth when he made this kind of excuse. "Say that they pulled the wool over your eyes, that the teacher who seemed so courteous and well-behaved filled your head with ideas that were never yours, that you only went there to learn and he hijacked you…"

But Father was stubborn. He was convinced he was innocent and had a right to think as he pleased as long as he didn't hurt anyone. They'd sabotaged his grocery store, what else could they do to him?"

"They left a summons for him to go urgently to the civil guards' barracks," said Mother, downcast. "They were looking for him. They'd come to get him. They turned everything upside down because they were angry when they didn't find him here. They know only too well we have nothing compromising here."

She now spoke to me as if I had suddenly grown up. She spoke to me as you speak to adults. And that, rather than the brutal police raid, made me realize how serious the situation was. Suddenly, that despondent woman had no warmth of feeling left to see me as the child I still was; overnight she stopped holding my hand, that she put else- where, and no longer carried me around her neck so I had to walk by myself; now there was no time for singing and hugging because all her attention was required for someone in a much more fragile state than I was, and at a stroke I felt exposed and unprotected. I understood in a vague, confused way that she was simply feeling a new, acute pain, that the wife now predominated over the mother, and a wife's harshness and tension overrode a mother's loving inclinations.

That was when the frantic days of wandering and self-vilification started. That very night when Mother left me alone with supper ready on the stove I simply had to warm up and ran to Can Tupí to tell the family about the tragedy on the horizon. I didn't go to sleep until she returned in the early hours. I stood by the windowpanes and glued my eyes to the stretch of road bordered by plane trees, lit only on the way out of town, scrutinizing every movement I could discern, inspecting every black shape that approached, recognizing a familiar form in every pattern the branches and leaves made, feeling a new kind of oppressive sadness, as if Mother had abandoned me and my happiness could only resume when she returned, with her presence.

After that first anxious wait, similar scenes of lonely afternoons and cold evenings were often repeated, when I pressed my face hard against the windowpanes and scrutinized that winding track, waiting for her dark, slender, slightly stooping figure to reappear with her burden of baskets and bundles. She came from the prison, from the farmhouse where she had gone for food, from Vic or Barcelona where she'd been asking for all kinds of certificates… I'd see her approaching exhausted, edgy, bags under her eyes, always half a smile on her lips and mentally inexhaustible. She would slump on the chair and say nothing. I sat next to her or in a corner of the dining room, asked no questions, listened to her panting breath and tried to decipher the signals she gave out, indications from the world of prisons or places she had visited, influential people, old friends, distant relatives, lawyers and doctors she'd been recommended, her hair messed up by the hand my father stuck through the bars, her glass beads and the bits of chaff stuck to her woollen shawl that Cío and Grandmothers' embraces had left, the folded documents in her pocket alongside the funds powerful friends had given her. Mother's return to that cold, silent house brought with it invisible images of dark, dank prisons, farmhouses yellowing with corn and ripened fruit, fine houses with carpets and heating and running water in the kitchen and bathroom, and as a backdrop the huge factory that awaited her early every morning with its vast, frosted windows that only sucked light from their workspace and shut out the rays of the sun and good cheer from the world outside.

After resting quietly for a moment, Mother got up a changed woman, as if she'd sloughed her old skin on the chair and went over to light the stove, asking me if I'd taken the buckets and pitchers to get water from the spring, and then she began to peel potatoes and fill the pot so she could put dinner on to boil, and only then would she slowly begin to unwind and tell me of all the manoeuvres she'd been attempting: "We'll get over this, Andreu," she repeated, as if she was trying to convince herself. "Everything can't possibly turn sour on us now. It would be a really big step if we got him out of prison. And even better if we could get him out in a healthy state! I know Lluís: he's not the kind for that sort of carry on. He's a man who needs people around him who love him. You know, he needs people to love him. I can get by without lots of things, I'm made differently, but he will fall ill if he can't leave that hell soon. We are what we are and some people possess hearts that freeze to death when they are abandoned to their own devices."

She never treated me like a child again. She spoke to me from the kitchen as if I wasn't there, and didn't wait for a single reply, comment or reaction. She spoke to get it out of her system, to relieve tension, to listen to the sound and warmth of her own words. As if cheering herself up after a hectic day.

She almost always went out visiting on a Sunday. And very occasionally when she asked me to go with her, she chose the trousers and shirt I had to wear, always the most worn and mended, and made me repeat what I had to say if I was ever asked anything, told me how I should greet people and focus my eyes when she spoke to the well-to-do folk we visited so my expression would be sufficiently forlorn and pitiful. I didn't need her to spell out that it was my role to inspire pity. Initially, I saw it as a piece of play-acting, but then I felt more of a con-man or trickster, and felt bad for a couple of days after the trauma, a migraine brought on by the obligatory change in my personality, the shame and degradation at being forced to inspire compassion like a beggar in a church doorway who had to act poor and seem poverty-stricken in his every gesture; it wasn't enough to be poor, a beggar had to express through theatrical mannerisms, clothes and submissive patter the social abasement he embodied and the alms he deserved. I couldn't accept that truth wasn't the only path to victory. If there was no justice worthy of the name in this world, one that was immune to deceitful flattery and hypocritical fawning, why didn't the vanquished accept their role as lifelong slaves and quietly adapt to the rule of their masters while, out of sight, they created their own realm of shadows, their avenging justice and secret order? Were adults incapable of doing what we children did at school, couldn't they build a silent, parallel life behind the backs of those who wielded power?

I never forgave my mother for exposing my childhood to that humiliating abasement out of love for my father, a tenderness she transformed into a saviour's passion. It was only a tad less embarrassing than the exhibitionist displays and charity-seeking forays in my First Communion suit or the self-interested spontaneity of our Easter Monday singing.

We paid our first visit to one of the factory managers, on a Sunday afternoon, in our town. Then to Vic and a chocolate manufacturer, an acquaintance from the days when we ran the grocery store. He lived in a mansion on the outskirts, in the middle of a garden, that seemed to have been designed by an artist's pen, with stained glass windows like a house in a fairy story. We weren't invited inside. The smiley, fair-haired woman I thought belonged to another world received us in the lobby and didn't even offer us a chair. Our visit must have been very inopportune because even a child like me could tell her attitude was contemptuous. In the air of that mansion I savoured a subtle aroma of chocolate that went gently to my head and made me feel pleasantly queasy. It was as if every door hid a cake shop full of delicious pastries. Nonetheless, my mother persisted with her refrain: "He's not done anything," "He's a good man who wouldn't harm a fly," "The other shopkeepers bear him a grudge, they won't forgive him for bringing competition or joining the town hall and all those fools whose heads had been turned by politics," and other such comments. Now and then she looked down at me, as if she'd just noticed I had a mark on my cheek or a hole in my pants, and then she'd rub my cheek or pull my shirt down so it fitted tighter over my trousers. Then she'd whimper, "Poor child, it's not his fault," "I'm not sure I can be a father and a mother to him," "a child needs a father by his side to keep him on the straight and narrow," and she always ended up asking for "a reference," "a bit of pressure," because "you, sir, have influence and the authorities take heed of you whenever…"

We visited a couple more acquaintances in similar vein: Mr. and Mrs. Manubens, the owners of Can Tupí, who welcomed us affably enough and were more interested in me than in my father, and an old priest who lived in a home and had been recommended to us by the priest, the head of the parish church school I went to who'd taken pity on my mother. The home where that skeletal cleric lived, with its vast freezing corridors, wooden benches and mean-faced nuns, seemed as sinister as the prison. One Sunday we even went down to Barcelona to see a lawyer recommended to us by the Saint Camillus Superior. We went bearing a letter of recommendation from Father Tafalla and the man invited us into his home on a day of rest and was the most agreeable of the lot. While he was talking to Mother in his office, he left me in a white, luminous kitchen where an old, smiley servant prepared breakfast for me the like of which I'd never tasted before: milk, biscuits, toast, mountain and York ham, jam, butter and hot chocolate… When we left, Mother seemed in good spirits and I'd surveyed the photos of the Generalíssim and of the lawyer in a soldier's uniform next to other comrades, all holding weapons, and concluded that we had at last knocked on the right door: one belonging to the real winners. A centre of power. In my vague, distant way, I grasped that, given the status of losers we'd assumed, the best way to survive was to keep our own convictions, even our personal dignity, to ourselves and willingly kneel down and lick our masters' boots. The winners didn't expect the defeated to think we were on their level, all they asked was for us to respect and obey them. Why did they dress differently if it wasn't to indicate in the clearest way possible that they wanted to be seen and treated differently? Was that so hard to grasp? Why did they wear blue shirts, black soutanes or tobacco-coloured uniforms if it wasn't to distinguish themselves from the rest of us mortals? Women factory workers and engineering workers also wore a kind of uniform, dirty, greasy overalls and housecoats, work clothes that were nondescript, just as rubbish carts were different to the tilburies and automobiles of the well-to-do, and the victors' uniforms weren't work clothes, they were garments to show off, to parade, to impress, another notch on the list of merits of society's upper echelons. Even a boy like me could understand such things and that was why I went along with the obedient, obsequious sheep fleece my mother had donned anew, and if I had any opinion about her performance, it was simply that she didn't need to abase herself as much as she did—or in particular made me do—to prove her acceptance of the new order. It sufficed for the victorious side to know that we accepted their victory, their power and their rule. That we weren't disputing *any* of their achievements or dogmas. Didn't grownups, Grandmother's rogues, know that the meek and the frail must always hide, must seek out hiding places "so they don't show their faces," and build huts in tree branches hidden by foliage, in places where nobody lives, so as not to disturb those people living in their mansions? It wasn't necessary to be so abject, to sink two or three degrees below the normal, as she did, to show we didn't question their authority and accepted their power without demurring for a moment. I felt that Mother's abject self-immolation before the powerful wasn't to the liking of those wealthy bigwigs; it made them uneasy because they wanted to enjoy their privileges as perfectly normal, not as anything exceptional, as if they'd been earned without trampling on anyone, and Mother's submissive behaviour reminded them of the attitudes of victims, of the suffering they had caused to climb up to the heights they now relished. I was always under the impression they felt her begging ways were overwrought, prompted more by the passion she felt for her husband than by any belief in his innocence. And that extra detail simply fuelled the repulsion they felt towards her behaviour, a woman so critical of those who "showed their faces" that she hated as much as the folk who "gave themselves airs," she who kept telling Father and me "never to draw attention to ourselves," how could she forget her own principles and so shamelessly display the passion, madness and thirst for love she felt for that man, my father? Only blindness and a sickly obsession with her husband, like a raging fever a patient incubates unawares, could have made her lose her senses like that. And I reacted quite spontaneously to her excess of love by rejecting all feeling and being afraid to show any tender, emotional attachment to another person. The lesson I'd learned taught me to flee emotional commitment: the more you loved, the more dangers you faced on every side. Keep well away and you won't get burnt. Love burns. Love destroys. Love kills.

15

What did Ció and Mother talk about in the course of those long goodbyes on a Sunday evening?

Obviously, they talked about Father. About him in prison and the consequences of the pressure they were exerting and the influence they could bring to bear, this man who knows that man who is a friend of the other fellow we met that day, and so on with a string of names vital to reach the key individual, the one who, in their opinion, could resolve everything.

I sat in the meadow and waited for the moment to give my mother a farewell kiss and go back to my cousins who were expecting me up the plum tree or by the pond. I couldn't understand how they could be so chatty. Now and then they let a phrase or new expression slip that to my ears didn't square with whatever they were pursuing so single-mindedly. I took no notice; they weren't talking for my benefit; I decided I didn't really understand what they were saying or that it was gossiping about more trivial matters, but gradually I gathered that they were referring to another problem they found upsetting, a delicate, secret subject, judging by how they cloaked it in veiled, oblique terms, as adults do, especially when discussing the mysteries of sex.

"Oh, no, no, no!" shrieked Ció, putting her hand to her forehead as if to chase off a fly or a thought. "If Dad Quirze finds out, you bet he'll kill them!"

"But haven't you talked to her?" Mother insisted. "What does she think? Has she stopped thinking about Pere Màrtir, now she's infatuated him again?"

"The truth is I'd say that Pere Màrtir and she…" Ció kept clasping the middle fingers of both hands together and separating them out as if they sent sparks flying at the first touch. "You know what I mean…"

Mother swayed her head pensively: "It's an illness like any other…even worse, if you think about it. What can I say? We two are like two idiots who've never seen beyond the walls of our house, I wouldn't know what we could do to stop them going off the rails again. I really thought he was back on track."

They were silent and then talked about Father again. The name of Pere Màrtir stuck in the junk box of my mind alongside a clutter of half-forgotten memories, strange names, peculiar phrases and scenes I couldn't make head or tail of.

Mother kissed me on both cheeks and urged me: "Be good!" Or else: "Behave yourself. Don't give them any reason to complain."

Then she did likewise with Ció and started to walk quickly off without once looking back. Ció and I stood in the middle of the path, watching Mother move away, and then returned to the farm the second she disappeared round the first bend. Ció always had something to say to encourage me, as she did now: "Don't you worry, you'll soon be able to go home." Or else: "It will all turn out right in the end, you just see. No good or evil lasts forever. And some day all this will come to an end, it can't go on for eternity."

I understood I shouldn't take her literally, that hers was wishful thinking, that the truth always hid beneath a hundred layers of darkness and could only be reached via strained, elaborate conversations, full of strange names like Pere Màrtir's and so many others. The long goodbye conversations between Ció and my mother seemed simply that: an onerous chore grownups took on to lay bare truths that were even concealed from them as adults. And if grownups found it hard to grasp how the world went round, we littl'uns, I told myself, had to be content to salvage the odd crumb of truth that fell from their after-dinner chat.

Quirze and Cry-Baby would sometimes still be waiting for me at the top of the plum tree, especially on the long, hot days at the end of spring and throughout the summer. When the weather was fine, they let us play there until dusk and on these occasions, when I climbed into the tree after accompanying my mother, my cousins said nothing until I was firmly in place on my branch.

As the first shadows fell, we gazed at the lights coming on in farmhouses, and played at guessing to which farm the lights belonged we could see scattered over the plain.

"That's the Can Tona window!"

"Now they're lighting up the cells the whole length of Saint Camillus!"

"That's the light in La Bruguera's gallery!"

Electricity had only come to the farms quite recently, and when men had to go to the sheds or pen, they still carried an oil or carbide lamp that gave off a smell that made everything stink.

"Who is Pere Màrtir?" I asked, in a neutral tone of voice, as if I didn't expect an answer, looking right up to the top of the tree.

I thought they'd not heard me, that my voice must have disappeared into space, because neither Cry-Baby nor Quirze answered. Until after a long silence, Quirze spat down: "A piece of shit!"

"What do you mean?" I responded.

"That he's a piece of shit," he spat again. "You see that gob of spit? That's what Pere Màrtir is."

"All right, but who is he? What did he do to turn himself into a turd?"

Quirze didn't elaborate. He jumped down from the tree and headed off home scowling. Cry-Baby followed him and then I dropped down too. I walked next to my cousin, a few steps behind Quirze, and whispered to her: "Do you know who he is and why everyone's so against him?"

"I don't know," she shrugged her shoulders. "I've only seen him a couple of times."

"Where?"

"Here and in the village. He came here one day and everybody started arguing and when he left all the women were in tears. I also saw him playing cards in a bar in town."

"Is he from there?"

"No, from the land. From La Coromina."

"What's he like?"

"Fair. Tall and fair."

"And you've only seen him once in these parts? What was he after?"

Cry-Baby shook her head. She said: "By the time I was living here, he'd stopped coming. I saw him the last time he paid a visit, but then they fell out so badly, he stopped coming."

I didn't really understand.

"You mean he was a frequent visitor?"

She shrugged her shoulders. Quirze was waiting by the doorway, buckets of bran by his feet and holding carbide or oil lamps to light our way to the shed to fill the pigs' troughs. I shut up. While Quirze scattered bran, Cry-Baby and I ran around the sty and played at making shadows with the lamps, shadows that lengthened or shortened depending on what we did with the lights, changing shape and looking like a horse, a skull or a goblin. Núria saw goblins everywhere.

"I saw the goblin again last night..." Cry-Baby whispered, so Quirze couldn't hear, as she pointed at the shadow she was moving on the wall.

"Oh, really?" I was amused by Cry-Baby's fears and the apparitions she saw, as much as they angered Quirze, who refused to listen to her talk about them unless it could be turned into an excuse to run and play. "Where did you see it? Did Grandmother see it too, or just you?"

"Just me. I was by myself…"

Cry-Baby and I were closer and she sometimes let me in on her secrets. Perhaps it was because we were both refugees in the grandparents' house, both had missing fathers, lost in a world of prisons or beyond frontiers. Fathers who had been sentenced and silenced, who were far away and absent.

"Last night I saw it run upstairs, through the sitting room, on its way to the attic…"

"What was it like?"

"Like a black dog. It ran like the blackest dog you've…"

"Did Grandmother see it as well?"

"Grandmother was in the upstairs dining room. We were lying in bed and all of a sudden, when we were about to fall sleep, after she'd told me a very frightening story, just when we'd shut our eyes, she said she'd left her headscarf in the dining room and got up to go and get it because she was feeling cold.

"So what happened?"

"As she was taking her time and I was scared at being alone, I got up to look for her. The sitting room was pitch-black and you couldn't see a thing. I stood rooted by the door and all of sudden the goblin came out of the lumber room, ran to the gallery door and rushed furiously up to the attic."

"Were you frightened?"

"I thought it was a cat or a dog. But it didn't leave by the cat-flap, it opened the door and I saw it leaving, big and black, like a mastiff."

"Didn't you say anything?"

"No, but I think it saw me because its eyes glinted when it crossed the sitting room."

"What did Grandmother say?"

"I ran and got into bed, and put my head under the sheets. I was terrified. When Grandmother came back she said nothing, she must have thought I was asleep."

"So what happened then?"

"After a while, as I couldn't get to sleep and Grandmother couldn't either, because when she's asleep, she snuffles and you know she's dozed off, I whispered that I'd seen the goblin run through the sitting room on its way to the attic via the gallery."

"And what did she say?"

"She asked me about the expression on its face."

"And what was it like?"

"Like a dog's."

"And what did she say?"

"She burst out laughing."

"She burst out laughing?"

"Yes. She laughed for a good while, so much so she had to loosen her small scarf—she was choking."

"What was making her laugh?"

"Later, when she stopped laughing and coughing, she said she thought that was funny, she'd never thought a goblin could have a face like a dog's. And she started laughing again, saying, 'A dog's face! A dog's face! If the goblins knew you'd caught them with a dog's face…!'"

Cry-Baby believed in goblins and witches and all those invisible, magical worlds. I did and I didn't, depending on the time and the place—I was very influenced by the people around me, if they believed, I made an effort to believe; if they didn't, I too thought they were idiotic. Grandmother was a total believer but in a different way. We both believed in them because it was a world we were discovering and found frightening; on the other hand, Grandmother Mercè believed because she knew that world and in some mysterious way had had dealings with it—in her own words—and now seemed rather tired of them and was slowly distancing herself all that. Grandmother herself said that growing old meant becoming rather tired of everything, that old people had seen it all before and nothing held any surprises anymore, they could find nothing new in life and that's why so many old people looked bored out of their minds.

"When I was a youngster," she'd say, "I'd never have thought these last years would be so hard. I'm tired, I mean, I feel tired when I've done nothing, I get easily tired and find everything more and more boring. What can we do about that? Luckily I take no notice and don't harp on it." However, she'd then react immediately and encourage us in a livelier vein: "It all starts with 'if it weren't...' When you reach the age of 'if it weren't for my back, if it weren't for my legs...' that means something is going wrong, you have to make an effort to ignore the ailment, whatever it is, and rush around more than ever. I try to, dear children, but find it harder by the day. I think I'll soon reach the age of 'if it weren't...for the whole caboodle,' 'if it weren't for the total disaster...'"

How could Cry-Baby and I not believe in goblins and magical wonders, if that's all we had? That fantastical world was the only thing of beauty we had. We could find solace only in our imaginations. Grandmother's stories and amazing experiences, Mother's songs and her ruses to put something on the table every day, the memories of my father and the phantoms conjured up by his painful absence...all that predisposed us to enter a space that was warmer and friendlier than everyday life.

Quirze was different. He was more like his Father: surly, taciturn, scheming, suspicious, blunt and brutal... But Cry-Baby and I were strangers in the farmhouse that was his lair. The first-born and young heir. Even Uncle Bernat respected him, and Quirze never deferred to Uncle Bernat, as if they both knew the young'un would one day be boss, would occupy the top place birth assigned him. Quirze was going to have to live there, that space would be his life until he died, and he seemed to accept that quite naturally. We were only guests who one day, we didn't know when, would have to depart, banished from that paradise that had welcomed us, where we found ourselves as a result of what grownups called "the circumstances of life." Quirze was like a clod of earth from those fields, he himself was part of nature; in contrast, we were simply distant spectators, temporary guests, and everything was more of a spectacle in our eyes, a novel experience as harsh and exhausting as reality itself. Quirze set no great store by what he saw around him and we saw everything with hopeful eyes, and that was why we embraced Grandmother's fantasy world and the ones we ourselves invented with such joy and excitement. They were a party in the mind Quirze didn't share, or did so with diminishing enthusiasm, as if the passing years rooted him more in the land and moved him far away from birds of passage, visiting guests, the second-born and his relatives from town.

"Rubbish! Always beating the same drum!" Quirze would say, when Cry-Baby and I repeated bits of Grandmother's stories up in the tree, that we always began with a "And what about if...?," "And what if the bailiffs or the phantoms from the war years drove up now, wanting to take you for a ride or extract your blood to give to the rich with TB who'd pay a fortune for it, what would you do?" "And what if the man who carried off children in a sack that he chopped into bits and roasted in the oven were to come out of the woods...?" "It's hard to believe you swallow this kids' stuff, big as you are! With all the work we have on! I'd rather break up sweetcorn or fill pitchers with water from the well!"

16

One day after lunch the Saint Camillus Father Superior spoke of the pleasure imagination brings—he actually said "appearances" because the subject of conversation was seamstresses and elegance prompted by Aunt Enriqueta's work, the fashion magazines she brought from her Vic workplace and the photographs in a film magazine of hers, but I understood him to have meant imagination— and when the friar spoke of the pleasure of contemplation I translated that into our act of sitting at the top of the plum tree and contemplating from that high vantage point whatever was happening in the house, or whoever was approaching along the paths.

"That is the sum total of the liturgy," harangued Father Tafalla, animated by the coffee and his tot of sweet anisette while he smoked the Havana cigar Dad Quirze had offered him before he'd left him in the gallery holding forth to the women and children: "Appearance, sign, form, the outward shape of a presence, a coin that hides one side and reveals the other… When we lay out a splendid spread on the table we assume we're expecting guests…in a way the guests are already there even though they're not there in person."

Grandmother kept on with her needles and wool and said nothing. Aunt Enriqueta looked at Xavier, his young Saint Camillus companion, as if to ask him to stop Father Tafalla's patter, that it was no time for sermons.

"Every day people want to be more fashionable," commented Ció, as she put a plate of biscuits on the table, a selection of tidbits, she said, reading the labels: "I don't know where they find the money. Of course, Vic isn't a village… It has powerful households who can live without the ration card, and get what money can buy on the black market. I've heard that the morning train to Barcelona is full of black-marketeers, women in particular, who hide bread, flour, everything they carry, under their skirts and before reaching the station in Plaça de Catalunya, the moment they hit the Meridiana, they throw their bundles out of the window to someone who is waiting between the tracks, so the police by the station exits don't catch them."

"And it's the same at the hairdresser's," said Aunt Enriqueta, "women spend more and more time there and want ever more extravagant hair-dos, a perm, an *Arriba España* or a French-style close crop."

"But this is worldly liturgy, in a manner of speaking," continued the friar, "mirages conjured up by the devil. Most temptations come to us through the eyes. That's what I meant, we sometimes allow ourselves to be duped by evil appearances. Why, say, do these women need to doll themselves up like that if they already have a husband at home? Some go without food so they can dress fashionably."

"Perhaps it's all they have…" whispered Grandmother, bemused, as if she was speaking for herself, "A hairdo is the only entertainment they have."

"What do you mean, Mercè?" the Father Superior looked round, half taking offence. "They've a screw loose, that's what they have. They could find their entertainment at the cinema, where there are lots of suitable films, and at the *festes* that seem to be held all the time, with concerts and good orchestras… The Bishop has even been forced to intervene and ban dancing cheek to cheek because people were going too far."

"I must have got it wrong," responded Grandmother in the same tone of voice. "As I never leave home…"

"It's dangerous to let the imagination stray, to trust in appearances. There are deceitful images, as well benign ones. That's why you must make the right choices and listen to the right masters. Now you tell me who would dare to wear the swooping necklines you can see in this magazine, for example, if they weren't already damned and couldn't or didn't know how to go beyond the crust of things?"

The crust of things. Did Cry-Baby and I go beyond that hard surface by dint of our belief in invisible worlds and swallowing Grandmother's stories as if they were true, or when we were scared out of our wits walking across dark, solitary places and saw goblins in every cranny, or were always being accompanied by a shadow, the presence of our missing parents?

In my case, and I expect in Cry-Baby's too, there was also the life we'd discovered in the countryside, the infinite nature of the woods, our bonding with animals, the serene presence of the mountains, the soulful life of trees... Compared to the precise order of machines and punctual, factory time-tables, the pleasant lack of order on the farm and the flexibility of time in the countryside were a joy as far as we were concerned. Grey hours existed in the country, chiaroscuro hours, that came like a gift from daytime, between sunset and the pitch-black of night, and didn't exist in the factory town. They were magical hours when you couldn't tell whether day or night ruled, hours when it seemed that anything went, that anything might happen, livestock could get lost, birds might abandon their nests forever, trees could lose their leaves or change colour, flowers fade, water disappear into the earth and people switch to another mood and adopt a character opposite to the one they'd displayed in the light of day. In the factory town everything turned on a siren blast or a bell's chimes. On occasions when I'd had to take Mother her mid-morning breakfast wrapped in a red-striped napkin at the bottom of a basket, and went into the factory that was as huge as a cathedral, with machines in straight lines and that large, round clock presiding over the hangar like a sun, next to the cross and two photos of the Generalíssim and the blue-shirted young man from the Falange either side, over the doorway, I felt I was visiting Mother in a prison. The siren blasted, the machines stopped and the women all had half an hour to eat their mid-morning breakfast. There was never enough bread at the farm and Mother would leave her basket ready in the kitchen and I only had to go to the baker's, on my way to the factory, just before it was time to go to school, take our ration of black bread or cut a few slices and stick it inside. Mother's companions liked to joke and fuss over me. The charge-hand was a fat, oily man, with a huge pointed moustache—so many long hairs sprouting impossibly above that lip—and he too came over to have a word with me. Thirty minutes exactly, clocked up precisely, to eat breakfast. On the other hand, on the farm, they had all the time in the world to eat and drink; nobody was clock-watching.

I felt strange in the factory—like a caged bird—and when I was leaving, carrying my school satchel, and the machines cranked back into action and filled the hangar with a din that drowned out all speech, Mother had to shout her goodbye which I could hardly hear, a couple of metres and no voice was audible, there was only that implacable din, and I'd come away determined I'd never work in a factory or in the mechanics' workshop I'd never visited, but which I imagined must be the same, if not worse. I thought that if they forced me to, I'd run away and live like a gypsy, like a charcoal burner who lived freely in the woods, or a rag-and-bone merchant, a thousand times better the life of a ne'er-do-well going from town to town shouting on street corners, "Rag-and-bone man! Bolsters, carpets, pots and pans for sale!" than that living death shut up in that arsehole of a factory, which was what Mother always called "that arsehole of a factory," saying "anything rather than turning into fodder for that arsehole of a factory," and I don't know if she wanted to pass on to me her loathing for the job she had, a dog's life as she called it, or else was underlining the way she was sacrificing her own life to sustain the family she now headed. At the time I never wondered why she hadn't escaped as I was thinking I would, but years later I began to understand the emotional or existential trap she'd fallen into and couldn't abandon. An arsehole of a factory or a dog's life were her words, and such language led me to decide it was a life sentence she'd not wanted.

I'd begun to savour the freedom of the woods when Mother sent me to the grandparents' farm years ago on a good three hours round walk to fetch food. I went alone, she'd shown me the way, we'd often gone together, and I had my favourite spots, the views I liked and the stretches of path where I quickened my pace, even ran, because I didn't like them; they scared me. The moment came when I'd let my legs go and start imagining things: the shapes of trees, the secrets of ants or crickets, the footprints on the track, the fate of birds… I learned to listen to the silence and value its grandeur. Would I bump into a thief? Generous bandits like Joan de Serrallonga or good-for-nothing tramps like the Kid from Sau were long gone. If I did come across a thief, how would I react? Would I stand my ground or would I run away calling out to anyone who heard me to come to my aid? And what if I got lost and didn't return home? I started imagining what lay behind the mountains, beyond those crags. On many a night I dreamt of fantastic landscapes hidden on the other side of the horizon, beyond the point my eyes could reach. A bright green country with dense, dark forests, and the highest trees…a land I longed for that I'd never seen, an ideal place that's never left my mind, that always appears when I'm in need of consolation, a friendly landscape where I can rest when I'm tired, meadows welcoming like clean, sweet-scented sheets that greet me without any ifs or buts… A gleaming, magical, unique wood of my own that is both hospitable and wild. Losing myself deep in the wood was my road to freedom.

Cry-Baby and I also needed to grow within ourselves, unlike Quirze who was happy with the outside world and proud of his own skin, of the ever stronger muscles he showed off to us like a circus performer, flexing his biceps or feeling his thighs, as if his body was the only territory he trusted. The crust of things. The world's bark. The skin.

On early mornings from spring to autumn, when the cold forced us to curl up at the bottom of our beds and tuck our noses in, when our feet felt for the hot stone Mother put in the stove for a while before we went to sleep and then wrapped tightly in an old pillowcase or a piece of jersey, before the cold invaded the house like an invisible flow of ice that seeped everywhere…when the weather started to be friendlier, sometimes, before daybreak, after the girls from the surrounding farmhouses had called on Mother and she'd gone to the factory, Father wasn't there, Father was rarely there—it was always a party when Father was at home, his body in the adjacent bedroom gave off a wave of warm, scented air, that dissipated the cold and loneliness, but in my memories Father was never there, he was always in prison, in the prison infirmary, working away—and in those hours when the air was as soft as silk, I'd take out of my night-table the toy theatre I myself had made from sheets of card and figures I'd cut and painted copying from the comics we swapped with our mates at the parish school, and invent the most amazing plays that inflamed my imagination, scenarios with dream-like palaces, castles and landscapes. A real ball.

They didn't regulate my free time at home. Parents let us village children go wherever we were allowed, whether it was to a dance—the few that were held because after the war they were a sin—to the cinema, the smoke-filled café, like flies buzzing around the men playing cards or billiards who didn't notice we were there, or to the parish theatre. The priest who ran the school had organized a moral, recreational theatre group—at least that was what he called it—that performed work by Pitarra, Benavente or Galdós, *Las joyas del Roser*, *La malquerida*, *Marianela*…, many of us knew whole scenes by heart, and they'd let us in for free because we'd joined the music and movement group of Maestro Llongueres. I was fascinated by the theatre and it sent my head into a spin. The cinema was something else. They showed two films, the first being the bad one and the second the good one. Those I liked,

I liked so much I'd see them again from end to end at night, trailers included, in my dreams. I'd sometimes leave the cinema as if I was sleep walking, not really knowing what I was doing, heading in the direction of home, my eyes still glued to the white canvas of the screen. Hollywood was a magical word, a new Latin liturgy to transform our lives. I drooled over the trailers posted on the walls of the cinema entrance with all those unpronounceable English names—Norma Shearer, Leslie Howard, Ronald Colman, Myrna Loy, Ginger Rogers, Mickey Rooney, Spencer Tracy... They must be the favourites of the gods, if they possessed such names, fabulous names from another planet, with scenes and photo strips— we called them the picture trailers—advertising the works for the following week that were more suggestive than the films themselves. Almost all the boys collected football cards; only two or three of us kept the publicity leaflets they gave out at the cinema. New ones came out every week. Back in the farmhouse Grandmother had *La Vanguardia* delivered every day from the factory town and the moment it arrived, if the weather was fine, she'd take her rickety chair to a far corner of the meadow so nobody disturbed her and spend half the morning or half the afternoon reading the news. When she returned to the house and put down the paper, I'd pick it up and open it at the film pages with the adverts for the films being premiered in Barcelona, a city that seemed like the navel of the world because there were always new films to see.

However the first time I visited the city, when I got off the train in the Plaça de Catalunya terminus, I was hit in the face by a repulsive gust of stinking air. Police and civil guards were standing on platforms in all the local stations in Barcelona as far as Plaça de Catalunya, to catch the black-marketeers and I saw with my own eyes what I'd heard people say about men and women throwing bags of meat or fresh bread out of the train windows to someone to pick up who was waiting between the tracks or on the sides. Then, when I went into the street, the racket and tumult of people and cars made me feel dizzy. I thought I could never live in that grey, smelly, never-ending city. I missed the sight of the woods, the backcloth of greenery and mountains; my eyes longed for a different place where I could lose myself. The city had no depths or green and the buildings dissected the sky, erased the horizon, blocked the view. The trees were spindly; I felt they were sickly and had TB.

Aunt Mariona was Mother's little sister and worked as a maid in the city; she couldn't go back to the small town, where she'd worked in the factory, because one day she'd run off with a married man, they eloped together, so people said. It led to an outcry, but the married man returned home a few days later and the local hard men forced him to run the streets tinkling cowbells; on the other hand, Aunt Mariona didn't dare come back and she stayed and worked as a servant in a well-off household. The first time we went to Barcelona with Mother, the three of us had lunch in a small, dingy bar and the two sisters shed a few tears, though I didn't really understand why, and Mother asked my aunt if she was all right and my aunt asked Mother about Father's problems, and that was about it. After we visited the gentleman who had to intervene to help Father, Aunt Mariona accompanied us to the station to catch the train back up to town, as they put it, back up to town.

Mother's family was much less easygoing than Father's. There were a dozen brothers and sisters, Mother was the oldest girl, born after the first-born and heir, and they all came to our house from time to time to ask Mother for help or advice; they thought of her as their mother because my maternal grandmother was very old, in poor health and into the bargain didn't get on well with her children, starting with my mother, who now and then let slip some comment about her defects, especially her fondness for booze.

"Sometimes she loses it," she'd say. "She doesn't know what she's doing. If only all families were like your father's!"

17

I do wonder why some things remain etched on my memory while I have forgotten others completely. And how can I know I have forgotten what I can't remember? Perhaps it's the gaps between memories, blank spaces between one scenario and the next, question marks floating aimlessly in the air, lulls between different emotions. Like the empty hollow left in a bed by a body that no longer sleeps there.

And why are there moments in life when we stop to look back and summon these half-lost images buried by time? What sort of nostalgia makes us recall horrendous years, hateful scenes, horrible people…? Given those sad vicissitudes why doesn't memory erase them for good, rather than bringing them ever more forcefully to the surface, tainted by an aura of regret? Does a law of memory selection exist that acts as a sedative, that lets what is best forgotten drop by the wayside and preserves what is significant, central to our life, its backbone? Does a kind of core marrow exist that acts as a storehouse, allowing a secret, lymphatic circulation of memories to impregnate our lives and compel us to be the individuals we are and nobody else, as we might be if we forgot things we can't relive, even in our memory?

And why does everything we remember, however chaotic and messy, finally assume a shape only we can recognize? Or does memory want to us relive past deeds like spectators reviewing our own prominence, and thus relieve us of the hurt they inflicted at the time, and seen like that, in the haze of memory, we try to understand them better, to extract some kind of light, and rid them of the grief, anguish and turmoil, like the sand deposit that remains at the bottom of a pond after a storm? Is that how the past might strive to give meaning to the absurdity of the present?

Does memory have a guiding thread or purpose? Why am I still haunted by Father's farmhouse, by its fruit orchards, by that impenetrable wood, and if it wasn't for the phantoms and fears crowding my head, by that pleasant landscape of sandy hills with its backdrop of invisible crags and blue mountains? What is the meaning of these memories that come so insistently to mind in no apparent order and from a hodgepodge of locations? Why haven't I retained with equally gentle emotions a vision of the farmhouse that belonged to my mother's grandparents and huge family? Why do some landscapes live within us and others not? Why do some individuals, family or not, hold the key to entering into our inner being while others are banished to the darkness outside, as the friars would say, rejected as miscreants, unworthy of crossing the threshold of memory?

Could that mysterious set of dead people Grandmother described to us really be true, exist invisibly, holding out hands to each other to avoid sinking definitively into the abyss, the last in the line—the one we knew in life—holding out an arm and an open hand, even tickling our backs and the soles of our feet, always beneath us, immersed in an invisible world and attached to a long necklace of which we only recognize the last bead in the rosary?

Sometimes it is simply a word that ignites the whole chain: azalea, don't forget to water the azalea, jug, a jug of milk, or pew, Grandmother always sits on the pew, or morel, we'll go to the woods to pick morels or we'll make a morel and hedge mushroom omelette, or a karakul, a Persian sheep that made us laugh, it's a karakul, its lambs have got the runs from colostrum, the first milk after birth, or mistletoe, wild lettuce and purslane that were for the pigs, but mistletoe was also a game played with folded belts, and Father Tafalla's frenzy, a word that only he used, the frenzy of the insurgents, a word that inspired fear, that was more than an insult…words that functioned like the first exercises pupils do when learning to read, the shock of discovery, a noun we've not heard for years that transports us far away and opens the floodgates to all those images and old words that are mired in oblivion.

Azalea, jug, pew, morel, hedge mushroom, karakul, mistletoe, wild lettuce, purslane, orange water, frenzy, crabapple, broody hen, looms, shuttles, lock-gates, hob, kitchen range, convolvulus and wild radish, herbs to ripen cheese in the churn, anvil to forge horseshoes, predators not to be trusted because they attack you, fertilizing land…

Like the small white pebbles in the story about children lost in the woods, that the youngest, trailing behind the line led by his parents, big brothers and sisters, dropped on the ground, the white stones he'd put in his pocket so he could find the path and his way home when his parents abandoned him.

Without parents, Cry-Baby and I were left with only words to help us get back on the right path. The secrets were but words, like every illumination. Small white stones. Stones. Smooth pebbles from the stream. Words.

18

There were word games, games that became the fashion and that overnight were replaced by others whose provenance nobody knew, not even those who'd brought them to class. That was the case with the nonsense game.

We all four joined in the round, because we only played when Oak-Leaf did, after we left school in the afternoon, in the clearing in the woods. The game was only interesting because of the words thrown up by the questions and answers we exchanged, following the rules of the game, and the comments Oak-Leaf often added, arousing our sense of mischief and appealing to our most hidden desires and a curiosity that was surfacing only now and even then against our will.

One of the four players whispered into the ear of his neighbour, so the others couldn't hear, "what use is our head?" or "what use are our legs?"; the individual questioned would reply just as warily, "our head is for thinking" or "our legs are for dancing." Once the round was finished, each person had to repeat a question and an answer, ignoring their own contribution, and only repeating part of the question to the people to their left and right, "He asked me what use our head is and she replied 'it was good for dancing.'" That way we came up with the silliest nonsense and the maddest responses.

First Oak-Leaf and then Quirze introduced new words that, camouflaged by fantastic definitions, seemed even more mysterious to Cry-Baby and me. And they, rogues or rapscallions, according to Grandmother, worked it so they got the most amusing or obscene. They directed the game and laughed the most.

So you might get, "What's the point of our bum?," and he told me, "It was to eat with," or she asked, "What's a male for?" and he told me, "It was an egg-making animal." The game started with innocent nonsense, then suddenly a secret, forbidden word cropped up, "He asked me what a cunt is for and I heard it was a hot, black sauce for dunking sponge-fingers in," or "she asked me what a hot chocolate delight was and someone replied it was a black hole women had." The words were uttered and immediately stripped of their obscene meaning—unless that was highlighted and caricatured by an arbitrary reply—and that dislocation of meaning and the surprise and laughter they triggered meant the game seemed quite ingenuous.

There were always words left at the end that Cry-Baby and I didn't know and we'd have to consult Quirze, or, less usually, Oak-Leaf. The whole repertoire of basic eroticism the two rogues or rapscallions would place on the table like a trump card to win a victory for the person who played it.

Once we'd run through the list of words referring to sexuality, our game took a turn that from the very beginning, from the first question and answer, felt as, if not more, exciting than the previous exchanges, and definitely more perilous. Nobody had set down the rules, but apparently after focusing on obscene words, someone decided it would be more fun with the names of the people who in some way practised the actions the words referred to.

"What is Madern the teacher good for?" introduced the first real person into our closed circle. Cry-Baby blushed bright red the second she heard me repeat the question Oak-Leaf had asked me. As I'd not suspected that her words carried any hidden agenda, I asked Quirze an innocuous question that elicited a ridiculous statement nobody found at all funny.

"Mr. Madern is good for opening your mouth when you've got toothache."

I grasped my opportunity to stick my oar in, "What is Pere Màrtir good for?," and when she heard that, Oak-Leaf gave me a surprised look and then continued with the game.

However, she saw to it that I got a surprise outcome: "He asked me, 'What is Pere Màrtir good for?' and someone said: 'he's good for nothing.'" When Quirze heard that, he glanced furiously in the direction of Oak-Leaf and she wrinkled her lip into a grin and defied his glare, and a moment later, as if they'd both said something to one another, they burst out laughing, she first, then he joined in, though less wholeheartedly.

Cry-Baby noticed the game had begun to follow a different pattern, and a few days after the inclusion of proper names, she got up halfway through a session and declared she was tired and bored and didn't want to play anymore. As well as Mr. Madern and Pere Màrtir we dropped into our round of nonsense, with varying results, Aunt Enriqueta, Father Tafalla from the Sant Camillus monastery, blond, bad-tempered Canary from the Civil Guard, the other one, Curly Lettuce, Gamundi and Siscu, a boy from school who was always trailing after Oak-Leaf, Xavier, the novice from Navarra, and a woman from the hamlet nicknamed Jump for Joy who was reputed to go with any man who asked for it, though she wasn't considered to be a whore, Cal Set, the official brothel in Vic, renowned throughout the district, Sweet Biscuit who sold sweets in the factory town whose body was like a sponge cake, whom everyone thought was effeminate and half-queer, and even Grandmother Mercè's goblins.

We vaguely acknowledged that the fact these individuals were named in our game meant they belonged to a special circle, shared something in common, possessed qualities that distinguished them from everyone else we knew, as if the fact we passed their names from our lips to our ears was a way to test our luck and see whether we could come up with a definition that threw light on the shadows surrounding those names or illuminated the dark zones that—in our view—they were concealing.

That was one distinguishing feature: all those named enjoyed a second life, an area of life we didn't know, one we found fascinating. Perhaps they were merely fantasies of ours, but we saw all those people in a murkier light than Ció or Dad Quirze, Grandmother Mercè or Miss Silly, Mr. and Mrs. Manubens, the masters of Can Tupí or Uncle Bernat. This second group were what they seemed, or represented everything they were: people without mysteries or shadows, of a piece.

It was the same difference that existed between Siscu, our schoolmate, and everybody else. We were interested in Siscu because his courting or rather larking about—in our village the first stage of courting was "larking about"—with Oak-Leaf had endowed him with flirtatious or seductive skills that surprised us, that we wanted to observe, just as we admired a hiker who goes on ahead on an excursion and opens up the path we will follow later. Conversely, our other schoolmates had yet to take that step forward and remained much of a muchness in the usual routine of the herd, in limbo.

So what did we want to find out about the adults evoked in our nonsense game that became a kind of magic spell? The fact that their names appeared with swear words that weren't a hundred percent insulting but that couldn't be mentioned outside our private circle, already pointed up, in our eyes, the hidden, sexual nature of the curiosity driving us on.

And so I began to get to know those people who on first sight seemed unsullied, and just as we thought it funny that Pere Màrtir was good for nothing or Mr. Madern was useful for opening the mouths of people with toothache, Cry-Baby and I didn't understand the shrieks of laughter prompted by the piece of nonsense that said, for example, that Canary, the blond civil guard on a short fuse, was good for letting the sparrow out of the cage. Cry-Baby and I had to intuit what lay behind the jokes and incongruities that made Oak-Leaf and Quirze laugh so much. In a similar vein we couldn't join in the laughter when it turned out that Father Tafalla was good for filling Grandfather Hand's shepherd's pouch or that Xavier the novice was good for catching butterflies in a cornet, Grandmother Mercè's goblins were good for carrying chamber pots to the lavatory and the Saint Camillus patients for spreading out clothes in the sun to dry. But most surprising of all was the combination that said Aunt Enriqueta was good for opening monastery doors to those who wanted to opt out, or, as they said in an expression that reminded me of Judas's betrayal, hang their habits on a fig tree.

After we'd squeezed all we could out of our nonsense game, Oak-Leaf started telling us what Siscu said and did to her when nobody was watching, and I felt her disclosures meant we were leaving our childish games behind forever and embarking on dark, unknown paths, that were more for adults, far from where we'd begun with our exchange of nonsense.

I was quite frightened—awed—by that adult world I glimpsed through the words of Oak-Leaf and Quirze, a world made of silent flesh and acts quick as the thrust of a knife, which I thought represented a threat and challenge to life at the farmhouse, as if a new, silent and invisible war was endangering our refugee status.

I knew things about sex from the dirty comments made by my schoolmates and a few scenes I'd observed by chance, apart from what the workings of nature in the countryside had revealed, like a mare or a ewe giving birth or dogs coupling, and it was a fascinating yet repugnant world. I viewed these adult goings-on as a spectator, as someone who knows that one day he will have to go to work somewhere, learn a trade, but who still doesn't know what kind of work that will be or whether he will choose it driven by a vocation or by more down-to-earth considerations.

And my short-lived experiences as a spectator told me that those things always bring unhappiness, or at the very least are linked to all kinds of chaos. Aunt Mariona, Mother's sister who'd run away with a married man, had been forced into shameful exile in a strange, distant city. And her seducer had suffered a public belling and a beating at the hands of his wife with the pole she used for washing, and that made him the village laughingstock, a cuckold and doormat they dubbed him, along with other choice insults. I found it the height of embarrassment when my mates in the parish school exposed themselves in the lavatories and compared sizes or when the big kids stopped thinking of us as "wet blankets" and let us listen to their conversations when they described the rude tricks couples got up to at night, what they do, how they do it, who does it best, what I would do, what I saw them doing, who told me and how he knew it for sure… In comparison, I found the boys in the Novíssima healthier, perhaps because in those first few years after the war we were still taught with the girls, and their presence imposed a different kind of behaviour and language.

The clearest demonstration of how adults in the grips of feverish love or sex—at the time I didn't distinguish between the two and stored all that information in a hodge-podge hard to unpack—went overboard was when Mother used me as a spy to check on whether Father was going out with other women.

Mother must have thought I was too young to really understand the mission she was charging me with, and the fact is I initially thought of it as an adventure, as Mother wanting to do me a favour and give me something amusing to do at an unusual time of day. It was precisely that element, the unlikely hour, unsuited to a child, which first alerted me to the real role I was being asked to perform.

Later, after my second or third sally, when she began to ask me what my father and I had done, which girl had sat on the seat next to him, where he'd stopped and what he'd said, and whether so-and-so was in the coach, I started to see what she was after, or rather to intuit the blind fury that was getting to her, that I interpreted as a form of envy or rivalry, a forlorn longing for Father's company.

When the war was over and factories were restored to their lifelong owners, who'd returned from the national camp, from the other side, as they said, and who now managed them from offices in Barcelona through executives, directors, foremen, clerks...and the whole strict hierarchy of bureaucracy they delegated power to, a time came when there weren't enough women workers in town to feed the constant expansion of the textile factories—the dyeing, starching and other tasks. So the directors organized coaches to pick up women from local hamlets and bring them home after the night shift ended. Later on they were forced to bring more people in, sometimes whole villages from Andalusia led by their mayor, who they housed in blocks of flats that were like matchboxes, as Mother called them, built expressly to accommodate them and built on the cheap.

A few months before the Civil Guard arrested and jailed him in Vic, carrying out the instructions of a judge or prosecutor who'd taken all that time to set him up, a coach firm hired my father. That's how he came to be a driver of one of those coaches full of women that drove to and fro from the textile settlements on the Ter, near our small town, and as far away as my grandparents' hamlet.

It all started one evening, when Father was about to jump in the coach he parked in front of our house, and Mother asked me in front of him: "Andreu, wouldn't you like to go for a ride with your father for a bit?"

I looked at them both, rather taken aback. It was the first time anyone had suggested I should go out after dark.

"Go on, tell him you'd like to keep him company and would love to go with him!" And staring at my father she went on: "Why don't you take him with you? In the meantime I'll wash up and mend clothes while I'm waiting for you to get back. Then he won't get in my way here. Go on, take him with you."

The expression on Father's face was half amused, half anxious: "What on earth do you think the boy's going to do in a coach filled with women who are filthy and sweaty after a day's work? Kids his age should be well into the land of Nod by this time."

"He can keep you company and you won't have to drive home all by yourself. He's got nobody to play with here. He just loves riding in a coach, don't you, Andreu?"

"But sometimes I have to stop off at the company repair shop in Vic that they only open late at night for us."

"All to the good, he can look at engines. Nowadays they say everyone must learn to drive a car, like riding a bike in our day. And, Andreu, you do like driving, don't you?"

Frankly, I didn't mind one way or the other, but faced with the tedious prospect of staying at home with nothing to do and going out with my father, I preferred to accompany him even though I was tired and beginning to doze off.

19

And so, reluctantly to begin with, and then as a habit that found favour with both Mother and myself, Father started to take me in the coach to the settlement, where we would wait for the siren blast and the women to leave, and as soon it was full, Father drove off as darkness fell over the local roads.

The women accepted me unreservedly, with alacrity, as if it was natural for a son to accompany his father. They all wanted me to sit by their side, so I'd flit from one end of the coach to the other, always in a window seat, and watch how the row of plane trees appeared, then immediately disappeared from sight, salvaged from the gloom by sudden beams from the coach headlights, concertina'd into a single mass by our speed that shortened the distances between them.

The smell of burnt oil, industrial grease and body sweat filled the coach. The women combed their hair, changed their coats, rubbed handkerchiefs over their faces and some even took a bottle of eau de cologne from their baskets and squirted a few drops on their hair, necks or cleavages. When they unbuttoned their coats or blouses to wipe away the sweat or rub in some scented water, they gave me a cheeky smile, sometimes winked and even made remarks that brought a grin to my face:

"Close your eyes, handsome, you shouldn't be seeing this!"

"But he's a little innocent…!"

"Not if he takes after his father…!"

"It's in his blood," they laughed.

"It's been passed on, like the colour of his eyes!"

Once they'd relapsed into an exhausted silence, one of the eldest started singing songs from the old days, and when we were nearing the end of the ride they always prayed an Our Father and three Hail Marys in remembrance of the three working women who'd died, beheaded by an unknown murderer on the path the women used to take through the woods before the bosses organized a transport service. As they finished, they'd say: "May Saint Anthony save us from all evil and mortal sin, Saint Joseph allow us a decent death and Saint Pancras keep us in work."

"But don't go giving us longer hours," added the younger girls, who were the one who prayed the least.

The same girls always sat next to the driver, my father, the ones who were nicest to me, Gracieta Rossic and Aurora Maions, both blondes with round faces, red cheeks and big green or blue eyes and breasts that seemed enormous, oversize and swollen. Both exuded enormous energy that had them bubbling away all the time, bantering, laughing, tidying their hair or blouses, painting their lips or eyes, changing their worktime espadrilles for high heels.

The women sometimes argued at the back of the coach and one of the oldest would laugh and shout: "I agree with what that comrade said!"

And that would end the argument and they'd all burst out laughing as if she had uttered a magic formula. It must have looked as if I'd not cottoned on, because the one next to me, after a repeat episode, told me: "Before the war, we had meetings, even mass meetings in the factory two or three times a week with the unions and the committee. We women were the loudest, the most revolutionary, and those of us who didn't have a clue about politics, when it was time to vote, would shout those words out to support the comrade most in the know."

If someone responded, vigorously waving their fist in the air: "Long live labour, down with capital!" the others shut her up immediately: "Be quiet, stupid! You can't say that now! Do you want to get us into trouble? You never know who might be listening. Remember the slogans on the posters: 'Spies are watching,' 'The enemy is always listening.'"

But I could see they were all tittering to themselves.

Sometimes there were incidents that appeared harmless enough that in fact revealed the vast extent of the invisible, submerged past, doomed to oblivion and destruction. Like the time when one of the older workers sang, quietly, almost inaudibly, so only those of us sitting near her could hear:

> The militia men's rope sandals
> are worth a sight more
> than the shiny leather boots
> butcher Queipo de Llano wore.

Horrified, the women nearby put their hands over her mouth to shut her up. A heavy silence descended that lasted the whole journey.

I repeated these phrases to my mother, and she'd repeat them slowly as if she wanted to memorize them, then she'd comment: "They're mad, they're mad! They're all stark raving... They'll get your Father into trouble making that kind of joke."

And she'd add: "Women lose their minds more easily than men."

She spoke as if she didn't include herself in that category of stupid women, as if she belonged to another class of women. And then she asked, as if my opinion was valuable: "Do you think Napkin Lolita or the wife of the owner of Els Boixets could stand eight or nine hours behind the machines in the factories with us? That's what those scatterbrains and your dad wanted. They went on and on about how the revolution wouldn't be worth it until the bosses started working alongside the workers. They wanted to see all the factory owners, and especially their

155

wives, transformed into workers, in blue overalls or dirty housecoats with a big basket, tying threads or placing bobbins on shuttles. How simple-minded can you be! And you see what they achieved, nothing at all, and they're lucky to have come out of it alive."

She looked up at the ceiling, and then down again, before launching into an interrogation: "Who did your father speak to most? Who sat next to him? Did Gracieta Rossic keep sidling up to him? Did Gracieta go off by herself when they reached town or did they wait for the other women? What did they say when they left? Was it only goodbye? Who did Aurora Maions go off with? Were they showing off their cleavage or did they wear scarves round their necks? And nylons? Did you notice if they were wearing nylons? Were they laughing all the time? Did anyone say anything to your father? And what did Gracieta have to say…?"

I told her what I'd seen, but took care never to mention Gracieta Rossic or Aurora Maions because I'd noticed that they were the ones who most preyed on her mind. It was a fact that Father bantered most with them and one day I even saw him put his arm around Gracieta's waist and playfully nuzzle her neck, but I didn't tell Mother because I thought I shouldn't, that he'd done nothing wrong, it was part of his leisure time when Father tried to be the young lad he'd once been and didn't want to let slip forever. I even sympathized with my father's fun that made my mother hit the roof. It was like when I was with my mates and I behaved differently to what I was like when I was at home with my parents, which didn't mean I was different and didn't love them anymore, it was merely that there are times and places when our parents, or our mates, or whoever, get on our nerves. How come Mother, who was so feisty on every front, so brave and determined, didn't grasp something so straightforward: that we all need to spend time with somebody slightly different at some stage in the day or in our lives? As she was always so busy and never left the house on Sundays, she knew nothing about the delights of the theatre or cinema and didn't understand how other people's lives can dazzle and seduce us.

When they saw me with my father, Gracieta Rossic and Aurora Maions would come over, pinch my cheek and say the same silly things to me the other women said, but in a different tone, that I thought sounded different, as if they had ridiculous siren voices, and then I knew it was time to leave my seat and go and sit at the back with the older women: "Hey, handsome, you can stay with your father, if you want."

"He's the spitting image of his father! The same eyes, the same good nature…"

And so on and so forth.

When we were by ourselves on the ride back, I sat next to Father who told me how to drive a coach, or else he left me alone on the back seats, where he must have thought I'd dozed off, and I stretched out on the longest and let the shadows of the roadside trees fill my mind; depending on the moon, they came through the coach windows and moved as they did in the cinema. These were special moments, feeling safe with my father in front, in an empty, transparent coach still impregnated by the strong smells of the women who'd just got out, the small lights of nighttime reflected in the windows like a shower of white petals, the deserted, silent roads, the empty village streets we drove through, the dark forest either side, and me speeding through the lot, you know, I felt like a prince in his carriage travelling deep into the night.

When I sat next to Father, he'd come out with some of his catchphrases that at the time I thought were really off the wall, though in a way they summed up a philosophy of life: "When I'm dead, I'll shit on the living!"

"The dying to the grave and the living to a fanny!"

"By your door I plant a cherry tree, by your window a morello tree, for every cherry a hug, for every morello a kiss."

"When you inherit, one eye laughs while the other cries!"

And so on.

Mother was more circumspect. When he came out with one of his sayings, she'd look at him and retort: "You like to complain so much about your father being a wastrel and not setting anything aside for his children when he died, I wonder what you're going to do for your own. Personally, I'd hope you'll cherish pleasant memories of me for the rest of your days."

One night, when the coach stopped in Vic for a checkup in the company's garage, Father went over to a huddle of men, mechanics and other coach drivers, and started to shoot the breeze and joke about whether they were going home or were off for a jar in a little café that stayed open to the early hours and even to daybreak. I'd stayed in my vantage post at the back of the coach, and could see my father pointing me out to the group as if saying he couldn't have a night on the tiles with me around, and the others glanced at me and said that one day he'd have to let me loose and teach me how to let my hair down. In the end he signalled to me to accompany him and put his hand on my shoulder, as if to protect or guide me, and we joined the group, three or four older men and two youngsters. I registered the excited way they spoke and gesticulated. They all smoked like chimneys. It was as if they took the fug inside the garage to the café next door. They bantered as we walked over. Every sentence or declaration was greeted with hoots of loud laughter I felt were unjustified. They were talking about things I didn't really connect with. They'd look at the youngsters and say things like "Wonder how you bright sparks will perform today!"

"You can never tell. Depends on the birds available."

"Perhaps there'll always be one who's not filled the form out right or who'll have to repeat the exercise because he spilt ink away from the dotted line!"

"The youth of today, lots of lip…and no spunk!"

"Follow the good shepherdess's advice. She's knows her flock."

Dad kept trying to raise a small objection, think up an excuse: "I've got to get up early for the morning shift…"

Or else: "Let's make sure everybody does their duty."

But the others were all up for it as if they'd only just got out of bed: "Hey, come on, you!"

"Strike while the iron's hot!"

"It's all right for you, you couldn't care less because they're always crawling over you."

The café next door was a real dive. The side street was dark and the dive's misted windows gave out a dull, yellow light that was tinged almost a pale blue. Inside was a marble bar-top in front of a range of shelves crammed with liquor bottles and a fat, greasy, paunchy, revolting guy was washing glasses one by one in a sink with a dirty cloth, moving his fingers deftly, as if they were sticky snail shells. It was a small place with four tables with tops made from that same white cemetery marble, where five or six men were sat who gave me quizzical looks but said nothing. Dad and I stood by the bar. He ordered a coffee and a glass of hot milk for me. Two of his colleagues stayed with us, while the others went into the street, larking about.

"We'll be back right away!" they shouted.

I watched them cross the road through a small patch of glass that an elbow or hand had rubbed clean. They shoved each other or slapped each other on the back as if they were going on an outing or to play football. They made for a more isolated house farther down the other side of the street out of which groups of men kept spilling. Whenever the door opened, a rectangle of yellowish light escaped that crossed the road like a moonbeam. Before walking in, one of the men in our group made a show of taking off his trouser belt, as if he were going to bring the livestock to heel.

Dad and his friends cracked dirty jokes about a couple of dogs who were sniffing around the café, until the fat waiter came from behind the counter and shooed them into the street. They said things like: "Those two are up for it too!"

Words that gradually opened my eyes to everything happening in that street and that house. Perhaps it was the house I'd heard the big kids at school licking their lips over, the famous Cal Set.

Someone laughed and said: "But they're males!"

"Perhaps they aren't what they seem and one's playing the part of one who isn't!"

That remark was like the theatrical gesture of the man taking his belt off before entering the house of ill repute. An equally theatrical utterance that left me on the doorstep to mystery. Words that began to lay bare a secret but only bared an inch of flesh to a spectator. A ray of light momentarily lit up the pitch-black street, allowed you a glimpse of the forbidden world within and then shut the door in the face of idle bystanders.

Father told me to wait for a second with his colleagues; he was going to the lavatory in the café yard.

While he was outside, the two men in the group who had stayed asked me if I wanted anything else, biscuits, another glass of milk, a sausage or chorizo roll, told me I could order whatever... I said I didn't, that I wasn't hungry, and thought Father was taking far too long to come back. But I expect it was because I felt tired and sleepy, and time drags more when you're waiting for someone and you feel out of place, and I did really feel out of place there. Now and then I glanced through the clean spot in the misty window: the street was empty and the door to that house hadn't swung open again.

Father came back through the door to the yard and put his hand on my shoulder. The other men returned shortly though I didn't notice when they left the house. Father said it was time we were on our way. The others said they would stay for a while until they'd finished their drinks.

We drove home in silence. Now and then my father slapped me on the back as if trying to animate me, but he said not a word.

Mother wasn't waiting for us in the dining room, as she usually was. The house was in darkness and Father carried me to bed and tucked me in. Then I heard sounds in the room next door and soon after the voices of my parents arguing.

"Have you lost your marbles?" Mother recriminated.

Dad's voice was softer.

"Have you forgotten what time I get up?"

I imagined Mother sitting up in bed, spitting on the floor and screwing her face up, like she did when she talked to me about Gracieta Rossic, Aurora Maions and those other cheeky bitches, as she called them: "Ugh, those hussies…!" she'd scowl. "They all want the same thing!"

Until they started arguing for real.

"We'll get nowhere," said Mother in a louder voice, "can't you see we'll get nowhere with that lot?"

"So what do you expect me to do, run after the Bible-punchers and lick their arses, after all they've done to us? They sank our business and did us as much damage as they could."

"That's not the way to get back on your feet, Lluís. That lot have never done us any good and they never will."

"What do you expect me to do? They're workmates, I have to get on with them…"

"But they never put their neck on the line like you. We all thought everything could change, that we were going to put an end to poverty. But now I realize my brain's too small to get round all that, that something's not quite right. I see things I don't like."

Dad paused a while, then piped up: "You women don't really understand."

Mother's retort came quickly, as if she'd been waiting for him to say that before she jumped and let loose: "Well, it looks as if Gracieta Rossic and those other bitches do. Far too well. Especially when you're the one doing the talking."

Battle was joined. The exchange of responses became so violent I could hardly hear what they were saying: "You're a jealous devil, that's your problem!"

"And your problem is that you're so weak-kneed. You don't stand firm anywhere: at work, with your family or with your wife… A bum on the run, that's what you are!"

"I only ever moved to get the best for you and the boy! Did you really want us to stay on like peasants, toiling from dawn to dusk, slaves to the boss and at your father's beck and call?"

"If I'd have known, I'd have preferred that to seeing you chasing after every bit of skirt. Don't tell me you were still at work at this time in the morning? What good's our boy going to get out of any of that?"

I heard noises and then Mother's voice, a voice rent by sadness and regret, a voice I only had to hear to feel queasy as if it were scouring my chest: "Where do you think you are you going?"

" … "

"What are you doing, Lluís?"

" … "

"Stop, for heaven's sake! Come here! Come back!"

I heard footsteps in the passage. I cowered in bed, frightened, pricking my ears up to try and hear what was going on. It was as if my parents had suddenly turned into dolls someone had put a match to. I imagined them going up in flames, burning in a strange fire.

Now their voices came from the bottom of the passage, from opposite the dining room.

"Don't do that, for Christ's sake!" Mother sobbed. "Please don't…!"

Dad's silence was like a bottomless pit.

"Please stop!" she implored.

There was a soft sound I couldn't identify, chairs being moved or a box being dragged along the floor, the friction from two forces in conflict, and their struggle to overcome resistance. I got up, shivering with cold, tiptoed to the bedroom door that was ajar and squinted through the crack into the passage

I could see into the ill-lit dining room thanks to the light from the kitchen and my dad brandishing a knife in the air. The knife blade gleamed like a broken mirror, shone much brighter than the miserable, yellow kitchen light. Then I heard Mother still sobbing and imploring: "No, Lluís, no…!"

That scene shocked me, like a mouthful of strong wine that goes to your head and burns your brain out. I shut my eyes and instinctively leaned on the door as if all my energy had drained away. The door closed the second I heard Mother shouting: "Shut the door, Andreu, shut the door!"

Then more chairs sliding and steps running towards me. I pushed the door bolt, but I can't remember if I managed to shift it. I hurriedly slumped into bed, curled up and pulled the eiderdown over my head, but kept listening out for shouting and noise in the passage.

"Your father has gone mad! Don't move," she said, "you stay put."

I heard a loud bang, like a fist hitting the wall, and then silence. After that, whimpering and footsteps in the room next door. Words being whispered. A brittle silence.

Early in the morning, when I'd half got to sleep, Mother paid me a visit. She was wearing a woollen scarf round her neck and a white, wrinkled knee-length nightdress. Her hair was dishevelled and her hands were shaking. She sat on the side of my bed, put her hand on my head and asked: "Are you asleep?" I said nothing, just moved my head, opened my eyes and looked at her. "Did you hear?

Father had a fit. It's over now. Understand? It was nothing to worry about. He's resting now. He's ground down by work and all the problems he's got. If he can rest for a few days, he'll soon get better." She leaned over, gently tucking me in, while she whispered, "Promise me one thing. When you see him tomorrow, don't say a thing about what happened. Not a word. Don't ever mention it to him. As if you'd heard nothing. He'd be really embarrassed if he knew you knew. And it was only a dizzy attack, a fit, a bad turn. It sometimes hits men like that…they get hot flushes, and flail out, strike blindly."

I nodded and lowered my eyes to avoid my mother's watery gaze.

Mother was right. Mother was always right. Without her good sense, Father's lunacy would have sunk our home long before they took him off to prison. And who kept our home going now, when he was rotting in a dingy prison, as she said, confiding in Aunt Ció when they said their goodbyes. The glinting blade Father had flourished at the back of the dining room, the braggadocio gesture of the man taking his belt off and shaking it gleefully like a whip before stepping inside Cal Set, the two male dogs sniffing each other's tails, the cheeky gestures of Oak-Leaf and Quirze when they burst out laughing when dirty words or references cropped up in our nonsense games…all that proved to me that my mother was right; emotional outbursts and intrigues of the flesh only brought unhappiness, chaos, headaches, separations, misery, longings, sickness and sadness in their wake.

Sex and its various manifestations were to blame for the fact that the world was one gigantic game of nonsense.

20

Some deed, some act, some mystery of nature precipitated events and shortened days as if there was no time left to waste. In a way, I felt a strange, unexpected conjunction of stars had ensured that that nonsense, that mess, those secrets, that adult world that was at once incomprehensible, opaque and fascinating, and so far had only revealed itself in short bursts, was now starting to pour down upon me like a storm bringing with it floods, avalanches and landslides. A downpour that caught me away from home, exposed and without shelter. A remote, concealed, fitful world I'd occasionally glimpsed, an apparently innocuous animal dormant deep inside me, now suddenly aroused by the scent of a hearty meal, ready to pounce with all its repressed hunger and hidden savagery.

The first time I saw Pere Màrtir, it was before lunch, when he was talking to Ció under the elder tree behind the farmhouse. I was off to the well with buckets and caught them whispering, just like Ció and Mother. He was tall, brawny, blond, blue-eyed and pale-skinned. He wore an unbuttoned greenish shirt, dark braces and well-cut black trousers. He looked at me for a second, then averted his gaze so I wouldn't see he was crying. I guessed he was because he kept wiping his eyes with his fist, eyes that sparkled like two glasses. Ció turned her back to me as if she wanted to shield him from my gaze. I turned my back when I bent over the well to hook a bucket on the pulley. Then I watched them out of the corner of my eye as I walked home with the buckets full. Neither budged, Ció with her back turned and Pere Màrtir, head down, rubbing his eyes with his knuckles.

I immediately recognized him. I'd never seen such a fair-haired, well-built fellow. And it could only have been him. The youngsters with TB and pliable bones who stripped off in the monastery's heartsease garden hoping the sun would restore their lost energy shared similar touches of nobility but some were emaciated, their pallid skin suffused by a sickly yellow and their elegance often marred by one woeful feature, premature baldness, a violently sunken chest, a swollen belly…that gave their naked bodies a hint of pathos and suggested they were in an endgame, that they couldn't hide the fire consuming their lungs or stomachs. In contrast, Pere Màrtir glowed with health, and his chest, arm and neck muscles seemed ready to flex, jump, swell and take flight. And just as the TB patients' wretchedness isolated them from others and inspired pity or disgust, rather than compassion, Pere Màrtir's tears and troubled face inspired admiration, surprise and even a kind of satisfaction in one's acknowledgement that perfection was vulnerable. He was like a god descending to weep like a mortal, and the TB sufferers in Saint Camillus were a gang of youths under sentence of death corroded within by a curse of destiny.

The word "martyr" somehow forged a link in my imagination between the white, ghostly figures of the young men with TB and the Pere Màrtir I'd just discovered whimpering under the branches of the elder tree. I immediately intuited something else: that his body belonged to the same species of muscular animal that possessed luminous, exultant, firm flesh like my Aunt Enriqueta. It was an identically heavy, dense bodily presence drawing every gaze with its harmony of movement and the magnetic allure of his eyes. In contrast, I realized that most of the other bodies I knew preferred darkness, concave spaces, voids, camouflage and erasure. Pere Màrtir and Aunt Enriqueta demanded light, exposure, ripeness, plenitude, adoration even.

The bodies of the tubercular youth in the Saint Camillus monastery, naked under the sun, lying on the grass, recklessly yielding to secret, curious gazes, had so far revealed a rather shamefaced nudity that could also seem placid, humble and fragile. Only the body of the youngest boy, an adolescent whose movements were precise and elegant, stood out from the rest in its low-key perfection. Generally, they were nudes that aroused respect and pity, like naked saints in church side-chapels or on religious prints: Saint Sebastian transfixed by arrows; old Saint Jerome, half-naked in a cave with a book resting on a rock; Saint John the Baptist, the waters of a river flowing over his feet and a sheep's fleece round his waist, holding a conch shell in the air and pouring water over the heads of gentiles; Saint Andrew, bearded and naked, nailed upside down on a cross; Christ himself crucified naked... I realized for the first time that Aunt Enriqueta and Pere Màrtir belonged to a different race: the race of radiant, gleaming, luminous bodies that spontaneously, involuntarily, radiated magnetic flows of energy and perhaps harmony. We other organisms were vulnerable to the actions of that radiation which captivated, destroyed or deactivated us. Weakened us.

The boy with TB in the Saint Camillus garden and even Cry-Baby participated in both worlds to an extent, one emanating solar rays, the other, a piety in peril. He sent out light and energy and called for no outside intervention; she was turned inwards, silently demanding compassion and warmth, loving looks and care. The tubercular youth and my cousin seemed to have been struck by an overlong, undimmed exposure to the rays of a beauty that had weakened, almost lulled them, but at any moment a strange hand or strange eyes might break the spell and restore them to their pristine plenitude.

Ció came for lunch by herself and sat in silence at the table. The men gradually arrived and took up their places without saying a word.

"Where's Enriqueta?" asked Grandmother when Ció placed the pot of stew on the tablemats.

"She's not feeling at all well," said Ció matter-of-factly. "She had a big sewing job last night. She arrived back in the early hours. She's exhausted and has stayed in bed. She isn't hungry."

Dad Quirze gave his wife a shifty look, which meant suspicion, or cunning in his way of communicating.

"She'd better stay upstairs," he said, "and not say anything until all the fuss has died down."

Cry-Baby and I stared into our dishes of stew. Quirze, on the other hand, kept grinning to himself. Bernat seemed worried, like Grandmother, and said nothing. Jan, the old hand, who often ate lunch with us, didn't let a single wrinkle mark his sunburnt face.

Halfway through the meal Grandmother plucked up the courage to speak: "Well, we really ought to do something about that lad! It was all pledged and he'd brought the rings and everything. This time it looked as if the wind was blowing kindly…"

A glance from Dad Quirze shut her up. After a while, when everybody had respected the silence, Dad Quirze started to mutter, as if he was talking to himself though he was clearly intent on replying to Grandmother, his mother-in-law: "It was blowing so kindly it's made a real mess of it! It's all gone pear-shaped. Fucking hell, we'll have to put a bomb under someone to save their bacon!"

Then he stared into his plate until the meal was over.

When we walked back from school that evening, Oak-Leaf went on ahead with Quirze and left Cry-Baby and me by ourselves.

"I told you," we heard Oak-Leaf repeat. "You see how right I was! You refused to believe me and now you've seen it for yourself!"

"What I didn't believe was that you'd seen it with your own eyes," replied Quirze spitefully. "And I still don't."

"I never said that," Oak-Leaf protested, "I s[a]
from the Rock of Light had told me, she walks a l
home through the woods by herself from the
where the coach drops her off."

"It's always the same story…"

"So why do you say I didn't spell it out to you? Maria
from the Rock of Light has been working for months now
and…"

"I know all that. Get to the point!"

"I told you that when she was walking by herself, she
heard a noise by a bend in the path, took fright and hid
behind some bushes, and it was then she saw two civil
guards appear laughing their heads off…"

"You sure about that?"

"I'm telling you exactly what Maria told me. Maria's no
liar. And she told me and nobody else."

"Oh, you don't say? Is that why there's so much gossip
in the village? It's even reached Pere Màrtir's ears."

Oak-Leaf stopped and looked alarmed.

"Did you say Pere Màrtir?"

Cry-Baby and I had got so close to our two friends
we only needed to stretch a hand out to touch them and
we'd been listening to everything they said for some
time. Apparently they hadn't realized because they didn't
stop talking for a second and the moment Oak-Leaf bent
down, gave Quirze such an alarmed look and put her
hand over her mouth, she must have seen us right behind
but she said nothing, nor did our cousin. And when they
resumed their conversation, they went on just the same,
as if they weren't worried whether or not we heard what
they were saying.

"Yes, Pere Màrtir. He came to our place this morning to
clear the air and Aunt Enriqueta refused to see him."

"You must be kidding…?"

Oak-Leaf reacted in a similar horrified manner and her
voice rasped like a hoarse old woman's.

"And that's all because somebody tipped the wink to that idiot."

"You can't say a word. You can't say a word in these villages. I promise you Maria from the Rock of Light swore and swore by God and all the saints that she'd only told me and not another soul. Villages are hotbeds of gossip; they're full of nosy parkers. Maybe it was the civil guards who spread it around. Canary likes to blab. They do say he loves to spend the whole day chatting in the village café."

"Oh, you don't say! Don't tell me they'd go blabbing to all and sundry!" joked Quirze. "Come on, tell me how many of them there were. How many?"

"She saw two. Two putting those belts with their weapons back on, that kind of strap they wear. One was Canary, for sure, because everybody knows him. And she says that fair hair looks white at night and they were both fair. But one came out first and then Canary, arm in arm with her."

"Did she see *her* as well?"

"At that time of night on that precise day she couldn't be certain it was her. It was a woman, for sure, but not necessarily her. However later, whenever she walked by that stretch of path, by day or night, she'd slow down or stop to see if she could catch them at it again. And at midday she did see them again a couple of times and the woman *was* her. Once she heard noise and giggling and she left the path and saw them lying down among the trees. And on another occasion she saw them walking along the path arm in arm and she let them go on, keeping way behind so they wouldn't see her, until they turned down the track to your house, towards Can Tupí."

"During the day?" asked Quirze, shocked. "In broad daylight?"

"Yes, she walked arm in arm with Canary, I'd told you that. But on these two occasions they were alone, there was nobody else, no other civil guard."

Quirze looked rather anxiously round at us.

"And you two, keep your traps shut," he said threateningly. "Not a word about this or I'll cut your tongues off. It's only stupid gossip. People in the village are envious of the good match she's made with Pere Màrtir and have done all they can to break up their courtship."

Oak-Leaf said nothing, didn't even look at us, as if what Quirze had said was an order aimed at us that was in no way determined by the truth of what had happened.

They mentioned a few more trivial details. Xavier, the novice from Navarre, was mentioned, but I couldn't see what that friar had to do with any of all that; I expect I didn't understand the ramifications. I was surprised by a comment Oak-Leaf made that I could only relate to Aunt Enriqueta's work as a seamstress: "According to Maria from the Rock of Light, she adores uniforms."

On the small path through the woods, Oak-Leaf asked us to accompany her as far as the clearing and play for a bit, but Quirze had gone all taciturn and said he didn't want to today, he'd got work to do at home, though we could do whatever we wanted. He said it in such a way we knew he couldn't imagine for one moment we might leave him all on his own, and for our part we didn't feel like staying alone with Oak-Leaf, so we followed him back to the farmhouse.

"So don't go gossiping now, right?" were Oak-Leaf's parting words from off the path. "Or you'll be to blame for anything that might happen. Quirze, you swore you'd not say a thing."

That left me with divided feelings, on the one hand, disgust at people's capacity for evil, their ability to invent anything whatsoever to hurt someone, and on the other, a strange fascination for what I'd been imagining—the sunbathed tossing and turning in the grass of the luminous bodies of Aunt Enriqueta and the blond civil guard and the other two nighttime guards I couldn't really fit into the picture. It was a gloriously sunny scene, with laughter and cries of ecstasy in the background, and gently moving arms and thighs that entwined in an improvised, impetuous, sensual dance. I also evoked that scenario at night, swathed in shadows, when their luminous bodies shone in the dark and lit up the night, like the light from the rock, from the Rock of Light, bodies of light. Pink flesh gleefully vaunting far from the pitch-black bedrooms and depths of night where I'd imagined these couplings taking place. I marvelled at the daring of the performers, their shameless unleashing of secret pleasures, the way they waylaid the sun over a clearing in the woods to illuminate their partying. The scene I imagined was based solely on fragments of what Oak-Leaf had said. It was forever imprinted on my imagination and throughout my life it continued to be acted out with joyous bliss, a rapturous dance of unknown bodies, like an array of classical nudes exhibited on a museum's walls, and it represented a first ray of illumination and soothing serenity amid the brutal, disturbing revelations people used in their various ways to talk about the facts of life.

21

It was a few days before Aunt Enriqueta joined us for a meal again. She went to Vic in the morning and returned at midday or in the evening, depending on the work she had on, went straight to her room and never came down to the kitchen for anything. We all assumed that Aunt Ció left her something to eat on her chest of drawers or bedside table.

"Women's ailments…" muttered Dad Quirze, chortling slyly, whenever Bernat was quick to comment on my aunt's strange behaviour.

Sometimes he'd add spitefully, "The monthly do. You can't trust animals that piss blood. An animal that bleeds every month and never dies…"

Ció said nothing and Grandmother simply nodded anxiously and came out with an expression we thought was a kind of short imprecation: "God help us…!"

Or else: "When God wishes, it rains whatever the weather. At least God created us."

Nobody mentioned Pere Màrtir and we didn't see him for quite a while. Father Tafalla and the novice were the ones who did come more often now, and always together, "Like the lovers of Teruel; where he goes, she's in tow," laughed Grandmother and no one knew where she'd got that saying from or who that couple were. The two friars were the only people Enriqueta wanted to see and she allowed them to go to the upstairs sitting room or first gallery, where she'd come out and chat for a time. The two friars always visited mid-afternoon on a Sunday or a holiday, after lunch, when the men went for a walk or a spot of fresh air or Dad Quirze had a snooze or took the opportunity to call on a neighbour or to go to the village café to play card games for a while—*la brisca, el truc, la botifarra, el burro, el set i mig*—and the farmhouse was almost deserted. We littl'uns were already playing in our plum tree den and we watched them come out on to the gallery and sit on chairs or the bench and begin a conversation enlivened by grand flourishes of arms and nods galore, while AuntCió moved cheerily among them pouring out lemon water with sugar or pop mixed with a drop of red wine. That pop was our holiday drink, because on work days we drank effervescent water in which little sachets of powder had been dissolved, that tasted just like pop and was much cheaper. The fact that pop was being served showed how important these polite visitations were and Quirze commented one day: "I wonder if Aunt's caught TB and one of these days will cough up blood like the noodles next door."

When we were bored, we jumped down and ran over to the hazel tree spinney, by the pond, from where you could see the meadow, what the monks called their kitchen orchard, the place where the sickly youths lay on towels as broad as bedsheets or curled up on deck chairs, like hammocks, half-naked and swathed in a pile of white sheets. A dozen skinny young men, and a couple of friars who flitted from one patient to another helping them to swallow a spoonful of syrup, adjusting their towels or sheets, or simply sat next to them and conversed for a while. Sometimes they were left alone, and that was when the silence of the afternoon and the stillness of the patients transformed the meadow into a kind of cemetery, a carpet of green grass strewn with white sepulchres.

"It's vice that's done for them," commented Quirze as if he was talking to himself. "They're all rotten inside."

Cry-Baby and I exchanged glances but said nothing. Perhaps the same thought had passed through our minds, namely that young Quirze, after our nonsense games and his secretive exchanges with Oak-Leaf, had become more mouthy, more aggressive and wilder, as if he wanted the filth and obscenities he voiced ever more freely to erect a wall between him and us, as if he wanted a terrain of dirt and mud to divide us into two opposed territories.

"Rotten?" I repeated, "What do you mean?"

"Are you stupid or what? Rotten means rotten, like apples or pears that have gone mushy inside. They look lovely on the outside, as if they are really lovely, but inside they've gone brown and squishy, the fruit is drunk, is full of shit."

I glanced at the ill boys in disgust. Even the tall spindle of a lad who always lay under the elm tree, by the gate, and looked to my mind like a ballet dancer or circus artiste, a performer on the trapeze or balancing wire, because of his elegant, harmonious movements, suddenly appeared like a haggard ghost, at once hollow and fake.

"I thought they only had shadows on their lungs and that was it," I replied while I wondered how to interpret what Quirze had just said. "Their lungs were kaput, people said, because they ate so little or were ground down by work."

"You idiot! Can't you see what those shrivelled runts down there are like? Do you think any of them has ever lifted a twenty-stone sack of potatoes? They all come from posh families in Barcelona or Vic that pay the friars for their keep so they can rest and breathe fresh air. They've got more five-peseta coins than a dog's got fleas."

"You mean someone infected them with that illness?"

"Their vices did, more like," he laughed, ridiculing my ignorance. "Don't think for one minute they behave any better here than away. Now they seem quiet and peaceful like little angels but you can bet they romp around at night like little devils. I expect they jump from one to the next as friskily as newborn goats."

"What do you mean? They're all men!"

"Ah, you're so wet behind the ears! There are men that act in reverse and play a woman's role. Or have you never heard of homos?"

I said nothing, as if I was shamed by my own naïveté. I remembered the night I spent in the misty-windowed café with my father and the comments the men made about the dogs that were sniffing each other.

"I've heard that people with TB are always hot for it, and that it's the disease that sends them into a feverish, randy state. They can never calm down and relax," Quirze enjoyed rubbing in his superior knowledge with these lessons on life. "They're hotter than we are. And as they have to let off steam more often, they're more addled with vice than we are."

Cry-Baby and I said nothing, submissive apprentices before their master. I felt sorry for her, for Núria, because I thought she was too young and couldn't understand such things.

"They say some die from so much..." now Quirze didn't find the word, or perhaps Cry-Baby's silent, humble presence put the brake on him somehow, "from so much... wasting of energy by themselves, because they must spend the whole night long rubbing their wicks."

"I'd heard a lot choke on the blood from their lungs that they cough up, like a haemorrhage, like a bleeding wound that won't heal."

"And because they've lost so much spunk their bones dry up."

He paused for a moment before elaborating, though he didn't contradict what he'd previously said.

"I've heard lots of them haven't got TB. Too much sun isn't good for people with TB. But they've got similar ill-nesses, cancer or brittle bones, contagious diseases they're ashamed of."

Quirze said that as a kind of definitive conclusion, before jumping off the wall and starting down the track through the hazel trees, hidden by the foliage; later we watched him emerge from the spinney by the side of the pond and walk off across the threshing-floor. He left Cry-Baby and myself all alone, without as much as a by-your-leave.

Núria and I walked silently along the same path, like two puppies following in their master's footsteps. My eyes still felt dazzled by the whiteness of the ill boys' clothing and their morbidly luminous bodies, now glowing in the aura of perversity and evil Quirze's words had bestowed upon them.

In the densest part of the spinney, along a stretch of path where we couldn't walk side by side because of the thick foliage, Cry-Baby went in front and without warning, as if she deliberately wanted to get lost or start some strange game, she opened a way through by lifting a hand up and moving the foliage aside on her way to a secret place she seemed to know, a hiding place or lair she had discovered. I followed silently, intrigued by the adventure she was initiating me into.

We came to a clearing where the ground had been trampled; the grass, flattened or uprooted, lay dry all around, under a ceiling of branches that was so thick it was like a grotto or natural cabin. The greenish darkness glazed over my eyes and the bittersweet scent of the hazel leaves stung my nostrils.

It was a hiding place I'd never visited before. How had my cousin found it? Was Quirze aware of that spot? From the piece of bare ground, the circle of flattened grass, the lower branches, whose leaves had been chopped off, and the pile of broken twigs, it was immediately obvious somebody else had used that den.

However, Cry-Baby said nothing. She let go of the hand which she'd used to guide me so far and stretched out full length on the ground as if she wanted to sleep or play at being dead. She closed her eyes and I sat down next to her, mainly because the hazel tree branches were very low and if you stood up, you had to stoop so as not to knock into the foliage or to ensure a sharp, pointy branch didn't gouge an eye out.

We stayed silent like that for a good while, Cry-Baby, her eyes closed, and me, by her side, completely bewildered. I couldn't imagine what we were waiting for or why we'd come to that unknown hideaway. My mind was a blank and I was filled with a sense of peace, as if we'd come to the end of the world, as if everything ended in that secret den.

Suddenly I noticed Núria was moving her hands. Almost imperceptibly, my cousin gently turned her hands without moving her arms that she kept either side of her body, and her fingers began to ease her skirt up, rucking the material, her hands holding it aloft, two clenched fists raising her skirt on both sides.

Now her legs were naked, she lowered her arms gradually so that the skirt rolled down to her waist, baring her navel, smooth belly and a slit half-hidden in the softest little mound of skin, whiter and more delicate than the rest of her body. She was wearing nothing underneath.

I sat and contemplated that revelation, spellbound. My cousin's eyes were still shut and she was motionless again, her hands holding her clothes above her waist. I felt my heart throbbing in my gullet as if blood wanted to rush to my head through veins that were too narrow.

I couldn't think. My cousin lifted my hand off the ground and placed it on her crack. Unconsciously I began playing with my fingers. She opened her eyes and smiled.

All of a sudden my mind was filled with the image of that sickly youth naked under the elm tree, his delicate, bony body, the pinkish pallor of his flesh silhouetted against a clean white sheet, a smile on his lips, as he stared into space. And as if that vision dictated my movements, I quickly stripped off my clothes and stretched out on the ground alongside my cousin.

The ceiling of our leafy grotto swayed slightly, lulled by the breeze. Sounds reached us from the farmhouse, men shouting, dogs barking, and closer by, bees buzzing as if complaining about the sultry afternoon heat.

Cry-Baby took my hand again and placed it back on her sex, and then stretched out her own hand to touch me. We both immediately burst out laughing as if we were tickling each other. She sat up, legs splayed open towards me. I did the same and felt a rush of blood to my belly.

The sheet of the sickly boy lying by the elm tree seemed to envelope the air in our hideout with its serene luminosity and distant warmth. I felt everything was within hand's reach and yet I anticipated a long wait. We gazed at each other as if we both possessed secret wonders hidden between our thighs. The sickly adolescent's dark tuft of hair, barely concealed by the end of his white sheet, heralded the next secret, the final mystery, the most intimate adventure. An unexplored continent hovered above the hazel trees, as far as the monastery garden, next to the skeletal elm.

"The schoolteacher says this is my nightingale's nest…" my cousin declared in a deadpan tone, gaze averted, as if she was talking to herself, while she placed her free hand on top of mine that was resting on her pubis and pressed it down.

I had to repeat what she'd just said two or three times, though I still didn't get it.

"What did you say the schoolmaster says…?"

"That there's a nightingale's nest down here," she repeated in a more animated voice. "Sometimes he also says it's a sparrow's refuge or a rabbit's burrow."

"You mean our schoolteacher…? Mr. Madern…?"

I turned my head to look at her and she did likewise. Her watery eyes glinted, as if she had a temperature, and little drops of sweat began to bead her forehead.

"Yes…" she answered, nodding to back up what she'd said, staring hard into my eyes.

"I don't believe you. You're making it up."

"Ask Oak-Leaf, and see what she says," she responded firmly.

It was a repeat of what happened previously, but I had to think through what I'd just heard several times. Did she mean that Oak-Leaf...? I replied forcefully: "I won't ask Oak-Leaf a thing. She's a gossip. She'd spread it all round the village. I don't want anyone to know."

We didn't say or do anything else that day. Before my cousin could say a word more, we heard Quirze's voice summoning us from the gallery with Aunt Ció joining in. We put our clothes on and ran off.

"We won't tell a soul," she repeated, from behind. "Not even Oak-Leaf will find out."

I turned round for a second to say: "But one day you must tell me how Oak-Leaf comes to know all these things." As I didn't hear Cry-Baby who was running a few steps behind me say anything in reply, I turned round a second time and asked: "And how come you know that hide-out among the hazel trees?"

I thought she nodded, but now we were focused on the gallery from where Quirze was signalling to us to put a move on.

As we went in, we could tell from the way the dogs were behaving that we had visitors upstairs. Aunt Ció came from the kitchen to welcome us: "Where were you two rascals hiding? We've been looking for you for ages." She ushered us into the downstairs kitchen and handed us two pitchers and a bucket: "Quick. We need some really cold water from the spring by the stream. Andreu, you take the pitchers and you, love, take the bucket to the well. And sharp about it."

It looked like important people were about. The kitchen table was full of tasty bites in the making to eat upstairs in the gallery, dining room or sitting room. Neatly folded party napkins, towels, the best glasses, bottles of wine, cold sausage and ham, cheese and nuts, slices of white bread, plates and knives...

"And what about Quirze?" I asked, because I wasn't at all keen to hump those pitchers to the spring all by myself.

"You leave Quirze in peace. He's got work to do upstairs," replied Aunt Ció nervously, as if she was not in a mood to stand any nonsense. "Quirze's been doing what he has to do for some time. Off you go!"

We ran out. On the way to the spring I reflected on what had happened under the hazel trees with Cry-Baby. It all seemed perfectly normal, something that had to happen one day or another. I was more surprised by the fact she'd taken the initiative than by any sight of her fanny. On the other hand, my strange fascination for the youth with TB or whatever it was lying under the elm tree, the delicacy of his movements, the harmony of his features, the mystery of everything he kept hidden under his sheet, that shouldn't have been a mystery to me at all, or even the aloof, rather elegant scorn with which he treated the other patients and the sense of rejection of him I felt I detected within the group…every detail that I could grasp, was etched on my brain, and made a much more powerful, more decisive impact on me than my adventure with Cry-Baby.

At the time I wasn't worried by these different experiences. I simply thought it confirmed the double life beginning to open up before me. Grownups, I'd observed, all had a secret life they never pursued in the light of day or in the presence of others. It wasn't just their sexual activities that they shrouded in darkness, it was also money matters, murky business deals, many of the connections between the Church and God, say, the confessing of sins and the confidences and guidance from that figure who simultaneously stood as a symbol of distinction, moral subtlety and lofty social status and many other questions that belonged to the secret side of this double world which all adults inhabited. Father Tafalla acted as spiritual director to two or three ill farmers' wives, and more than once he'd laughed and let slip that we too could do with a spiritual director in ours, and that would put an end to a lot of the squabbles and suspicions, and that he was volunteering himself to point the souls in our house towards the straight and narrow road, particularly the women's, those who were better disposed, but nobody took up his offer. And now I was becoming aware, quite unconsciously, that Cry-Baby had already entered the duplicitous realm of grownups and easily navigated their sinuous maze of deceit.

Even on that issue the adult world was difficult to understand and interpret. And I grasped that if I was growing up, it wasn't because I had learned how to comport myself outside the home, far from my parents, but because I sensed that I was taking ever more confident steps forward into that slippery, ambiguous world.

22

When I got back from the spring, I found Quirze idling under the elder tree behind the house. The moment he saw me, he said: "Hurry up, they're waiting for you! You look as if those pitchers have brought you to your knees, as if they were a couple of saucepans. They're not that heavy!"

I ignored him. I was surprised to find him there. "What are you doing down here? Don't you have anything better to do?"

He leaned back on the trunk of the elder tree, arms folded and one leg doubled under him with his foot resting on the tree and laughed. "And what business of yours is it what I do or don't do? Hurry up inside or they'll be mad at you!"

"Are you expecting more people? Who are you waiting for?"

I hadn't stopped. I talked as I walked and was just about to go round the corner.

"Who do you think I'm waiting for, you idiot? I'm not waiting for anyone, that's why I'm here. You think you're so clever, the first in the class, see if you can work that one out," he laughed, delighted by his turn of phrase, and repeated: "I'm here because I'm not waiting for anyone."

I was surprised he was so talkative. Quirze was usually as surly and short on words as his father; that night he seemed to want to talk sixteen to the dozen.

Aunt Ció relieved me of the pitchers the second I walked into the kitchen, tight-lipped, as if she was at her wits' end.

"What was Quirze doing back there under the elder tree?"

Ció was too busy to answer my question. Grandmother, who was sitting by the table washing glasses, answered after a while when she realized Aunt Ció was taking no notice: "The four bigwigs from the village are in a meeting upstairs with Dad Quirze and Uncle Bernat and don't want anybody disturbing them. Young Quirze is keeping an eye out, in case the flocks come back early, to make sure they don't create a din. And if the men come back late, he'll have to lead the animals to the mangers as well."

It didn't seem a very satisfactory explanation because Quirze could do all that from elsewhere. I must have looked puzzled because Grandmother added, as if it was an afterthought: "It's best if nobody comes near the house while we've got strangers here."

And she cheerily asked, as she would do when she wanted to get us to do something: "I thought you could do something fun now. Can you guess what?"

I gave her a cheeky look as we all did when she inflected her voice in that way, as if she were a young girl once again, to persuade us that the job she wanted us to do was easy enough, a winning tone we couldn't refuse.

"The light's gone again. The power's gone. I expect there are cuts and nobody bothered to tell us. They leave us in the dark every two or three days. It would really help if you went up to the sitting room, so as not to disturb the meeting in the dining room, and lit a candle to stop the mosquitoes flying up there at this time of day. They might zing into the meeting and upset our gentlemen visitors."

I stood and stared at her trying to guess whether or not she was being serious.

"Come on, do it!" she insisted. "When it's late in the afternoon, the mosquitoes fly upstairs because there's only stale air, the day's fug, when the animals go out to the trough and those creatures fly to wherever new lights come on. If you don't, they'll go straight for the oil lamp they'll light in the dining room as soon as it's dark and irritate the big cheeses. Take a candle and matches from the chest in the entrance. That will be fun and give you something useful to do."

"And what should I do after that?"

"After what…?"

"He means, when they've stopped talking," chipped in Ció, who had now got all the trays ready for upstairs and hadn't seemed at all interested in our conversation up to that point. "Come with me and I'll tell you where best to stand to attract the mosquitoes. When you hear them winding up the meeting, you must run downstairs and tell us, so we can show up and give them a hand. And all the better if they don't see you."

A question came to my lips quite spontaneously: "What's Núria doing? Where is she?"

"You leave that girl in peace!" shouted Ció, angrily, as I'd rarely seen her.

"She's doing the same as you," said Grandmother as cheerily as before. "She's in the attic with a candle scaring off insects."

"She went up to the attic to get a basket of potatoes," Ció corrected her, though no longer aggressively. "She'll be down in a moment."

Ció helped me get the candle and matches from the chest in the entrance and we both went upstairs to the sitting room.

The afternoon now seemed more expansive and tranquil. The blue of the mountains melded into the blue of the sky, a fusion creating the lightest shade of blue that wasn't sure whether to thicken into darker hues or fade into dirty greys and whites. The breeze was cool and soft like a clean pillow that had just been ironed. Ció made me stop in the centre of the sitting room and told me to wait there until she came back. She walked into the gallery and I heard her open the dining-room door, and the sound of chairs greeted her entrance with the trays of refreshments.

"They haven't lit the oil lamp yet, or even a candle," she whispered when she returned. "They'll light up when they find their words are getting nowhere and they need to see people's faces. You should light up now. The more mosquitoes, the better, and the more that fly near the flame, the better, and the more that singe their wings or burn to a cinder, even better."

While I stood rooted to the centre of the sitting room,Ció went up and downstairs three or four times with fresh dishes and whenever she walked by she smiled and was once again the pleasant, friendly Ció I'd always known, as if finishing her chores and receiving the visitors' thanks had restored her usual poise.

I now wondered who the visitors were that merited so much attention. Perhaps the owners, I conjectured. Bored but intrigued, I gradually eased my way towards the gallery door. The candlelight was weak and flickered whenever I peered outside. The voices in the dining room got louder and louder as if the initial conversation was degenerating into an out-and-out argument.

At first I paid no attention to the voices because I knew I wouldn't understand what they were saying and I was happy in my role as the frightener away of mosquitoes and I let myself be carried away momentarily by the feeling of calm, lightness and fulfilment that suffused my body, as if I'd been transformed into a transparent, aerial, invisible being, like the goblins Grandmother said inhabited the farm, the surrounding woods and above all her stories, that were as real as anything else, as far as we were concerned. I detected in my unusual state of bliss a point of pride because I was alone, abandoned by everyone, far from home, practically without a family, and the fact that they burdened me with those negligible, even dispensable tasks, a matter of routine courtesy, like holding a candle in the centre of the empty sitting room to fend off insects, was proof I too was dispensable, and was a bother, although they never said as much, and that I was alien with respect to the close family that had always lived in that farmhouse. I was a Johnny-come-lately, a hanger-on, a refugee, as some villagers said and Oak-Leaf repeated. And the approaching silence of night already falling over the gallery helped me to see myself as an outsider who'd come to that house by chance, who realized that nothing there belonged to him, a quite fortuitous presence, who after time—"and whatever had to pass, had come and passed," or, as Mother and lots of people were always saying, "we can do nothing, it's out of our hands, what will be, will be"—would leave that place and that family; consequently, when they left me alone and my thoughts wandered off in whichever direction boredom or nostalgia took me, I had fun imagining myself as that outsider, a gypsy or charcoal burner in the woods, and roamed far from my immediate surroundings and escaped to places that were unknown, fantastical and inaccessible…

A loud thump on the dining-room table brought me back to reality. It must have been a fist crashing down. And after the ensuing silence, a familiar voice that wasn't Dad Quirze or Uncle Bernat, remarked in a tone that now rang out more loudly and directly than before: "Don't try to persuade me that the horse rode out of the woods by itself, as if by magic, that it was reared without a mother or a master and never bedded down in any stable?"

A different, tense silence followed, and then I heard Dad Quirze's voice. It was the voice he adopted on special occasions, obsequious, almost gentle, smarmy even, a quiet voice unlike his usual sullen, prickly tone, and it immediately seemed fake, his way of mocking his interlocutor or showing that whatever he said and heard went in one ear and out the other.

"You know only too well that Grandfather Hand is the one who drives the flocks up and down the valleys, a long way from here, and that he doesn't recognize the dead horse. We've never traded in horses on this farm or had dealings with the people further up who take them to graze in the Pyrenees."

"So how do you explain the appearance of the disembowelled body of an unknown horse on the bend in the road? We have our own ideas about how it got there. And why it got there."

"Then you know more than we do!"

A voice started speaking in a more clipped Spanish accent and I couldn't hear what it said at all clearly because the individual must have had his back to the door. When I heard that voice, I remembered it was the village mayor's, Filthy-face and the one now speaking in Andalusian Spanish was the head of the local Civil Guard, Martínez— whom people simply called Martínez—and he was notorious because his daughter's skin was so tanned it was almost black—people called her *Negrita*—and her hair was blacker than coal, and according to the biggest lads in the village she was always ready to 'let herself be felt up,' or 'give a blow job,' as they put it.

"*Otroz asuntoz…*" said the civil guard, "*…rezpecto a otroz asuntoz…, habladuríaz de pueblo…*"

"I completely agree with you, sir, village gossip," said Dad Quirze when the civil guard finished his little speech.

"I must insist yet again on our need to conduct a search, if only to put a stop to the accusations coming our way from the Administration," said the mayor in a more conciliatory tone.

"As you wish," responded Dad Quirze, "Our house and stables are open to everyone, come whenever you like. Right now…" Dad Quirze paused briefly before adding: "I mean, right now if you turn the electricity back on, because with the power coming through now, we don't have light anywhere, we're in the dark… In the pitch-black you couldn't tell a sow from a suckling pig. We're still forced to use oil and carbide lamps. You should tell the company to extend the cables from the Saint Camillus monastery to here…"

"We've already discussed all that," said the mayor. "They must change the posts for the cables. That's the responsibility of the owners and the company."

Dad Quirze emitted a strange noise I couldn't interpret.

"To get back to the matter at hand," resumed the mayor, "you ought to know that the horse was stolen from a farmhouse in the lower reaches of the Pyrenees, near Setcases."

And I so learned there were animal thieves who stole horses or heifers, oxen and also sheep that were easier to transport when they were taken to mountain pastures and brought down to the plain to be sold to butchers or breeders. They'd even steal pigs and suckling pigs, so they said, but those thefts tended to be between neighbours or people in the same village because they were animals that were too noisy—they never stopped squealing—and difficult to transport. Horses were the most valued though, I gathered, particularly if they were studs that had shown their worth in mating, and also because they could be used for transporting heavy loads and by the army. The army had an entire cavalry regiment stationed near the Lleida Pyrenees, the Vall d'Aran, Esterri d'Anéu, Viella…and other place names I didn't recognize. People in this country, so they said, weren't used to eating horse meat like the French. They drifted from one topic to another as if they had lost their thread. It seemed like a courtesy visit, but I was sure that the mayor and the head of the Civil Guard hadn't come just to shoot the breeze with Dad Quirze, who couldn't stand the sight of them. Then it came to me in a flash that the horse business was only an excuse and that what had really brought them to the farmhouse was the scandalous behaviour of the young civil guards and Aunt Enriqueta. I listened hard but I don't think they mentioned that. Perhaps they did but not overtly, as was the wont of adults when they discussed delicate matters. But they didn't know young ears were about, that I was eavesdropping.

Suddenly some thing or other made them change tack, they started talking about whether the CNT, the CEDA, the POUM, the FAI, Esquerra Republicana, or other parties…names I'd not heard in the factory town or perhaps I didn't remember because they were never mentioned at home or in the neighbourhood. They also talked about the phantom pickup truck that drove around the district at night with the militia patrol transporting the people they dragged from their homes for a little ride: that meant driving them to a suitable place to shoot them in the back of the neck. They didn't say 'the individuals arrested,' they used the word *nacionales*. Priests and *nacionales* were the words they used. They also mentioned communists and anarchists.

"You were fortunate not to get involved in anything, Quirze," the mayor said at one point in the argument, as if that were praise indeed.

"I…" answered Uncle Quirze, "…haven't a clue when it comes to politics…" and then he added, as if he thought his first comment hadn't gone far enough: "People should be left to get on with their business…but respectfully, they shouldn't be bawled out or roughed up."

Then suddenly the conversation returned to the horse. To the strange way it had died, disembowelled.

"It must have been exhausted…" said the mayor, "Pure exhaustion. It was on its last legs because it had been ridden too far."

"*Y del pezo de la carga*," added the civil guard, though I'd first heard *caga* or shit.

"But what heavy load could a stolen animal be carrying?" Dad Quirze's voice seemed artificially soft and even, soft and even as it went in the Christmas carol. "Or perhaps they did overburden it and forced it to ride down from the mountains with a couple of miscreants on its back."

The mayor laughed for the first time in all that while I'd been listening. And as if Dad Quirze's comment had brought that particular conversation to a close, he added in a conciliatory tone: "Fine. Best if you follow our advice and sign those papers and that will be the end of the matter. You've got precedents in your family and you're not on good terms with the village priest. Fortunately you are a friend of the Superior at Saint Camillus, who gives you a helping hand, or we'd have been forced to send in reports that would have really upset the apple cart."

"Me…?" Uncle piped, whispering again. "But I never get involved in anything. Don't I just work all the hours God sends like a pack mule? The fact is I don't like those ceremonies, parades and stuff. I don't feel happy away from the farm."

"I'm not referring to times past, to the war," rasped the other man, "because you were very clever at sitting on the fence, nobody knew which side you were on, the whites, the reds or the men with the black and red flags. I am talking about now, these years when we are cleaning up the Fatherland, when we all have to pitch in together and move forward in unison. I reckon you learn every way you can."

I hadn't noticed that Aunt Ció had positioned herself next to me, two steps away from the gallery door. Night had fallen over the sitting room and it was pitch-black everywhere. Outside you could hear the first nocturnal sounds: crickets, sheep, owls… Aunt Ció put her hand on my waist, as if she wanted to stop me taking a step forward, though she had gone to where she was now listening. I thought she was about to scold me because my candle hadn't singed a single mosquito wing.

I understood perfectly that the mayor had been referring to my father and Cry-Baby's father when he mentioned the precedents the family had, and my heart had missed a beat. Not out of fear, but rather regret, I reflected, because my father rarely entered my thoughts, yet those strangers were badmouthing him as if he was a nuisance, an irritation and a bother. Remoteness had transformed my father into an object. Memories withered and turned into the kind of yellowing photo you came across in your pocket when you were looking for something else and you really don't know what to do with it, whether to put it somewhere to be revered or in the drawer for odds and sods.

Aunt Ció pushed me back, whispering, as she strode out into the gallery: "Go downstairs and get rid of the mosquitoes in the porch and don't snuff the candle out until you hear them walking downstairs."

Now the men's voices were audible in the gallery and seemed animated as if it had all been a friendly conversation. I went slowly down the stairs and stood holding my candle in the doorway where I felt stupid and ridiculous yet again as I peered into the night from where the two dogs eyed me in amazement. I could still hear voices up behind the balustrade. Aunt Ció had joined the conversation. When they were walking downstairs, I put out the candle and went into the orchard, climbed up the plum tree and stayed there until the big cheeses had left.

23

Sprawled in the plum tree I could see the house's black façade and the gaps made by the two galleries, repeated like a frieze. A candle flickered in one of the attic gallery arches. It must have been Cry-Baby doing what she'd been told. Aunt Ció was holding an oil lamp in the entrance and the civil guard and mayor waited a minute for Uncle Bernat to get the colt from the stable, harness it to the trap and light the lamp by the side of his seat. The two big cheeses got in through the little rear door while Bernat jumped on in front, flourishing his whip. Dad Quirze and Aunt Ció stood by the door for a moment dutifully waving them goodbye as the trap disappeared behind the house and along the path to the hamlet.

The moment I entered the kitchen, I could feel a storm brewing. Dad Quirze was sat at the table frowning, Aunt Ció was bent over the sink washing glasses and plates, Grandmother half-sat on her pew and nobody was saying a word. I shut up too. I sat down at one end of the table and soon after Cry-Baby and Aunt Enriqueta walked in with a basket of potatoes they put on the floor by the kitchen range and then started tidying the kitchen. A little later Quirze showed his face, grabbed an empty bucket and announced without looking at anyone: "I'll make a start on milking the cows as Bernat's not back."

Dad Quirze swayed his head a fraction as if he wanted to tell him something but then said nothing and sat taciturn and scowling across the table again.

Grandmother spoke up: "Don't worry your heads about this… We just have to let time go by and all this will slowly go to the dogs. One day the allies will sort this lot out and that will wipe the smiles off their faces. We just need to be a bit more careful, that's all."

But nobody took any notice of what she'd said and the heavy, unpleasant silence redescended.

Dad Quirze suddenly slammed his fist on the table and swore: "The fucking…!"

The women looked round from the range or their chores to see what happened next. But Dad Quirze got up in a temper and walked out of the kitchen shouting: "You can't say what you think—not even in your own home!"

The women stood there in silence and resumed their chores. Only Grandmother commented eventually: "Their visit has really got to him badly. He couldn't tell them what he wanted to say because the people at the top don't want to hear certain things. They only want to be flattered and soft-soaped."

When it was dinnertime, we heard the sound of the trap coming back and Dad Quirze went out. He was back in a flash followed by his son and Uncle Bernat. They all sat down in silence while AuntCió and Aunt Enriqueta lay the table.

"How did it go?" AuntCió asked Uncle Bernat.

Bernat nodded as if to say they could imagine how it had gone. *How did you expect it to go?* he seemed to be implying. It was obvious that Dad Quirze and Bernat had had words in the entrance, perhaps when they were taking the halter off the colt and putting the trap in the shed, because Dad Quirze didn't react as if he was interested in finding out the answer, andCió didn't repeat her question.

They ate dinner in silence, glancing, gesturing and uttering monosyllables, and that helped reintegrate Aunt Enriqueta into the group, since it was the first time she'd stayed for a whole meal since the rumours about her had been rife in the village.

"This mayor is a wet blanket and a rank fool," said Grandmother almost at the end of the meal, when the heavy silence was too painful and the bleeding inflicted by the strangers' visit to house seemed to have been staunched. "I've known him since he was a nipper, he was a skinny little piece of shit. They've always been church-goers in his house; they couldn't survive without the whiff of a sacristy. That's why they put him in charge of the town hall. He's got only one idea in his head and he doesn't want to lose that. His brain is pure mush. He's his master's perfectly trained dog. He does what he's ordered. He's an arse-licker who wields no power. They told him to take a sniff around the farm, so here he came. Of course, the Civil Guard is another kettle of fish. They belong to another race and I don't get what they're after."

"What do you mean?" asked Aunt Enriqueta, and we all assumed she'd said that to stop Grandmother probing any further, to stave off danger. Or perhaps she wanted to show she wasn't afraid of talking about whatever and was simply saying she wasn't guilty of the accusations against her; it was her way of saying it was slander. It seemed like a kind of victory that the boss of the Civil Guard and the mayor had come to the farm, after the uproar there'd been in the village, and she wasn't implicated.

"It's like the friars next door, the ones in the Saint Camillus monastery. What are that lot doing here so far from their own land? I can't understand why someone would leave their village and family to look after sick castaways, administer the last rites to the dying and dress the dead. It's just like the civil guards, what's the point of watching the borders if all those who wanted to escape have already made it to France? And what are they supposed to do in the village if they killed off all those who didn't think like them at the front or on the road? They're not even any use when it comes to stopping the starving entering a field of potatoes at night to dig up the land and get a good bag of spuds."

"They're like the priests and the military," said Aunt Ció, making an effort to string out the conversation, because what Grandmother had said had changed the atmosphere in the kitchen, had made it lighter and more relaxed, as if the previous silence had started to sour things and their voices now cleansed the air of any invisible bad or rotten bits, "they don't belong to the village either, and do their work and don't cause any strife. Nobody finds that odd."

"It's different. Priests and clergy don't come from so far away, are often from the locality, particularly priests. But these civil guards, for example, come from the other end of the earth and live imprisoned in their barracks, a kind of castle on the outskirts of the village, with that notice on the door that says: *Todo por la Patria*, as if it was an enclosed order of nuns. There's one of those convents in Vic, and just through the door you can see a notice that says: *Hermanos, una de dos, / o no entrar o hablar de Dios / que en la casa de Teresa / esta ciencia se profesa*, more of the same, some are all for the Fatherland and the others for God and Santa Teresa, but it makes no difference, what I mean is that these people, friars or monks, military or Civil Guard, don't fit anywhere, no land is theirs, they're like birds of passage or animals with nowhere to graze…"

"I don't see why that's so peculiar," said Aunt Enriqueta in more of a whisper, as if she didn't dare join in or was apologizing for speaking now we all felt more spirited after Grandmother's sparky words and even Dad Quirze's eyes had brightened and he now raised his eyebrows wondering what other amazing things might be simmering in his mother-in-law's brain. "People like that have always existed. There's work that nobody else would do, if people from away didn't do it."

"There must have been a time when people started leaving their homeland to travel far away and do next-to-useless jobs," Grandmother insisted.

"Next-to-useless?" echoed a shocked Enriqueta.

"I mean villagers would never do them. Who would want to spend the whole blessed day parading around with a gun over his shoulder and a pistol in his belt spying on his neighbours? And who would want to devote their whole life to caring for sick strangers who are never going to get better and would give up being close to their own family, father, mother, brothers and sisters, wife, children, because when they fall ill and need a helping hand, they probably won't have them at their side, probably won't have anyone and will die lonely and forsaken like stray dogs?"

"It's what they call vocation," chipped in a less brusque Aunt Ció. "Father Tafalla, for example, though he's Navarrese, he doesn't stick out like a sore thumb. People who don't know that think he's from the village or locality."

"But they do give up their home comforts, their own family, their own land," Grandmother wouldn't relent. "I reckon the Fatherland is about being comfortable and even God must enjoy being somewhere with somebody. Don't tell me the Fatherland is a a completely unknown quantity or that priests and monks shut themselves up burning the midnight oil for years only to discover they don't know who God is or where they can find him?"

"But that's got nothing to do with it..." began Aunt Enriqueta, apparently out of sorts.

"These people with restless bums can never sit still anywhere," Grandmother resumed the same lunatic argument, "and can never really love anything or anybody. Nobody is their guardian angel. They've got one idea in their bonce, a single thought screwed into their skull, but neither their skin nor their blood ever warms to what's in front of their noses. Perhaps they see further than we can, but they understand nothing about what's happening in their own backyard. Father Tafalla is a bit different because he touches the mouldering skin of the sick and is infected by their stinking breath and that explains why his head isn't as cold as the people whose brains are only full of God's bubbling cauldrons or fanaticism for the Fatherland."

The children and men listened in silence to the three women conversing. I felt we all understood that rather than a conversation, their chatter was an attempt to keep silence at bay, to stop the stone slab of silence redescending upon us. The women spoke in the same way as they waited on table; it was yet one more domestic chore, as if they were duty-bound to enliven the repast, when the men couldn't or wouldn't talk.

Dad Quirze seemed interested by Grandmother's disquisitions, bore the expression of a keen pupil, like when Xavier the young friar explained the direct and indirect rule of three. He smiled, but said nothing, as if Grandmother's words were stimulating his brain. Remote and intriguing, a bagatelle, like the rule of three he would never use.

In a barely audible whisper Dad Quirze commented, keeping his head still, as if it was a comment for his ears alone: "If Father Tafalla wasn't like that, we wouldn't be on speaking terms…"

Everybody waited for a moment, because it seemed he wanted to add something, but he didn't, and Grandmother continued, ignoring what we'd just heard: "The Fatherland is the land that gives you your food, and it just occurred to me that priests say God is a lump of bread, he turned into a lump of bread, I mean, longing isn't enough for a god or a fatherland to exist, something more substantial is required, the land you tread, the bread you bake, the wine you decant…"

Dad Quirze waved his hand, as if wanting to point out that Grandmother had gone too far this time. We kids listened to her as if she was spinning one of her yarns about fairies or murders, with decapitations and revenge…

"No, I'm not really so wide of the mark," she laughed, looking at us. "My goodness, if only I'd been able to study like you! The only thing I regret is having to leave this world without have studied. If I find reading the newspaper every day is like taking a look at the world out of a window, just imagine what I'd feel about books that explain everything, give you all kinds of insights. I had to learn to read all by myself, letter by letter, full stop by full stop. Even so I can write a letter if it's not too long and make myself understood, you bet I can! When I was young, I learned how to so I could write to Grandfather Pep, my first husband, when we were courting, because he had to go a-soldiering in Africa, and we couldn't see each other and had so much to say…"

Perhaps she was tired or feeling sad, because she no longer spoke so vigorously. She added, almost moaning: "That's why God won't forgive those who went to school, are literate, and declare wars and do evil and want more territory, more money, more of everything…rather than finding a way to make everybody happy. Right here, in the village, amongst us, not very long ago they were all killing each other for the sake of big idee-als, idee-as… What was the point of the idee-as they filled their heads with? If I could have studied…"

Dad Quirze slowly got to his feet, as if reluctant to go and take a last look at the animals. Uncle Bernat followed and Quirze ran behind them both and now only the women and littl'uns were left.

"What a to-do that was with the Germans on the Russian front, for example," continued Grandmother as if intent on keeping silence out of the kitchen, "the poor wretches, and the Americans on the Normandy beaches too, you tell me which fatherland either lot were supposed to be defending so far from home. You can understand the Russians and the French, but the Germans and the Americans! You tell me if it wasn't idee-as, good or bad, that drove them so far from their homes!"

She looked round towards the door to see if the men had left and added: "And all those folk scattered throughout France, and the ones who stayed and hid like rabbits because they couldn't cross the frontier, can you tell me where *their* fatherland is? I'll die without ever getting to the bottom of it: what kind of God are they talking about, what kind of fatherland are they defending, if we should all do our best to find a heaven and an earth that are more liveable and more enjoyable."

The men had gone off with the carbide lamps and the kitchen was half in darkness. Ció and Aunt Enriqueta were still at the sink washing up. After a silent pause, Ció said: "You know, I think it's time everyone was in bed!"

We went up to the sitting room with Grandmother, Cry-Baby, Aunt Enriqueta; I went in front carrying the candle. Ció stayed and waited for the men to get back from the stables. The moment we entered the sitting room, Ció ran to pick up a black pile in the middle, intrepidly, as if she'd seen what it was despite the pitch-black.

"It's the knitting basket!" she exclaimed.

It was the first time I'd seen that basket full of skeins and balls of different coloured wool, with long, sturdy needles stuck in the hole in the middle of a thread spool. Aunt Enriqueta and Grandmother exchanged looks of surprise.

"Good heavens!" shouted Grandmother. "What's that knitting basket doing there?"

"Before, when we went up to get potatoes," explained Cry-Baby, "it was up in the attic, on top of a table in the gallery.

"And what was it doing there?" asked Grandmother, taken aback, as if asking us, in the voice she used when she was telling her stories and stopped from time to time to ask, "So what do you think happened to Cinderella?"

"And how on earth did it get down here all by itself?"

Cry-Baby and I looked at her as if we expected her to tell us what the secret was. Aunt Enriqueta started to grin.

"It must have been the goblins," she went on, taking the basket out of Cry-Baby's hands. "These goblins are cocky little devils and turn everything upside down. Goblins go mad when there's a full moon. Isn't there a full moon today?"

We all went out into the gallery to watch the round coin of the moon move across the waxen sky, big as the top of an Easter candle.

"It's Salut's basket, the girl from La Bruguera's. She left it at the tailor's because she wanted me to teach her to do some thick knits she'd seen in a fashion magazine," said Aunt Enriqueta half apologetically. "She wants to knit a winter jersey for her fiancé. I left it upstairs so it didn't get in the way down here and I didn't lose any skeins. I must have brought it down earlier on and left it here so I don't forget to take it with me in the morning, when I'll be seeing her."

Aunt Enriqueta picked up the basket and, when she was giving us a kiss before retiring to her room, Grandmother said: "I'm sure that's what it was. Tell Salut to knit some bright and cheerful jerseys for the children as she does every year. Good night."

However, I could not get to sleep. I tossed and turned in my bed as if I had a temperature. For the first time I felt that room was a prison and Quirze's presence was annoying. I couldn't stop thinking about Cry-Baby's sex yet something else, like the white veils of the sick youths in the monastery garden, prevented that image from really gelling. My curiosity about Cry-Baby's body had aroused an interest in my own, that had been almost dormant till then. I remembered the older lads' dirty talk in the school in town. Big and little were all lumped together in the same class, "unified" they called it, and it was difficult to avoid the displays the big boys put on under their desks, away from the eyes of the teacher-priest, or not to hear their conversations about their latest discoveries, or ignore their precocious remarks—if you didn't want to be called a ninny or a coward—that they threw out as a kind of challenge to see who could say the rudest things, or to pay no heed to the things they insinuated to tell you grownups' secrets, teach you to be a man, or go with them to their get-togethers in local caves where they'd take tobacco and nobody could spoil their fun.

I'd always kept on the periphery of such goings-on. My more childish appearance and the fact that they *were* older than me created a kind of protective barrier. And being there but not joining in was fine by me. I sometimes registered the insalubrious stuff they talked about and the bragging by the biggest boys was too raw and crude for my delicate stomach, but I'd put on a brave front and take it as right, as gospel, the umbilical cord connecting me to a knowledge of the facts of life. However, I always thought that my time had yet to come, that maybe all that was perhaps not for me, and in any case I intended to dodge most of the quagmires and hurdles where I saw my older companions come a cropper.

That night in my room I realized I had got it all wrong.

24

I began to suspect I'd never thought about my teachers the way I did then. Before, that is, before Cry-Baby's revelation, I accepted the presence of teachers in the classroom as naturally and unthinkingly as I contemplated statues of saints in a church. A church was unthinkable without those images in altar niches, but saints never assumed dimensions that were more impressive than the church itself, except for miraculous or highly venerated images. We were called after saints and also had them on prints and illustrated pages in our only reference book, the *Enciclopèdia Universal* published by Casa Dalmau Carles Pla S.A. from Girona, and the images or saints were a humble, useful, commonplace presence, like that of teachers in schools.

What Cry-Baby had told me assigned Mr. Madern, the schoolmaster in the Novíssima, to the category of the miraculous or highly venerated because of a quality I couldn't pin down. Strange new thoughts buzzed round my head. Thoughts that created feelings of repulsion and envy and in my delirium I even decided one of their professional tasks was perhaps to open our eyes to sexual matters, in the same way that teachers, in their pedagogic enthusiasm, often tackled subjects they apparently should never tackle, out of an excess of devotion to their pupils, like going to mass with us every Sunday, as they did now, or visiting the Eucharist chapel of an afternoon, or arranging excursions on the last Thursday before Lent or making us sing patriotic hymns and raising the flag every day and beginning class with the sign of the cross, the Lord's Prayer and a Hail Mary, all things that went beyond teaching us to read and write, the basics we needed to be accepted in the adult world, "the day after tomorrow," as they all called it, or "useful knowledge to open up the path in life that awaited us," as if our school years weren't part of our lives and only represented an approximation to the real life we'd live later on, in years to come, when we'd know about living, when we'd discover what real life was about, which was something everybody kept saying, "What do you know about life?," "You'll know what life is soon enough," "Life will teach you," it was always life, another life, never this life, as if we were human larvae encased and entangled in the threads of a silken chrysalis drowsily waiting for life to burst out for real, the genuine, definitive article.

Don Eladio Madern, Senyor Madern, the teacher at the Novíssima, unlike the priest at the small town parish school, never hit anyone, didn't even have a pointer—we called it a stick—like the priest had to rap you on the hands or the tips of your fingers as they tried to wriggle away. Mr. Madern was a nice man and that was obvious when he explained a subject close to his heart or did so out of duty, under compulsion. He gave us tasks, such as problem solving, filling our exercise books with beautiful calligraphy—Roman, Gothic, italic script…we learned a dozen different styles—or wrote dictations, while he played chess. However, he'd also spend an hour every day telling us about something, mostly lessons from history, particularly Alexander the Great, Pericles, Julius Caesar and Caesar Augustus. On the other hand, when he had to explain religion or sacred history he did so reluctantly, dutifully, and never missed a chance to introduce a note of skepticism we, his pupils, never quite grasped. I once commented on the number of animals of different species that had to cohabit in Noah's Ark and wondered how was it possible for tigers and lions not to eat the deer and rabbits, or even more prosaically, how could a wolf and a chicken, or a fox and a hare, coexist in a state of hunger, and he'd give me an intrigued look and answer as if talking to a drinking friend:

"Well, that really isn't so crucial. If you can accept that the ark and all the paraphernalia around its construction, sailing and final salvation existed, you can swallow the minor detail."

At the time I didn't see what he was insinuating. I didn't say anything, but I felt he'd not only not addressed my question but had treated me like young innocent abroad who requires an adult to teach him different kinds of "truths about life." One sort of truth I guessed went much further than the mysteries about sex. What I was learning from the big kids and bad boys about sex was all about curiosity, and the movements and perversions of the flesh. What the teacher posed related to doubt, the perplexities and mysteries of thought. I was frightened by the idea that perversions of the mind might be even more fascinating than those of the body.

Our teacher made such remarks on a number of occasions over time and when he did so I understood he was establishing a kind of complicity with me, that by only addressing me he was treating the rest of the class with open contempt. For example, when he stopped in the middle of a history lesson, changed his tone of voice, looked me in the eye and launched into,

"Considering that history is written by the winners, and the defeated don't have the right even to a footnote in the big book of history…"

Only to add, even more knowingly, as a provocation: "Be aware, nevertheless, that I'm always on the side of the winners. They must have had something going for them over the others, if they managed to win. Victory is never neutral or unmerited. *'Vae victis!'* said the Romans. Woe betide the defeated! They spread the plague. Steer clear of them!"

Or else: "The rich have slightly more merit than the poor. Their money, at least!"

Or: "If we allow ourselves to be affected by our feelings, we are done for. We should strongly resist ourselves. And never listen to our hearts, suffice that it beats!"

Grandmother found Mr. Madern's *boutades* amusing and when I came back from school, she'd often ask me what his latest shaft of wit had been. As she got to know him better through our banter, she started to drop the nickname of Puppeteer, as if he was gaining respect in her eyes. When we discussed what he'd said or done, she seemed to think it was really funny and she'd comment that that fellow's sour jibes—the teacher who spent half his time at school glued to his chessboard—were down to the fact that the Novíssima was under sentence of death. Grandmother meant that the authorities had decided to close that school and we would be forced to go to the national schools in the neighbouring village—always in the plural, because there was one for boys and one for girls—as there weren't enough children in the outlying farmhouses to sustain two classrooms for girls and boys and two salaries for the schoolmaster and mistress.

"Teachers eat very little," laughed Grandmother, "so they say, but that clever-clogs teacher of yours must get something to keep the wolf from the door, he doesn't look as if he's starving."

She sometimes asked us what we thought of Mr. Madern, whether we thought he was a fascist or a revolutionary, whether he was a reactionary or an anarchist, she'd add more precisely.

"That's to say," she went on so we could grasp the distinctions she was making, "whether he couldn't care less what he says and doesn't worry about the consequences, because he's covered his own back like all the regime's reactionary supporters, or on the contrary whether he does care and lets others get on with it because he believes in absolute freedom and in nothing, neither God nor master, perhaps not even the Fatherland. He couldn't give a toss and wants to let freedom organize itself following its natural instincts, without laws or compulsion, like a wood nobody plants and nothing hinders where trees grow more proudly, finding their own place and their own light."

We glanced at each other, at a loss what to say. We didn't understand that someone's behaviour could be dictated by inner convictions. We thought people did what they did out of boredom, sloth, routine or self-interest, that they only came up with the arguments after they'd done something, in particular to justify themselves, make excuses, express regret or boast about their feats, depending on the outcome.

"Sometimes he even dozes off, thinking about his next move, his eyes glued to his chessboard," was all we could think to say.

"He must be a man who's fed up to his back teeth with everything," concluded Grandmother, "with politics, religion, his profession, life… Is it true he has a photo of José Antonio hanging next to the crucifix, and no portrait of the Caudillo?"

"He says his photo was ruined by damp and he's taken it to be restored or replaced…"

"Now that's a good one!" laughed Grandmother, as if she alone got the joke. "He must be one of those disillusioned Falangistes who didn't want to hitch up to the Generalíssim's chariot alongside the Moors, the Carlists, the Bishops, the military top brass, the Falangistes in faded colours, the rentiers… and the whole crew of hangers-on."

However, after finding out what I now knew about Mr. Madern, I avoided these conversations with Grandmother and was amazed Cry-Baby had been able to withstand that banter and gossip in the past without ever blushing.

One day when I still hadn't managed to get straight the exact relationship between Cry-Baby and Mr. Madern, the latter asked me to wait in the classroom at the end of school because he wanted to speak to me.

The first thought that came to mind was that I should scarper as fast as I could. The figure of the teacher was all mixed up in my mind with prints and images of the giants and ogres in Grandmother's stories, who gobbled live children, swallowing them in one gulp. However, it was these fantasies and similarities that gave me the courage to wait patiently behind my desk while my mates left because I was ashamed I could take those children's stories seriously. What's more, I told myself, if he'd wanted to do something on the sly, he'd not have asked me in public in the middle of the class to stay behind and talk to him. I'd told Quirze and Cry-Baby not to wait, to go home, that we had to sort out a couple of problems. True enough, he had approached me on the quiet, but Gamundi, who shared a desk with me, and those nearby, had heard him. Though my schoolmates always ignored the jousting between the teacher and me, they reckoned he liked me because of the high level of knowledge I'd brought from the parish school. As far as they were concerned, being held in esteem by a teacher and receiving praise for one's schoolwork was something to be ashamed of; they preferred not to have anything to do with arse-lickers, as they called them, the know-alls and seminarians, which was the worst they could say of someone. My mates from the country hamlets were sure I'd end up in the seminary if I continued to be so fond of books and school. However, the teacher never mentioned that, nor did the priest in the parish school.

The classroom emptied out and I hung around tidying the things I kept in my desk. The teacher had gone out to the entrance to say goodbye to the class and when he came back, he sat on his dais, and gave me what I felt was a warm look, full of expectation, the kind parents adopt when they summon you to give you a present on the night of the Kings, however miserable, scant and disappointing you remember it being on that night for giving presents that weren't given, but grownup eyes shine in a special way because they know what you don't, they have the key to what you're hoping for, and that knowledge shines in their eyes with a mixture of hope and the fear they may not match your expectations.

He didn't ask me to come nearer, but simply said: "I didn't know your father was in prison."

I looked at him and didn't know what to say. *Ah, so it was that!* I thought disappointedly. Those political things that got Grandmother going.

"I hope he's lucky," he continued, as if he was turning the page of a book and starting a new chapter. "I wanted you to know that Mr. and Mrs. Manubens came to see me to ask after you. Your schooling, your ability, your behaviour… in a word, your future."

My future? I repeated to myself. In what way were the owners of the farmhouse involved in my future? I'd seen the Manubens two or three times at most. The husband was plump and pleasant with a bald, shiny pate that looked as if it had been varnished. His wife was conceited, buxom, plump too, her eyes, mouth and cheeks were always made up, she wore dresses with swooping necklines and loose skirts, dripped with necklaces, rings and bracelets, and sported a curly fringe and a perm at the back that looked rather ridiculous as it gave the impression she wanted to hide her age; her voice piped and juddered. The Manubens had courted me whenever they paid us a visit and I now recalled that day when the wife looked me up and down as if I was an item she wanted to buy before she'd said: "Poor little thing! If you could eat the odd decent steak, you'd be even nicer! Your cheeks would be more handsome and your eyes sparkier."

I smiled and ignored the empty feeling in the pit of my stomach, as if a piece of flesh or inner organ had been torn from me. I couldn't articulate it, but I felt that large lady had no right to interfere in my private life, while at the same time I thought she was right, that I ate very badly in the factory town, Mother's sawdusty gruel, her potatoes and stinking greens with a knob of tasteless sausage, black maize bread, onion omelettes, and rabbit legs on the occasional special Sunday…but steak, never.

"The Manubens…" continued the teacher in a strangely gentle voice, as if choosing his words carefully, "own the farmhouse where your grandparents live…do you know them at all well?"

"They're friends of my uncle and aunt…and Grandmother Mercè," I replied hesitantly, unable to imagine where my teacher wanted to take me. "They've sometimes visited the farmhouse to see them."

"Come a bit nearer," he told me in a friendly tone I'd never heard before, because he always seemed to speak in a deadpan way as if giving out orders; now he wasn't issuing an order but an invitation.

I shuffled closer to his little platform and stopped in front of the table, not daring to rest my hands, let alone my elbows on top. The teacher moved my chair closer and bent over me, his arms folded on the table.

"Listen," he said. "I'm now going to talk about things you may not understand. I mean politics, laws, the world of adults, the business of life…"

He looked me straight in the eyes to see if I grasped what he was saying or to check on the effect his words were having on me, words I thought were boring, repetitious commonplaces of very little interest.

"The most important thing for a man is freedom," he continued. "Most wars and revolutions have been fought in the name of justice and freedom… But it's not wars I want to talk to you about. I simply want to say that the Manubens are taking an interest in you, in your studies, in your life and your future."

The teacher stared at me keen to make me grasp what he was saying, but I couldn't imagine the agenda hidden behind his words. As far as I was concerned, the Manubens treated me pleasantly enough, Mother had instructed me to arouse the pity of the rich and of factory owners, and to behave as if I was a victim of the circumstances of the war, to weave a saccharine web of feelings of compassion and commiseration whenever they stopped to speak to us and gaze down on us as if we were relics from the war and examples of the consequences of the envy of those who'd revolted, so I wasn't at all surprised that the Manubens should take an interest in my schooling or in my life on the farm. The rich had lots of time to kill, Mother would say, and had different obligations to the poor, particularly the need to preserve their world so it could act as a model to the poor who aspired to draw close, because if there wasn't a mirror of a perfect world which they could look into and aspire to, in which other direction might the aspirations of the poor lean?

"They have asked me, if the situation arises," continued the teacher more spiritedly, "whether you would agree to them taking charge of your schooling, watching over the progress you make, ensuring you have everything you need...so you can go on to study at university."

Now I looked at him, intrigued. I felt a stab of fear somewhere in my chest and a pit in my stomach, though I couldn't identify the cause, nor could my brain pinpoint any real danger.

"It looks as if your father's cause won't prosper," said the teacher, his voice faltering, "well, you know, a reprieve might come at the last minute—that has happened in other cases—but if it doesn't, what we don't want to happen, might very well come to pass."

He lowered his eyes so as to avoid mine. I thought of Mother's long conversations with Aunt Ció—how was it they'd not told me anything? Was what they called the sentence, the appeal against the sentence or the execution of the sentence really so imminent?

Was that why they both whimpered in the middle of their conversations as if their sobs were contagious? Was that why they looked down and shut their eyes as if they were privy to a horrible scenario? Was that why they hugged as if they'd not seen each other for ages or wouldn't be meeting up again for months or years, a long time before they actually said goodbye…?

"The Manubens don't have any children and they are looking for someone to adopt…"

The teacher twisted his neck slightly and his eyes softened as if he wanted to make what he was saying more palatable. However, I couldn't get my head round what he was saying. It was like the farewell conversations between Mother and Aunt Ció, I was used to being left out, to them not expecting me to react to whatever they were saying, and now was perhaps the first time I was being spoken to in person about a serious, important matter, and I really didn't know how to take it. I couldn't decide if it was a proposal or a possibility, fact or fantasy.

"I don't think they've spoken to your mother as yet. But I'm sure they have talked to your uncle and aunt, and if they know what the Manubens are intending, you can be assured your mother is in the know too. They must think that, if things turn out badly, she'd be able to cope better by herself… that is, without you." said the teacher, immediately adding, possibly to soften the impact of his words: "Oh, don't think I'm speaking on behalf of anyone! These are simply my own reflections, ideas prompted by a visit of the Manubens to express an interest in your schooling, your behaviour… I felt I should tell you, that you should be aware, that you ought to be ready if the situation arises, so you aren't taken by surprise. What do you have to say for yourself?"

"I don't know," I replied like a robot, the truth is I *didn't* know what to think. Quite unconsciously, I noticed I was spontaneously smiling at the teacher, as if I owed him something, and I was really annoyed at myself for such knee-jerk reaction.

"I spoke about freedom at the beginning of this conversation because you should consider what you can gain and what you can lose in this situation. They'll tell you, if they haven't already, that you'll now be the man in the family and that everything that may happen will make you mature very quickly. Don't take any notice. What you must think through is whether you want to continue with your schooling or want to stay at home and work like the other boys, in a factory or on the land. That is the only genuine decision you have to take. If you like studying and want to go to university, this is a good opportunity." He paused and added: "You will find the way to keep your freedom."

He cleared his throat and continued: "I mean there are lots of ways to do what you want while at the same time pleasing those who are helping you out. You must be clear about the extent you can please others without curtailing your own freedom, the things you don't want to share with anyone."

A noise in the playground made us both look round and out of the window. Quirze, Oak-Leaf and Cry-Baby hadn't followed the teacher's advice and were running and shouting at each other on the gravel.

"They're waiting for you," said the teacher. "I won't keep you any longer. You think about what I've said, when you have a moment of peace and quiet, just in case things don't turn out as we'd like them to. Be brave. You can get over this. I too lost my parents when I was very young and now I regret not putting up more of a fight to do what I wanted to do rather than going on to do what I do now. Fight and don't let anything get in your way."

The teacher stood up and I moved away from his dais. He silently accompanied me to the door and as I left he patted me twice on the back and that was that.

Quirze, Cry-Baby and Oak-Leaf had run off to the playground gate and were giving me curious glances. When I joined them we started to walk, not saying a word until the Novíssima was out of sight.

"What did he want?" asked Oak-Leaf first. "Why did he make you stay behind?"

I shrugged my shoulders. I couldn't think of an excuse.

"Yesterday, at midday, at lunchtime, Father came and talked to him," said Quirze. "We didn't see him because he took a shortcut so as not to bump into us. I heard him talking to Mother about it last night."

From time to time Cry-Baby looked round at me, her eyes glistening, but she didn't speak up.

"Perhaps he wanted to talk about you," I said, without much conviction.

"They spoke about you, not about me," Quirze answered firmly. "And about your father."

Once again I felt a heavy weight in my chest, as if I'd suddenly been landed with a burden that was bigger and heftier than my lungs and heart. A horrendous weight that choked the words in my throat.

"You haven't been to see your father for quite a while, have you?" asked Oak-Leaf.

I couldn't come up with an answer. My chest weighed heavier and heavier.

"They'll let you see him now," continued Oak-Leaf in a voice that was a combination of a desire to please and cloying curiosity. "They always do when it's people they're never going to let out. You just see how they'll summon you and your mother to the prison one of these days."

I suddenly broke into a run down the path, irrationally, as fast as I could and on the first bend I disappeared into the woods, into the mass of trees.

My friends started shouting, half out of fear: "What's getting at you now?" asked Quirze. "Hadn't they told you anything?"

"Come here!" went Oak-Leaf. "We didn't mean to upset you!"

And Cry-Baby's gentle voice, the one that meant the most to me: "Andreu! Andreu! Andreu!"

25

I stopped at what I thought was the most secluded spot in the woods. Branches were so high and thick the light struggled to get through. The round clearing was full of tall, damp, bright green grass. I stretched out on my front and buried my head in my hands. I didn't want to see anyone, hear anyone or think of anything.

My father, my father…if my father was going to leave forever, I must be the first to distance myself from him. Now for the first time his absence was hurting. His sentence seemed like a betrayal. Now more than ever I was conscious of the void left by his absence. I felt he would leave a hole it would be impossible to fill. A hole that wouldn't go away. A scar that would never heal.

Tears didn't well up, because I'd not planned on crying. There was a dull whimper, a hoarseness irritating my throat. I could see my mother, frightened, on paths in the darkness beyond, carrying baskets of clean clothes and food to the prison, to the hospital, to the hideout, wherever Father languished. An invisible father. Father's face. Father's loving voice. His hand's rugged warmth. His trusty gaze. His skeptical, mocking smile. Images of him etched on my memory, one with his back turned, in a spotless gabardine, leaving the pharmacy with a gentleman one autumn afternoon, and another with him in a blue overall and a loose jersey laughing with the mechanics that night in the bar opposite Cal Set. The memory of my father. Just a memory. A memory that was already on the wane. I couldn't even hold on to the memory. The memory was also fading, escaping, dying. Memories also die, I now saw, and that frightened me.

When I lifted my head, darkness had fallen. I thought I'd heard Quirze, Oak-Leaf and Cry-Baby calling out to me, searching for me, but I could hear nothing now. What if I got lost and couldn't find the path back to the house? What if I got lost on purpose and never returned? What if I never ever returned…anywhere?

I walked instinctively and emerged on the path to the farm quite by chance. Round two bends, and the house came into sight. I slowed down as I got nearer. I didn't know what I was going to say. My uncles might have gone to look for me. What can Quirze and Cry-Baby have told them? I felt embarrassed about walking in and having to invent some excuse or answer their questions.

I lingered under the elder tree and the intense scent, like bitter, vegetal incense, cheered me up. As if the elder tree's unexpected smell was restoring something I had lost. Perhaps that *is* what memories were about, the sudden presence of the unexpected, an invisible realm that hovers above us, out of reach and deaf to the desires of our will.

"You're late back…"

That was the voice of Jan, the old hand, who was looking at me from the lumps of rock salt scattered around the troughs.

"Quirze and the lass arrived a while ago," he said, not at all reproachfully.

I said nothing and hurried towards the entrance. Quirze was in the doorway playing with the dogs. He looked at me askance, and said nothing. Cry-Baby was sitting on the stone bench and got up and stood next to me when she saw me. We went into the kitchen together.

"Your bite-to-eat is on the table," said Aunt Ció, rubbing her hands on her apron.

Grandmother Mercè was sitting on her pew with her balls of wool.

"Eat something, even just a mouthful," she said gently. "If you aren't hungry, eat as if you were, chewing will bring back your appetite. Eating always brings back your appetite."

There was a pile of folded napkins on the table and a plate with a slice of bread, a piece of cold sausage and a glass decanter of wine. I sat down without touching a thing. I sensed they were all looking at me and scrutinizing my every movement. Cry-Baby sat next to me, on the bench, clasping her face, her elbows digging into the table, her eyes staring into mine, not saying a word.

"Your mother will soon be here," said Ció, keeping her eyes on the oven. "And if she can't make today, she'll be here first thing in the morning."

"You see...?" added Grandmother ever more affectionately. "We won't abandon you, we'll be at your side the whole time."

However, her voice tapered off and she had to rummage in her apron pocket to find a handkerchief to wipe her eyes and nose, as if she was blowing her nose.

"It can probably still all be sorted out," continued Grandmother on a stronger note. "Let's hope so. I've not put my rosary beads down since I heard them say yesterday that time's running out. In case that might be any use..."

She took a deep breath, as if hoping her lungs would give her the energy to continue. Ció looked round, so I would hear her: "Eat something, love, let's not allow sadness to get us down. We've never hurt anyone, not even a little scratch, or a single bruise. They'd really like us to have empty heads, of course, they're annoyed when people think what they want to think and keep their minds on their own business! They'd prefer us to have heads full of sawdust so they can boss us around better. Damn and blast them! Dozens of wild horses should come down from the mountains and kick and stamp on them..."

Ció slowly turned round as she spoke, as if her increasingly violent words made her fear she'd have a stroke. But then all of a sudden she shut up and turned her back on us again. I started nibbling the slice of bread.

Dad Quirze walked into the kitchen and the second his feet crossed the threshold he halted when he saw me. His cheeks flushed as if he'd had a rush of blood. He stared at us all for a moment, then turned round without uttering a word and walked out mumbling almost inaudibly as if talking to himself: "I'll be back in a jiffy."

I nibbled the bread but didn't touch anything else. Grandmother's knitting needles were going at a quicker rate than ever and now and then she took her glasses off and wiped her eyes, as if to complain her eyes were weary. Aunt Enriqueta arrived and went over to Ció and whispered in her ear, as if she didn't want to disturb the order and silence reigning over the kitchen. Then she walked over to Grandmother and sat next to her. Bernat also came in for a moment, before rushing out like Dad Quirze.

Death was like that, I reflected: the sudden quiet, the unravelling of life, usual routines turned upside down so no one knew how to react, what to say, or where to put themselves in order to find the comfort zone in the house or the world. It was a radical dislocation, a displacement from the world one had known hitherto. A mysterious force that threw everything into chaos and burst invisibly upon the scene like cold snaps in the first days of winter, transforming everything, though everything appeared to be intact… It shrouded in anguish and sadness those who noted its presence.

The tranquillity and silence were broken by a crashing sound. The clean, piercing noise of glass. Cry-Baby, sitting at the table, had moved an arm without thinking and had knocked the decanter onto the floor. We all looked at her, taken aback. Then after a moment of confusion, Cry-Baby burst into tears, as if something baleful had happened, as if she wanted to take the blame with her tears and avoid recriminations.

"That's nothing to worry about," said Aunt Ció, arriving with a cloth and broom to clean up the mess.

"That's right, it's only wine," smiled Grandmother, "we've got more than enough! Come on, no need to cry!"

But Cry-Baby cried disconsolately. Aunt Enriqueta sat next to her and gave her a loving hug until the tears became whimpers muffled by my aunt's bosom, almost imperceptible shudders. And we all knew the weeping wasn't simply about a smashed decanter, that the clatter of glass was a focus for something broader and more diffuse, a brittle, rarefied atmosphere of dire omens and repressed fear now fighting their way to the surface, unleashed by the dramatic crash to the floor.

Aunt Enriqueta helped Cry-Baby to her feet and led her out of the kitchen.

"Just lie down in your bed for a bit and rest," she said, "till it's time for dinner."

"Andreu, you should do likewise," said Grandmother. "Go on, the two of you, upstairs and lie down for a bit, till you get over the upset."

"You've hardly eaten a thing," said Aunt Ció when I got up to accompany Aunt Enriqueta and my cousin. "It will be all for the best, you'll be ravenous at dinnertime."

We both walked out into the pitch-black entrance.

Dad Quirze and my mother were whispering by the foot of the stairs next to the door. Mother was carrying an old bag, a kind of clothes basket, crammed to the brim with parcels wrapped in newspaper.

Aunt Enriqueta stopped for a second, as if wondering whether to turn tail, but the moment she saw she couldn't hide my mother's presence, she glanced quickly and silently my way. Then she gave Cry-Baby a push and vigorously swept upstairs, leaving me behind.

I stood there still and tense because I was afraid of Dad Quirze. My mother came over and silently put her free arm round my back and squeezed me against her tummy.

I shut my eyes and let myself luxuriate in the sweet smell of clean clothes and cheap soap impregnated with factory oils and crates of industrial cotton that my mother's body exuded. A homey smell that took me far away from that farm and reminded me of where I came from. An invisible path returning me home.

"We can go and see your father tomorrow," she said wistfully, after standing silent and stock-still for a few seconds.

26

Vic Prison was a ramshackle ruin on the corner of an out-lying street. If it hadn't been for two or three turrets with lookout slits and battlements on either side, like a castle transplanted from the mountain to the plain, you could have mistaken the building for one of the many convents for enclosed orders scattered across the city.

We had arrived at the prison entrance early in the morn-ing, my mother carrying the basket of parcels and me gripping her hand tight, as if the place threatened danger. Outside, the roadside was packed with people, relatives of the prisoners, all holding bundles and crumpled sheets of paper and looking harassed, waiting for a signal or the time to go in, peering at the closed windows on both levels and the movements and suspicious glances of the civil guards walking round the turrets, trying to work out what was happening inside the jail. Now and then shadows filled the long slits and people assumed a line of prisoners or civil guards must be parading behind. The glinting to-and-fro of bare bayonets that stood out like knives raised above the battlements were threats that even filtered down to us.

That night my mother and Aunt Ció had stayed alone in the kitchen chatting late into the night. Before falling asleep, I heard the two women come up the stairs, and even then they went on talking for a good long time in the sitting room. I imagined them, as I'd seen them so often on the path by the cherry tree, amid the oak trees, heads bent, two shadows blacker than the surrounding gloom, confiding in each other, arm in arm or holding hands, nod-ding or shaking their heads, but above all, downcast, as if oppressed by the weight of the words they uttered. Now and then a deep sigh, a muffled lament, interrupted their conversation, suffusing it with tragic resonances.

Mother and I positioned ourselves by the crowd of people waiting on the roadside. Most were women wearing black dresses and headscarves. There was the odd young lad like me, with patched trouser bottoms and messy hair, and we looked at each other timidly, almost on the sly, as if to acknowledge that we belonged to the same race of losers, were abandoned and stranded on the roadsides of a city that was progressing without us.

After so much waiting, I noticed people were stirring, straining their necks, moving their hands, lifting their arms, taking one or two steps forward so as to be in the middle of the street. Mother grabbed my hand and, as she looked up, she stared into my eyes and said: "Look… They're walking in single file. Watch out for him."

They'd opened the shutters to the first-floor windows and you could see a line of men filing past, shapes that were repeated from one window to the next. A group of women crossed to the other side of the road and some even shouted out a name two or three times, though the line of prisoners never came to a halt.

"Can you see him? Can you see him?" Mother asked, and I noticed how nervous she was from the way her hand clasping mine shook.

One or two prisoners turned their heads in our direction, and that led people to move back towards the ramshackle prison building. When the men under sentence had disappeared, the group outside seemed deflated, plunged into a kind of disappointment that made them bow their heads, shut their eyes and stoop their shoulders. A gloomier than ever silence descended over everyone.

Mother gripped my hand tighter and said nothing.

They didn't open the prison door for what I felt to be a very long time, and the whole crowd pushed and shoved their way inside as if it was the New Year sales. Mother still held onto my hand, quietly but firmly defending the place we took in the queue that the civil guards forced everyone to join.

In the entrance, police in dark grey uniforms were opening every parcel and rummaging in every one. They took the packets Mother was carrying. They tried to calm her down by telling her not to worry, that it would all make its way to the inmate's hands. They said inmate, as if they'd stripped my father of his name.

The inside of the building seemed icy cold. The whole edifice seemed freezing and deserted. Stone stairs, flaking walls, passages without a stick of furniture, bars everywhere. We entered a large rectangular room full of people. The women were crammed against an iron bar that separated most of the room from a series of large, barred windows that formed an empty passageway, guarded by two policemen with guns over their shoulders who strode up and down, keeping at bay anyone who tried to walk through and approach the big windows.

Prisoners were on the other side of the barred windows, two for every opening, one on each side. Mother and I walked up and down looking in every window to find my father and when we'd tracked him down, my mother elbowed her way through to the front row that was leaning against the iron bar. I stood next to her. The bar came up to my chin.

Father's eyes were large and shiny, his face pale and gaunt; his bones, cheeks and jaw jutted out, trapped between the two thick bars of the grille, as he grasped the iron further down. When he saw us, he got up, still clinging to the bars. He tried to smile, and I thought his yellow teeth looked rotten or false.

Mother and he had to shout so their voices rose above the incessant din that seemed driven by a machine. I only caught the occasional sentence like: "How are you? Have you been back to the infirmary? Don't worry, I'm knocking on doors every day, and lots of people have put themselves about to help you. I've brought you clothes and food. Your mother and everyone send you lots of kisses. Don't give up hope now, bear up. We'll find a way... You just see how we will."

Father nodded while one hand fell away from the bar, then he gripped it again, and his face and eyes lit up strangely, like a hollow pumpkin with a dismally flickering candle inside. At one stage he must have said something important I didn't catch, he moved his lips in my mother's direction and I didn't hear him, they must have been talking about me because my mother put her hand on my shoulder and lowered her head slightly so I could hear: "Don't you worry about that. Andreu is keeping up with his schooling, both the teacher in the Novíssima and the priest at the parish school are being very good with him and say he's doing well, that if he goes on like that, he'll be able to do whatever he wants..."

Then Mother looked down both sides of the passage and when she saw that both guards had their backs turned, she pushed me under the iron bar and said: "Run, go and give him a kiss...!" as she put a handkerchief in my hands, adding: "Give him this, if you can...!"

A couple of big strides and I was opposite him and my speed helped me to stick my hand through the bars and Father grabbed the handkerchief and leaned down to give me a kiss. I felt how bristly his cheek was because he'd not shaved, and his skin was bluish, almost transparent, and his hair grey and sparse. He didn't look at me, but quickly said: "Look after your mother! Make sure you look after her!"

I beat my retreat before one of the police could come and yank me away. When the policeman was level with my mother, he stood in front of her and said it was forbidden to go close up to the booths, I then learned that they weren't windows, but *locutorios* as the Civil Guard put it in Spanish, and that she shouldn't play the fool anymore if she didn't want those inside to suffer as a result, and that our visit was at an end, other relatives were waiting.

We walked away reluctantly, and Father looked at me two or three times and lifted up a hand with a single finger sticking out as if to remind me of what he'd asked me to do. Mother and he looked into each other's eyes right to the last moment, and it seemed their eyes would never separate.

The police ushered everybody out of the waiting room, the booths emptied, and we slowly walked downstairs, as if we'd left our eyes behind.

Once outside, we walked on in a haze, and my mother asked me things as if she was talking in her sleep, and never waited for my reply, as if they were questions she was asking herself: "How did you find him? He looked better, didn't he?"

Mother had forgotten I'd not seen him for over a year. The last time I'd seen him in prison was in the infirmary, in a clean bed, after the operation, only a week after he'd left hospital. Mother kept walking and her questions were contradictory. She said: "He seemed a bit the worse for wear, downhearted, don't you think?"

We stopped in a front of a café full of the same people who'd been in the prison visiting room and on the road outside. Mother asked: "Are you hungry or thirsty? Do you want anything? I don't remember if we had any breakfast or not at Grandmother's."

I said nothing and followed her in. We went up to the counter and she ordered: "A cup of coffee for the boy!"

The waiter asked her what she wanted and Mother said she didn't want a thing. Some people sitting at a nearby table got up and Mother made me sit down. She stayed standing by my side. I pointed to the empty chair and the waiter also suggested she sat down, saying it cost the same standing or sitting, but she said not to bother, it wasn't worth sitting down, she was fine standing.

I quickly drank my coffee, uneasy at the presence of my mother rooted there, as if she wasn't worthy of the luxury of a seat and a drink.

As if her earnings didn't permit such expenditure.

I felt my mother was withdrawing into a zone of darkness, was refusing to join in the futile round of social life, was absenting herself from any activity that wasn't factory and housework, and that from now one she'd exist only for me, the family at Can Tupí and the memory of my father.

She had to get back to work on the afternoon shift. She had switched her morning shift with a colleague and would have to run to get there on time. She left me on the bus that went from Vic to my grandparents' hamlet, the stop by Saint Camillus monastery, where I'd get off. She repeated, as if instinctively: "Remember, remember…"

But I didn't know what I was supposed to remember and later on I thought she might perhaps have said, "Remember him, remember him." She ran her dry lips over my cheek and went off to the station where the bus to town stopped.

I travelled back to the farm, pressing my cheek against a window in that half-empty coach. I was tired, though I'd not done anything requiring physical effort. I was overcome by a feeling of powerlessness, alienation and moral collapse. I don't know why but my head was full of the faces of the priests who taught the catechism, the priest at the parish school and the Camillus friars from the monastery, who preached forgiveness, forgiveness, repentance and forgiveness, mercy, providence…and what else? And of the three theological virtues, charity was the most hallowed, the most prized, the most vaunted, but I could see forgiveness or mercy nowhere. Why didn't people notice? Even I could see that clearly enough and Quirze and Dad Quirze as well, and all the men I knew, from Uncle Bernat to the teacher at the Novíssima, Mr. Madern, knew the score as well, and perhaps that's why they always seemed grave, surly, unfeeling, and immune to the fun and jokes that bring cheer to life, that seemed as brutal as the thud of an axe. They all knew mercy and forgiveness didn't exist in this world and that everything priests said was like Grandmother's fireside fairytales, pleasant, cheery chatter to pass the time, entertainment for our leisure time, but totally nonexistent.

In fact, that was the source of the intangible beauty and virtue of Grandmother's imaginary characters that were as evanescent as a dream.

27

Days passed and we all felt we were in a state of vigil. On the surface everyone went on living normal lives, followed the necessary routines, but from the moment I got back from the visit to my father, I felt I was surrounded by a bubble of cold air that isolated and protected me. From Grandmother to Uncle Quirze and my two cousins, everybody treated me with a barely perceptible extra degree of consideration I easily missed if I wasn't really on the alert. It was the sum of small details that made that subtle distancing quite tangible.

Ció put more on my plate than on others' and insisted I ate heartily; Dad Quirze avoided giving me orders or any kind of work; Cry-Baby looked at me gone out as if she were seeing me for the first time or had noticed a pimple on my face; Jan, the old hand, smiled whenever he bumped into me, that enigmatic smile of his that wrinkled his face and shrank his eyes, transforming them into closed slits that hid his two dots of light; like his father, Quirze never addressed me, though he never ignored my presence and always let me climb into the plum tree first; Oak-Leaf hummed songs or told dirty stories the whole way back from school, but never suggested new games or told us anything new; Grandmother Mercè stopped knitting or mending and sat staring out of the kitchen window at the cherry tree path, as if expecting a piece of news, her eyes languid, blank, and drowned in dampness.

One night, at dinnertime, I noticed that Aunt Enriqueta had yet to come and that Ció was doing everything early as if she'd some reason to be in a hurry. Grandmother, on the other hand, seemed more cheerful and took me and my cousins to the sitting room upstairs immediately after dinner because she wanted to tell us some new stories, some of which would make us laugh and others that would have us shaking with fear, and Quirze listened, head down and silent, as if relieved he didn't have to help the men for a while as he usually did day in, day out.

Grandmother Mercè sat on a chair by the gallery door, in the shadows, and we stretched out over the floor on sacks, close to her voluminous black skirt. A blue light shone in from outside outlining every shape like a low mist and a cool, pleasant breeze blew in the new season's scents.

To begin with, Grandmother's voice seemed to tremble but she soon warmed to the task and was the first to laugh at the stories she told. That woman who went to confession at the Saint Camillus monastery saying she wanted to see the face of God, that if she didn't see the face of Our Lord, she would be unable to repent for her sins, like Saint Thomas the Apostle, who had to see in order to believe, and her confessor told her she could never see the deity, that was the privilege of saints, maybe later on if she persevered in her devotion and penitence she might see the sacred face, but maybe if she came back on another day at such and such a time, as a special favour, she might be able to touch, that's right, touch the divine countenance, and the woman returned on that day at the assigned time and kneeled by the confessional and asked through the screen whether she could touch the face of God, and her confessor said yes, she could, that she should stretch her hand out into the front of the confessional, lift up the curtain and feel the holy face, and there the confessor was waiting for her, soutane lifted and trousers dropped, bum in the air and when she touched his plump rump, she exclaimed in astonishment: "By the Holy Virgin of Monserrat, what a lovely face and such a flat snout!"

We laughed our heads off and repeated the punchline, "By the Holy Virgin of Monserrat, what a lovely face and such a flat snout!" when we told the story to Oak-Leaf; we pissed ourselves laughing in the middle of the woods.

Grandmother was irrepressible. The story of the Countess of Tornabous, from Tornabous Castle, not far from us—the richest woman in the realm—the realm being an imaginary terrain that didn't fit the district or national boundaries or any other of the administrative specifications we were taught at school, but was where Grandmother located her fantastic stories. The Countess of Tornabous was the richest, sweetest-toothed woman in the realm, and as she was a widow and her husband the count had left her everything upon his death, land, property, everything, and an instruction to do whatever she wished with it, she, the Countess of Tornabous, spent her entire fortune, land, goods and everything she had and could borrow on banquets and gourmet food and drink she ordered from afar, delicious liqueurs and titbits—Grandmother was the only person who ever used that word, titbits—and it came to pass that as the Countess of Tornabous spent her life eating and never bothered to manage her wealth or keep an eye on her servants, one day she realized that all her doubloons had gone—another word that only cropped up in Grandmother's stories, doubloons were the legal currency in all her yarns—she was ruined and forced to abandon Tornabous Castle as poor as a church-mouse and set about begging, in gypsy dress, with a tatty little basket. Now you saw the poor Countess of Tornabous on byways and street corners asking for alms for the love of God, who'd have thought it, the haughty Countess of Tornabous, once the grand lady and mistress of the entire realm, now transformed into a beggar who survived thanks to handouts from her former servants and vassals, all because she'd stuffed her guts and frittered away her whole wealth on lavish feasts and fancy new dishes that cost an arm and a leg, and hark ye now—magical words we only heard in these stories, hark ye now, like "once upon a time there was a king…" were the warning bell, the fanfare, the call to attention that heralded the long-awaited ending, the miracle, words from the world of fables that we never found elsewhere—and hark ye well, for one day when the Countess of Tornabous was asking for a crust of bread for the love of God in a farmhouse doorway, the farmer's wife gave her a linen bag with a crust of white bread and a handful of walnuts, and the countess walked off so happily and on a bend in the track she calmed her hunger on that gift from the farmer's wife and found the bread and nuts to be so good, so tasty, so really delicious, that she bawled out: "If I'd have known that bread and walnuts were so scrumptious, I'd still be the Countess of Tornabous!"

We would repeat the punchline: "Bread and walnuts are so scrumptious, if only I'd known, I'd still be the Countess of Tornabous!" that were a wonder in words, summing up the whole fable with a couple of lines that would be etched on our brains for evermore, the moral and poetic lesson, the beautifully closed world of Grandmother's fireside tales that left no margin for doubt, a rounded-out world where everything fitted, that left a taste of perfection in our mouths, the image of a more complete, more fully finished planet than the one we inhabited and one which we could only reach through words, an imaginary world the door to which only her words could open.

Like the goblin in the shape of a monk who guarded the space in the attic where hams, sausages, apples and grapes were hung to dry, and if you dared to go in without permission from a grownup, he'd appear and push you outside, saying:

> I'm a monk big and fine,
> who gobbles in a flash
> all who cross that line.

Or the one about the knight who had to go on a journey and he leaves a chickpea with a neighbour to keep it safe, and on his return, when he asks for it back, he's told the hen ate it, so he says, then give me the hen, a hen for a chickpea?, they go to the judge and he's granted the hen, and on another trip he leaves the hen in another house, on his return, a pig had eaten it, and so it goes with the pig an ox eats, and the ox is eaten in a girl's wedding, so give me that lass, that lass for an ox? I got a hen for the chickpea, a pig for the hen, an ox for the pig, that lass for the ox! And the knight, in an act of amazing lunacy that can only be understood in terms of the mystery of those tales, rides up to a crag and throws that lass over, saying:

The lass will rise,
look at her writhe!

We repeated the words though we didn't understand their meaning, aware they hid a secret, wondering at the crazy act committed by the knight and the lass's miraculous writhing, a fantastic end, only possible in a world of story-telling that could transform cruelty into happiness, laughter and hope. Death, into life.

And the stories about trees in the woods. The Sweet Chestnut of Fullaraca, near Viladrau, in terrain full of dry pine leaves, that was over five hundred years old and its hospitably hollow trunk that offered a grotto-like haven in bygone times to witches and in the nineteenth century to Carlists and not so long ago to a charcoal burner who lived there. Or the oak tree of Fussimanya, in the remotest depths of the Guilleries, that is a medicinal tree, like lots of herbs, with a branch shaped like a cradle, like a small bed, where people placed ill children, leaving them there a while so the curing sap of the tree and all the energy it carried wrapped round the child, who thus emerged cured. Adults also approach that tree, whose age is a total enigma, reaching far back beyond the times of the Moors and Romans, and give it one big, long hug as if it were an old friend until the strength of the tree passes into their body and they feel invigorated and want to jump, run and race around as never before, after they'd gone to the tree feeling drained and floppy and the same strength that flowed through them now distances them from the trunk, from the branch they'd embraced, as if it were a raging bonfire. And, above all, the lovers' tree, the one Grandmother preferred, also in the Monseny mountains, in another beech grove, on the edge of a forest of firs, that was created by the embrace of a fir and a beech tree, that became so entangled they'd become a single tree, all of which happened because two young lovers died there persecuted by their feuding families who refused to let them court, and they had frozen to death in the very spot where the fir tree and beech tree immediately sprang up, and then never separated out, were always together, united for ever as the two young lovers had wanted to be.

Grandmother was irrepressible. She even let us sing songs she'd previously forbidden because they were so filthy, like the one we found so funny that went like this:

> Once there was a king
> who had a bright red thing,
> he shat in dribs and drabs…
> A pox on any man who blabs!

Or the one about the tailor from Manresa that Aunt Enriqueta had brought from the seamstress's, that told of a dirty old tailor from Manresa who one day "when he was leaving his shop" went after three young girls and asked "if they wanted to come with me" and when they were halfway along the path, the threesome began to "turn on him" and "now they pull his pants off, hang them from the top of a pine, and beat his bum with a white espadrille," and we found that incredibly exciting and ended up repeating the humbled tailor's complaint, "I'll never chase young girls again, I wanted to have some fun but they gave me pain," and we laughed ourselves silly.

In the end we started to doze off, we were so exhausted. Then Grandmother told us all to go to bed, that she'd stay up for a while as she wanted to tell her rosary beads. We got up, completely at a loss, and as we went to our bedrooms, Cry-Baby in the centre of the sitting room starting shouting: "The shadow! The shadow! I've seen the goblin's shadow!"

Quirze ignored her and walked on and into the farm-hands' bedroom, but I gripped Cry-Baby's shoulder and looked in the direction of the lumber room, where she was pointing her finger. I thought I saw something move.

"It's the door," I said to calm her down, "it's only the door that's moving."

"Cats run up and down the whole night," said Grandmother, not budging an inch. "The pesky creatures never stop. I hope nobody has left the pantry door open."

Cry-Baby went into Grandmother's room and I followed Quirze into the hands' room. The liberal way we'd been treated that night, especially by Grandmother, who'd been readier than ever to meet our every request, made me suspect something wasn't right.

Early next morning Uncle Bernat woke me up. He came over to the room where Quirze and I were sleeping, pushed the door open and shook me, saying: "Hurry up, Andreu, it's time we were off!"

He said that as if he knew what it was all about. I looked at Quirze on the mattress next to mine; he was sleeping like a log. From the faint light coming through the cracks in the shutters and the door, I guessed it was really early.

"What's wrong?" I asked, rubbing my eyes.

"Nothing," Bernat was tucking his shirttails into his trousers. "We've got to go to your town. Your mother wants to see you."

I refused to read anything into his words. I hurriedly washed my face in the bowl, splashing sleep from my eyes.

We went down into the kitchen. Ció and Grandmother were already up, with breakfast all set, bowls of hot milk and slices of garlic bread, oil and chocolate, something quite unusual because chocolate bars were only appeared on important festive days.

Ció was wearing a different dress, the usual grey but cleaner and better ironed, with black shoes she never wore, with her hair combed further back and gathered into a bun. Grandmother was in different clothes too, with a dark headscarf, a black skirt almost down to her feet and a shawl that was black too.

We ate breakfast in total silence. When we'd finished and were leaving, Grandmother spoke to me: "Be brave, because you'll have to help your mother."

The trap was ready outside and the colt was all harnessed up. Dad Quirze, in his usual garb, walked out of the stable and came over after we'd jumped on, and said: "Off you go then, take care!"

We went to the factory town almost in complete silence. Now and then Aunt Ció and Uncle Bernat said something I didn't really understand, words with hidden meanings that didn't expect a response, simply a slight nod, like this:

"Let's try to get there before they do!"

Or else: "Best if you drop us off at the house. I imagine they'll take him there first before anywhere else."

Or: "Father Tafalla said there was nothing doing, no way to make them see sense."

I gathered that Aunt Enriqueta was already in our small town, that she'd gone the day before. Grandmother was all quiet and simply fingered her rosary beads. I felt in a state of anticipation, not daring to guess what was going on, stunned and depressed by the suddenness of it all. I became increasingly aware of an uncontrollable force that was suddenly oppressing us and crushing our lives in a cruel, blustery fashion, in the face of which we could only cower and receive the blows raining down, a force transforming us into leprous, thick-skinned animals at the mercy of that very same ruthless cruelty. The only way out, I thought, was to react by being sly, cunning, two-faced and deceitful. I now understood why Dad Quirze was so surly, so aloof, so prickly, so sarcastic, as if nothing could affect or move him. He kept out of everything, like Father Tafalla from the Saint Camillus monastery, positioning himself at another level, higher in the case of the friar and lower in my uncle's, but both outside the norm, from which they deliberately distanced themselves, one using his knowledge, the other his guile, both within their respective hideouts, in the monastery or the fields and animals' stockade, to ensure they didn't see or get distracted by anything that might upset them. Perhaps that was why they got on so well together: they recognized they were both on the margins of society, were both masters of their own territory, one with the sick and the other with the crops and livestock.

I thought I should protect myself like them, in exactly the same way, guilefully, by never revealing my aims that were simply to survive far away from that irrational force that governed our lives. Both of them, their supreme aloofness in particular, and the total indifference towards everything around him displayed by Grandfather Hand, made it obvious that life would only be worth living the way I wanted if it was my way of life. Mine.

28

We reached town when the mist had come down: it wasn't a drizzly mid-winter mist, the pissy sort, as people sometimes say, but a soft, pleasant streaky mist, like strips of cotton wool, that settled over the winding river. The trap went straight to the house, on the outskirts. A group of women were chatting in front of the entrance. When the trap pulled up, two neighbours came to the rear door, and before we climbed down, they informed us, misery written all over their faces: "He's not here, they…"

"They took him away a few minutes ago. They're in the cemetery."

Bernat pulled the reins and turned the colt towards the opposite direction from which we'd come. Grandmother took a handkerchief from her pocket and held it over her eyes so we wouldn't see her crying. Ció gripped her arm, saying: "It's happened, although we were afraid it would, weren't we? Perhaps it's the best that could have happened… Don't cry, Mother, we've got to be strong."

Then Ció took my arm, caressed me for a second and said: "Be brave!"

I felt guilty because I shed not a tear. I couldn't cry. It seemed I'd forgotten how to. Rather than sorrow, I felt embarrassed, embarrassed because of the looks and comments I'd have to suffer. Deep down I wondered whether it would lead to a violent change in my own life.

We made our way up a dirt track in the upper part of town. We left the houses behind and the tops of the cypress trees behind a whitewashed wall beckoned us to the cemetery.

We alighted by the wrought-iron gate and Bernat helped Grandmother as far as the path leading to the chapel, where Ció and I took her, one each side, and he retraced his steps to tie up the colt.

The sandy path, between two rows of white cedars, sliced through a grassy field, with mounds of freshly dug earth and wooden crosses that bore rudimentary inscriptions, like homework written in a rush. A wall of niches signalled the end of the cemetery, with a chapel in the middle where people were milling outside. The second they saw us, the public stepped respectfully aside to let us through. A priest and two well-dressed men seemed to be arguing, some way away from the niches. When they saw us, they shut up and bowed their heads as if to acknowledge us.

Grandmother couldn't stand any longer and we sat her on the back bench in the chapel. It was a small space, six or seven benches, a grey-stone altar, a wooden Christ on the cross hanging from the ceiling, four candles, and nothing else.

The wooden coffin was set in front of the altar, near the front benches, on the ground and all alone. The box was made from cheap wooden planks, and the heads of the nails stuck out for all to see like flies crushed around the rim and huge cracks showed how hurriedly it had been made.

Cracks, I thought, feeling increasingly guilty, I couldn't stop my flow of thoughts, why does it need those cracks if the dead don't breathe. I also thought about the time when Mr. Manubens, the owner of Can Tupí, had once told us, to illustrate the lack of feeling of anarchists—and, he had added, of godless people in general—about when an officer of their stripe had given the order for a hole to be left in the side of his coffin, when he was buried, because doctors were sometimes as silly as gravediggers and buried people who looked to be dead but weren't, they might have had a fit—an illness that was new to me—and would awake from apparent death a few days later. That was how Mr. Manubens began, but even more incredibly the man had ordained his coffin should be positioned feet first in the niche with his head pointing outwards because he wanted to hear the chatter of people strolling through the cemetery, be they ghosts or the living; he wanted to have as good a time after dying as he'd enjoyed alive. And worse still, added Mr. Manubens, his face reddening with indignation, he insisted that, if people brought flowers for his tomb, they should turn the flowers towards the wall with the stalks pointing at the general public, because those offerings were for him, not for them; the general public could go to hell.

It was pure madness for my brain to be thinking such things at a unique moment like that! Perhaps I was the only one thinking such untimely thoughts, which showed what a mixed up-lad I was.

The men were separated from the women, and Grandmother sat on the front bench next to Aunt Enriqueta and other women I didn't know. They all wore black and mourning shawls, or *un cèfiro*, as it's called in Catalan, over their heads. Ció insisted on sitting me next to my mother. Her face was waxen white, her eyes swollen and her cheeks bluish, but she didn't shed a single tear. Mother, I suspected, was like me, and didn't feel like weeping, or perhaps she'd used up all her tears. She stooped over to kiss my cheek and took my hand and placed it on her skirt. I noted she was wearing a dress that wasn't hers, strictly mourning attire, that was longer than the ones she usually wore, hers were never so far beneath the knee, and its sleeves and collar sagged loosely. Aunt Ció sat next to Aunt Enriqueta.

The priest walked down the central aisle, flanked by two sacristans, all wearing white surplices, the priest's over his soutane and the men's over their everyday jackets. The priest also wore a purple stole around his neck, like a scarf, with two strips hanging down on each side. They stopped in front of the altar opposite the coffin. One of the sacristans brought the priest a sprinkler from some hidden corner.

Before the ceremony started, a man came over—one I recognized as being from the neighbourhood—and told me I should change pew, that it was my duty to head the mourners on the men's side. I looked at my mother, who nodded, so I switched pews.

The man responsible for my move sat beside me, on the front male pew that had been empty to that point. The few men there were sat in the back rows and had left the front two free. Bernat sat right at the back, accompanying my grandmother.

"I'm the chief mourner," said the man from the locality, leaning towards me, "we didn't have time to print any cards. We'll give them out next Sunday, if they let us have a funeral service."

I gathered that it hadn't been straightforward. The priest took the sprinkler by the handle, began reciting lines of Latin and started to shower the sides of the box with holy water. Once he'd done that, he indicated we should stand, and recited the paternoster. He walked over to my mother and gave her his hand, then turned round, put one hand on my head while he blessed me with his other and walked out without more ado. The two sacristans summoned the burial men, two scowling, unshaven, ill-dressed men, and between the four of them they lifted the coffin up and carried it outside.

Mother and I followed the box, and the rest of those present lined up behind us. I was shocked to see neither Grandmother nor Bernat sitting on the last bench. The niche was at the bottom of the wall where we had previously seen the priest arguing with two men. Only seven or eight people accompanied us that far. The others stood in the entrance to the cemetery or departed.

The chief mourner seemed like a master of ceremonies who wanted to take charge of everything, even the way the box was lifted up to its niche on a ladder. Before it was lifted, they placed it on trestles, and two men stepped up—that I thought were my mother's brothers, members of that large family of hers, most of who I'd only seen once or twice in my life, at my other grandparents' house, and they asked: "Can we take a look at him before…?"

I was surprised by my mother's firm tone. She replied curtly: "No. If you'd wanted to see him, you should have done so when he was in hospital or prison."

And she turned round to me, pushed me in the direction of a fat, smartly dressed, buxom woman I immediately recognized, and said: "Say hello to Mrs. Dolores. It's thanks to her that we've been able to bury your father. She lent us the niche. If it hadn't been for her, they'd have buried him in the ground like a dog."

Mrs. Dolores or Napkin Lolita smiled shyly. When the burial men had finished their task and closed off the niche with four large bricks, we slowly made our way out of the cemetery. Two young girls came over to Mrs. Dolores and accompanied her along the path that went straight into the town.

I couldn't see the trap anywhere, or Grandmother and Bernat. Perhaps Grandmother had felt sick and they'd left. I was puzzled.

The mist had lifted. The road from town had been swept, with no obstructions, and cultivated land on both sides sloped gently down to the first houses around the bulky mass of the parish church and the ribbon of river, factories on either bank, driving the lock-gates, then twisting and vanishing into the Guilleries woods.

We went into a huddle with Mother in front; small groups of people from the town and Mother's workmates followed on behind. Some people stood on the sides of the path and greeted us with nods and faint smiles. Mother walked past them, didn't look round or say a word, staring ahead, lost in thought.

Suddenly she turned round and the whole group followed suit. Mother looked back at the two men and the priest who were talking away from the path, in a field full of farming implements. Mother glanced briefly in their direction and the three men seemed to break off their conversation and return her glance, heads lowered, as if expecting her to take the initiative, to show respect, reverence or some acknowledgement that they seemed ready to accept and reciprocate.

However, Mother strode towards where the priest and men were standing. I now recognized that one was the mayor and the other, the head of the local Falange, a Mr. Brull, with his neat little pencil moustache, who came to the parish school early in the morning and made us line up in the playground to salute the flag and shout out the slogan of the day, the words of which we didn't understand, oaths he suggested like:

"The stars at dawn will shine eternally on the youth of our imperial destiny!"

And things of that ilk, that to us little kids were like weird gobbledegook. When we finished, he hoisted the flag and shouted even more stridently: "Fallen for God and the Fatherland!"

And we all had to respond in the most brutal, disciplined military style: "Present and correct!"

Mother headed straight for the little band of big cheeses. Ció tried to stop her with a "No, Florència, don't! Not now!"

Aunt Enriqueta tried to grab her sleeve that was hanging loose, but Mother pulled her arm sharply away. The two women followed on two paces behind her. I stood rooted to the side of the path, severely embarrassed.

Mother came to a halt in front of the men. They looked at her respectfully, even fearfully, I felt. When the priest tried to say something, my mother erupted in that harsh tone I'd only heard once or twice, that made you shake with fear, a calm, rage-filled voice, a firm voice that didn't stammer once: "What more do you want? You've finally killed him! Are you happy now? You dragged him from his home fine and healthy and you return him to me battered, twisted and lifeless. Pray tell me what you gain from his death? Does it serve any purpose? I'll tell you what purpose it served. It helped deal with the envy you all harbour, trampling yet again on those who refuse to bow their heads before you! If there is a God out there, I don't think he will forgive you. He won't ever forgive you!"

Mother broke off for a moment, took a deep breath and then continued, ignoring Ció who kept repeating behind her: "Florència, let it go!" and she addressed the three men, imploring them: "Please don't take any notice of her. Don't hold it against her. She doesn't know what she's saying. It's not her. You must see she's gone crazy…"

But Mother continued, ignoring them all: "So what do I have now? What state do you leave me in? You should have killed me by his side. Why did you leave me bereft? Do you still not dare kill a woman? Can you tell me what he did that I didn't? I don't understand. Do you? Come on, tell me, I'd like to know why. I thought as he thought… And why not? Aren't *we* allowed to think? I'll tell you what I think: I think you have torn my life to shreds, *my* life, do you hear? The only life I had because Lluís was my life, and without him… If that's what you wanted, then you don't deserve to be alive, your children should spit in your faces, that's what you deserve… You disgust me!"

Mother stooped slightly so her gob of spit would hit them, but nothing came out of her mouth. She tried a couple of times, as if she were coughing, but her throat was parched and it was futile. As red as a woodpecker, Brull took a step forward to stop her but the priest grabbed his arm and kept him by his side. The three men were silent now. The mayor's face had gone livid, as if he'd suffered a heart attack. The vicar was the only one who remained

composed, smiling his fake, well-rehearsed, patronizing smile. When Mother turned round to walk off, he
remarked two or three times: "We won't hold this against
you. We'll take your state of mind into consideration. We
will talk all this through later…"

Mother, with her back to them, was about to turn
round and answer, but Ció grabbed her arm and pulled her
forcefully away. I gripped her hand.

"Let's go," said Mother, "we should go. We've no place
here. It's disgusting, they disgust me!"

The remaining relatives and neighbours were waiting
on the verge, with Aunt Enriqueta in front, and welcomed
us with their appalled expressions.

"You shouldn't have done that," muttered Aunt
Enriqueta, beginning the retreat with us.

Mother took her time to respond. Finally she said:
"What did you expect me to do? Go and lick their boots?"

We walked home in silence. Before we got that far,
some of Mother's friends and neighbours left us to go their
own way.

The house door was open and a band of women,
mostly neighbours, were in the dining room and kitchen.
They greeted us as if we were ill. They had put a cloth on
the table and set out glasses of hot milk and slices of bread.

"Come on!" they begged us. "You just sit down and
have a bite to eat. Would you like us to stay and get lunch
ready?"

Mother smiled sadly in gratitude. She said nothing as
she walked by each of them and caressed them with her
hand, tears streaming. When she came to the last neighbour, her face was awash with teardrops that dripped from
her nose and chin. Her back and head began to convulse,
as if she was having a fit, and the moans from her lips grew
louder and louder.

Aunt Ció and the neighbours caught her before she fell,
as if she was fainting, and they took her to her room. Her

laments and convulsions got more and more violent; her whole body shivered as if she'd caught a chill. They lay her on the double bed and sat next to her, placing handkerchiefs on her forehead and rubbing her arms and legs. A neighbour and Aunt Enriqueta ran to the kitchen and put water on to boil and started scouring the cupboards for orange-blossom or El Carme water to calm her down.

I'd never seen my mother in such a state; she seemed to have gone mad. The women strained to keep her still and AuntCió hugged her as if she wanted to hold her down. I looked on from out in the passage, feeling powerless, wretched and totally devoid of hope. As if the world were crumbling before my eyes. As if a vast desert had begun to take over my life.

"It's impossible!" Mother stuttered. "Can't you see it's impossible?"

A neighbour began unbuttoning her dress and another shut the door so I couldn't see. They tried to soothe me saying it was nothing serious, that she'd soon get over it, that I should go to the kitchen and eat.

I sat on a chair opposite, which the table had been laid. Aunt Enriqueta came from the kitchen and sat next to me. She ran her hand over my head, as if tidying my unruly hair, and said: "It's all nerves. We'll go back to the farm soon. We must take all your clothes with us. We must sew black bands on the left arm sleeves and dye those that can take the dye. You'll have to wear mourning clothes for a year; your mother must do so for life."

29

I stayed at home that night and slept with my mother.

When Mother calmed down, the neighbours began to leave until we were finally left alone with Aunt Ció and Aunt Enriqueta. The neighbours had got supper ready, but Mother refused to eat anything. She got up, sat in a corner of the dining room and watched while we ate.

"My brothers are terrible," moaned Mother, "only a couple came and they disappeared as soon as they could. And poor Mariona, who wanted to come, couldn't bring herself to because she's still afraid of showing her face in the village.

Ció and Enriqueta made excuses for them saying they lived far away, that they probably hadn't heard the news, that at least the two did come who were in a position to… and other similar arguments.

"But what about Felisa?" Mother asked sorrowfully, "Why didn't Felisa come?"

Felisa was her youngest sister and Mother was particularly fond of her, even though they saw little of each other, because she'd looked after her from birth; my maternal Grandmother died soon after giving birth, exhausted by bringing so many children into the world, or so people said.

"Felisa has to run a household," protested Aunt Ció, "what with all those men and all working on the land…"

"You can be sure she'll come as soon as she can. Everything happened so quickly. Even I," continued Aunt Enriqueta, "couldn't get here until yesterday evening. I only found out because you phoned me at work in Vic to say they were taking him from prison in a van.

They argued for a while about whether it would be better for me to stay a few days or a few weeks to keep my mother company, or whether I should go back to the farm in the summer holidays that were almost upon us, saying that time would decide most things. They seemed so convinced that time solves so many problems but I didn't understand how time by itself could solve anything, I felt the hours and days went by and nothing changed; I was impressed by the fact that clocks were there to calculate time and only went round and round to the same points, it was always six or twelve again, I felt the hands turned in a void, a labyrinth of hours from which they could find no exit, and that the only signs they left of its passing over things and people were layers of dust or wrinkled skin, so I thought it was stupid when a grownup said time was the great healer, when even I could see how the passage of time only ravaged everything, messed everything up, put everything out of joint. Time only mattered when you looked back. Time was our anxious longing for Father to come back, time was Father's death. Time was death.

After lunch, they decided it would be best for me to go back to the farm the very next morning; after everything that had happened in the cemetery with the priest and two dignitaries, it would be best not to show my face in the parish school so soon. Aunt Enriqueta could stay on a few days to keep Mother company. Bernat would collect me the next morning and that night I'd stay alone with my mother. Aunt Enriqueta would return to the farm that night to collect her things so she could spend the necessary time with my mother; as soon as she finished work in Vic she'd catch the bus, rather than return to the farm. It seemed like the right solution for everyone.

While they said their goodbyes, Mother andCió took the opportunity of a moment when Aunt Enriqueta was combing her hair in the bathroom to have a few of their quiet words on the side.

"It will do her good to spend a few days away from home and the village gossip," commented Ció. "See if you can persuade her to go back to Pere Màrtir. Tell her where her bad ways might lead her. And that she'll never get a man like him again. She must set her stall out soon. She's no time to waste."

"I hope she listens," said Mother, "but I don't know if I can pull that off."

The two aunts walked off arm in arm as the mists settled over the village again. And no sooner had the door shut than two neighbours who must have been watching out called to ask if we needed anything. Mother said no, thank you very much, that she was feeling better now, and from the doorstep she looked out towards the path that climbs up the nearby hillock and her eyes locked on an approaching figure, a basket over her arm, walking rather on the tilt, as if she had a limp.

"Ay!" Mother put her hand over her mouth and her eyes lit up, as if she'd seen a ghost. "I'd swear that's Felisa!"

She rushed out to greet her with open arms and the neighbours discreetly shut their doors behind them. Aunt Felisa, with her hair combed back, her sunburnt face, small eyes, simple black dress, thick grey stockings, black espadrilles and shy smile, put her basket on the ground and silently swayed her head as she hugged Mother. She looked on the wild side, just as I remembered her from the two or three times I'd seen her; Mother used to say that her family were a difficult peasant lot.

"You shouldn't have come!" said Mother, showering her with kisses. "You have such a lot of work at home, and it's a long walk to get here, you shouldn't have bothered. I'd have come to see you."

Aunt Felisa patted me on the head and we all went indoors.

The basket contained eggs, a bottle of milk, a white loaf and a couple of fresh cheeses. While Aunt Felisa spread them on the kitchen table, Mother told her what had happened, but left out her final skirmish with the bigwigs. Aunt Felisa listened in silence. I felt exhausted and listened with no real interest, sitting on a chair from the dining room.

"We found out last night, when Peret came back from the village. I couldn't escape any earlier. Peret and Pau came, I expect you saw them? Feliu sends his apologies, and says you'll soon be seeing him."

Peret and Pau were the uncles who had come to the cemetery and had a strip torn off them by Mother when they asked for the coffin lid to be lifted so they could take a last look at the deceased.

The two sisters stayed in the kitchen for ages, and talked everything over while they heated up a saucepan of milk and toasted bread on the grill over the oven. They kept lamenting and exclaiming and remembering what had happened from the moment he was arrested and put in the infirmary to his death. By the time they took their supper into the dining room, they seemed to have wrung that story dry.

"He perked up for a couple of days, just before he died. As if he'd made one last effort to see us outside the infirmary."

Mother kept repeating that Aunt Felisa shouldn't have put herself out to come, and her sister said she couldn't stay to sleep, that she'd be off straight after supper.

"But it's pitch-black out there!" erupted Mother, alarmed. "How can you go back at this time of night, you won't be able to find the path, or see where you're putting your feet? At least stay here until early morning."

"I'll feel even less like it in the morning. I can't abandon the house, you know, I'm the only woman and as soon as dawn breaks, the men will expect everything to be ready. They all get up when it's still dark."

"One day won't matter," insisted Mother. "We've got so much to talk about! We've both been so rushed off our feet we've not had time to get together."

"I've so much I want to tell you!" sighed Aunt Felisa.

I started on my supper while they went in and out of the kitchen on any pretext, telling each other things in a tone that seemed both complaining and reassuring, slipping sentences in that didn't make any sense, until I realized they weren't really saying what was on their mind—my presence prevented them. They sat down at the table for a moment and Mother pecked at a piece of bread or took a sip of milk but that was all; she said she wasn't hungry, that she couldn't get anything down, and Aunt Felisa didn't manage even that. When I had finished, Mother told me to go to sleep, to lie on my bed and rest, I'd fall asleep soon enough, fast asleep at that, she said, and I realized how much I was in their way and went off to my bedroom. From my bed, I could hear their whispering, which got louder and louder as if they felt they could confide now they were all alone and confident I wasn't listening

"This is hardly the time to tell you," wavered Aunt Felisa. "You've got enough problems of your own, poor thing, after everything that has happened."

But Mother protested that it didn't matter, that she should go ahead and say whatever she wanted, that in fact she found their conversation distracting, that she would have to get over her grief eventually. I imagined my mother playing the big sister role I'd seen her take on so often, as second mother to all her brothers and sisters, particularly the younger ones, welcoming, strict, soothing, experienced…, handing out advice left and right, sharing in the others' problems as if they were her own, a kind of mother hen puffing out her feathers when her chicks seek refuge under her plumage.

"It's a friend of Feliu," said Felisa.

Feliu was the big brother, the first-born and heir, the most difficult of the bunch, an authoritarian master who'd been widowed five or six years ago; I couldn't even remember his wife, I don't think I ever saw or met her. The period when Feliu became a widower led Aunt Felisa to establish herself as the centre of the household, mistress over everyone and everything. The other sisters were married, lived far away and the heir's strong character didn't make being in contact easy. "Everyone in his own home," was one of the maxims Feliu liked to voice in the presence of relatives, alongside similar expressions like, "The less you need family, the better," or "Brothers, sisters and in-laws, out of sight, out of mind," or "Absence doesn't make the heart grow fonder," or else "Outlaw the in-laws!" The heir's attitude had strongly infected the whole family and that's why I didn't know most of my cousins on my mother's side. The excuse, according to Mother, was they were such a big crew, we'd spend our entire lives visiting each other so the solution seemed to be to disconnect from everybody, and, above all, never pay them a visit, the phrase "going to someone else's house" was a criticism, a kind of invasion of the privacy of others, except when there were deaths and funerals, the only occasion when those who could got together.

Nevertheless, despite the heir's prickly character, which was the main reason why her family was so scattered and at odds, my mother always warmly welcomed brothers and sisters who came to our house, and I even felt she was delighted to do so. The contrast with Father's family, which was infinitely more open and generous, made me realize that Mother could have been different, more loving, more outgoing, more caring, if she'd not been driven out from an early age by that sour, harsh element they'd sowed deep down. Mother was never given to kissing or any kind of physical contact with our relatives or with me. Expansive moments, when she opened up, were few and far between, and only with a select group of people. She got on with people or couldn't stand the sight of them; there was no happy mean. She could be, and in fact was, extremely unpleasant towards the second category. And those in the first never plumbed the depths of her feelings, how much she loved them, because she didn't know how to communicate that, was terribly shy or felt emotionally inhibited and that chilled all her relationships.

"Feliu will soon be marrying the young girl from Can Passarella, as I expect you know."

"Has he told you how it's going?" asked Mother, suddenly perking up.

"You know what he's like. He never talks about his business. But we can all see what's going on. He spends more and more time with her at Can Passarella and he's getting the house ready for when she comes."

"Do you know her? Have you talked to her?"

"Not very much. Only the time of day."

"What's she like? What do you make of her? I know nothing about this lass. Will she be able to run the household?"

"What can I say? I don't know. She's a young thing, you know? It means she's not used to doing certain chores!"

"Do you mean you think she's not right, that Feliu shouldn't have got all hot and bothered over a sparrow like her, that he's aimed too high?"

"Who knows what he's playing at. Perhaps he's got one eye on the dowry she'll bring with her."

"You'll keep me posted, right?"

"When it's all signed and sealed, you bet I will. You never can tell otherwise!"

There were sudden silences, pauses when I imagined them going into the kitchen, or perhaps nibbling something. Sometimes an almost inaudible mutter told me it was a fake pause, that even though they were by themselves, they only broached the darkest secrets in hushed tones.

"He came for lunch once," resumed Aunt Felisa, stopping the whispers, more relaxed as if she'd just shed a huge burden, "which was the first time I saw him and I didn't take to him one bit. He's a widower, like Feliu."

"A widower?" asked Mother, disappointed. "That means…how old is he? Does he have children?"

"Two, an eight-year-old boy and a ten-year-old girl," Felisa's voice sounded mournful, "at least that's what he told me."

"Did he tell you how old he was?"

"I didn't dare ask."

"I bet he asked soon enough how old *you* were! It's obvious, he's looking for a woman to do the housework and a nanny to look after his children!"

"They're well out of their nappies."

"How old do you reckon he is?"

"Well into his forties," Aunt Felisa guessed, "closer to fifty than forty. He's got a full head of hair but it's all grey. And he's quite round-shouldered, with a crooked spine."

My aunt laughed, as if she'd been caught doing something wrong.

"His face is round and chubby!"

"But what about his hands?"

"Why do they matter?" Aunt Felisa seemed surprised, as if she'd left out an essential factor. "Should I have looked hard at them? I'm not sure…big…a farmer's hands…like everyone's around here, I'd say. I do remember his nails were long and yellowish!"

"That means he is a chain-smoker. You should check out everything before you make another move. Strong hands means he's hard-working, that idleness doesn't keep him in bed. And they make a man of him, big hands mean he knows what he wants. I expect he stank of tobacco?"

"I didn't get close enough to smell his breath."

"Didn't you speak to each other alone for a second?"

"Yes, we did. Feliu left us in the entrance for a while, before he left. And then he accompanied me to the wash-place in La Solana. He carried the basket of dirty clothing the whole way."

"And what did he say?"

"That if I didn't mind, he'd come back another Sunday to see me. That Feliu thought it was a good idea. He's now been back four Sundays on the trot."

Then they reverted to their secretive whispering. Then suddenly, Aunt Felisa's voice, shaken by her sobbing, like a lament: "Ugh, that's nasty! I don't know if I could do that! It would be beyond me!"

And Mother, in her role as guardian angel:

"Yes, you could… You just see. We've all gone through that, you little silly."

"I sometimes think I'm too old for some things and too young for others. I don't think I even know myself."

"Now you *are* being silly! Nobody knows what they're like till the time comes…, right to the very last moment."

"And what if it doesn't work out? Look at you and Lluís." Aunt Felisa immediately regretted mentioning the deceased's name. "Oh, I shouldn't have said that! I'm sorry, please, I didn't mean to. I didn't want to make you feel miserable."

"Don't worry, it doesn't matter…that's all memories now. And the best were of our first years together. It seems that was only yesterday, but it was over as quickly as a gust of wind."

"Were you sure right from the start?"

"We were two young kids and from the first time I saw him at the salamander spring, there was never anyone else for me. I saw right away he'd follow me to the end of the world if I asked him to."

A silence ensued I imagined was full of tears and cuddles.

"I shouldn't have mentioned that."

"Yes, you should, I want to remember… They say memories also die but I think I'll carry him inside me till the day I die."

"I wanted to hear you say that, so I could finally persuade myself… I don't feel I'm capable of what you felt. Or that I could jump through all those…hoops as you called them."

"Didn't Mother ever tell you?"

"Mother, poor dear, you know as well as I do, was more into the next world than this when I was beginning to worry about such things."

"Of course, but you shouldn't worry your head. Men know what to do, know only too well... Don't be afraid, they're good teachers."

Suddenly, after a mysterious silence, they seemed to burst into an uncontrolled spate of sobbing. I thought it was Mother, but when I heard her voice consoling Aunt Felisa, I realized the tears were my aunt's. She cried like a young child.

"No, no..." she repeated, as if they were dragging her to the slaughterhouse. "I don't want to, I don't want to, don't let him take me away. I don't want him, I don't want him!"

"Nobody is going to let him take you away, if you don't want it to happen. Calm down. It's nothing to worry about. You're afraid, and that's normal. It's always a bother to leave one's house to take charge of another. But men are easy to keep happy if you give them what they want. You're younger than he is and you'll soon get him used to what *you* want. You'll get over it, you mark my word. You'll get used to it in the first few days and then it will be plain sailing, nothing to it, like getting rid of a bad cold. Shush, shush, my sweet child."

The tears kept streaming.

"If it's not him, it will be someone else, it's bound to happen one of these days. Don't you see that if Feliu brings another woman into the house, he'll cast you aside like an old broom. And you're used to being top dog, you'll find it hard to buckle down to orders given by a stranger. You'll be very unhappy. On the other hand, a house that's only yours, whatever headaches it brings at the start, will be a different life. Feliu must have thought that when he met..."

"Josep."

"...when he met Josep and decided that he'd do for you."

More silences and sighs. Mother kept insisting, and I began to find her insistence rather distasteful. I felt sorry for Aunt Felisa, I felt she ought to understand, in the translation I always had to make of adult conversations, that she was being driven out, with the best of excuses, from her own house, far from the woods, driven out to ugly factory towns, to a wasteland of superficial exchanges with people who meant nothing to her and who she didn't care a fig for, accustomed as she was to living in the middle of silent, protective woods, surrounded by family and acquaintances. Tree of life, tree of Paradise, white poplar, Judas tree, alder tree, herb of the host, tree of love... And her instinctive fear of marriage seemed a very proper protest against the exile they were sentencing her to, swept off by that man with the big hands and head of grey hair. Aunt Felisa, whom I'd always thought as a wild, cunning, silent, untamed animal, with a fox's fearful eyes and awkward gait, now seemed very akin to me, a vulnerable victim of the injustice of life.

30

The "injustices of life" was a phrase I'd heard hundreds of times on everyone's lips that I adapted to my situation by applying it to the punishments meted out by the parish priest who hit us with a small cane or ruler on the palm of the hand or on the knuckles in the most serious cases, or to my resigned acceptance of Mother's refusal to give me money to go to the cinema or buy comics—that she called *Smurfs*—from the town's only newsagents-cum-bookshop. Now, as I listened to Aunt Felisa sobbing in the dining room, I realized that greater injustices existed, like being driven from one's house and family to make a new life far from the woods in the company of unpleasant strangers. I don't know why but Cry-Baby came to mind, as distanced as Aunt Felisa or I myself were from all our familiar landscapes.

While Aunt Felisa continued to moan and Mother to advise and cuddle, I stumbled around my pitch-black bedroom looking for a cranny where I could absorb the latest victim of life's injustices, and then another word suddenly came to me that I'd heard on the grandparents' farm, in Can Tupí, and only ever used by men, I don't recall whether it was Dad Quirze or Father Tafalla, in a conversation about the war that must have gone completely above my head, from which I'd only retained a single word: infiltrator. Infiltrator. For a long time I hadn't known when to use this word, and now, suddenly, I grasped that Aunt Felisa, like Cry-Baby, Aunt Mariona in Barcelona and myself, had infiltrated the places where we lived. We didn't belong to the families or homes that had taken us in, we were no more than infiltrators, like little animals rescued from the woods and lodged in cages in the stables or kitchen, or domestic pets, tolerated as long as we behaved well and didn't cause too many headaches. Infiltrators could be dispossessed at any moment of everything they had and expelled from the places where they lived; it all depended on chance, on the injustices of life that were extending their domain, on a man who went after a woman to marry and bring into his home, on the outcomes from a war we'd not been involved in, but had, willy-nilly, to suffer the consequences of, on Father's imprisonment and death…, everything took us away from the original woods of our childhood, from the safe haven of its foliage, the welcoming silence of its depths, the intense greens of its leaves and grasses and the thickets that carpeted the ground.

I thought my father's death was something that went beyond one of the injustices of life that I'd faced and kept facing. To an extent, one could fight against those, offer resistance, alleviate the pain. For example, my classmates who were obliged to hold out their hands to receive their punishment from the priest-teacher would previously wipe them with garlic, as if they were slices of toast; they reckoned that way the pointer or ruler slipped and the blows didn't hurt as much, or else, to resist being expelled from your home, you could run away and refuse marriage, or to avoid staying at your grandparents you could hide in the woods or escape over the mountains to France, like those who'd lost the war, and become a tramp without roof or family. In other words, the injustices of life depended on the will of someone else, on an enemy or person in authority, a schoolmaster, a parish priest, a suitor…but how could you dodge death? Death was much worse than any of life's injustices, death was the negation of life, the antipodes of life, the contrary of life, nothingness, non-life. It was more horrendous than any other injustice because nobody could offer resistance, nobody could run away or hide from such an act because it didn't come from outside, you carried it within, death turned you into your own enemy and executioner, it was a mountain that crumbles and collapses or a wood ablaze that turns to cinder. It was *the* great injustice, the unique injustice, on which all the others depended.

Death, I thought, was the unique injustice for the moment, but perhaps there were others, however few, that were as monstrous and inevitable as death. I felt my chest shudder at my gradual discovery of these inevitable, unique Great Injustices, when I realized how my scant experience had already extended the list of the common injustices of life. And when that thought struck me, I shuddered again, because the image of the boy with TB came to mind, with his pallor and lethargy, lying on the grass, like a church angel whose wings had changed into white sheets. I didn't know why I most remembered him from all those sickly bodies stretched out in the monastery's garden of heartsease, I thought it must be because he seemed the youngest, the frailest or sickliest, something made him special, as if his body wasn't irradiating a light that made him almost transparent. My father's death had triggered the image of the living dead, as Dad Quirze described them, and that was why the figure of the sickly youth lying on the lawn now appeared, like a Saint Sebastian who'd been humiliated, thrown to the ground, broken in two, his lungs gouged by wounds that bloodied his lips and ribs. But one source of sorrow lingered at the back of my brain, like an almost imperceptible blemish, which only worried me when it erupted into my consciousness, namely, the presentiment of another unique, grandiose injustice like death, another source of emotional devastation, like Father's death, and that couldn't be death in general, the death of everyman, or illness, because incurable illnesses belonged to the same category of great injustices as death, to which it was merely the prelude, a warning and anticipation, and if it was only a passing illness it didn't merit consideration as a common injustice, it was a mere accident of life, something familiar, when an injustice should be a sudden, unexpected event, that annihilated hope, and the presentiment I felt whenever the memory of the languishing, tubercular youth appeared wasn't connected to death, that I'd almost taken on board, but to a dark side of life, to an injustice even more punishing than death, one I had yet to discover, which is why the vision of that luminous, sickly body preyed on me and fascinated me so.

Aunt Felisa finally departed. It was pitch-black by now and she and Mother, on their way to the door, stopped in the passage opposite my bedroom to see if I was asleep. I acted as if I was completely out of it, tucked up in bed, a pillow over my ears, and they went up the passage resuming their whispered conversation: "What will you do with him?" asked Aunt Felisa, and I felt I was being treated as an alien, as an obstacle, and anxiously waited for my mother's reply.

"I haven't decided yet," she answered, rather limply. "For the time being he'll go back to the farm with my mother-in-law. Lluís wanted him to continue his schooling, but I don't know whether I can take him very far by myself. I'll have to find someone to give him a helping hand."

They moved away down the passage. Aunt Felisa said something I didn't catch and Mother commented: "Don't do anything, don't commit yourself. But try not to get rid of him until you're really sure. Much better a good man you're not wild about than being sold on a man who's worthless. Infatuation and rapture are short-lived, last only a few days, and a family has to pull together for a lifetime. And, you know, the crazy pangs of courting and infatuation are for young people, for people in their first youth, I mean."

"But you…" Aunt Elisa tried to protest.

"Don't look to me. If you only knew what I have suffered! But I'm a special case, and I recognize I am special and that not all women have to do what I did. Everything

I've done I've done because I wanted to. I wouldn't wish what I've suffered on anyone."

Their muttering turned into the distant sound of voices in the porch, until I heard the key turn in the lock and the door open. They must have stood outside for a while, because the door didn't shut for some time.

Mother was moving around the house and I couldn't think what she might be doing at that time of night. Finally all the lights went out and silence descended. But it didn't last very long; I'd just fallen asleep when I felt someone get into my bed, and push my side to make space. I thought for a moment that I must be back in the grandparents' house and that Quirze or Cry-Baby was fooling around. It was my mother, and I guessed as much from her smell, that mixture of cheap soap and bleach, factory oil and the usual scent from her skin that reminded me of the bushes that flowered in the woods, rosemary, thyme, broom…as if she used scented water, though in fact she rarely used any kind of perfume.

"I can't sleep in such a big bed…" she whispered, as if that was her excuse, "Go on, make room for me. I'm not a bother, am I?"

I didn't reply but quite spontaneously gave her a hug. We hugged for a while, until I felt my chest was shivering as if I was cold and I thought I must be holding back my tears. I couldn't cry; I was quite empty in that respect. I also thought I must have caught a chill and hugged her even more tightly.

I felt responsible. I wanted to remember my father's precise words in prison, when he asked me to look after my mother, but I sensed they weren't the exact words he had used. And then I thought how that was the first time I'd slept with her, and I was suffused with a kind of regret from some of my earliest memories, fleeting moments, lightning flashes that briefly lit up the void of that era of unconsciousness, and I saw myself forlorn in the house of the kind old babysitter, Beneta, while my mother went to work, and then, at night, when she came to fetch me after finishing her shift, and my father whom I never saw, absent, remote, alien, like a shadow you couldn't distinguish from the black of night.

I felt that Mother's coming to my bed that night was a kind of making amends for the way she'd neglected me in my first years. She owed me days and days of her presence. Could she make up now for those solitary afternoons on the terrace at Beneta's, my only distraction being the sight of nearby orchards and distant mountains? I don't remember any toy next to me, while I longed for the presence and woodland scent of my mother who never came, who always appeared later than my hopes of ever seeing her again lasted and my terror at staying the night with Beneta, that always meant much more to me, because nighttime was a huge, impenetrable universe as far as I went. She owed me something else, but I wasn't sure exactly what.

And that debt, that my mother was probably unaware of, made me keep aloof from her. Quite unintentionally, driven by the injustices of life we all suffer, she'd taught me to do without love. I suspected, in some way or other, that she could have avoided that, and also, that my father could have looked after her rather than roaming the streets and spending hour after hour trying to put the world to rights, and then she wouldn't have had to leave me with Beneta, but she'd not done that. My father preferred to spend his time solving other people's injustices of life and thus brought injustice into his own home. Those injustices fell in turn, like a row of dominoes, so nobody was ever left standing, ever, anywhere.

That's why I didn't cry over my father's death, or at least that was how I justified myself. And at the same time I also withdrew from my mother's embrace and turned my back on her.

31

When I returned to Can Tupí I got the impression I was even more of a temporary resident. The first day everybody treated me like a convalescent who'd just survived a serious illness, but the day after everything went back to normal, as before, as if nothing had happened. The only thing that jarred was that nobody mentioned Father's death and the effort not to do so forced everyone to be careful with their words, or perhaps I only imagined all that. Before going off to spend a few days with Mother, Aunt Enriqueta gave me four items of clothing that had been dyed black and a waistcoat and a brightly coloured jacket with a large band of black cloth sewn on the top of the sleeve, a kind of official strip for those plagued by misfortune, as if I'd suddenly signed up to the sad brotherhood of the relatives of the dead.

Mr. Madern, the teacher, shook my hand very formally, uttered a polite formula of condolence and made no other comment. Miss Pepita, Miss Silly, greeted me at playtime and said she was very sorry there'd been so much pain, I didn't know whether she was referring to my father or me. My schoolmates said nothing, gave me curious looks, as if I'd undergone an experience none of them wanted to live through and had come out of it too well, like winning a fight with friends or surviving an accident unscathed.

"So your father died," Oak-Leaf said the first day we walked down the path home, in a neutral tone, as if commenting on some everyday occurrence. "I thought they'd execute him, he'd been sentenced to death. I didn't know he was ill."

I simply nodded and agreed in a feeble, feigned matter-of-fact voice. My cousins said nothing.

"Did he die from lung failure, like the TB patients in the monastery?" she went on in the same vein. "They say there are lots of sick people in prison, and they infect each other and nobody gets out healthy. And they're so cold and hungry, their lungs get into a real mess."

"I wouldn't know," I replied equally limply.

I didn't know which sickness had killed my father. I imagined it was the one they'd had to operate on in a rush a couple of years before, stomach cancer, and I remembered Mother explaining the details to Aunt Ció at the crossroads where they always said their final farewells and the way my aunt scowled and screwed up her face when Mother described the wires and needles they stuck in him to "take a sounding," a new word that was to horrify me for evermore, and I shut my eyes and distracted myself by sitting on the ground, uprooting grass and herbs or hunting crickets while I listened to their conversation, and Mother went on, "It's more difficult for men, it's such a small hole, it's terrible, it makes you grit your teeth," and I imagined the details that appalled me and told myself that what I was thinking couldn't be true, "and they can do nothing," they repeated as if they couldn't resign themselves, "they can do nothing," "it's a tricky illness," "a nasty illness."

"What will you do now?" asked Oak-Leaf with her usual lack of tact. "Will you go back to your town or stay in Can Tupí? If you stay on, they'll soon make a farmhand of you, that's what the men do."

"And why are you sticking your nose in?" interrupted Quirze angrily. "What business of yours is it what he does or doesn't do?"

Oak-Leaf stared at him defiantly. The irritation in their voices led me to suspect they'd had a bust-up. Cry-Baby continued walking along the path, as if she wasn't listening.

"There's no harm in asking," said Oak-Leaf, all meek and mild. "Everybody is saying that Andreu will go back to his town, because you let him stay in your house to help his mother while his father was in prison."

"And what's that got to do with you?" Quirze was getting more and more aggressive. "Do we stick our noses in what you do or don't do in your house? You shouldn't interfere in what we do in ours."

Oak-Leaf shrugged her shoulders and replied by pointing at her ears: "Everything you say goes in one ear and out the other, just so you know how much notice I ever take of you."

"So why did you ask me, clever-boots? Don't ask if you don't want to know."

"I wasn't asking you. I was asking Andreu and Núria."

Quirze looked at us both, at me by his side, and at Cry-Baby, who'd stopped a few yards farther on and was playing on the grass verge with her foot, amusing herself, while she waited for us to stop bickering.

"All right, ask them, and see what that twosome has to say," replied Quirze in a defiant tone that was also telling us to act belligerently towards Oak-Leaf.

"I've asked him and he knows nothing," said Oak-Leaf, turning to me, "or acts as if he knows nothing."

Oak-Leaf took a step towards Cry-Baby, who was still playing with her foot as if she didn't know what was going on, and said: "And *she* won't open her mouth. You won't tell me anything, will you?"

Cry-Baby lowered her eyes further, avoiding her gaze, and moved her foot more intensely, as if she was trying to flatten every single blade of grass.

"And *she* doesn't even know where her father is. And her mother fled over the mountains to look for him, and right now we still know nothing, they've both vanished, as if the earth had swallowed them up, like an enchanted prince and his princess."

"Shut up, you spiteful bitch!" rasped Quirze. "You're the devil's own kind, everybody says you're the devil's own. And a lot more besides."

"They can say what they want! As if I took one blind bit of notice!"

Oak-Leaf shrugged her shoulders again. We stood rooted there for a moment and I was convinced the three of them must have squabbled or had a really bad falling out while I'd been at home in town, an obstacle now stopping them from moving on. In the end, Oak-Leaf turned tail and headed along the path across the woods, bawling: "She refuses to talk to me, so that shows who's the one behaving badly! Did she think I was going to chase her? I'd never chase after that lump of beetroot, I don't need that rotten walnut one bit. She's the one that needs me, you bet she does, because I know all there is to know about her and she only knows what I decided to tell her about myself, which was all lies!"

Quirze stooped down to pick up a couple of big stones which he threw angrily at her. Oak-Leaf retaliated, and the rocks fell next to us, and sent us scattering. Suddenly Quirze ran after her, caught her, pushed her to the ground and started pummelling her, while he screamed: "Shut up, you vicious swine, don't say another word about us if you don't want me to smash your face in, and I'll bash your head in too if you don't shut up...!"

Oak-Leaf whimpered on the ground and said things we could barely hear: "If you don't leave me alone, I'll tell everything! Leave me alone, or I'll spread it round the village! You idiot, you animal, you savage, leave me alone!"

Quirze left her on the ground and walked back to us. Oak-Leaf silently pulled herself to her feet, shaking the dust from her dress. I thought she was crying. Quirze strode past us and shouted, as if it was an order: "On our way!"

Cry-Baby and I followed him without glancing back once. A good way on, when we were within sight of the farm, I asked Cry-Baby, who was walking next to me, two or three yards behind Quirze: "What ever happened? Did you fall out over something?"

A moment later, Cry-Baby answered almost inaudibly: "It's them two…"

"What on earth did they do to you? Why are those two so angry?"

"They squabbled the other day as well. Oak-Leaf repeated that she'd seen Aunt Enriqueta in the woods with blond Canary, and he didn't believe her, he said she was making it all up to get at us."

I didn't know what to say. A few more steps later Cry-Baby added: "She said I'd do the same."

"You? But when?"

"She told him about what happened with our teacher and I said it wasn't true. That's why they squabbled. Oak-Leaf said that Quirze ought to know, that the teacher had done exactly the same to her, that he was a louse, a rat…"

Now Cry-Baby did raise her head slightly and looked out of the corner of her eye to see how I reacted. When she saw I didn't flinch or say a word, she added in a more strained, hesitant voice: "Oak-Leaf…wanted to…do it with Quirze…"

I looked at her in shock, as if I'd not really understood what I'd just heard: "Both of us, she and I…with him."

I stopped for a second and she turned round to spell it out: "As you weren't around…"

I walked back to her again. She went on: "But I burst into tears and ran to Can Tupí. Quirze squabbled with her. I saw them rolling on the ground, they were scrapping like a cat and dog, in a rage, insulting and swearing at each other."

And then: "Quirze caught up with me before I got home and he made me promise not to tell anyone, that everything Oak-Leaf had said was a pack of stupid lies. She's evil, more evil than Old Nick, he said, everybody knows she's the devil's own, and I should stop being her friend forever."

Now eight or ten paces in front, Quirze suddenly stopped and without turning round put his hand up to signal to us to stop as well. We stood there for some time, silent and stock-still in the middle of the path, near the farmhouse, looking towards the house to try and see why he'd given us that alarm signal. It was early evening and a bright sun was still lighting up the landscape, a gentle, delicate, silken light that melted the colours of the woods and slowly faded. The sun fell on to the blue mountains of the Pyrenees in the far distance, as if it had cast off that light that was so tranquil, thin and fragile, like a covering of snow that would only melt with the morning sun. Despite that brightness, an oil or carbide light was hanging in the gallery, like the point of the tiniest needle, as if it had been flickering all night. We couldn't see the entrance because the hazel trees near the pond and the hayrick blocked our view. Quirze beckoned us to walk to where he was standing.

"Can you see anything odd?" he whispered when we were level with him.

"The lights…" I replied.

"Why have they lit them so early?" asked Cry-Baby, perplexed.

"The electricity's not been working for days, perhaps the power went again," I added.

"Can you hear anything?" continued Quirze.

We stretched our necks and listened hard, but I could only hear the familiar quiet sound of the livestock in their pen, a kind of skyscape of dull humming, like a layer of dust thrown up by sheep, the odd tinkle of a bell, the bleating of sheep, clucking of hens and the odd distant bark, the rest was a protective bubble of silence enveloping the farmhouse. Cry-Baby didn't seem to have heard anything unusual either.

We both shook our heads at Quirze.

"I can sense something… The dogs are very on edge, as

if they didn't dare whimper."

We listened hard again, but with the same result.

"It's the usual," I said. "They bark now and then because they're hungry."

"Let's go on," ordered Quirze, striding towards the house, "but I smell something isn't right. I can't see any of the hands, it's deserted. Somebody should be on the threshing-floor at this time of day, or on the hayrick, getting the mangers ready for the night."

As we approached the farmhouse we heard the same noise of animals we'd heard before, but louder. Perhaps the animals had a reason to be anxious, though they didn't seem scared or frightened.

As we walked under the elder tree we heard a ruckus inside the house. Quirze burst into a run and we followed, on tenterhooks.

32

Two civil guards were sitting on the stone step in the front entrance smoking and looking jaded.

The moment they saw us, they jumped to their feet and grabbed their guns from the nearby wall.

We stopped in our tracks opposite them, shocked and speechless.

"*Sois de la casa?*" one of them asked, whom Quirze must have recognized, as he glanced at his colleague. He spoke in a very clipped Spanish.

"*Esperad un momento,*" replied the latter as he walked inside without returning the glance.

"What's up?" asked Quirze in a tone I thought was wonderfully firm, not showing a hint of fear.

"*Un registro reglamentario,*" said the guard quite impassively, as if he were behind the counter in an office.

Quirze took a step forward as if to go in but the guard barred his way, saying: "*Espera.*"

The second guard came back with Aunt Ció in his wake. Her face was red and she seemed angry. She was lifting the corner of her apron, as if she'd just been cleaning something.

"Go and have a bite to eat in the kitchen," she told the three of us, her voice trembling, "I'll bring you something right away, but best not go upstairs until...these people have finished...what they have to do."

The guard accompanying her gestured as if authorizing us to go in and the three of us silently followed Aunt Ció.

We saw the large baskets in the entrance were open and empty by a number of boxes that had been strewn all around. We could now hear the muffled mooing and bleating of the animals.

The kitchen cupboards had been thrown open and a heap of firewood scattered over the floor, the cloth curtains under the sink had been drawn back and dishes, pots, pans and buckets tipped all over.

"They've turned everything upside down," said Aunt Ció as she washed some glasses and looked for a milk jug. "They've not left anything in place, they messed up the lot… I don't know what the hell these people think they're going to find."

We stood straight-backed by the side of the table. Staring at the basket of bundles of wool and knitting needles abandoned on the floor, next to the empty pew, Quirze asked: "What about Grandmother? Where's she?"

"She went to lie down," answered Ció, placing the glasses and milk jug on the table. "So she could rest and not have to speak to anyone. Sit down and have a bite to eat. They'll soon be finished, now they've turned everywhere topsy-turvy."

While she sliced bread and took cold sausage out of the drawer and put it in the centre of the table, she added: "All this malarkey can't possibly go on much longer."

"What are they looking for?" asked Quirze.

"They're looking for what isn't here," she exploded. "How the fuck do I know what they're looking for! They must think our attics are full of flour we're going to sell on the black market or tobacco smuggled from South America, the stuff people often bring down from Andorra… You can. be sure someone had it in for us and informed on us."

"Are the hands upstairs as well? And my father? And Bernat?" persisted Quirze while his mother walked to the kitchen door to catch the noise coming from the sitting room and the gallery.

"Your father and Bernat are with them, keeping an eye on what they're doing," whispered Aunt Ció from the doorway.

"The hands must be cleaning out the stables, that's what your Father told them to do as soon as this palaver started."

The noise upstairs got louder, as if they were dragging sideboards or boxes around. Aunt Ció turned and told us: "Don't you budge from here. Wait for me and keep quiet."

She left the kitchen.

Cry-Baby and I started to pick unenthusiastically at our snack. Quirze waited for a moment and then went over to the door, as his mother had just done. He stood there for a few minutes, silent, head bowed, trying to make out the movements and noises, and finally he decided to leave, without saying a word, or even giving us a glance, as if we didn't exist.

The noise upstairs gradually dropped off. Now we only heard footsteps going up and down and the sound of conversation. Cry-Baby and I glanced at each other, not knowing what to say or do. Suddenly Quirze ran in, as if he wanted to hide or was being chased, he sat down next to us and started wolfing the food down until his mouth was stuffed and his cheeks puffed out. Presumably they must have caught him spying on something and now he wanted to put on an act, in case somebody came into the kitchen to check on his whereabouts and what he was up to.

However nobody else came. We heard the footsteps of people coming downstairs and then a conversation in the doorway that was hard to hear, in Spanish with snatches of Catalan, and what we could hear most easily was Dad Quirze's clotted, rudimentary Spanish repeating: "*Nada, nada... Todo está aclarado, verdad que sí?*"

When we saw the gang of civil guards accompanied by Brunet Who Never Stops walking past the kitchen window and round the house to take the path to the village, we knew the raid was over. I thought Brunet looked angry, with his little pencil-line, mousey moustache and a shirt as blue as a mechanic's overall, and registered that Canary and Curly Lettuce weren't there.

But the grownups didn't come into the kitchen for a while. Someone went upstairs and we imagined they must have gone to look for Grandmother, and an even more secretive, inaudible conversation now reached us from the front porch. This time not even Quirze dared get up from the table. We looked from the window to the door and back but saw nothing. We heard the lids of the big laundry baskets slam down, angrily even, then AuntCió finally walked in, still looking very on edge, her face a paler shade of red, wiping her hands on her apron even though they looked dry and clean.

"I don't know… I don't know…" she mumbled, ignoring us, "I don't know how we'll get out of this. This time God or Lady Luck took pity on us, we must thank Father Tafalla for his supplications. I don't know what we're going to do, I really don't."

When she walked over to the table to clear away the glasses, leftover crumbs, the piece of sausage and milk jug, it was if she couldn't see us, her eyes were open and staring blankly into space and she walked like a sleepwalker.

"What about Grandmother?" Quirze asked again, now wanting to catch his mother's attention than out of any real curiosity.

"She stayed in her room. She wants to rest for longer. She probably won't even come down to supper. She's lost her appetite. Those people clattering around totally overwhelmed her."

She paused to sigh and then added: "This raid has knocked me out, too."

She went on with her chores by the stove keeping her back turned on us. Quirze looked to see whether Cry-Baby and I had got over our bewilderment and were doing or saying anything. He couldn't stand sitting still any longer.

He got up quietly and went to the door as if he was going to make a run for it. He bumped into Pere Màrtir, who was coming in, on the doorstep. We'd not heard any footsteps, and Pere Màrtir stood there, stock-still, opposite Quirze, as polished and gleaming as a silver tray, as Grandmother said he always was. Pere Màrtir and Quirze stood opposite each other as if paralyzed, but after the initial shock, both took a step back to let the other pass. However, Quirze took a couple more steps back, encouraging Pere Màrtir to go in, which the brawny young man did with a grateful smile.

AuntCió looked round and when she saw Pere, she shouted in gleeful surprise and hurled herself at him in an embrace that Pere Màrtir welcomed with an even broader smile, hugging her gently, and when our aunt started whimpering against his chest, he stroked her head, slowly and lovingly, as if wanting to tidy her dishevelled hair.

"What are you…?" AuntCió shouted. "In my heart of hearts I knew you'd come, but I thought it would be tomorrow, not this soon. They left only a minute ago."

"Yes," he whispered, as if his words were only for her, "I saw them, the whole patrol, going off empty-handed…"

"You passed them on the path?" asked Aunt Có, panicking.

"No. I came on the shortcut through the woods so I wouldn't bump into anyone. I took the turning just outside the village and waited until they'd all gone by."

Aunt Ció let go of him and wiped her tears on her apron. They both exchanged silent, knowing glances and when she shook her head, he smiled cheerfully again. It was obvious, even to us, that their eyes spoke of things they were already party to and that they needed no words to understand each other.

"Sit down and have something to eat," reacted Aunt Ció, her hand on his back directing him towards the table where we were sitting. "They've finished. Why don't you stay for dinner? Dad Quirze and Bernat will want talk it all over with you. These cheeky brats will be off right now to help young Quirze with the animals. You just go and sit down."

But we ignored her big hint and stayed put. Quirze came back and sat next to us.

"I can't," replied Pere Màrtir, standing at one end of the table, "they're expecting me back tonight at home. I only wanted to know how you were and to see whether Enriqueta was around."

"She's still at Florència's. She's keeping her company," Aunt Ció went back to the range, opened the cupboard and took out a tablecloth, "she's been going every day after work. She'll be back today because Florència is slowly recovering. What else can she do?"

"So she's not back yet, right?" Pere Màrtir looked at us out of the corner of her eye and at Aunt Ció as intently as before.

This time the young man's question caught Aunt Ció off guard.

"No, I was telling you…" she began until she read into Pere Màrtir's eyes. "No, nobody else has paid us a visit!"

"It's just that someone was murdered in Vic this morning," he replied as if that piece of news was a kind of explanation. "Hadn't you heard?"

"What's that? What's happened? We've heard nothing," said Ció, sounding interested, looking at us as if she wanted us to share in the news. "We've been chasing our tails all day, really under the hammer from the second we found out they might turn up at any moment…getting everything ready…until just a few minutes ago."

Both now addressed us as if they'd finally condescended to acknowledge us, now we seemed vital, as if an increase in the audience would spread the impact of the news. We were so excited by the word "murdered" that I, and I imagine my cousins too, hardly paid any attention to Aunt Ció's sudden rush of explanations; she was probably so alarmed she'd not really thought through what she was saying. She left a difficult conundrum in the back of my mind that I struggled to resolve; in any case, nothing squared over those few days.

"Early this morning, before daybreak, the Civil Guard shot a man to smithereeens who was leaving the Hotel Colom in Vic."

"What on earth?"

"They were clearly keeping an eye on the whole square and the vicinity of the hotel because they'd been informed Massana might be spending the night there, he'd crossed the border to prepare a couple of attacks, and was pretending to be a landowner from Collsacabra. Evidently the square was covered in mist, you could hardly see a thing, and the second the man left the hotel, the civil guards shouted to him to halt, he put his hand to his chest, they thought he was going for his pistol and shot to kill, didn't even give him time to raise his hands and surrender."

"My God!"

"The man dropped dead on the spot. When the guards went over, they saw he was the owner of the Reguer de Pruit estate who was on his way to the station to catch the first train to Barcelona that leaves at six. He was going to see his son who's a boarder at the Escolapian School in Sarrià."

"What's that? You mean he was the owner of the Reguer de Pruit and they mistook him for…"

"That's what I said. The man clearly put his hand to his chest to get his papers from his wallet, his pass or whatever, the papers he was carrying in his inside jacket pocket, and the guards thought he was armed and was going for his pistol."

"Of course, I expect he stayed the night in the hotel so he could catch the first train to Barcelona."

"That's right."

"So how come we only just got to find out? It must be the day we've had… But Brunet Who Never Stops and the civil guards were here and they never said a word."

"And they won't, if they can help it. We'll see if it comes out in the newspapers. And if they do ever mention it, it's because they can hardly hide what has happened from the people of Pruit and the whole district, but I'd be interested to see if they mention it further afield."

"How did you find out?"

"Canary told me. They put all the barracks round-and-about on alert and ordered all the civil guards to patrol the woods in case infiltrators were about. It's a joke, because no group has crossed the border... The Pyrenees aren't up the road here as they are in the Vall d'Aran."

"So perhaps that's why they came here today..."

"I don't think so. They'd planned this raid in advance, according to Canary."

Aunt Ció looked down, as if embarrassed by what Pere Màrtir was saying or didn't want to hear; the young man clammed up immediately.

"We were very lucky..." mumbled Aunt Ció keeping her head down, and then she looked up again, stared at Pere Màrtir and said: "You realize you and Enriqueta have given us some bad turns, but know what?, if we get out of this unscathed I'll forgive you all those headaches and sleepless nights."

Pere Màrtir smiled shyly, his half-rabbit grin that made him seem so vulnerable, that transformed a sturdy, compact, perfectly proportioned man into a defenceless child.

"How can we repay you?" asked Aunt Ció, walking over to us, but focusing her head and conversation on the visitor.

"Don't you worry about that," said Pere Màrtir, shaking his head. "If everything turns out all right, don't you worry."

"Let's hope so... We've got more tricky business coming up."

Pere Màrtir shrugged his shoulders, signalling that he was powerless.

"Are you sure you don't want anything to eat?" asked Aunt Ció, putting the cloth on the table, but not unfolding it, waiting for our visitor to decide. "Come on, stay for dinner. You'll be able to talk to the men."

"I don't think I will. We'll meet up later, if everything turns out..."

"I hope God's listening to you, my love..."

Pere Màrtir bid us farewell with a nod in our direction and Aunt Ció accompanied him to the front entrance. As they left the kitchen, she said: "Shall I tell Enriqueta you came, when she gets back?"

We didn't hear what he replied. Perhaps he didn't say anything. They both stood and talked by the door for a time. What could they have to talk about that was more terrible or more exciting than the accidental murder of the owner of Reguer?

When Aunt Ció came back, she scolded us because we'd not gone to help the men with the animals, as if she'd only just noticed we'd been there for heaven knows how long. She grabbed Cry-Baby and said: "And you can go upstairs to keep Grandmother company."

Quirze and I walked to the stable but I sat halfway down the stairs and watched my cousin flex his muscles and fork up the hay, spread it over the ground and divide it out before putting it in the mangers.

Dad Quirze and Jan, the hand, let him get on with it, didn't say a word. Bernat wasn't around. I was afraid Uncle Quirze would start baiting me; he often did when I tried to help the men, he made comments about weak-kneed students that shattered with the slightest effort they made as we were made of glass, or my particular clumsiness that he said came from "being born with a silver spoon in my mouth," or from "being all mind and no muscle," and such like, that were surprising from a hulking man as taciturn as he was. His comments, nevertheless, came wrapped in a film of irony, that distanced them, as if he was talking about someone else, and that made them less hurtful, as if rather than insulting me he was indirectly praising my ability to study.

"This young man," he'd say, looking at me askance, "when he arrived here, couldn't tell a mule from a gelding, or a filly from a foal. They don't teach you that at school, do they? You had to learn that here. Townsfolk don't even know what hoofers are."

"Animals that hoof," I repeated, joining in the game and touching my ears to show I did remember what the difference was between mules and geldings, foals and fillies. He liked bantering with me, and I sensed it was his way of getting closer to me, and I was glad he didn't force me to help his son, or compete with him over the tasks in the stables or on the land.

At dinnertime, while she was serving up, Ció explained blow by blow what Pere Màrtir had told her about the mistaken murder of the owner of Reguer de Collsacabra. Dad Quirze, Bernat and Jan, the hand, listened carefully, didn't raise an eyebrow, only grunted now and then, which was their way of approving or booing according to the level of sound they emitted, just like mardy children.

"The rats!"

"The swine!"

"The evil beasts!"

Cry-Baby went down to the kitchen to get Grandmother's food and also her own, so they could both have supper in her bedroom.

When we'd finished eating, Quirze and I went up to see Grandmother. We found her in bed, leaning back against a pile of pillows Cry-Baby had put in place, and their plates and glasses of milk were on the sideboard and the bedside table. Cry-Baby sat by her side on the turn of the sheet.

"I don't feel like doing anything," Grandmother wheezed. "I feel everything I've suffered over the years has come back to haunt me. As if it all happened today… I reckon this war will never ever come to an end."

Her exhausted eyes glanced lovingly at us and then she added, cracking one of her jokes, no doubt to make sure what she'd just said seemed more tolerable: "I don't even feel like telling stories! Such shocking things happen, I lose interest in my stories. Right now, I wouldn't know where to start. I don't remember a single one. When the war was going at full tilt, I felt exactly the same; with all that blood and gunfire outside, my stories evaporated inside me, as if they'd no strength of will or were afraid to show their faces."

33

Oak-Leaf stopped going to classes at the Novíssima. Mr. Madern, the teacher, gave us no explanation why. When she'd not been for two or three days, somebody asked after her and the teacher replied most matter-of-factly, as if it were the most natural thing in the world: "She's been put to work in a local factory."

And we all thought that was an explanation with substance, as definitive as the cold of winter or heat of summer arriving. All the boys and girls accepted their fate in the factory, on the land or in a small family business with a kind of meek resignation, a fate they couldn't escape; the oldest even gleefully anticipated the end of their schooling. They could see no possible way to dodge that burden, let alone to rebel against it. They had no other horizons and didn't long for a different outcome. It was the future destined for them. There was no other.

My heart was somewhat sickened by their complicit acceptance of a tediously predictable adult life. Those schoolmates of mine—in both schools—seemed to think they lived in a rounded, orderly universe where everybody sooner or later found their slot; they simply had to slot into the gaps that were produced in society in clockwork fashion, as if the way one generation relieved another was a precise law of nature that couldn't be defied. Their only aspiration was that their minimal presence should perpetuate an established order that from some superior, hidden place made the world revolve smoothly. They let themselves be swept along by the movement of things—society, the universe, destiny— and only tried to ensure it never sped up or braked to a halt.

They had learned from the "defeated" generation that they were only pawns in the game of life, and they viewed the world above them, shaped by the bosses, the powers-that-be, the church, the enemy, the law, with respect, and found it quite normal to jump to their orders because bosses were the only people who understood how to pull the strings that governed the world.

My experience of prison made me see them as the defeated, and the defeated were different to those in prison; they were the defeated who hadn't even put up a fight, as far as I was concerned. I was under the impression they would have submitted to any flag, the only proviso being that it should come with victory on a plate, one they could take on board without taking the slightest risk.

I felt I was different, though not necessarily more courageous or superior. Deep down perhaps I even envied them their submission and the way they bowed their heads before the superior forces of society and nature, which, I thought, made them happier. I'd seen the faces of relatives waiting to visit those under sentence in prison, the gestures of insubordination that made them clench their fists on the pretext that it was a cold morning, eyes that spat fire as they reviewed a brutally hostile world and sparse, pointed words that wounded like sharpened knives. I'd seen there was another world of simmering rage, of constrained violence, perpetually on the alert, waiting for the moment to rise up. I didn't consider myself to be either strong or courageous enough to be like them, but I had learned that the providential, orderly universe that my agricultural-labourer or factory-worker schoolmates intended to inhabit was an illusion, and that if I wanted to survive, I should only trust in myself, that my strength lay in my powers of dissimulation, my inner struggle, my partial, oblique adaptation to the moment and the concealment of my true intentions; my weapons were treachery, sleight-of-hand and deceit, if need be.

Oak-Leaf had absconded with her secret concerning puppetmaster Mr. Madern, and Cry-Baby also lived a hidden, secret, elusive life, and I suspected Aunt Enriqueta led a dark life in the depths of the forest, and all that only reinforced me in the option I had chosen. Nobody told the truth, everybody lived double lives, one on the surface, one in secret. Only Mad Antònia walked naked through the woods, openly declaring the secret behind her sickness. I'd have to be mad like her to expose my inner state. What did I know of the life Pere Màrtir lived and all his hidden crevices and crannies? And the adolescent with TB in the heartsease gardens, with his archangel face and body branded by all manner of obscure sin, what did I know about them? Only my fascination with the shadow their lives projected over mine, and that alone.

And I now imagined Oak-Leaf crossing the woods in the early morning, when it was still pitch-black, coming out onto the road at some point to catch the coach, and making that journey every day with her colleagues on that shift, joking and singing the whole way or praying Hail Marys and Our Father in remembrance of the girl murdered years ago on the path to Cós in the days when the factory girls walked through the woods—they still called them factory girls in the country, contemptuously, just as they sang ditties dubbing them "steam bugs" and "tramps and pigs" when they saw them walk past with their lunch baskets. Grandmother knew a stack of insulting limericks invented by country folk who didn't want their girls to abandon work on the farms—I imagined Oak-Leaf chained for life to the line of women who had joined the sad, brutalizing factory routine, like my mother, hard labour that stole away their good cheer, their good health and their time, and sent them home in a bad temper, tired and unhappy, like a river returning to the surface the bodies of the drowned, eyes gaping but lifeless.

My memory would get entangled with my imagination, and sometimes the mixture played tricks on me and

I was afraid I couldn't remember things properly, say, for example, the memory of my father, the last image I clung to, of him behind prison bars, separated by that empty space I'd run across, his wan face, the bags under his eyes, his two- or three-day-old stubble, his sallow, emaciated skin smelling of dank cells and the lukewarm sweat of caged men; all I remembered about him began to fade so quickly, and sometimes I could only see a hazy outline of him, as if my picture of him was disappearing, and I took that to herald a second death, the death of his memory; the dead fled my mind, were erased, turned to shadows, to ashes, to oblivion, to non-things, and it was horrible not to be able to evoke those beloved images, as if they'd never existed, and that was the greatest injustice ever, a pit deeper and darker than death itself, the death of memory, the death that was definitive.

And so Oak-Leaf had left us too, and I could still see her in the clearing in the wood where we used to play and argue, I remembered words I'd heard at my father's funeral, when somebody had spoken incomprehensibly about him "passing on to another life," and those words now came back to me and I felt they were more appropriate to this situation because Oak-Leaf had changed her life and passed on to adult life. We were all fated to pass on to another kind of life. Even the mischievous brats sitting behind desks in my class would one day pass on to adult life, quite unawares, from one day to the next, they'd be transformed into grownups, young adults, old people and would behave like the genuine article, would smoke for real in the café in front of everybody, not hiding in the lavatories or playground as they did now, and court a girl, spending their Sundays strolling together round the main square, making public his emotional commitment to that girl who would be his fiancée, his legal wife for life, his widow...rather than swapping information about sex and exposing themselves in secret.

Quirze was the second to leave school, even though it was a temporary measure, or so they said. That happened when the farm was invaded by reapers, gangs of reapers who'd come from all over, mature men and young men, strong and bare-chested, who slept in the barn or woods and gathered on the threshing-ground every morning to be divided into groups and share out the corn fields; they made sheaves in the crook of their arm which they then heaped into stooks, everyone with a scythe in one hand and a wooden half-glove on the other, and the women would come later to pick up the ears of corn left among the stubble; they were women from the village and sometimes Aunt Ció, Cry-Baby and I joined in on days when there weren't classes, and Aunt Ció and Cry-Baby brought them a drink mid-afternoon in a basket covered by a napkin, and when the reapers saw the basket coming they'd whistle and laugh, stop working and sit down on the edges of the field to eat and drink, they called it having a swig and wetting their dry throats, and they were sweaty, dripping in sweat, and gave off a tepid smell that was a mix of corn, grass and their own brawn. Quirze had to help them that year, by his father's side or Bernat's and the hands', he had to learn, they said, and it was high time he started, school could wait, he'd be back when the harvest was over. However, after the reaping came the threshing and for days the whole farm was transformed into a beehive when the carts came with sheaves of reaped corn, the threshing machine was set up in the middle of the threshing-floor, and we thought it was huge as a steam engine, and the shouting and the sound of baskets and mounds of corn and large sacks of grain filling the barn and the granary even reached as far as the entrance to the house, full of chaff, chaff like drops of dry dusty rain that impregnated everything. From the gallery Cry-Baby, Grandmother and I watched the men moving and the most exciting moment in the threshing was when the straw started to stream nonstop from the spout of the machine which they directed to one side with straw streaming out that they shaped into a haystack, what would stay a haystack for the whole of next year, next to the pond, by the hazel tree spinney.

All those men from elsewhere radiated an energy that was felt throughout the house; the women didn't stop for a minute, were always on the go, and women from the village came to help because Aunt Ció by herself couldn't cope with even half what had to be done, and the men didn't come into the house for a single meal, didn't stop the whole day, we never saw them, and Grandfather Hand never appeared on such days, because he'd been told he wasn't of an age to help, that he'd be more of a nuisance than a help.

Cry-Baby and I rushed home from class every afternoon because we knew we'd find something new in the farmhouse, new reapers who'd found quail or partridge nests among the corn or undergrowth and brought them home where the haystack got higher and higher and was almost finished. Aunt Enriqueta washed their shirts and patched their trousers, and we listened to Grandmother's news about what had happened during the day. We never played on the path like we used to, we never dawdled, as Grandmother put it, and without Oak-Leaf or Quirze we felt lonely, orphaned, and ran so as to be back at the farm early.

Afternoons were drawn out and mid-afternoon was what midday used to be. Mr. Madern, the teacher, hadn't kept back Cry-Baby or me, as if he understood with all that hustle and bustle we had no time for him or anybody else. And deprived of Oak-Leaf's brazen lack of shame and Quirze's coarseness, neither Cry-Baby nor I dared to begin a round of the nonsense games that had once filled our conversations.

The men didn't even stop on Sundays, they only stopped if it rained, because they said the rain made the straw stick to the machine. Then they crammed into the barn or the pen, perching their bums on rocks, itching to return to work, with cigarettes on their lips and a jug of wine that was always being passed around, and they told stories about the peculiar people in their or another gang, and that made them burst into loud, belly-shaking guffaws, like the one about the day-labourer who never washed and when they scolded him and said he'd soon start breeding lice, and didn't he feel ashamed to be always so filthy? and he replied "Nobody knows me here, I go as I please," and when the gang came to his village to work, he didn't wash there either, because, or so he said, "They all know me here, they know what I'm like," and other cases that became famous like the one about the man who didn't do up his fly and when people told him it was open, he retorted he would never button it up, that once a woman with the hots for him had cooled down in the time it had taken him to unbutton, the laughter was even louder and people slapped their knees.

When the gangs departed, the farm seemed to relax for a few days. At siesta time on Sundays, when the house went quiet because the reapers had gone and it seemed bereft, when the sun was motionless in the sky and the yellow light burned like a red-hot brand-iron, Cry-Baby and I went to play in the hazel tree spinney. We made our escape from everyone on the excuse that we were going to play hide-and-seek. It was the signal for us to go and sleep under the low, deep shadow from the hazel trees. Mother, who'd arrived that morning, stayed in the kitchen to help Aunt Ció and they'd chatted until it was time for her to go. Quirze took a nap, like the grownups. And without him, without the tension he created with his older knowing ways—Grandmother said that Quirze was our trouble-maker who sowed seeds of discord—we weren't so keen on climbing the plum tree. Our new life now belonged to the shadowy arbours in the hazel tree spinney.

We never said a word. Núria stretched out in the depths of the spinney and waited for me to follow. I lay by her side and we stayed still for a while, as if we were expecting something to happen. She sometimes said, "Do you want to play at teachers?"

And she let me put my hands on her and explore her whole body. She hardly ever moved, and only occasionally showed any interest in my displaying myself. We held each other tight, as tight as we could, and after a while, as if disappointed that our embrace hadn't melded us into a single body or that the two opposing forces had only produced exhaustion and tensed muscles, we separated out with a mixture of satisfaction and frustration, like a schoolboy who has done homework that his teacher then doesn't bother to read or mark.

We'd run off at speed to poke our heads over the wall at the end of the spinney and spy on the sickly figures lying in the heartsease garden. We grinned and pointed out the most naked, the sickest, the hairiest, the most emaciated... I don't know why but Cry-Baby never mentioned the boy lying under the elm tree, the boy who seemed the youngest and as lithe and white as a river of silver. Perhaps Núria also felt he was a special case, that he didn't fit in that whole scenario, as if his sickness wasn't the same as the one affecting the others who seemed to lack something... conversely, the boy—whom I already considered to be mine, ours—seemed to suffer from an excess, from an abundance, the others had neither colour nor flesh, didn't look well or at all special, yet I felt that chosen boy had just the right colour, body weight and gaze, the right *tout ensemble* and exuded a warmth, a sheen, that attracted every eye. Each small gesture he made was just right, not a single millimetre too much or too little; the others, on the other hand, moved awkwardly, slovenly, as if they weren't in control of their limbs. It was obvious that all the TB sufferers, except for him, had lost a vital, irrevocable struggle, unlike our young man, who acted as if he was resting after a prophetic skirmish with a divine saviour who had entrusted him with the mission of salvaging perfection in a world full of all manner of mutilation.

One afternoon, he wasn't there and the garden seemed deserted. I felt a void in my chest, as if I'd lost something crucial that I needed in order to live, a pint of blood or half a rib, and the wound was sore. I didn't understand why I felt all that or why those things happened. I felt guilty because that sense of loss hit me more than my father's death. It was different, my father represented the disappearance of a being I'd once had and now lacked, the young TB sufferer represented the appearance of someone I hadn't been expecting, didn't know, and was a revelation of something strange and disturbing.

Luckily, he appeared on another day as if that had only been a blip, a rise in temperature or medical advice not to take so much sun. That re-encounter filled me with joy; I experienced a new, hitherto unknown fulfilment.

Days before, shortly after my father's death and the civil guards' raid on the farmhouse, when Grandmother had been out of sorts and didn't leave her bed the whole day and declared that all her goblins and fireside stories would disappear from our land, annoyed by so many deaths and unable to breathe air so full of hatred, resentment and revenge, Grandmother summoned the three of us to her bed, to her side, for a while, and said she didn't have the strength of will or oomph to tell us a tale or recall a comic or horror story, she just wanted us near her because she hadn't seen us for days and was now starting to feel better and wanted us to keep her company for a bit.

Cry-Baby and I climbed onto her bed immediately, half-undressed, but Quirze felt mardy, said he wasn't in the mood for all that baloney, and AuntCió had to insist he stood next to us, barefoot, he didn't have to get in bed if he didn't want to, and that's how the three of us came to be next to Grandmother, and from where she lay she laughed and told us to get some sleep, that she was going down to the kitchen to prepare a herbal drink that would help us to dream some lovely dreams.

The three of us sank into the soft mattress and laughed as we remembered the prim little princess, the crème de la crème of all true princesses, who couldn't get to sleep if she found there was a pea or pebble under the ten or twelve mattresses she'd been placed on. Grandmother didn't come back and we fell asleep.

I suddenly woke up sensing that somebody was looking at us. At the very first when I opened my eyes I saw it was much darker in the room, as if night had turned a jet black. But immediately, my half-open eyes saw Grandmother with a small oil-lamp at the foot of the bed staring at us, with a strange man by her side who was smiling at me, a friendly, trusting, motionless presence. It only lasted a moment because Grandmother and somebody in the sitting room were hurrying him up, the man smiled and said nothing; his smile wasn't the same as Grandmother's. Hers was a forlorn, weary grimace, his was cheerful, determined, and very, very loving. He was dressed for deep winter and his head was wrapped in something like a hood or sack turned inside out, which gave his face a cheeky, facetious, fantastical aspect because it looked quite solitary, amid the shadows, a stray face that had come to the foot of that bed to spy on how we slept, like a character from a fairytale, a denizen of the depths of the forest. The man carried something in his hands or under his arm, bundles or bags, which were hidden and made him stand really straight, a stiffness that only emphasized even more dramatically the sense of unreality.

Grandmother whispered something, then someone muttered in the sitting room, hurrying him up. His was the smile of someone who is observing a miracle. It only lasted a second because Grandmother tugged his arm and they both suddenly disappeared. It was so quick and so fantastical I thought it must have been a dream or mirage. Before falling back into a deep sleep, I felt the flickering light disappear into the sitting room and melt into the pitch-black night. I didn't have the courage to check whether Grandmother was in bed or not, or to look at the face of Cry-Baby who was by my side, or Quirze who was farther away, to confirm they'd seen what I'd seen.

Next morning when I woke up with Grandmother on the other side of the bed, I remembered hardly anything, and a voice inside me urged me to say nothing and ask nothing, first because it had surely been a dream and everybody would laugh at me, and second, because my heart told me it was a grownups' secret, that unwittingly I had glimpsed a secret from the adult world, just like when you are older and discover it is your parents who organize the presents on the night of the Three Kings and they don't tell you because they simultaneously want you to open your eyes yet also preserve the illusion, and they banter about whether you do or don't know, and now I felt in a similar situation and needed time to decide if I wanted to cross that border or not and insist on the truth that would bring me closer to their world or stay quiet and maintain the fiction of prolonged innocence that allowed them to tiptoe over our dreams at night.

"You slept like logs all night!" said Grandmother when we got up.

"I thought somebody stroked my hair," said Cry-Baby suspiciously, "or that people were caressing my face."

"The goblin," laughed Grandmother, and now her smile was happy and relaxed like the nighttime visitor's, "it must have been the goblin who came to say goodbye. I bet it was him."

"Rubbish!" said Quirze, storming out of the bedroom. "I never want to sleep here again, I'm much better in the hands' room. These two never stop tossing and turning and, Grandmother, you got up at least two or three times during the night."

34

At the start of summer, when we had to decide whether I was to stay on at the farmhouse or go and spend the holiday months in town with Mother, Mr. and Mrs. Manubens, the landowners, said they would pay a visit.

Days before, Mr. Madern, the teacher, bid farewell to all his pupils because, as he said, he'd won promotion to a city school on the fringes of Barcelona, a permanent post, and wouldn't be returning the next school year. Miss Pepita, the ex-nun, the infant class's Miss Silly, as he also told us, wouldn't return either because she was going back to the convent, though she only informed us much later, because she stayed on at school throughout the summer for all those infants and juniors who wanted help with their summer homework or to learn how to type on the two typewriters the Rural Town Hall put at the disposition of the class.

Mr. Madern seemed in a good mood on that last day of school and organized games in the playground, even though he was the one who never showed his face at break-times, preferring to remain hunched over his chess game; that was a special day when he helped lead games like world flags, hundred-metre sprints, shot-putting, jumping... We did nothing the whole day, and suddenly, after the games, at lunchtime, he produced bottles of fizzy pop and wine and gave out small glasses he filled with a mix, either only wine or pop depending on the age of the pupils. He invited Miss Pepita too, and she came in, all smiley and embarrassed, and drank only fizzy pop, not a drop of wine.

"I told them you're going back to the convent," he announced in front of everybody.

She blushed and replied: "It's still not decided. I spoke to the Mother Superior at the Clarissa's and I spend Sundays with them. I think it will be best for me. In these missionary times, lots of sacrifices, lots of vocations are needed to clean up the country and make it Christian once again."

The class was creating a racket and almost nobody listened to what she was saying. I'd walked over to the dais because a moment before I'd seen Mr. Madern speaking to Cry-Baby, I didn't know what he said to her, and I felt anxious, driven towards them, as if I had a right or a need to know what they were saying.

Miss Pepita talked to herself, because the class didn't take a blind bit of notice and Mr. Madern listened for a second and then called to someone or busied himself tidying exercise books on the table. When I went over, before returning to her infants, the ex-nun told Mr. Madern: "I feel increasingly at a loss, I've told you that more than once. Inside, in the convent, I mean, there is order, discipline, a path…"

The master laughed and responded quietly: "Yet more order…! But the country is like a millpond compared to what it was. We'll die of disgust and boredom if things don't soon change. I'm hoping that in my new post, I'll be able to slip off to Barcelona every now and then and let my hair down."

"You're different," she frowned, "you men *are* different… I drown in a glass of water, I even lose myself in this tiny village I find too big for my liking… I've got my religion, you've got your politics."

"Politics!" scowled Mr. Madern. "Can you call this politics? It's the death of politics. I'll be able to look up my old comrades in Barcelona and find out whether the Provincial Delegates have sold out as people say they have. According to the rumours…"

Cry-Baby stood next to me but said nothing. I listened to the teachers' conversation and was surprised by Mr.

Madern's disillusioned attitude, and found him, by my lights, to be as disenchanted as Dad Quirze on the farm, as if the world appalled him, as if he wanted to isolate himself from it differently to the way silly Miss Pepita was hoping to: both wanted to shut themselves up inside a secure, impregnable fortress, both were seeking a safe bolthole, she, I felt, in renunciation, and he, in action, a self-imposed prison and barracks, both dissatisfied with the life they led, disappointed by something they'd been expecting from life that had failed to materialize. What on earth could they have expected from life that they'd yet to find? I didn't really understand whether life had *betrayed* them—one of the words I'd heard repeated on so many lips, starting with my mother, when she was at her lowest ebb, and that I was always astonished to hear, like when someone in Barcelona or any big city said they'd been bamboozled on the street by con men or tricksters, something I found ridiculous and pathetic, because they could have avoided such deceit if they'd gone about their own business and not been distracted by anything or anybody, particularly by the first stranger who waylaid them in the middle of the street—or that they themselves had been betrayed by life as a result of bad luck or lack of savoir-faire. They were both teachers, couldn't they guide and advise us so we could avoid the dangers they'd not managed to sidestep themselves? I reckoned that grownups who complained of such ephemeral discontent were ridiculous and pathetic. Mother, for example, would be more than happy and fulfilled, if only they returned her husband to her. Her workmates, another example that came to mind, would jump with joy if only they could get up at eight or nine every morning, and not have to spend half their lives standing by a machine, slaving like animals. So what did that couple of puppeteers have to moan about? That they didn't have everything they'd wanted?

When Miss Pepita left and Mr. Madern accompanied her to the door, I asked Cry-Baby: "What did he say?"

She shook her head as if she was chasing a fly away.

"Don't you want to tell me?"

"Nothing much, just that he's leaving," she piped softly.

"Is that all? So long for so little?"

"That maybe he'll come back to see us one day."

"To see us, who exactly?"

"Everybody at school, the new teacher, at the start of term to tell him how everything works and what we're like…"

"Was that all?"

"Yes," she replied more firmly. "When he does things, he doesn't speak, he does them and that's that. He told me I shouldn't tell anyone. That we should never say a word."

I now felt Cry-Baby was more brazen than ever, as if she'd suddenly had a growth spurt and was beginning to speak bluntly like Oak-Leaf always did. I made no comment, dismayed by the thought that Cry-Baby was changing and would change even more. Perhaps Mr. Madern the teacher went after Cry-Baby because he didn't want people or the world to change so quickly. I'd also rather my cousin never changed, and would always be as she was during those years on the farm, a shy, frail, thin, fair-skinned individual, hair a straw yellow, sky-blue eyes, legs amazingly shapely from her knees upwards and a lovely tummy that undulated gently. I didn't want Cry-Baby to turn into a young woman like Oak-Leaf, who had always seemed like a tomboy. Mr. Madern must have swapped Oak-Leaf's company for Cry-Baby's when Oak-Leaf turned into the cocky sort she was before her latest transformation into a young working woman with her lunch basket, the last in the line of factory girls, in rough, oil-stained clothes, coarsely spoken because she was angry and exhausted but not from any fun and games, like those we had in the clearing in the woods. Everything was changing, and Cry-Baby would change too. And the world was also changing, I could see that now, it was a summer of changes, with me out in the open waiting for change as well. I'd never thought that the world grew as we did, and changed and was all of sudden faced by difficulties and obstacles on every side. The only thing that didn't change was sickness, the infirm in the heartsease garden, and my young man with TB under the elm tree who was always the same, white and motionless like a marble statue. Sickness and death, only sickness and death ever emulated perfection in that changing world.

·When we returned to the farm we found the owners sitting in the upstairs dining room, with napkins on their knees and new cups and a lace table cloth on the table. Grandmother was in the downstairs kitchen, on her pew, and she warned us: "The owners are upstairs. I think they want to see you, Andreu."

That shocked me and she added: "Listen to what they have to say and be on your best behaviour. Then we can talk about it all when your mother comes on Sunday."

As Cry-Baby seemed keen to accompany me, Grandmother was quick to add: "You stay with me. Keep me company. Don't you worry, the day will come when you'll be the centre of attention."

I walked slowly, reluctantly, up to the dining room. I vaguely remembered the advice Mr. Madern the teacher had given me a few days before, and didn't dare speculate beyond my recollection of that memory because everything he'd said that day was coloured by an equivocal revelation I'd been expecting from him, after Cry-Baby had confessed. As on that occasion with my teacher, I wasn't expecting anything tangible; I only had a vague impression that the masters, Mr. and Mrs. Manubens, had taken this strange interest in me. I felt that I was about to go on display before them, just like when my mother made me flaunt my First Communion outfit in a number of well-to-do houses or with women friends in the town, so I'd move their hearts and they'd give me alms. My chest weighed heavily, like stone, because I was tired of play-acting to arouse pity and pious sentiments.

Lolling back on the only wicker armchairs in the dining room, Mr. and Mrs. Manubens were eating biscuits from the tray and sipping sweet wine from the glasses Aunt Ció had put on the table. She'd also set down a basket with slices of bread and a couple of sausages.

Mr. Manubens wore a gleaming white linen jacket, a white shirt and a sea-blue tie. A sizeable paunch peeped out from under his jacket and the braces holding up his trousers were as blue as his tie. White socks and weave shoes, summer-style. He'd hung his hat on the back of a nearby chair. Almost bald, with his ruddy cheeks and watery blue eyes, he always seemed to be crying a bit. When he twisted his mouth into a kind of grimace you never could tell whether it was an incipient smile or his elegant way of showing distaste.

As voluminous as her husband, Mrs. Manubens wore a metal-blue dress with half-sleeves covered in white polka dots, that Aunt Enriqueta called her "mole" pattern; she was dripping with jewels, earrings, white necklaces, bracelets, rings and an ostentatious medallion on her bosom that was slightly décolleté though never threatening to trespass the bounds of decency, white high-heeled shoes and fine nylons, I couldn't tell whether they were what Aunt Enriqueta called "sheer"; her lips were painted a pale red and her eyes a deep lilac. Her skin was wrinkled, as if her bones gave no support, and I felt she was what people call a rag doll, with a face, bosom and legs made from remnants. Flesh-like clothes in need of an iron. She always smiled pleasantly, but when she spoke, hers was a loud, warbling voice, full of cackles and trills, like a singer of operetta clearing her throat, and above all it sounded fake, originating in her gullet not her heart, a voice you couldn't hear for long without feeling hers was one long stupid comic act in which she voiced the most awful clichés and tawdriest social attitudes. If you listened for any length time, you simply felt she was making fun of you.

"Come in, come in," said Aunt Ció as soon she saw me hesitating in the gallery doorway.

Uncle Quirze was also sitting at the table, at a far corner. He'd changed his shirt for a clean one, but wasn't wearing the cap he always sported when in his Sunday best. He kept his head down, his blue ferrety eyes looking up as if he was watching out for his prey. When I walked in, he shuffled on his seat and said nothing.

"Right on cue, as if your ears were burning," said Aunt Ció with a welcoming smile. "Mr. and Mrs. Manubens were just talking about you."

She pointed me to an empty chair next to hers, and I sat down.

"I was telling them how your mother and you had had a bad time over your father's death and that you were now coming to the end of your schooling at the Novíssima with Mr. Madern, who has taught you very well, like a proper teacher."

It was plain that Aunt Ció was talking to pass the time and let Mr. and Mrs. Manubens take a good look at me and reflect on the best way to broach the subject. Finally, Mrs. Manubens leaned slightly towards me and kicked off: "But that's all in the past, isn't it, boy? You feel better now, don't you?"

I nodded and felt I was replying to a doctor, everything was so spotless, so neutral, so disinfected, like a doctor's consultancy.

"Your mother, poor dear, will find it harder to get over it," she rattled on, "but don't worry, everything will eventually turn out hunky-dory. She's a brave woman, your mother, a woman with drive, and extremely deserving. She has kept the household together all these years in the face of all sorts of obstacles."

Aunt Ció nodded as if she were in complete agreement, Uncle Quirze didn't flicker an eyelash and trained his beady little eyes on my face, and Mr. Manubens, his eyelids half-closed, seemed to have hung his eyes from the rafters.

"Obviously your mother has been fortunate with your family," added Mrs. Manubens, "without the help of relatives in this household, she would have found it much more difficult to stand firm after all she's had to endure."

"And you have been very understanding towards all of us," interjected Aunt Ció, but a tendentious gesture from Mr. Manubens, held out his open palms, as if to defend himself against sudden danger, cut her obsequious little speech dead.

"Please don't, do stop..." his wife added, with a self-deprecating flourish of the hand.

I tried to keep my head clear, to not think of anything, but the idea kept bugging me that perhaps those people, the owners, the bigwigs, as my mother and Grandmother called them, were the only ones who didn't feel betrayed by life and that life couldn't betray them easily as it could everybody else, who had no resources to pit against adversity. They were the only ones who knew where they were going, what they wanted and how to get it, they possessed the power and the strength to decide their own futures and adapt the world to their needs, at the very least their world, that united, privileged contingent floating like an opaque, enclosed bubble over the rest of us mortals, unique, admirable and self-regarding because it could do nothing or very little for the wretched of this earth, could only grant them the leftovers, charity, crumbs from their banquet, because everybody knew "there wasn't enough to go round," that wealth, like beauty and well-being, was in short supply and that the world, all the beauty and goodness in the world, existed for a very few, for three or four in every town, who acted as mirror and example to the rest of the country. Besides they were the only ones who could recognize and appreciate beauty and goodness; years of training or a terrific stroke of luck were necessary if you were to attain the superior heights from which one could see deceit and disillusion coming and properly resist.

"It has occurred to us that you too could help your mother," interjected Mr. Manubens in an affably authoritative tone. "You could do much to help her. So far you have received support from your Aunt Ció and Uncle Quirze, they have lent you a helping hand. And you have shown your gratitude by working hard at school and getting high marks... Wouldn't you now like to continue with your schooling?"

I nodded, looking into Mr. Manubens's jaded eyes. I hadn't really thought about continuing at school and at that moment in time I didn't know where that led to or even what the next stage could be. My agreement was prompted by two images. The first was of the filthy factory and the section where my mother worked, the production line, with its stench of wet cotton and sweat from the fifty-odd working women who spent their life tying threads along the machines, rows of which filled the space on both sides, and all nonstop; the boredom of so many hours of routine toil under large closed windows and frosted glass, that obliterated the view of the river flowing alongside and the woods on the other side; the constant racket of the engines, cogs and wheels powering all that machinery, and the two or three young lads, three or four years older than me, who'd entered as assistants to the mechanics, turners or milling-machine operators and ran around the building in their oil-stained, patched blue overalls, with dirty faces and black, calloused hands, acting like cocky young sirs though their expression was in fact taciturn and surly, a result, I imagined, of the arrant brutality of the world that they had just entered. The second image was of the priest in the town's parish school, who in one of my periods there at the start of that year, before I moved to the farm and continued my classes at the Novíssima, had asked me to enquire at home if next year they would like me to go to secondary school in Vic, he was beginning the preparations for entrance to the Institute in Manresa, as there was no national secondary school in Vic and all the students had to take their entry exams in Manresa, and that two boys had already enrolled, the son of the town hall secretary and the son of an accountant in one of the biggest factories, but I had been unable to give him an answer because Mother, when I asked her about signing up, said that right then with my father sick in prison, she couldn't think or decide anything about what we should or shouldn't do, that we'd have to see later on, that now there were other more pressing problems to resolve, and when I went back to the Novíssima with Mr. Madern, I didn't give it another thought, until the day the teacher summoned me and told me that the masters, Mr. and Mrs. Manubens, were taking an interest in my education, and I understood I'd have to go with the flow and wait for the opportune moment to decide on my secondary schooling. My present acquiescence represented a total rejection of the factory and my desire to join the company of the best-regarded boys in town, those destined to administrate, who wouldn't dirty their hands, who said an office was perhaps the finest place in a factory, or perhaps the town hall, or who knows…

"What would you think to starting your secondary school next year at Saint Michael's in Vic?" went on Mr. Manubens, who perhaps didn't understand, I thought, that I couldn't make a decision about that, that it was way beyond any of my possibilities.

"We'll look after everything…" added the mellifluous Mrs. Manubens, "your mother won't have to worry her head about a thing, no expenditure, no worries…"

"You'll be able to go and see your mother from time to time," Mr. Manubens pointed out. "Her village isn't far either from the school or our house."

"Just give it your consideration," said Mrs. Manubens, "you don't have to decide immediately. We understand only too well that it's not easy to decide on such a big change in your life."

"Later on you could study for a degree…" continued the master. "You could also study for a degree by enrolling in the Junior Seminary in La Gleva, and moving to the Senior Seminary in Vic… But if you've not yet felt a vocation, you'd find boarding-school discipline rather harsh, washing with cold water, freezing, frosty mornings, hours spent kneeling in prayer in the chapel, food ill-cooked by the nuns, companions straight from the land or remote villages…"

He straightened his back in his chair and resumed his harangue in a more moderate vein, as if he had realized that his description might seem like a criticism: "It's not that I think a life of self-denial is a bad thing, not for one minute. But at your age you must feel the vocation if you're to cope with it. A vocation or tough demeanour that only the sons of agricultural workers can bear at this age…"

"Vocation will come later," explained his wife. "Given all that has happened, it's hardly surprising you've never given all this a thought. You'll see everything much more clearly once you've seen a few exemplary individuals and received good advice. One must give God time to make his presence felt. We are contributing to the rebuilding of the seminary, and you'll be able to enter whenever you want, when you feel the vocation, because clearly we do understand that a seminary is not simply a matter of bricks and mortar."

"Your secondary school certificate will help you do whatever you want, whenever you want…" said Mr. Manubens, now opening his arms in an all-embracing gesture.

"We have a big house and you'll have plenty of room to study and accommodate everything else."

Uncle Quirze swayed the top half of his body as if he was sitting in a rocking chair, forwards and backwards, gently, nervously, his palms splayed over his knees, his eyes closed, as if he was feeling uncomfortable. Aunt Ció was quick to interject: "Of course, we've already talked it over with your mother, and she will do whatever you say, whatever is best for you. It will also be a sacrifice for her, you being away from home and not seeing you so often, but you've got used to that in recent years, to being apart, I mean, and seeing each other only at Christmas and a few festive holidays…"

"But you should also see it as your way to help her," Mrs. Manubens was quick to add, "one more mouth to feed is a burden, whatever people may say, particularly if it's not bringing in a weekly wage, and more work after a day in the factory and everything that involves, cleaning, washing, mending… The poor woman needs a bit of respite now. Think of it as a sacrifice you are making on her behalf, for her well-being."

"And, of course, you'd be able to see her whenever you wish," chimed in Mr. Manubens in that patronizing tone of his, as if it was impossible to envisage that wasn't part of the deal, "just as she can come to see you whenever you want, you'll be in regular contact. I don't think you'll pine for each other."

"It will be just like it is now," concluded AuntCió out of good will rather than any conviction, "but different. Instead of being here with us, you'll be with them and will be able to continue your schooling. Here you'd end up on the land, like Quirze your cousin, or in town, you'd end up in an arsehole of a factory, like most people."

"From that point of view…" said Dad Quirze, who'd not said a word in all that time and now spoke hesitantly, as if duty-bound to take part, "one sees it in quite another light, naturally."

But he didn't pinpoint what that light was previously, or now. He seemed about to say something else, and everybody looked at him, convinced he would, but he shut his eyes again, rocked to and fro and said not another word.

"Lady Luck has passed your way," added AuntCió, looking into my eyes, "and people say she only passes your way once, and then flies off for evermore if you don't take her up. It's an opportunity not everyone gets, with people you know, friends, who are doing what they do out of good will."

"In that case, I say…" Uncle Quirze spoke up once again, though he didn't open his eyes or stop rocking.

I thought I caught a glimmer of sadness in Aunt Ció's eyes, something that prevented the bright spark of her usual good temper from sparkling. A moment of silence ensued, as we waited to see if Uncle Quirze wanted to add anything, but when a while passed and the silence began to weigh heavily, Mr. Manubens went on: "If you like, we can enrol you in the school for next year, so as to safeguard your place, and we will ask for an appointment to see Mossèn Vinyeta, the headmaster, so he can meet the boy and tell us what we must do to get him properly ready for his entry there."

"If needs be, we will pay for a private teacher," his wife chimed in, solicitously. "And a clever young seminarian will come to our house every week and give you extra lessons so you can make the grade."

That offer seemed to be the final touch that clinched it with everybody. A private teacher and a clever seminarian were the icing on the cake! Who could ever afford such an expense? How could anyone refuse the avalanche of good fortune now on offer? To reject all that wouldn't just have been crazy, but a mark of disrespect our masters didn't deserve, something their tenant-farmers couldn't allow themselves. Our masters were our masters! Look out if you refuse their offers! It was as if a horn of abundance had been opened. Even Uncle Quirze opened his eyes and nodded, repeating: "In that case, it's the best…the best solution all round."

"Isn't it just?" said Aunt Ció. "So what do you think, Andreu? What do you say?"

I felt a pressure that wasn't going to go away and nodded. I'd like to have seen the scenario rather more clearly and had time to think it over by myself and talk it over with someone else, Mr. Madern perhaps, but the presence of Mr. and Mrs. Manubens compelled me at the very least to show my gratitude, but the words weren't forthcoming. In my heart of hearts, in the depths of the forest, as Grandmother would have said, something dark and secret existed that I didn't understand, an insurmountable obstacle I'd yet to discover, though my instinct warned me it was lurking round a bend on that path. I only managed to articulate a "Whatever you want…, yes…"

Mr. Manubens stood up and we all followed suit. Aunt Ció came over, took my head and squeezed it against her tummy while in her most loving voice, the voice I knew she kept for occasions of utmost despair, she murmured softly, as if she didn't want the others to notice any change of tone: "Everything will turn out fine, you just see. We'll help you get on and that's all there is to it!"

35

Mr. and Mrs. Manubens were travelling in a new car they'd left in the shade from the elder tree, a black car the Quirzes, father and son, stared at as if it were one of the seven wonders… It was driven by an oldish chauffeur who declined to enter the house and waited outside smoking, leaning against the tree. They stood and admired the car as it drove away into the distance, enveloped in a cloud of dust it threw up; then father and son went down to the stables and my aunt and I walked to the kitchen. Cry-Baby stretched out her arms helping Grandmother to skein her wool. Neither asked about the visit, but AuntCió started to tell her how it had gone, before Aunt Enriqueta arrived. Grandmother listened but made no comment.

"It all went very well," AuntCió put it briefly. "I think everybody was pleased. The owners will see to everything. They'll treat him like a son, you can be sure of that."

Grandmother looked at me and I thought her eyes shone more intensely behind her glasses. After a few seconds she muttered: "If it's for his good…"

Later when Aunt Enriqueta came from work, AuntCió told her about the meeting in greater detail. Aunt Enriqueta had stopped going to keep my mother company a few days ago: they had agreed that once the first mourning was over, as they called it, she'd pay the occasional visit and if she needed her company, she could send her a note via the errand boy or conductor on the local bus service that went to Vic two or three times a day.

Aunt Enriqueta sat at the table and listened carefully to every word her big sister uttered. When she finished, she stood up and shouted in a voice that shook with repressed rage: "So what did you expect poor Florència to say in the state she's in?"

Her reaction surprised everybody in the kitchen.

"What do you mean?" asked Aunt Ció, taken aback. "We addressed everything we had to address and reached an agreement, what's wrong with that?"

"Have you forgotten what these masters of ours are like?" retorted Aunt Enriqueta, as if it was an issue they'd argued about before. "Quirze and you have spent years complaining about the conditions they impose on you, that you are tied to the land like donkeys, and now you bow and scrape before everything they suggest. They are a couple of damned parasites on the poor, and you know that only too well."

"This is different..." replied Aunt Ció in self-defence, "it's something that isn't connected to our situation."

"You should have done what Lluís and Florència did years ago: leave the land and fuck off to town, to the factory, earn a guaranteed wage and none of your head-aches... Do you think Bernat or young Quirze will put up with all you've put up with?"

"As if it's been a bed of roses in town. They've relied on us for their hot meals every day... And I don't say that resentfully, God forbid, we've done everything we've done out of love, but don't you say it's all gone smoothly for them because it hasn't, not in their case, or in Fonso's, and who knows where he is now, and if it hadn't been for the shelter they found in this house..."

"The war did for them," agreed Aunt Enriqueta in a more conciliatory tone but as firmly as ever. "Those are things that didn't depend on them, but what about the way they took off in the first few years? Don't you remember how we envied them? Lluís and Fonso were about to be made may-ors in their respective villages! And if the war hadn't caught them, they'd both be laughing at us here and now!"

Grandmother stopped knitting and listened attentively as they argued. Cry-Baby and I sat frowning next to her, by her knitting basket, and pretended we weren't listening. The grownups were arguing in front of us, yet again. The only precaution they took was to suppress names or words that were too familiar, too loaded, and their words floated in the air, hazy and inconclusive, giving their squabbles the aura of an unfinished story we had to round off in our imaginations. A hollowness separated our two worlds, a space like an empty chamber where the air got colder or hotter depending on the temperature or the interest in the issue at stake and the tone of voice. In my view, Aunt Enriqueta's reaction was incomprehensible, in Cry-Baby's too, as I could tell from the look on her face. Perhaps, I thought, it showed how that hollow void was bigger than I suspected, much more significant than we realized, like those islands of ice that only reveal the peak of the mountain hidden under the water.

"Blasted politics..." mumbled Grandmother without looking up, "it was blasted politics that brought on the war."

The two sisters shut up to allow Grandmother to speak. Both turned round to look at her, sitting on her pew and listening. It was more out of respect than any readiness to heed what she said.

"Politics is a very confusing business and maybe they weren't ready to get as involved in it as they did. We were in no position to keep them in school, and ignorance is the mother of all evil."

"Don't say that, Mother," said Enriqueta, as combative as ever, "both sides had their educated and non-educated. And some who'd never crossed the doorstep of a school made it to general... Effort and courage also count for something."

"Don't, love," Grandmother insisted, "things would have turned out very differently if they'd all had a good profession. Idee-as..." She used to say "idee-as." We all spoke like her. But we never spoke about idee-as. "Idee-as...idee-als from what I've read, I gather idee-as have as much or more power than weapons, and the hotheads we had to listen to were donkeys with only one idee-a in their heads, and that was to put an end to the grief in their bellies, and they could only repeat party slogans and trot out fantasies, just like the clergy now and the blue shirts..."

Grandmother stopped, and the two sisters waited a second before resuming their bickering, now in a less strident, calmer tone.

"That's why it's so important for someone in the family to get some schooling," concluded Aunt Ció. "Not everyone can study, or has the brain to do so."

"I don't know what's got into you," Aunt Enriqueta wasn't relenting, "to make you think that schooling is the solution to everything. Lots of people get rich now, from black-marketeering or smuggling, and they don't have any schooling. And all the old soldiers who work in the town halls and unions and the regime's offices don't have a diploma between them and only know how to wave a pistol... And they are the ones giving out the orders!"

"I don't understand where you're going with this..." said Aunt Ció, sorrowfully.

"I don't want to go anywhere. It's only that I'm amazed the way you jump to orders from masters who only want to keep you tied to the land, *their* land, forever. Don't count on me, or, I reckon, on Bernat to follow suit! Any day now he'll land a job in Vic or a small town, and you'll be left on your own with Jan and a couple of hands. And young Quirze will do the same when he sees the kind of life he can expect."

The two women turned to look at Grandmother, then shut up. Grandmother had picked up her needles and was knitting head down, as if she wasn't hearing a thing.

"Now's not the time to talk about all this," said Aunt Ció, seeming to want to put an end to the argument.

"Quirze has got other things on his mind, and we can't pile any more on him. It was as much he could do to go upstairs and put on a performance for the masters. And haven't Mr. and Mrs. Manubens behaved considerately given the hue-and-cry we've had here… in all the time we've had the water up to our necks? Have they ever said anything or interfered with us, or asked whether we were on this side or that, or held against us what Lluís and Fonso got up to during the war? And they weren't exactly shrinking violets! Even though they, the masters, that is, were persecuted and forced to go into hiding, like so many in the war! Not a single word of recrimination! Not *one* word! They said nothing, even at the time!"

"Because they didn't know what the score was here. If they'd have known, we'd soon have seen how they reacted…" started Aunt Enriqueta, but then she suddenly broke off. She gently leaned her body to one side, as if she wanted to grab a chair to sit on, and Ció, who was opposite her, with her back to the kitchen door, looked at her, speechless. Until, a moment later, she swung round and saw Uncle Quirze poised in the doorway, quiet and still as a mannequin, his face red and his eyes aflame.

None of us budged and finally Uncle Quirze stepped forward, hands in pockets, staring at Aunt Enriqueta, who kept her head down and said nothing.

"We were saying…" stammered Aunt Ció, apologetically, as if trying to draw a veil over the argument. "Enriqueta knew nothing about the boy's schooling… she's been away a few days keeping Florència company…"

But Dad Quirze wasn't listening. Keeping his eyes on Aunt Enriqueta, he took two more steps forward, until he was standing next to his wife. Aunt Enriqueta looked up and now looked sadly at him, as if regretting everything she'd said, but then she stiffened her back and prepared to meet the onslaught. Keeping his hands firmly in his pockets, as calm as could be, in a determined, harsh voice,

Uncle Quirze said: "So we should be off to live in the factory town, should we?"

Aunt Enriqueta said nothing, was deathly silent in the middle of the kitchen. Aunt Ció walked quickly over to where Grandmother, Cry-Baby and I were, as if she wanted to protect us: "Don't react like a bull to a red rag. It was only her way of talking."

But Uncle Quirze appeared to ignore her, as if he'd not heard what she'd said. He waited a moment and then launched into Aunt Enriqueta: "As far as I know, we chain nobody to this house, nobody is here under compulsion and if someone reckons they'll be treated better somewhere else, the doors are open and they can clear off when they want to run, no need to wait a minute longer, nobody will stand in their way.

"Drop it," begged Aunt Ció, helping Grandmother to tidy away her wool and needles. "It's not worth devoting another second to it. They were idle comments. Talk for talk's sake."

Aunt Enriqueta's voice seemed tinnier, more strident than usual, though not at all weak or fearful. She spoke resolutely: "And why can't we say that these masters screw us for as much as they can, and that you'd be much better off in town, in a factory, in any job in fact, with more free time and a regular wage? The tenants in La Bruguera have already left, and the ones in Can Tona are thinking about it, and at least they have stood up to their masters."

"All this only makes people restless and unhappy at home. Makes them dream that outside their farm, in any town or city the streets are paved with gold and all is fine and dandy. The La Bruguera folk will do what they want and so will the Can Tona crew, everybody knows what's wrong there and how they've got to get their act together. Have the people in La Bruguera ever helped you, or the masters or tenants in Can Tona for that matter?"

"I'm not saying..."

"No, you say the first fucking thing that comes into your head, you never think, you do your own thing, as if you were the queen, and to hell with everyone else."

"I never said that."

"But that's how you act. Where's the dank flat in some town in the back of beyond that could take all of us—old'uns, kids, uncles and aunts—the whole tribe? Has it ever crossed your mind how so far everyone has fitted in this place, where you have lived and done whatever you wanted, and how we've helped everyone leave who's come here because they had nowhere else to go and never sent them off without a full basket?"

Grandmother had stood up and Ció accompanied her to the door. Cry-Baby and I followed, not really understanding what was happening. I saw it as yet one more landslide in the slow collapse of that world after Father's death. Like a change triggering more changes when nobody knows when it will end or what the final landscape will look like. For a second, I thought that Mr. and Mrs. Manubens's welcoming proposal might offer an escape from a universe that was going under. A bolthole. The soothing calm of an alien abode that could protect me from these people who were changing like the world around them, adults I understood less by the day.

"So I've only done what I pleased, have I?" repeated Aunt Enriqueta, becoming increasingly aggressive. "So I've only done what I fancied, have I? Haven't I worked and helped every way I could and for whatever end, haven't I done my stint at the seamstress's and in the house when it suited?"

"When it suited *you*," it was now Dad Quirze's turn to seem calmer and more poised. "You've lived your life and gone to and fro doing what you wanted and we never said a word, it was your life and that was an end to it, someday you would marry Pere Màrtir and feather your nest elsewhere, we've not interfered in what you earned or what you spent, we helped you save a little on the side because when you leave here Grandmother and us won't be able to give you a dowry, so you could set up on your own if you wanted, if Pere Màrtir agreed…, but Pere Màrtir is too easygoing, Pere Màrtir has waited too long to put the reins on you, now Pere Màrtir hasn't a clue which hand to play…, and you've fooled around with him, with us, and with the first comer who lifted your skirt up, and if he wore a uniform, better still, you fucking whore…and now you think we should follow advice from you, whether the masters are this or that or beyond the pale, whether we should all move to town, as there's no future for us here, and now Andreu should say no to the offer they're making? Are you right in the head? Have you got a screw loose? Aren't you muscling in where it's none of your business? What should we have done, in your book, shut the door in the masters' face the second they showed up our doorstep, pour a bucket of boiling water over them from the gallery when they got out of their car, tell them that we're fine, that neither we nor Florència would accept anything from them and that the boy can study on his own account because we've got more than enough money, we've had a good turn up for the books and our pockets are full? Is that what you're saying we should have done, you little scatterbrain?"

Aunt Ció whimpered silently while she led Grandmother by the arm into the upstairs sitting room. Cry-Baby and I followed them, our ears glued to the kitchen and the words and sounds shooting out from there. We stopped briefly at the foot of the stairs for Aunt Ció to pick up the oil-lamp and light it. They were rationing electricity again. Grandmother said nothing, pretending she couldn't hear a thing. She kept her head down, held her knitting basket on her arm, and seemed older and more hunchbacked than ever. Aunt Ció spoke quietly, put her head next to Grandmother's: "This was always going to happen," Grandmother nodded. Aunt Ció added: "That Enriqueta pushed her luck too far."

While we walked upstairs extremely slowly, keeping pace with Grandmother, we could still clearly hear the shouting in the kitchen.

"You're clever enough to know what you should or shouldn't be doing. How come poor me has to give advice to you, the brain-box?" Aunt Enriqueta seemed quieter now she'd been told a few home truths. "Apparently, there's nothing you don't know. You know who I should marry, who I should befriend, who I should be seen out with, perhaps even who I should be courting. You know everything there is to know."

"As if you ever waited for us to tell you which man was right for you!" Uncle Quirze had lost his temper and seemed more and more annoyed, on the point of losing it completely. "We should have put the leash on you before your goings-on became the talk of the town!"

"What on earth do you mean? Did you want me to spend my whole day sewing and washing like crazy? What about all the times I've taken the washing to the fountain, loaded down like a donkey, with baskets of dirty clothing belonging to the reapers, threshers and all that rabble you hire every summer, and you never came once to offer me a single drop of cold water? Don't tell me that was the kind of toil that suited me! Did you ever worry about who I went out with or was seeing when I was next to that fountain working like a mule? You were as silent as the grave because that's what suited *you*, it wasn't costing you a day-labourer's wage, everything was wonderful and you turned a blind eye…"

"Forget all this crap!Ció does that all year and never gives a peep."

"Ció isCió and I am me. And Mad Antònia is mad Antònia. I don't want to end up like her. I haven't married you, or Pere Màrtir, or anyone…yet. And in case you didn't know, I'm not planning to stay shut up in this place like some dowdy spinster kowtowing to every order and waiting for my bridegroom to be brought to me on a tray, overcooked, tasteless, with lots of gravy and condiments so I can't tell he's seconds. I'll choose my own, thank you very much, and if I don't like the one who's chasing me, I'll find somebody else, and if he knows how to lift up my skirt, that'll be a big improvement on those dreamy-eyed dolts who can't make up their minds to ask you for the first dance."

"Don't muddy the waters, it won't do you a scrap of good."

"And don't you make me talk about Pere Màrtir, because I know what I know now, and you don't know if butter wouldn't melt in his mouth or if he's a Johnny-come-lately. And when it comes to uniforms, you're on even rockier ground, because you'll never appreciate the favour Canary did us when he alerted us to everything..."

"Fonso is your brother, in case you've forgotten..."

Their voices faded in the sitting room. Aunty Ció sat Grandmother in a chair and before going back to the kitchen she told us stay with her: "I'm going to separate them, they're like little kids... They're arguing over nothing, and it won't solve a blind thing."

We sat on the floor next to Grandmother's armchair for a while, with the gallery door open and the dark of night before us. My aunt and uncle's shouting match reached us from downstairs, now joined by Aunt Ció, but we couldn't make out a word of what was being said. We stayed silent and still opposite the pitch-black outside. The orchard's fruit trees were silhouetted against the night and farther away the dense woods melded into the same shadows. A warm breeze blew in, and seemed full of small specks, perhaps dust from the threshing floor.

We were stunned by the presence of Quirze who'd come up to the sitting room unnoticed by us. He stood straight-backed by the side of Grandmother who put her hand around his waist, as if she wanted to lean on him, as if he were a stick or tree-trunk, and she whispered words we strained to hear: "Ay, Quirze, my lad! Lucky you and I are still here to keep this place going. In the end everybody will be off and only you and your parents and the odd hand will stay, if they last out, I'm sure Jan will but I wouldn't bet on Bernat. Lucky I'll have you to the end of my days. Who can I rely on, Quirze, if not you, Quirze?"

Quirze said nothing as if he'd not heard what she'd said. Grandmother sighed and added: "War rots everything, that's what Father Tafalla says, and he's right. Blasted war spares nothing, saves nobody, simply kills…and…everybody scattered to the four corners…brother and sisters, sons and daughters, grandchildren…flung all over the shop, like thunder, lightning and hail that leaves not one plant standing."

We noticed how Grandmother was squeezing Quirze tight around his waist because he stooped slightly forward and his shirt wrinkled where her hand pressed tightly. But he said nothing, not a word, and seemed as serious as ever. Cry-Baby and I looked up to see what was happening, and Grandmother's eyes met ours and she smiled, as she always did, she always laughed in the end and that effort she made calmed us down, nothing could be that bad if she could turn it into a joke: "Even the goblins have scarpered, my children," she laughed, "even they have cleared off to get a breath of fresh air, and now you see how old and rickety this big house is if the goblins, water maidens and witches don't want to hide here. Everyone must do what they must do, must make their own path in life, must soldier on…it's a law of life."

Then Cry-Baby asked timidly, as if she knew she was crossing a forbidden frontier: "Won't the goblin ever come out again, Grandmother? Won't we ever see him again at night?"

"You will, my dear," she laughed again, as if her sadness and sorrow had suddenly evaporated. "Of course, you'll see the goblin again. Not here, because he's already left, but you'll be seeing him again—somewhere else."

"Where? Whereabouts?" my cousin reacted in surprise until she grasped the kind of riddle Grandmother had invented: "Oh, I get it now! In the woods, I'll see him in the woods, in the depths of the forest, in the darkest depths!"

Grandmother laughed again, as if cheered up by her little game, and replied: "We… Now you say that, I reckon it will be some time before he's back. Goblins like a quiet life and flee houses and places where people shout and bicker. They want to be the centre of attention, and that means it's harder to catch sight of them, especially when there's squabbling, that's when they're quick to scarper!"

"And will only *I* be able to see him?" Cry-Baby seemed hooked on the game. "Won't Andreu be able to see him? And what about Quirze? Or Oak-Leaf?"

"You poor little jenny-wren!" said Quirze keeping stock-still. "Oak-Leaf isn't one of ours anymore. They've put Oak-Leaf out to work. You can bet she has no time for ghosts now. And, as far as I go, I don't want to see anything. Father says I needn't go back to school if I don't want."

"So now I'll have to go to the Novíssima by myself?" Cry-Baby asked fearfully. "Every day? All by myself? Oak-Leaf says nasty things happen in the woods."

"Oak-Leaf is out of her mind," Quirze interrupted, "and a liar. Don't you know everything she said was stupid nonsense? She never saw anything in the woods, and never met anyone either."

Quirze's voice was unwavering. I sensed he was starting to align himself with the grownups, in particular with his father, who divided people and the world into two halves, the good side that supported him, and the bad side that didn't. Everything was black or white, there were no greys, no in-betweens. How could he say that when we all knew some of those things had turned out to be true?

"What about the dead horse then?" asked Cry-Baby, as if she'd read my thoughts, "and the civil guards?"

"Are you still scared of the civil guards, you ninny?" Quirze laughed, but he was play-acting, not for his benefit, but to make fun of her. "If you see them walk by, just ask them to go with you and that will be that."

"Now that dead horse was a very strange business," interjected Grandmother. "There are thieves and Republican soldiers who cross the border and come to steal... Perhaps Grandfather Hand will tell us something eventually, when he comes."

Our conversation had made us forget the quarrelling in the kitchen. Aunt Ció's voice, from the lobby, at the foot of the stairs, brought us right back to it.

"Quirze!" shouted Aunt Ció who we could tell was really angry. "Come down right now, Quirze, you've got to run to the monastery."

"Right now?" he whelped, wearily. "At this time of night the monks are all asleep!"

"Shut up and come down at once if you don't want your father to tell you!"

Quirze muttered and grumbled his way downstairs. We remained still and silent to see if we heard more voices. But we heard nothing else until Quirze was halfway down and Aunt Ció hurried him up with another exclamation that sounded odd from her lips: "And don't you answer me back unless you want a good hiding!"

Then we heard her at the foot of the stairs telling him in a more subdued tone to fetch Father Tafalla from the Saint Camillus monastery, and to ring the little bell for the sick that's by the front door, because they always have someone on standby in case they needed to rush off and give the last rites to someone who is dying.

36

Grandmother bade her time, until the figure of Quirze at full pelt disappeared around the corner of the house and the noise of squabbling voices in the kitchen became barely audible once again, and so remote it might have been restless animals in their stable.

"Perhaps we should all go to bed," said Grandmother limply, as if we ought to be doing something.

"Before we've had dinner?" asked Cry-Baby, who really didn't seem to feel the tension in the air.

"Are you very hungry?" smiled Grandmother. "Because I reckon the hottest thing at suppertime tonight will be the kitchen sink. We'll have to eat grass. The oven's not for lighting. Anyone want to test out that saying—sleep on an empty stomach, dream of the dead and gone?"

Cry-Baby scowled in disgust and wasn't exactly overjoyed at going to bed so early on an empty stomach.

"You know what we could do?" asked Grandmother, as if she'd had a brainwave. "Andreu, you find your way downstairs and fetch a light from the kitchen..."

I didn't budge because I wasn't thrilled at the idea of returning to the kitchen if I didn't know what kind of reception I would get. I imagined Dad Quirze's face and those cold, hard eyes that looked as if they could sting, strip and nail you to the ground in front of him. Dad Quirze rarely argued, his gaze had been enough to get his way on the few occasions I'd seen him row or shout at someone, it only needed a couple of insults or snarls from him to crush anybody who tried to cross him. That's why I thought the row in the kitchen that night was quite out of the ordinary. Something terrible must have happened, something unspeakable, some dreadful, dark deed had undermined Dad Quirze's taciturn sullenness and made him go red with rage and raise his voice to his sister-in-law. A part of the obscure, hidden magma of the adult world had revealed itself in that outburst triggered quite fortuitously, on a minimal pretext, like a small crack that leaks liquid from a full tank, and it was all my fault, because of the visit paid by Mr. and Mrs. Manubens, the masters, who were opening their powerful wings to protect me. What else lay behind all I'd seen and heard?

"What do you think, lad?" persisted Grandmother.

However, before I could respond, we heard someone on the stairs, and a light getting ever closer and brighter. Aunt Ció was coming up to the sitting room with a smelly carbide lamp.

"What are you all doing here in darkness?" she asked, her voice calmer now voice, as if the earthquake was over and done with. "Don't you want any dinner?"

"We were only just talking about that…" said Grandmother, hesitantly. "I couldn't care less. But these two tummies have been rumbling for some time."

"It will be ready in a jiffy," Aunt Ció put the light down on the old sideboard. "Can you wait a minute? Andreu, you come down with me and have a bite to tide you over. They do say the longer you wait the better it tastes. Empty guts, down in the dumps."

She said that in an amusing fashion but we weren't in the least amused. You could tell it was forced, an expression that didn't fit the situation or moment. I reluctantly levered myself up from the floor and stood next to Aunt Ció.

"We've gone to get Father Tafalla," said Aunt Ció, slightly changing her tone, before she left, as if she would be sorry to go without passing on the latest news about what was happening downstairs. "He always gives good advice."

"At this time of night?" Grandmother asked, rather surprised. "Won't they think someone's fallen ill and is on their last legs?"

"No, we can rely on him, and when he sees Quirze, he'll understand."

Aunt Ció looked round and said: "Come down and fetch something."

I followed her silently to the kitchen. She only made one comment in a hushed tone, that I didn't really understand, as if she'd said "as we will see," or "let's wait and see," or some expression of the sort.

My legs were almost shaking with fear at the idea of confronting Uncle Quirze's rabid expression and Aunt Enriqueta's half defiant, half phlegmatic stance. However, Aunt Enriqueta was alone in the kitchen, sitting at one end of the table, arms folded, head lowered, as if she was waiting for someone. Uncle Quirze wasn't there.

"Andreu is going to take something upstairs for Grandmother and the little girl," said Aunt Ció, opening drawers and taking a plate from the rack, and she spoke blankly, as if duty-bound towards her sister, or as though she was apologizing for turning her back on her or making a friendly gesture. "A couple of pans of milk perhaps."

Then I noticed that Aunt Enriqueta was crying. She was crying silently, her tears hidden behind her loose hair and bowed head. You could tell she was crying by the way her body shook and her hands rubbed her eyes.

"Andreu, love…" I heard her say and my heart leapt as if suddenly someone was about to blame me for everything that had happened.

Aunt Ció swung round, surprised. Aunt Enriqueta looked up, and her red eyes stared at my face: "Don't take it badly…what I said wasn't about you. We all want you to continue with your schooling and go to university, whatever it takes. It was just that I was sorry I couldn't help you more now your father isn't here, and that between us we can't find you what you need. I'd have been so pleased to help you… we… your mother…"

Her sobs choked the words in her throat and Aunt Ció went to give her a cuddle, as she said: "Love, Andreu knows that… He will think it over, you've seen how we've helped them as much as we could, I mean, everybody, Núria, him, the brothers and sisters, everybody. Don't worry, he didn't hear a thing, you didn't hear a thing, did you, Andreu?

I shook my head.

"They were upstairs with Grandmother," continued Aunt Ció, returning to the kitchen range.

I didn't know what to do or say. A wave of red-hot fire seared me from chest to face. I was stranded in the middle of all that, and felt similar to how I'd felt some time ago at home when I overheard the conversation between Aunt Felisa and Mother, her sister's laments, doubts and the fear aroused by a giant of a man—that's how I imagined the widower, from what they'd said—they wanted to marry her off to. I'd registered, if rather hazily, though it was much clearer now, that Aunt Felisa's panic stemmed from her ignorance of the new role awaiting her that provoked appalling fear, a sense of inevitability and frustration at being unable to flee the trap they'd set her. I intuited that Aunt Enriqueta was facing the same situation and same trap, with a similar fear. I knew perfectly well what she'd said about my schooling wasn't behind her tears or anxiety. Why would they have rushed to get Father Tafalla, if I and my future had been the reason for the confrontation? Images of Pere Màrtir and the naked youth with TB beneath the elm loomed at the back of my mind, I didn't exactly know why, as if they were responsible or even saviours with respect to the misunderstandings that had arisen like the small spark that had lit a conflagration, or perhaps they came to mind to protect me and indicate an escape route with their silent example.

"Take all that and carry it up to the sitting room," said Aunt Ció, placing a tray of biscuits, chocolate and three bowls of milk in my hands. "If you want more or need something else, give me a shout. Off you go now! Take the candle too."

Before leaving the kitchen I tried to make eye contact with Aunt Enriqueta, as if to say goodbye, but her head sank down and her eyes stared vacantly.

I slowly climbed the stairs, frightened I might fall with the candle dangling from one of my hands that supported the tray.

Grandmother had got up and she told me to put the tray on the sewing table in the gallery. We all three sat on the bench facing the fruit orchard, and Cry-Baby started dunking biscuits in her milk, I did likewise and Grandmother still said she wasn't hungry. We stayed silent for a time, until we heard somebody running towards the house.

It was Quirze, who ran into the house without glancing at the balustrade where Cry-Baby and I were standing, our mouths full.

"Sit down, sit down…" Grandmother urged. "Quirze will be here any minute and we can go to bed right away."

"Won't anyone else be coming?" asked Cry-Baby.

"Father Tafalla will take his time, that is, if he comes," replied Grandmother. "He's the only one who doesn't go out at night to give the last rites to the dying. He tells the other monks to go. And as he informed us one day, he advises them not to hurry when it's their turn, to take their time getting up if they are in bed, to give their faces a good wash to wake themselves up and dress properly against the cold if it's winter or the heat if it's summer… And when we asked him why he took it so calmly, what if they didn't hurry and arrived at the sick person's bedside when he'd already cocked his toes up, he replied that families who sent out an alarm call in the middle of the night would have had days, weeks and even months to ask a priest to bring the dying individual the last rites, Eucharist and unguents, but they always did it in a rush at untimely hours because they were slothful and apathetic and didn't altogether believe in the healing power of the sacrament; for them the Eucharist or extreme unction were like the last port of call, the end, the final farewell, the last sacraments that meant nothing else could be done, and that's why they waited until the very last moment and it never occurred to them that the Saint Camillus community also dealt with bodily health, doctors of bodies and souls, healers and curers, and when they came to the bed of the dying they should have clear heads so as to decide whether to call a doctor, take the sick to hospital or give them an injection, if that was in order, so they couldn't be half-asleep, or risk exposing themselves to catching cold or to gusty winds and return to the monastery ill themselves, every monk was needed, they had lots of work and couldn't fall sick or give up their toil in the monastery or outside, because the convent is also a hospital full of ill…"

Grandmother rambled on, rather deliriously, as if she was afraid of the silence that would start to pressurize us if she shut up and was afraid of what we might ask Quirze now he was back.

She did shut up when Cry-Baby said: "Someone else is coming."

My cousin and I couldn't stop ourselves from looking over the balustrade. We heard the footsteps and chatter of two people wearing surplices who walked into the house.

"There's two of them," Cry-Baby told Grandmother.

Grandmother waited for a moment before she spoke. First she closed her eyes out of exhaustion, and then said: "Priests never go out alone, they always take a companion, like civil guards. As our Quirze can't accompany them when they go back…"

"But Quirze went and came all by himself," commented Núria knowingly.

"He's different. Our Quirze is like a cat that sees in the dark and knows every turning. The monks are more fragile. It's another kind of male."

Quirze appeared in the gallery doorway, leaned on the frame, staring silently inside.

"Sit down, lad," Grandmother urged him. "Have something to eat."

But he said he wasn't hungry, that he was tired and was going to bed.

No sounds or words reached us from the kitchen. As if the two visitors had melted away. We waited for a while, unsure what to do or say. We nibbled away in silence and now and then Grandmother took deeper breaths, as if she was sighing, her eyes open wide but looking at nothing. When she finally stood up she seemed more tired than usual and told us to leave our scraps on the tray, right there on the table, that we could take all that to the kitchen in the morning. She told Cry-Baby to take the lamp, that I didn't need it, and they went to their bedroom. I went to the hands' bedroom, which is where Quirze was.

The sitting room was in darkness and I had to feel my way out. Quirze wasn't asleep, I could tell because he kept tossing and turning in bed. I stripped off, as quietly as I could. Then, lying on the bed, I waited to see if my cousin said anything, but he just kept turning over like one big bag of nerves.

I didn't really get to sleep that night. When I did start to doze off, something woke me up and left me weary-eyed, with my mind racing. Quirze's turns, the creaking doors and windows, the dogs' barking...the slightest noise woke me up. I tried to block out what was happening in the kitchen and whether the visitors were still there or had left, but I couldn't and they were all present in the recesses of my brain, sitting around the long table, and I wondered what on earth was happening and why the Saint Camillus pair had come here in the middle of the night, as if some misfortune had blighted the house, and how come you couldn't hear any shouting.

Suddenly, when I had sunk into a black hole of sleep, a body shaking next to mine woke me up. Alarmed, I opened my eyes and saw the shadow of Quirze sitting on the bed, with the sheets at his feet and the palms of his hands splayed either side of his legs, as if he was afraid of falling.

"Do you hear that?" he asked, gaze averted, as if he was talking to himself.

I looked up. At the very first I heard nothing. Moments later, I heard a noise in the sitting room. And very gentle whispers, like a hand caressing silk. Then, the noise faded, I imagined as they went downstairs. I knew that Uncle Bernat and the hands hadn't come to sleep there because in summer they preferred to stay in the barn or village where they were free to do what they wanted. And Jan had his cave—what he called his cave—next to the stables, with his belongings, where he didn't want anyone sticking their noses inside.

Silence fell over the house again. Quirze turned round and repeated his question: "Did you hear something then?"

It came from the front entrance. It sounded like a door slamming but the dogs weren't barking or anything. And then right away, a distant noise, outside the farmhouse, as if they were chopping up the elder tree. I thought I could also hear the wind whistling through the woods, as if it were a comb parting the leaves and small branches to one side. I imagined the tops of the trees bending over driven by the gusts, huffing, as Grandmother said, or puffing.

"Wait," said Quirze, standing up.

Barefoot and wearing only the patched underpants they forced us to wear, made from yarn they brought from the factory, which we took off in summer because we got overheated, Quirze opened the door cautiously, and disappeared into the pitch-black sitting room. I waited on my bed, my ears straining to hear what my cousin was doing and where he was heading. But time passed and I heard nothing. My naked feet felt like cotton wool. My eyes bulged wide open, as if my forceful gaze could penetrate the darkness. I didn't know whether I should get up and rush to my friend's side. He'd not asked me to do anything, and I wasn't sure whether my impulse to follow him was curiosity or merely a wish to imitate him and do as he did—be determined, daring, fearless and unabashed.

When I was about to get up, Quirze came in with the same expression as when he'd left. He stretched out on his bed panting and waving his legs in the air, as if he were kicking out at an invisible enemy. I waited for him to calm down, then asked: "What…?"

Quirze took his time, as if he were deciding whether to tell me or not. In the end he spoke in a deadpan tone, as if passing on news that was neutral, that didn't affect anyone: "Aunt Enriqueta has beat it."

I didn't know what to say or how to react. I stretched out next to him, bewildered, and said the first thing that came into my head: "But why…? What happened? Where's she gone?"

Now he did respond immediately: "Didn't you cotton on? She couldn't wait any longer. She's gone and that's all there is to it. They'll tell us why in the morning."

"How do you know she's gone? What did you see?"

Quirze turned his back on me, to indicate he wanted to sleep.

"Why has she left?" I persisted.

"Let me get some sleep. We'll find out tomorrow."

"How did *you* find out? Did you see Father Tallafa and the other friar?"

"I've seen nobody. My parents are in the kitchen by themselves and they are still chatting. Grandmother got up and is in the rocking chair, but she's not rocking, she's crying. And Aunt Enriqueta isn't in her room, she's not touched her bed and her chests of drawers are all empty."

I didn't dare ask anything else. I shut my eyes and tried to imagine the scenes Quirze had described. Why hadn't I noticed what even Quirze had got a whiff of? What had he meant when he'd asked if I'd not yet cottoned on? What exactly had I missed? Cry-Baby had clearly missed it as well, because if she'd noticed anything strange she'd have told me.

Then, as night proceeded, I began to think how of late, since Father's death, Aunt Enriqueta hadn't set foot in the house; after working at the seamstress's, she went to my home in town and kept my mother company. It was inevitable I didn't cotton on, because she was never here, Aunt Enriqueta never even came to have supper with us.

Or perhaps, a little light started to flash, as Grandmother used to say, in fact, perhaps that was why what had happened had happened, but if that was the case, how come Quirze had cottoned on?

When the cracks in the door and window shutters began to show up in the dark, with the first hesitant light of dawn, I fell asleep.

37

When I woke up, Quirze was no longer at my side. Light was now streaming through the cracks brightly enough to illuminate the whole bedroom. These were the last days of the school year, and Cry-Baby and I ate breakfast in silence, while Aunt Ció served us, looking glum and saying nothing. Grandmother was still in her bedroom and I didn't dare ask whether or not she'd soon be down. She sometimes waited for Aunt Ció to go up and comb her hair so could leave her room all spic and span, as she put it. The men, Quirze included, had gone off to the fields long ago.

"Off you go!" Aunt Ció bid us farewell. "And don't dally on the way, or the teacher will start crying."

I found it odd our aunt was in a mood to say these things you usually say to young kids or when you want to crack a little joke.

Cry-Baby and I walked for a while, not exchanging a word. When we were round the first bend and the house disappeared behind the woods, I asked her: "What happened last night? Were you asleep all the time?"

"For a bit. But I woke up when Grandmother got up to talk to Aunt Enriqueta."

"What happened?"

"I don't know. I was half-asleep while they were whispering to each other. Then Aunt Enriqueta came over and kissed me. And Grandmother stayed in her rocking chair because she couldn't get back to sleep."

"Was Aunt Enriqueta by herself? What was she carrying?"

My cousin looked at me as if she didn't understand my question.

"What do you mean, what was she carrying?"

"Suitcases or bundles of clothes."

"Oh, I didn't notice." After a while, when she saw I didn't persist, she piped up: "Oh, now I get you! Are you asking me because Quirze went to fetch Father Tafalla? Do you mean did I see the two friars? She was by herself. I saw nobody else."

"The Saint Camillus friars must have returned to the monastery, I suppose."

I knew more than she did. But for the moment I decided to tell her nothing, until I'd found out more. If what Quirze had said was true, they couldn't conceal Aunt Enriqueta's departure for much longer.

At school, Mr. Madern, the teacher, read us a story from a reading book, the title of which was *The Last Lesson*, one about the last lesson a teacher gives to pupils in a rural school, like ours, in a French province that had become German because of a war the French had lost—I couldn't decide if it was the world war with the allies or fascists that preoccupied Grandmother so much or a previous war—and the teacher in the story, a Frenchman, was forced to leave the school because a German was on his way and would change everything, starting with the French language, that he'd replace with German; I didn't understand how pupils and teachers could be at fault in the turmoil of that war, as if they were dead or wounded, or a mortar shell had fallen on the poor school, but I liked the story a lot because it moved me differently than the fireside tales about mischievous goblins, wondrous water-fairies or horrific crimes that Grandmother told, a new emotion flooded my heart and eyes with tears, one I'd never experienced before. Grandmother's yarns were full of mystery and aroused my imagination, conjuring up marvellous worlds that, even though I knew they didn't exist, seemed alive and fascinating in my mind and left an after-taste like happy memories of a journey to unknown places you had never dreamed of, of fantastical excursions; on the other hand, that story about the teacher seemed for real, was surely true, I could understand and empathize with it, it spoke of people like Mr. Madern and me, and the story seemed to tell us something about what happens when a war is lost, the evil wrought by all wars, even if wars, guns and battles were never mentioned, and I understood there were struggles that were just as important as those fought in the trenches and invisible weapons that damaged the brain and the soul, like the French teacher's sadness and his moving farewell, that also allowed me to glimpse the love the teachers felt for those forlorn children and the profound message embedded in their lessons, that didn't simply help to teach us how to read and write, as Quirze and Oak-Leaf and most of the pupils in the Novíssima or the parish school thought, just as the teacher-priest wasn't only teaching us the basics, but also wanted to make us good Christians, as he always said, which was why he obliged us go to mass and catechism, and I wondered why Mr. Madern was read-ing us that French teacher's farewell speech to his pupils, what in fact did he want to get from us, and suddenly the image filled my mind of Núria with her skirts rucked up, the gentle slope of her belly and the pink mystery of her slit, and I felt rage as heavy as a lead weight stir in my belly against Mr. Madern, and the pity and tears I was feeling because it was his last lesson vanished and I began to hope with gritted teeth, in a kind of curse, that German soldiers would come and kick their way into that school, destroy the dais and carry the teacher off as a prisoner, drag him over the floor and cover the blackboard with insults, swear words and jibes against the French and French *civilization*, the word Mr. Madern was reading at that very moment, the whole of one civilization under the boot, and I laughed and fought my tears and that feeling of weakness, out, out, out.

I was shocked to find such hateful rancour within me, it was like the discovery of sex, an unexpected discovery, bewildering and magnetic, convulsing my entire body, taking me out of myself and leading me to strange new places where it was hard to keep a grip on the reins of reason, like when Quirze taught me to ride a horse without a saddle, bare-back, when you didn't know if you could control the animal or where it would take you, yet at the same time, if you succeeded in taming and breaking it in, it gave you a magnificent sense of mastery over the world, of having all that strength and power in your hands, a communion between your upright, open body and the space around, that was transformed into the universe, the only one on the planet who counted, everything subject to your will, all power, all pleasure, all potency. All revenge.

I felt I ought to conceal that unexpected strength I'd just discovered on my last day at school, the final, true moral of the story, and use it when I needed to, at my convenience, just like sex, to help me keep away from my feelings the people I didn't like or who wished me ill—beware of those who wish you ill, Grandmother always advised me, though she never specified which ill or which individuals we should be wary of—and also of those who didn't fit my way of being or doing things, but above all it gave steely energy for self-defence, to forge breastplates of contempt and rejection against any who acted as my enemies, more secure, comforting protection than any good words and deeds I'd been taught in parish catechism classes, because it was a weapon that only depended on me, that nobody else had access to, I alone could recognize its potential and the determination impelling me to apply it.

I had to pretend: nobody must know I'd found that strength, like a solid, resistant rock within me I could produce when I wished, like the sexual secrets adults knew about and practised yet never mentioned, never spoke about in public, as if they didn't exist. A wave of satisfaction coursed through my body and I reflected how this new ability to hate, to stand up for myself and say no, even if only silently, was a huge step forward on the road towards the conquest of the outside world, towards growing up.

In that maze of thoughts, driven by the discovery of that hidden vein of unspent fury, I missed the end of the story about the French teacher giving his last lesson in the region of Alsace-Lorraine before he left the school in the hands of the German authorities, I think that's what Mr. Madern, our teacher, said, Alsace-Lorraine was the name of the provinces that had been lost, nor did I draw out the conclusion or moral—*Faules i moralitats* written by some canon or other and the *Catecisme de la Doctrina Cristiana* from the bishopric were the only books in Catalan I'd ever seen at school, remnants of the old town-hall library, the only ones saved from the bonfire they lit at the end of the war because almost all were on the list of books banned by the bishopric, written by atheist authors, *Autores buenos y malos* was a handbook the teacher-priest at the parish school used to consult and he laughed his head off when he mentioned the duly banned Don Impío Baroja and Don Miguel Unamierda, and the mere possession of such books at home, not even the act of reading them, led to immediate excommunication, *ipso facto* said the priest, *ipso flauto* we muttered, that meant expulsion from the brotherhood of all baptized Christians, they said, terrible grief that brought eternal condemnation simply for owning a book!, and lending it to someone else was even worse, because that was to lead a soul into perdition, as if you were murdering someone, and there was no forgiveness from God for that; consequently, I could only guess what our teacher Mr. Madern had meant to imply by reading us that story.

In my view, he'd wanted to say something about the task of the teacher, a kind of praise for the importance of teaching snotty kids—Grandmother sometimes called us snotty runts and said we stop being that when we cleaned away our snot and she occasionally referred to classes at the infant school as the snot-nose or dirty-pants brigade, and when somebody mentioned a word or phrase only approximately following the sound, as when someone in the village said intransigent for in transit, she said they spoke in snotty sounds or as it sounds, and I thought he was trying to establish continuity between his labours and those of the teacher who'd take his place, a little like the parish priests and Superiors of religious orders—Father Tafalla always said that—it didn't matter who stood before the parish or the community, or the school in this case, it was continuity and constancy in our work that counted, individuals came and went but institutions went on forever, institutions, a word I'd never heard used in either of my two schools, though it was always on the lips of priests in church, were *over and above* individuals, an expression I struggled to understand because I couldn't imagine what importance or what use a church or school could have without individuals, an obvious example was the hermitages scattered over the plain—where Saint George and Saint Francis had died by the small spring that appeared miraculously because the saint was dying of thirst when he walked past that spot, the Casserres monastery with the holy body of a child embalmed like a mummy, that they said was once a grandiose monastery, thronging with hundreds of monks and extremely influential in bygone times… What were they now if not abandoned, half-ruined, useless buildings, where solitary images of saints and Virgin Marys draped dirty, crumbling altars, cobwebby naves full of creepy-crawlies, sometimes transformed into animal pens or dung heaps…that without people, priests or a village were no use at all, were nothing at all, nonentities, mere relics of a dead past that had been buried forever?

What indeed would become of the very school we attended—la Novíssima—if all its pupils were moved to the national school in the nearby town? So what then did teachers and priests mean when they said there were things like institutions that were above individuals and more important than people? However, I think Mr. Madern, the teacher, had meant to say in his last lesson that the school still survived though the master who had given it life in those borderlands between France and Germany, Alsace-Lorraine, was now forced to leave, something I really didn't understand. There were things I didn't grasp, that I couldn't get my head round, and anything that went beyond the boundary of individuals was of no interest to me, and perhaps that was why I understood nothing I couldn't imagine as a person of flesh and blood. For example, when they spoke of justice, I always imagined judges and prisons with Father inside, when they spoke of wealth, I saw Mr. and Mrs. Manubens, the masters, or Napkin Lolita and the factory owners once a month dropping by their offices in their shiny new cars, when they spoke of illness, I always imagined the stark naked, languid youth lying in the heartsease garden, under the elm tree, and likewise with everything else. That was why I had great problems with religion, because I was beginning to suspect that everything I imagined when I heard priests talking about heaven, hell, God the Father, God the Son, God the Holy Spirit and the Most Holy Trinity, and the whole celestial gang—a phrase Dad Quirze used when he was swearing—didn't exist beyond First Communion prints or statues in church that bored me, I'd seen so much of them that even now I found they were caricatures or childish efforts, and I wondered: if there was something superior and more important than people, why did they represent heaven and hell everywhere with images that were only the faces of individuals who looked like figures straight out of a Bethlehem crib and who, if it weren't for their clothes, looked just like us? Where then was the institution they kept talking about if they couldn't make it visible without the help of people? They even explained eternity, such a hazy concept, by recourse to the figure of a child trying to empty out the sea with a small saucepan, and however many years and centuries the child spent extracting water, supposing that one day, when the boy was an old man and had spent his life, plus his children's, grandchildren's and great-grandchildren's, extracting water nonstop from the sea, they still wouldn't have scratched the surface of the time that eternity endured, that never ends, that we cannot conceive, that means forever and ever and ever. And if we cannot even conceive of the extent of eternity because it doesn't possess one, everything was eternity, was the ever more of ever more, how could that invention that went by the name of Institutions be at all important for flesh-and-blood individuals—Father in prison, the owners in their factories, the lad dying from TB in the monastery garden? What were Politics, the Church, Grandmother's *idee-as* and *idee-als*, the State, the Fatherland the teacher in Alsace-Lorraine defended in his last lesson…if not thoughts without bodily substance? If institutions couldn't live without individuals, how dare they say they were above flesh-and-blood men and women?

There was one other thing that worried me about the teacher's last lesson. It was an invention like eternity and that was why I regretted not paying enough attention so as to catch what he'd meant to say through that story of an expelled teacher giving his last lesson in the school in Alsace-Lorraine. It was the feeling of loss the French teacher experienced, a feeling, I understood from what our teacher Mr. Madern read, that wasn't limited to the fact he was being forced to leave his beloved school and change pupils and place, but referred to something much more profound and intense that, although I could account for it, I guessed was linked to the name of Alsace-Lorraine. Was Alsace-Lorraine lost because France lost the war, I wondered? No, it wasn't lost, it simply ceased to be French and began to be German. All that was lost was the French teacher and the pupils who liked him. But those who didn't like him, those who'd discovered he had a defect, a blemish, as Grandmother called it, an individual act of treachery, as I had with Mr. Madern, even if I thought he was a good teacher, why should they lament his departure so vociferously? At the end of the day the change was simply annoying and I thought the teacher's speech in his last lesson was overblown and self-interested.

Later on I reflected further about such issues and concluded that the problem arose when the different representations you were shown to help you understand the big concepts—institution, religion, justice, illness, wealth, poverty...—were mixed up with other images you didn't expect to be at all connected, yet if they appeared in your mind allied to those initial figures, though you hadn't summoned them on purpose, there was, in fact, a connection and this mix of images and concepts sent your head into spin, erased the boundaries of the representations and feelings they provoked, and that was the only way you could understand the sorrow of the French teacher in the Alsace-Lorraine school because his suffering over the loss of France was additional to his grief at being forced to abandon his work and all that became entangled with the image of my father's defeat, fixed forever in that last image I retained of him, skinny and unshaven in prison, and not only the failure of his side in the war, but the failure of his ideals, what Grandmother called *"idee-als"* and sometimes "blasted politics," and Mother would chip in with "stinking politics" and complain about Father getting stuck up to his neck in it, he'd paid dearly for that, said Mother, and that was the confusion present in the case of the French teacher defeated in war, mixed up with the figure of my father, another loser, both sidelined by blasted, stinking politics, something we had to abstain from and keep at a distance because it only brought headaches, sadness and appalling last lessons. In a way, it all made me think that the ills they suffered were their own fault: Father, for sticking his nose in where it wasn't wanted, and the French teacher, for choosing the losing side and remaining loyal, stubbornly so, to the French who hadn't even been able to defend a small rural school in Alsace-Lorraine.

Mr. Madern, the teacher, closed the storybook and gave us his commentary. His voice was hoarser than usual and he coughed to clear his throat two or three times before starting to speak. He kept homing in on me in particular, but I'd been thrown into turmoil by all those thoughts hitting me like waves of fury tempered by caution and the scrutiny of the new connections now rushing into my mind, and I didn't really understand my teacher's speech, or rather, I didn't want to, I didn't want to let myself be swayed by his words or to welcome them, now I had discovered the satisfaction of saying no, of refusing, of closure to the outside world and the pleasures of remaining embroiled in the twists, turns and combinations of my imaginative world.

"There are other stories in this book," said Mr. Madern, the teacher, "that I am sure you might like, like the one entitled 'The Tiny Florentine Scribbler,' or another by Juan Valera, 'The Mirror of Matsuyama,' but I chose this one because it describes a teacher bidding farewell to his pupils, and that's what we are experiencing here today. It is another country, and the teacher and pupils are different. But what is memorable is the legacy the teacher leaves behind, what he has taught them…"

He paused to clear his throat. He gave the impression he hadn't finished what he wanted to say or didn't know how to. So many twists and turns lost me, or perhaps the fact was I didn't want to listen to him, didn't and did, as Grandmother would say.

"Wars always leave a trail that lasts for years, that's a struggle to overcome and can sometimes be as hurtful as open warfare, but that period is drawing to an end… Some episodes… I mean, the war…"

I felt he was referring to me, but there may have been other cases among my schoolmates, "episodes," as he said, that only the teacher was aware of, and his message was aimed at everyone.

"I am sure you'll like the stories I mentioned before, I'm sure you'll like them if you read them carefully. You've got these two books and I'll add a couple more so the school can start a small library. Perhaps some of you will be able to continue your schooling elsewhere and will have to read a great deal. You will have other books and other teachers. However, most of you will stay and work in town or will travel to Vic or other towns on the plain, to find work. I'd hope you could all move on."

I began to pay more attention to the ebb and flow of my thoughts than to the teacher's vagaries. I wanted to rediscover that stream of anger that had flowed a moment ago so I could be sure I could unleash it whenever I wanted. It wasn't very hard, I only had to summon up the image of Cry-Baby clinging to the branch of the plum tree or sprawling in the deep shadows from the hazel-nut trees and a fire flamed in my chest and it was hard to conceal the burning I felt in my eyes, my neck and lips.

"The subject of all these stories is the same," Mr. Madern, the teacher, now continued, "men's struggle to move on, to overcome some mishap, to go forward... This struggle can sometimes be about knowing ourselves, about finding out who we really are, and that's what Juan Valera's story in the book is all about."

Quite spontaneously I flitted from the dense shadows in the hazel tree spinney to the heartsease garden, and visualized the figure of the naked boy with TB resting on his immaculate sheet, and I thought how my cousin's nudity and the sick boy's had a common source, one I still couldn't pinpoint, but I felt they were identical realities I could only express for the moment through words like beauty, emotion, curiosity, sickness, arousal, friendship...friendship, for sure, but not love, love was too grand and was out of my reach, friendship, for sure, and also companionship, closeness, attraction…the representation of love was still a blank, and I thought how love for one's country, for France, and Alsace-Lorraine, that the teacher had read about, was adult business, remote feelings, somewhat futile fantasies, like their hollow, lifeless institutions, but on the other hand thanks to Núria and the boy with TB, I now knew what beauty, emotion, sickness, longing and desire were and could thus in some way understand why Cry-Baby put up with the teacher's groping without complaining, even though she disliked it, just as the boy with TB disliked his sickness, but both said nothing, enclosed and protected by their pain, finding refuge in mystery, and this silence, this acceptance endowed them with a total, pure, definitive beauty, an aura of penitence and generosity that transcended beauty itself because it was beauty that had been sacrificed, was gratuitous, orphan, sacred abandonment to the desires of another—the teacher, sickness, the sunbathing, the shadow from the hazel trees… yielding to the desires they inspired and that made them more desirable, marble perfection like statues of Saint Lucia, her eyes offered up to everyone on a tray, Saint Sebastian, with his naked torso exposed to lethal arrows, staring into the sky, scorning the arrows of his executioners, exposed like the Holy Sacrament in the monstrance, or friar Saint Camillus of Lellis, bending over a half-naked, swooning, bloodstained leper who clung to his white habits.

"Things always return to their rightful place however much we mess with them, especially if a force exists that is determined to establish its order and impose its law," the teacher, Mr. Madern, now continued, with respect to something he'd said previously that I had missed. "The force of will, the force of things, the force of reason, the force of law, the force of truth, it's all the same, however you phrase it, force always win out in the short term or the long over misdeeds and secret conspiracies."

He spoke of misdeeds, secrets and mischief, and I thought this must be aimed at Cry-Baby, but my cousin in the back rows seemed half-asleep, bored by that rant. Núria's drowsy face, their secret and the name of France suggested the existence of an enemy. Till then I'd not thought of anybody as my enemy, at most there were nasty or scheming people I was at odds with, friends who were not so close or friends I didn't talk to, but as yet I'd had no out-and-out enemies. Mother had told me that Father had had some, and they were the cause of his misfortunes, of our downfall. I had seen Mother's rage when she attacked the four bigwigs, as she called them, and Grandmother, the fascists, on our way out of the cemetery the day Father was buried. But those were *their* enemies, my father's or my mother's, not *my* enemies. I didn't know how one was supposed to deal with an enemy. There had to be a more forthright stance than simply turning one's back or not speaking to them. And now I had discovered that hatred within me, I knew I was capable of having enemies, that now I could hate somebody and channel in their direction the vigorous energy suddenly pouring from me like the revelation of sexual potency or attraction of naked white bodies. That energy had a purpose, which was to defend me against my enemies, and right then I thought how the closest enemy I had in the present was the teacher, Mr. Madern, and to test out the intensity and extent of my hatred I should perhaps decide to hate France, an entire nation, despite the initial loss of Alsace-Lorraine—had the teacher sanctified the martyr-provinces, or was he referring to other provinces I'd missed through my lack of attention?—because he seemed to sympathize with that war and I'd decided to remain aloof and curse everything he loved. So then, it was also possible to hate an entire country, and that capacity to hate was extraordinary and a revelation that brought me such bliss, such a great feeling of superiority, that there was no need for me to lean back against Dr. Caminals' garden gate, as I used to with my mates in town, when we cut a notch in the wood with a knife, to see whether we'd grown a little or a lot over a given period, whenever we remembered to measure ourselves, because I now knew I had really grown up, and that the hatred within me could grow to match the stature of my enemies.

38

After he'd wound up his final speech, the teacher let us go and create a racket in the playground, while he stood in the doorway watching us, as if he was supervising us, but I noticed something special about his gaze and couldn't think what it was.

When it was home time, we cleaned out our desks and the teacher also stuffed an old leather briefcase with the equipment from his table, books, rulers, pens and nibs, rubbers and blotting paper, all he had, and put the chessboard and the box of pieces next to it, as if he was about to set out on a journey. Then he positioned himself at one side of the door and shook our hands; the teacher had a farewell word for us one by one, "goodbye!," "be good!" or "work hard!"

Cry-Baby was one of the first to leave and the teacher, Mr. Madern, stroked her cheek as he told her something I didn't catch. Núria blushed, looked down, and shook his hand. When it was my turn, he stared into my eyes as he held out his hand and that was when I regretted being bereft of everything I'd just felt, even of the words to express a glimmer of that hatred, but I couldn't, my rage had melted as if his presence had spirited away all my evil thoughts, and thus disarmed, I simply squeezed his hand and listened to what he had to say.

"I know it's all going well," he said, and I listened to him from afar, as if he were speaking to somebody else or standing elsewhere and his words were coming to me from a way away, "Make the most of it and get on. Think of all the boys who have to live in a boarding school, far from home, in order to keep on studying. I'll be in the village for a couple of days before I leave. If you need anything, come and see me. As you know, I live at the inn."

I nodded, and was angry at myself for so doing, but I couldn't help it, and when our hands parted and I was leaving, he added in a gentler tone: "Your cousin, Núria, is a good lass."

That was like a stab in the back. I couldn't understand why he said that. Cry-Baby waited for me at the start of the path to the farm and she followed me, not saying a word, when I walked by. Later, past the first bend, I asked her: "What did he say to you?"

"Nothing," she said, averting her gaze. "He wished me luck, in case we don't meet up again."

I hesitated, trying to find something to say in reply. In the end, I asked: "And why should you two meet up again?"

This time she did look at me, and didn't seem in the least put out. Now she asked: "And when will *you* be off?"

"Next term, I reckon," I said reluctantly. "But we'll meet up again. I'll probably come and play with you on Sundays."

"Quirze says you'll never come back."

"What does that idiot know! He knows nothing."

That year the summer holidays didn't open up an endless vista of light, the days and days of fun and games that usually awaited us. Summer was the time that most resembled the eternity priests, teachers and friars talked about. Months without end of parties and possibilities offered by a sunny season that even lit up our nights. That final year was the end of eternity. We'd just begun our holidays and were already thinking about how they were going to end, of a different beginning that might part us forever.

All in all it made us forget that Aunt Enriqueta had vanished. They were days when rather than her absence, we felt a dense, malignant atmosphere throughout the house. Silences were longer and dragged more; conversations were tighter-lipped. Nobody mentioned Aunt Enriqueta, only Grandmother said something one day to Cry-Baby and me, as if someone had already told us something about her situation: "She'll be back, Aunt Enriqueta, she'll be back. They've taken her to Vic and Barcelona for a few weeks where she's got work to do, work that's urgent, because apparently Father Tafalla has ordered clothes for an entire monastery that is departing to the Americas. She'll be back."

That Sunday Mother came and spent more time with me than usual. On other occasions, when she arrived, I sometimes didn't even notice her, and bumped into her in the kitchen talking to Aunt Ció or Grandmother, and I'd say hello and go back to playing with my cousins up the plum tree or in the stable if we had work to do, but that day Mother didn't let me out of her sight. She kept her arm round my waist while we sat on the kitchen bench talking to Aunt Ció, who was preparing lunch with her back to us. In their usual fashion, they spoke about Aunt Enriqueta without naming her, in an indirect, dispassionate way, as if she were a distant relative who was ill, with an illness that couldn't be named

"You didn't expect that, did you?"

"Not in a thousand years would I have expected anything of that sort. I was expecting everything but that."

"You'd never have imagined it was *him*, would you?"

"He'd been here a few times, not that much, and he seemed like a wet little sparrow, a lambkin, with his short ears and nice as pie... And look how he's turned out! I'd never ever imagined he had it in him to play such nasty trick."

"Had you ever seen them together?"

"Never, I tell you, not once. You know he never came by himself, he couldn't, it wasn't allowed. He always came with the other older...the big..." Aunt Ció swung round to look at Mother, and smiling sweetly made a round belly shape with her hands. "They were always together. He was his companion. A kind of secretary, almost, you might say."

"They must have met up somewhere else, in the woods…"

"I began to have my suspicions when she was so quick to agree to go to your house in town and keep you company."

"You caught a whiff…?"

"Do you mean…? I don't think so. She always arrived at the same time, on the dot. On the coach."

"Heavens knows what she told them at the seamstress's in Vic. She had the whole day to herself. To herself and to do whatever she liked, clearly. I'd bet my right hand she didn't go to the seamstress's at midday or on many an afternoon."

Aunt Ció, her back turned, made a gesture of resignation, as if to say that must be right, that there could be no other explanation. I acted the innocent but hung on each word and gesture, trying to extract some sense to work it all out. I thought they were referring to Canary, the blond civil guard, and his colleague, since they always went about together.

"Dad Quirze lost his rag. You can't imagine how furious he was. We didn't get any sleep all night. We had a huge row! It made my poor mother ill, and she doesn't know the half of it."

Once again, my mother's presence introduced the enclosed world of adults, with its language of hidden meanings and knowing references, to events only they knew, interpreted and evaluated. I felt excluded from that world and my exclusion removed any responsibility for the fates of those people, whether present or absent, as if they were saying I didn't belong to their kind, wasn't party to their worries, their interests, their dangers, their blood, and their prerogatives, as Grandmother Mercè would say. Each hour that passed I felt cast farther adrift. Was this one way to force me gradually into the world of Mr. and Mrs. Manubens?

"So then, there's nothing we can do, right?"

"Now we must let time go by… It's all we can do."

"And what will you do? I mean to cover it up, when what must be, must be… Have you tried…?" Mother asked, insinuating something or other. "King's crown works wonders in these cases. It really does the business. And there's a woman in Vic you can rely on…"

Aunt Ció made that resigned-to-fate gesture once again. Now she turned round, rubbed her hands on her apron and said: "You know what these people are like. They don't want a hue-and-cry, or anything putting them in a bad light. And you know that we owe them a lot of favours. They've done deals with Dad Quirze on both sides of the mountains, and Grandfather Hand acts as their messenger boy though he's not a clue what he's carrying. It seems they need to send lots of things over the other side on the quiet, no people, just things, papers, banking stuff, that is, all underhand. That lot trust nobody, not even their own. Fonso couldn't have escaped without their help. We owe them too many bits of help. We can't do a thing without their blessing."

"Of course, we went through all that with Mariona and it is a pain. And you haven't had the gossip yet, we even had a belling of the husband."

"I never expected all this, I really didn't. After all we had to go through over Fonso's plight, it's not fair we've got another disaster to face now."

Aunt Ció left the kitchen as if she and Mother had planned they would leave us alone, saying: "When the time comes, we shall return to all this."

"Poor Ció, so many headaches!" Mother exclaimed, squeezing my waist even more tightly, as if I understood everything they'd talked about.

I said nothing. It was the first time Mother and I had met at the farmhouse since Father had died. She removed her arm and I sat at the table, opposite her.

"What do you think about all this carry-on?" she asked, looking into my eyes.

I felt she was thinner, with sunken cheeks, a pointier nose and the bags under her eyes seemed more puffed up. Her hair was combed back, with small curls on her neck like remnants of an old perm, and she was wearing a dress dyed black that left smudges on her nape and wrists. I found the look in her eyes and her attitude in general much less vigorous, as if she was suffering from days of exhaustion.

"I don't know…" I replied, simply to say something. I couldn't think what she expected me to say.

"Grandmother still doesn't know the whole story," she suddenly added. It was one of those changes I wasn't sure how to interpret, when I went from being an ignoramus to a confidant, which made me reflect that the grownups, my mother, weren't sure how to treat us littl'uns, "be careful not to say a word to her, we don't want her having a stroke."

I nodded, with little conviction. I found those changes disconcerting.

"They've told her Enriqueta had to go to Barcelona for a while for work reasons. However, she knows nothing about the novice from Saint Camillus. She'd not cope with the idea of those two scarpering off in an underhand way. We'll see what kind of a go they make of it."

I didn't react on the outside, in front of my mother. Inside, I felt I was collapsing, as if that would-be monk had gutted me or my heart had switched sides. Xavier, the little friar from Navarra, so silent and unassuming, so well-mannered, with his fragile white face, long pianist's fingers and green eyes like a couple of olives? Did this mean they could leave the closed order, if they wanted, that anything was allowed, if they dared try it on? In a flash I saw the naked youth with TB lying on the sheet under the elm tree in the heartsease garden. I didn't know why I was connecting those two right then, what the sick boy was doing next to the Navarrese novice, or what link existed between the two of them apart from the fact they lodged in the monastery, one within the community and the other in the infirmary. There must be a secret connection I couldn't identify, like the hatred unleashed within me by the teacher in the Alsace-Lorraine school's last lesson and Mr. Madern, the teacher in the Novíssima, who seemingly weren't linked, but were like distant twin brothers embroiled in a peculiar mix of politics and education, of war and schooling, and, as I was beginning to grasp ever more clearly, in the kind of seduction they practised over their pupils, sexual in the case of the man in the Novíssima, and political and patriotic in the Frenchman's. Two forms of violence I found repugnant. That's why I was at a loss, and didn't know what to think about the new secret link I was now discovering, but there must have been a reason why the unassuming and seductive novice and the sick adolescent whose fragile nakedness now came into my mind together.

Mother must have noticed something was going on inside me, because she asked: "Hadn't anybody told you?"

"They told Quirze to run to the Saint Camillus monastery in the pitch-black to fetch Father Tafalla and another friar," I let slip, following the thread of my own thoughts.

Mother opened her eyes wide and leaned towards me.

"Now let's talk about you," she said, in a voice that showed she wanted to move the conversation on. "Let's talk about what directly concerns us. Mr. and Mrs. Manubens came to see you, didn't they?"

I nodded, avoiding her gaze.

"And…?" her voice sounded less of sure of itself now.

I looked at her, willing her to help me guess what she was thinking, but I didn't say a word.

"What did you think? What did they say? Did you come to an agreement?"

"You knew them already, didn't you? Hadn't you spoken to them? How did you leave it?"

Mother must have imagined the opposed emotions that were paralyzing me. She explained: "I went to see them in Vic with Aunt Ció. They'd sent me a note to go and see them as soon as I could. They were very nice. Didn't Aunt Ció tell you?"

"She never tells us anything," I couldn't soften the touch of rancour in my voice.

"She must have left it for me come and tell you. Aunt Ció has also had days with lots of work and lots of upsets, like us, so don't blame her for anything. I expect she intended telling you about it but with all her ups-and-downs she couldn't find the right moment."

She paused. In the meanwhile she changed her stance, as if trying to get more comfortable; she folded her arms and rested her elbows on the edge of the table, in a stiff, authoritarian pose, then unfolded them, lay her palms upwards on the table, looked at the ceiling, and said: "I won't do anything you don't want. If you want to go with them, I'll let you, but if you'd rather stay at home, you can. It's your home. Grandmother, your uncle and aunt, have done enough, far too much for us over these last few years. You can't stay here any longer. Núria will be off too, as soon as your Uncle Fonso has settled into his new life in France, I think he's already found work in a vineyard near Perpignan. You must tell me. As I am now, by myself, I can't do any more for you, in terms of your schooling, I mean. I've also spoken to the priest in the parish school and he thinks that if you have an opportunity to study, you should. When he told me what the books cost, and only the books, I took fright: almost two weeks' wages from the factory. What would we live on if I had to pay for all that?"

Mother's face was a blur, a fog of anxiety erased her from my field of vision. It was that same voice, that same spiel, the leprosy of poverty one couldn't jettison, that neither of us could jettison because her voice, her anguish and laments passed the infection to me. Her voice brought me back yet again to the streets in our town showing off my First Communion outfit, strutting my stuff before friends and acquaintances, pressuring them into giving me a small present, a memento, charity. Or the visits, by her side, to the local toffs, factory owners and powers-that-be, to beg them to do something to get Father out of prison, out of hospital and off the death sentence. When I was with her I was always under the impression that I was witnessing a mammoth struggle, one that was lost before it was started, to cast off the wretchedness, penury and misfortune that had pursued us ever since the pair had foolishly left the grandparents' farm, had gone far from the silent, tranquil refuge of the forest. I admired that woman who fought tire-lessly, fiercely, in her battle against the scourge of poverty, yet rebelled when for convenience's sake, or clear-sightedly, she floundered in that parasitic swamp of shame, as if the fate we confronted was inescapable.

"It'll only be for a period and you can come back when-ever you want, naturally. It will always be your home, you know. I'll come to see you. Mr. and Mrs. Manubens have been very generous. They don't have children and want to help you to get on in life, if you can manage it. Didn't you say you'd like to be a doctor?"

I shook my head. A doctor? Perhaps I did once say that, I expect under the influence of the mystery of Saint Camillus, the young man with TB and the superior man-ners of elegant, affable gentlemen, the doctors I'd met in town. However, I now felt quite differently, I was now beginning to feel the bitter taste of hatred I'd discovered at the Novíssima, although less intensely, though I knew I *could* stir up that inner fire now fuelled by Mother's words. I didn't want to, the need to do justice to my mother pre-vented me, but it made it crystal clear that I must distance myself from her if I didn't want her to infect me with the filth of poverty. Even though I didn't like books and found studying hard, I would clear off so I could find work else-where, far away, where the annoying, flattening fumes that reduced me to zero couldn't floor me.

"You must get used to the idea that they are like god-parents. I think their idea later is to see if they can get you into the Seminary, they're the people who've given most for the new building…but that's because they're so pious—and reputed to be sanctimonious—it would seem odd if they didn't try to hook you into all that, apparently they are already the religious godfathers of two or three seminari-ans, but don't worry your head about that, make the most you can of your schooling and when you see where you're heading, we can talk again."

"They never mentioned the Seminary to me."

"No, I'm the one telling you. You'll live with them, in their house, and they'll send you to a good school… the Escolapians of Mercy, they said, for your secondary education."

"I thought it was going to be Saint Michael's, everyone goes to Saint Michael of the Saints, in Vic."

My mother looked taken aback.

"St. Michael's? No, the Escolapians are in Igualada. Mr. and Mrs. Manubens have had a mansion built on the city outskirts, and that's where they're going to live, if they haven't already. They own a knitting factory there that's going very well, it's what brings them the most money now, much more than their farms, and they want to extend the business, Napkin Lolita told me. So you thought it would be Vic? Perhaps they said Vic so as not to panic you, because that would be closer to home."

I nodded. I didn't know whether to be overjoyed or dis-appointed by the latest news. I hadn't a clue where Igualada was, but I didn't feel disappointed. I had decided to leave, to go wherever. I started to be intrigued by this unknown city.

"Igualada isn't very far, but there's no direct train, you have to go to Barcelona and catch a train in another station, they're not the same trains from Puigcerdà, it's another company. I don't know what it's called."

I stiffened my resolve, looked her straight in the eyes and said: "Yes."

Mother seemed mightily relieved.

"Are you sure? You're not doing it for my sake? I told you I didn't mind one way or the other."

I nodded once again. What else did I have to say for her to understand that I accepted the deal and wanted out.

Then she got up, went over to the sink and poured out a glass of water. She walked back to the table with the glass and placed it in front of me as if I'd asked her for it.

"Drink this," she said. "Your throat's dry and you're finding it hard to swallow."

I took the glass, reacting mechanically, and downed it in one gulp.

"You see?" she said, removing the dirty glass. "Now we'll go and tell Aunt Ció and Grandmother what you've decided. They'll be so delighted."

39

From the moment everybody found out I'd accepted Mr. and Mrs. Manubens as my godparents, they all started to treat me differently. Initially I thought I was imagining that, because the decision I'd taken to distance myself from the world I'd known to that point made me more of a loner, a more reflective, self-absorbed individual, as if I'd been branded with a distinguishing mark or was surrounded by the luminous aura I'd seen in religious prints of the saints or God's chosen.

However, they *were* looking at me differently. The comments they made on any matter whatsoever seemed to touch on the issue directly or indirectly: "Eat well, we don't want the masters to think we've taught you to be fussy," "Don't dirty your hands, that's not the kind of work for you," or "Keep your clothes tidy, we don't know what you'll have to take or if you'll need new outfits," and so on. Even Quirze, who'd never put himself out over anything, now tried to take on the hardest jobs when we had to work together, and Cry-Baby, who already seemed to be living in a different world, when she found out we'd not be seeing any more of each other when the new school year began, dragged me along to play among the hazel trees more often, and our encounters in the deep shadows from the leaves and green hazels were more sensitive— Grandmother always said "sensitive" when something moved her deeply or she said "he's very sensitive" when she spoke of someone who was deeply affected by life's adversity or spiteful remarks made by others—as if our first play and tentative explorations had been transformed into profound interpenetration, total trust, a much more intense emotion than the contact between our bodies. She continued to offer herself passively, as if she'd lost her will or was daydreaming, but she responded to everything I initiated, coupled into my movements and reacted to my every gesture, eyes closed and a loving smile on her face.

In the language of the playground—the only first-hand information we had about sexual matters—when a boy ejaculated for the first time they called it "spurting," "he's spurting now," they'd say, and they'd said "she's butterfly-ing" for the girls' arousal, and we extracted unambiguous expressions from the adult conversations between Uncle Bernat and the hands or seasonal labour that filled the house at harvest and threshing time, like "going to give the reed a squeeze" or "rubbing the sparrow" or "carding," or "he's well juicy" and many others my schoolmates brought from their respective hamlets. In the velvety shade of the hazel trees, we tried out all the actions suggested by the words that had come to us in an obscene, partial, or rather laboured manner, and with my cousin they became beau-tiful, serene acts with no sense of guilt, the naturalness of the pleasure erasing any shadow of sin or remorse, they were simply games, experiments, childish experiences and tentative moves that gradually brought us close to the bodily knowhow displayed by grownups, which we would have to master one day.

We also realized that our games were ephemeral, involved no commitment or consequence, and could stop at any moment, just as the wind changes, depending on the other's mood or taste and that made them more intense and enjoyable, because each game might be the last.

However, during that final summer on the farm, Cry-Baby played our games more passionately and I thought she gave herself up to them with real enjoyment, despite her inertia. It was unconditional, absolute surrender, and that offering in itself satisfied me, after the first moments of mutual exploration. I wondered what else the world of grownups might hold in their adult bedrooms, if I felt we'd already exhausted the content of all the words we knew.

Sometimes, before or after entering our grotto of hazel tree branches, we'd look over the wall around the heart-sease garden, to see whether the ill young men were sun-bathing on the grass. Depending on the time of day, they'd not yet come or had already gone. When I saw them, I breathed more energetically, as if the air rushing to my lungs was reinvigorating, and the sight of the naked boy brought on a feeling of fulfilment I'd never experienced before. When I was hugging Núria I forgot everything, but there was always a fissure momentarily occupied by that frail, astonishingly beautiful figure, that found strength in its own defencelessness, exactly like my cousin, and the more vulnerable, exposed and helpless he seemed, the more powerfully he struck me, as if his cure, his very life depended on me, exactly what it felt like with Cry-Baby.

This feeling of incompleteness, of imperfection, could be experienced as a kind of mutilation which I interpreted as an aspect of my immaturity, I thought that later on, when I was more experienced I'd know how to fill that gap, that lack, and that adult couples must have managed to do that, to make it whole, without any fissures, because people couldn't possibly live peacefully with another person for so many years if they were suffering the anguish caused by having one's body in one place with a person and one's thoughts in another with someone else.

As I was left alone that summer and on the farm they took care not to burden me with any jobs, even Dad Quirze's ferrety eyes looked at me more wryly and he thought twice before speaking to me, and I started to fantasize about whether I really was my parents' child, or if it was simply a coincidence I'd come to be with them. I found the idea I was an adoptive son very appealing, that I was somebody now simply changing direction and going to live with a family that was as fake as his first one, even though some experiences and memories were too vivid and striking to allow me to push my fantasy much further. In a way, those thoughts were a way of punishing my parents, a kind of revenge for the losers' fate they'd inflicted on me, and the height of satisfaction I reached in these fantasies were greater than the remorse triggered by the potential betrayal they represented. I'd discovered the power of hatred and now developed a liking for betrayal, for the arrogant flourish of pride embodied by the rejection of my family, my roots, of my entire past. I thought how it was like what I'd felt as a child when I really wanted something I was being refused and later when it was allowed, I wouldn't accept it, as if I'd never wanted it in the first place, as if my final refusal was a deserved pay-off for the initial denial I'd been forced to suffer. "I don't want it now," were my exact words, "I don't want it now! I am the one that doesn't want it now!"

That summer I spent a week with my mother in town, the week my mother was on holiday, and those few days served as the farewell to my other family landscape. My friends in town and our neighbours already knew I'd be going to study in another city at the start of the next school year, sponsored by some very pious folk, the masters of my paternal grandparents, and they all treated me in the same distant way I'd noted on the farm, that was perhaps even colder and more intense, as if I'd wanted to distance myself from them and their fate, and once again I felt like a traitor and deep down I accepted I was. "I am the one who doesn't want you now!"

When Mother's holidays came to an end and she went back to work, I returned to the farm to see out the holidays. Cry-Baby informed me of the big news of what had happened to Pere Màrtir in my absence. They'd not talked about anything else for a couple of days. They seemed very worried about him, evidently he'd been found on a solitary side street in Vic, in the early hours, lying on the ground because he was so drunk he couldn't stand up. They said he'd left a café where the local first-born and heirs gambled their *duros* and doubloons away, a café for card sharps—the expression was Grandmother's—that organized clandestine games behind closed doors, after official closing time, when the usual customers had left. The card sharps played on till the first light of dawn, sometimes till the café opened in the morning and the farmers going to market came in for breakfast. They also commented how Pere Màrtir was on his way to losing his bulls and his bells—another local expression, this time from Aunt Ció—and that Aunt Enriqueta was responsible for the lad's lunacy. "That joker Enriqueta will lose the lot, whatever she had and whatever she's got now, because the friar-boy who hung up his habits on a fig tree won't last her a couple of months!" Dad Quirze cursed, and they talked about going to fetch her from Barcelona to see if she could help the poor lad, Pere Màrtir, pull through, so he didn't meet a bad end like some stony-broke rake.

The news surprised me because I thought of Aunt Enriqueta and Pere Màrtir as figures from my past, and I now found it a strain to think about them, a bit like Uncle Fonso, who'd fled to France, or Cry-Baby's mother, who were never mentioned, as if they didn't exist, like my own father, who, once dead, had turned into a memory, I now had to abandon all these people I'd come across in life, forget those waifs and strays on endless, dark streets in big cities and distant countries, separated from me by the frontiers of age and invisible mountains; I'd exhausted my curiosity about them, they no longer meant anything to me.

However, the detail of the nighttime gambling den in the bishop's city, with the ever-attractive image of a dejected Pere Màrtir, laid low by misfortune and abandoned in the middle of the street, revived the sympathy he'd always inspired in me and I found room for him in my private oratory, on the altar reserved for hapless heroes, stricken down by sickness, desertion, the death sentence, or sexual offers, alongside the boy with TB in the heartsease garden, Cry-Baby and her white, gently sloping belly, Father striped zebra-like by prison bars with his blue stillborn stare and sunken, unshaven cheeks, Aunt Mariona ravaged by the big city and transformed into a sticky saccharine pudding, Aunt Felisa crossing the woods at midnight to come and cry in Mother's skirts because she didn't want to marry the ogre they'd chosen for her, or Mad Antònia from Can Tona walking naked through the woods searching for the ghost of a boyfriend who'd been executed right in front of her eyes.

And apart from that addition of a new image to my private universe, questions came to me like why were they insisting on mixing Aunt Enriqueta up in that episode, if she'd already paired up with the Saint Camillus novice and, as we'd deduced, her belly was even swollen because "she was expecting," as Aunt Cío and Grandmother said, wasn't that enough to withdraw her from circulation? This meant Aunt Enriqueta might appear to us as easily as a witch from the woods as a fairy working miracles with her hands on a sewing machine or wherever she was now, hands of gold, everybody said, hands that would never allow her to go hungry, a fairy's fingers, in fact, and I didn't understand what powers she possessed to save Pere Màrtir from anything at all. And how come Pere Màrtir couldn't get Aunt Enriqueta out of his head—he carries her deep in his blood, said Grandmother, and Dad Quirze said she would drive the lad crazy—what had she given him, what kind of love did he harbour for her that he couldn't disentangle himself from her or couldn't live without her? The madness of love, like the lunacy of gambling, must be an infection, an illness like tuberculosis that dried out some people's lungs and conversely let others breathe quietly and peacefully—a mystery. And it was my fascination for this unknown world that brought me close to Pere Màrtir or the boy with TB in the monastery or Mad Antònia or Cry-Baby, my conviction that they were beings fated to carry a burden through life that others were unwittingly freed from—like someone born into an untrammelled existence who thinks his state is perfectly natural, who never reflects that he was born with a drawback—and that's why the former live their lives more frivolously, more unconsciously, skating over the surface, and struggling to grasp the submerged, melancholy, daydreaming character of those who carry the burden of a ballast of lead.

The latter seemed like beings fated to self-sacrifice, who travelled the world with the air of dogs without a master, starving and battered, but irradiating a mysterious attraction that only other victims destined to similar sacrifices could appreciate. This explained why boys and girls entered seminaries and convents, drawn by the magnetism of figures like Saint Lucia with her empty eye sockets and erect forehead awaiting an invisible light, or Saint Sebastian tied to a tree, his chest and legs full of arrows that pierced his flesh with an array of red flowers, who despite his suffering, held his head high with a strangely happy smile on his face, or Saint Camillus of Lellis in his white habits clawed at by the skeletal hands of the sick and wretched and yet he smiled blissfully and turned his eyes to heaven as if grateful for the suffering strewn on his path and the dozens of crosses bearing the Son of God crowned with thorns, beaten, nailed through his hands and feet, his ribs split open by spears, and transformed by this Calvary into a Redeemer, King and Saviour.

I wondered rather apprehensively whether I too wasn't fated to join this select group of the chosen few marked out by their difference. On the one hand I was attracted by the idea, on the other, I was afraid I'd be unable to behave like them—my models—with similar dignity and elegance, unable to bear the suffering or hardships with the strength they displayed when they welcomed their pain, like the village lads who on Saint John's Eve walked barefoot across the embers of fires lit a while before and never complained, always smiled, and never burnt themselves.

Father Tafalla turned up one afternoon after lunch, at siesta time, and they seemed to be expecting his visit, as if he'd been invited a couple of days before. He was accompanied by another old Saint Camillus friar who said hello to us all and then, on the excuse of being behind with his prayers, walked up and down the cherry tree path, gripping his breviary. The Saint Camillus Superior sat down in the kitchen for a minute and then went up to the gallery to the sitting room with Dad Quirze and Uncle Bernat, who helped Grandmother up. Aunt Ció followed. Before leaving the kitchen, Uncle Bernat told Cry-Baby, Quirze and me: "You can go and play in the barn or the fruit orchard, because we've got work to do. And let us know if you see anyone coming."

Quirze muttered, as if to complain about his deliberate exclusion from the meeting they were about to begin: "You want us to go to the barn in this heat!"

"Go wherever you want," he replied, "but don't get in our way."

Cry-Baby and I climbed up the plum tree and Quirze called the dogs and went into the stables. Quirze had stopped playing with us. Cry-Baby and I took over the branch at the top of the tree our cousin had abandoned. It was the highest and strongest and the best place for watching the goings-on of the grownups in the gallery, Dad Quirze, Bernat and Father Tafalla, seated around Grandmother's armchair and Aunt Ció coming in and out with glasses and jugs of water with honey and lemon. We couldn't hear a word of what they were saying and their gestures weren't expressive or dramatic enough for us to guess the subject of their conversation. Cry-Baby and I were quiet, our eyes glued to the gallery, until eventually she said: "They're talking about Aunt Enriqueta."

"How do you know?"

"Because AuntCió told me this morning that Father Tafalla would come this afternoon and bring regards from my father."

I was taken aback for a moment. What was the connection between those two things? I sometimes felt my cousin hadn't a clue.

"What do you mean?"

"Aunt Enriqueta had asked how my father managed to cross the mountains and hide in France. She and her novice want to do the same."

"How do you know? Who told you?"

"Grandmother told me last night in bed, before we went to sleep."

"What else did she tell you?"

"That I should be ready too, because depending on how things go, the three of us might go to France, with my father. She says he's expecting us."

"The three of us? You mean you, Aunt Enriqueta and the young friar?"

Cry-Baby nodded.

"But she said," she continued, "it's more than likely I would cross the border with a...I don't remember what she said, a mountain ranger or guide or smuggler, a priest who's a friend of Father Tafalla and Grandfather Hand. During the war the priest learned how to ferry people to the other side, because he had to do it time and again to save the lives of priests and nuns they were planning to execute, though he's stopped doing it now and is the priest in a small village church near Andorra, but he'd do us this favour out of friendship for Father Tafalla and Grandfather Hand, who've become close friends since the war."

I glanced at Cry-Baby and was intrigued. She knew more than I gave her credit for. We all thought she was gormless when she wasn't. I was pleased she seemed more alert as I'd already begun to regret I'd be moving a long way from her, especially because I thought she always seemed so hapless, and the notion that she'd learned to cope by herself meant going our different ways didn't seem so upsetting.

"You'll have to learn French," I said, testing how resilient she was. "Where will you go to school in France? If you don't know French, nobody will understand you."

"My father didn't understand a word and he's not suffered as a result, and Mother's been living there for some time and nobody's ever said they don't understand her or that she's having a difficult time."

I was surprised by my memories of her mother. They never say how she's faring, I thought. That was another family story, or rather, family mystery they never fully explained. Would Cry-Baby be all right with her mother in France? In order to move the conversation away from her mother that I guessed was dangerous territory, I said: "At the village school, with the priest, we read a story called *La chèvre de Monsieur Seguin*, and it was easy to understand. French is written one way and read another…"

While I spoke, I evoked the fantasy of a France that was within hand's reach, just around the corner from the farm, yet so different, or so people said, a country of freedom and a haven for all fugitives and people on the run, a land of priest-eaters and stern-minded, arrant Republicans, of freedom, equality and liberty, Grandmother sometimes repeated, and I'd even think the air was cleaner there, and life easier, and people better behaved, and I could already imagine my Cry-Baby transformed into a distinguished *mademoiselle*, with fairer hair and bluer eyes, transformed into a citizen of France in the centre of a little box lined with pink silk that was liberal and welcoming, *la douce France*. I was happy for her sake, she deserved that, in fact she was already French before she crossed the border, simply because she was so different, tactful, free, and always ready to please. I'd hunt her out some day, I didn't know when, as soon as I could flee this horrible country that forced people to change family and flee shamefully, stealthily, on foot, under cover of darkness like thieves or murderers.

Cry-Baby sat on the trunk and said: "Look, they're leaving already."

Father Tafalla, Bernat and Quirze had got to their feet and were talking around the bench where Grandmother was sat. Aunt Ció was waiting for them by the sitting-room door. A couple of jumps and Cry-Baby and I were on the ground and rushing over to the front-door. Meanwhile, Aunt Ció leaned over the balustrade and shouted: "Children, come and say goodbye to Father Tafalla!"

We waited by the entrance because the grownups came downstairs very slowly, still tying up what we imagined must be the final threads in their conversation.

"I didn't mention the ex-cloistering of Xavier because she wouldn't understand," said Father Tafalla.

"I wouldn't be so sure," protested Aunt Ció, "at her age, she understands everything. But, you're right, it's better if she doesn't hear the details. She will suffer less."

After a silence, Aunt Ció continued: "She found work straight away. And he says he will too and soon, as a nurse, or a teacher in a local private academy. They've been lucky. They're renting a flat that relatives of his are subletting."

The last steps of the stairs weren't hidden by the wall with the mirror, the second they saw us, the Superior of Saint Camillus beamed and lifted his arms up as if he was going to bless us.

"Here they are!" he exclaimed, as if he'd not realized his arrival had been the reason why we'd been banished. "Our two travellers, our two students."

Dad Quirze and Uncle Bernat both stooped to kiss the Superior's hand in farewell and the Saint Camillus Superior smiled, acknowledging their gesture as he placed his hand on our heads.

"Are you ready to leave?" Father Tafalla asked bluntly.

Cry-Baby and I smiled shyly. Had he been given the responsibility to tell us when and how we were to leave?

"Those two live wires are always ready for anything!" said Aunt Ció, walking towards us. The friar accompanying Father Tafalla stood a prudent distance from us, seemed to be awaiting his orders.

Father Tafalla looked into my eyes. He spoke especially to me: "You have been extremely lucky," he said. "The past is past. You know what I mean, don't you?"

I didn't really understand, but I nodded. The Superior glanced at me ironically, as if wondering whether to continue his sermon or leave it, and he went for the last option, turned round to Cry-Baby and said: "And how are you, little girl? Are you too ready for your new life?"

He stopped, no doubt because Núria's bulging eyes that stared at him in amazement made him realize the young girl didn't understand his involvement in all that.

Aunt Ció put her hands on Cry-Baby's shoulder, as if to bring her closer to the Superior, and said: "We don't know what will happen to this young lady, so far away…"

Cry-Baby's eyelids flickered nervously open and shut.

"May God bless the two of you," concluded Father Tafalla, signalling to the friar accompanying him that they should leave. "And let me know as soon as Grandfather Hand arrives, because there are a lot of loose ends still to tie up."

"Kiss the Father's hand," Aunt Ció told us, as she herself stooped down to kiss it. "And thank him. I don't know how we can ever repay his goodness."

Cry-Baby and I kissed the back of the Superior's hand and waited on the spot until he'd disappeared round the corner of the house, flanked by Aunt Ció and the friar who followed on a couple of paces behind. Aunt Ció whispered to Father Tafalla, as she did in her endless goodbyes to my mother, and the friar listened, slightly tilting his head to hear her confidences. What could he still have to tell Aunt Ció that they'd not been able to say before? What secrets might they be?

The second we were left by ourselves, Núria and I ran upstairs to Grandmother. We found her alone, despondent, with her knitting basket by her feet and her needles and wool abandoned on her skirt, with her hands folded on her lap. We walked quietly over and she greeted us with a nod, as if to say yes, she had registered our presence, and we stood silently by her side until she whispered: "They make smoke, rather than giving out light," and I understood she was referring to the Saint Camillus friars who'd just left, because I'd heard her use the same phrase when she found out about the way Xavier the novice was implicated in Aunt Enriqueta's flight, and I immediately understood why she said that.

And then she added: "I'm not a shadow of what I was…"

And after a sigh: "My body no longer does what I tell it to."

She raised her hands in a theatrical, exaggerated manner, and went on: "But I'm still the young lass I once was on the inside, it's only the memory of the girl I once was, that I still am deep inside. I believe our youth never abandons us, the passing years simply bury it deep down and it finds it harder and harder to get out. That's what happens to us old folk, you young'uns don't notice, but we carry our youth within us, we really do—always!"

She squeezed our hands and shook them as if she wanted to tell us something that was beyond words.

"Father Tafalla and Mr. and Mrs. Manubens think they are the masters of the world, and we should let them think that, we should let the Emperor's clothes well alone… you know what I mean? Fonso, your father, Núria, was always very good with his hands, as a young child he was already making boxes and cages and all kinds of gadgets, his hands are worth a fortune, and when he lived in hiding here for a time after the war, he learned to knit, he knitted jerseys to while away the time, jerseys for everybody, did you think I was the only one doing that? Poor little me, I could never have made so many, not in a month of Sundays! He went at it much faster than I did and dressed the whole family, and he was the one who couldn't budge…oh, dearie me!, and the monastery blankets for the convent he folded for the refugees crossing the border and hiding in the woods…"

She lapsed into silence for a moment and behind her spectacles her eyes seemed to pierce the horizon and see everything she was telling us.

"In the old days, all us brothers and sisters lived on the land, we were all near the house, and I felt like a mother hen, like a mother hen with all her chicks around her, but youngsters grow up and want to fly off on their own and find shelter in other nests, the whole coop scattered… Now Bernat is the only one left, and he feels out of place and any day now he'll find a young lass and will fly her a long way away, like all the others. The folk were right who predicted that factories and roads would kill everything, and that cities gobble everything up and are the root of all evil. I won't live to see it, but I'm sure this place will be a desert in a few years, machines will do labourers' work and nobody will want land work. The world goes round and round and life goes on, everything changes and nothing stays as it was."

She let go of our hands and smiled that mischievous smile that was her way of seeing off her bad moods and grumbles: "Crikey! Why am I telling you all this? I wanted to tell you something else, but the nonsense Father Tafalla and the others stuffed my head with this afternoon made me forget. Now what did I want to tell you just now? You'll be saying my head's not right and my brain's gone to pot? Ah, I think I do remember now!"

She took our hands once again but gently now, as if she'd passed on all her energy to us before.

"The allies can't delay much longer before deciding to intervene. I'd like to see it, but I don't know if I'll still be here. Whatever happens, remember that Father Tafalla helped us a lot. Grandfather Hand has been considerate towards him and transported papers across the border, but without Father Tafalla we might never have raised our heads again. When we were ground down, he helped Dad Quirze get going again with livestock and timber and perhaps as a result he may become a master one day. Don't you ever forget that!"

One Sunday in late summer Mother brought a bundle of clothes for me and said I should get ready because any day now Mr. and Mrs. Manubens would come to take me away.

When it was time for her to leave, I accompanied the two women as far as the place with panoramic views by Can Tona, by the bend that hid the farmhouse out of sight. AuntCió and Mother continued chatting away, and I didn't even try to catch their words now, as if all that no longer belonged to my universe and I wasn't fired to find out the latest twists and turns in the lives of my relatives and the acquaintances who seemed linked to their existence by knots they couldn't undo, a thread that was too tight or too loose, broken strings or new cords, links and bonds that frightened them as if stability in their lives depended on them and couldn't survive without those tensions.

They dropped names and expressions that meant practically nothing outside their conversations and that stung my brain like a bee, creating a welt or wart of suspicion I tried to stroke or squeeze like an annoying pimple you try to remove with your fingers.

"You mean…?" said one, panic-stricken.

"You can be dead sure," the other affirmed.

"Wouldn't…!" exclaimed the former.

"Wouldn't…? You'll soon see! Remember what I just said."

"You don't mean wouldn't…?"

Occasionally they let slip something more explicit: "You mean he won't…?"

"Are you sure she…?"

"She won't put up with him for very long, I know her too well. She's not made for that."

"She's not like us two, that I do know..."

"We've been a couple of beasts of burden, that's what we've been..."

"We've been two complete asses, let's be clear about that!"

"Now, they won't truck any nonsense, they..."

It was like a cobweb, and with patience you caught a detail, a fact, a name to help decipher their language of gestures, grimaces, exclamations, hints and half-words. As far as I was concerned, they always spoke about the same thing; just as once almost the only topic used to be my father's illness and imprisonment, now conversations were all centred on Aunt Enriqueta's lunacies and the unhappiness of Pere Màrtir, the boyfriend they preferred, even though they'd huff and puff and complain about the behaviour of the masters, Mr. and Mrs. Manubens, the upsets suffered by my mother's two sisters, Aunt Felisa and her marriage of convenience to a widower—"She cried all night," said my mother, "they spent their first night in Barcelona, at the Hotel Jardí, a cheap little hotel, don't be under any illusions, no big spending, 'cause I reckon he's so mean he even finds it a strain to give you the time of day, and she cried all night, the poor thing," and Aunt Mariona, who lived in Barcelona and now missed country life, "The crazy dear says she sometimes runs away to the top of Tibidabo to see if she can catch sight of our woods, and tears come whenever I tell her about the village and farm," and sometimes about France and the people in France.

"Mariona will tell me everything when I see her," concluded Mother, as if she possessed an older sister's right to clear up the chaos in the family. "I'll keep an eye out to make sure this couple of innocents don't go barking up another wrong tree."

If the sun hadn't set, they'd have gone talking for hours, because they never gave up, it beggared belief that what I thought to be such petty existences could generate such long debates, and I noted the regret in their gripes and reproaches, as if they were lamenting they'd not lived more, that they'd not dared open any closed doors, as if life had slipped through their hands when they still felt it beating in their hearts, as if work had wasted them away and they now had to console each other for the loss of the lives they had once led as girls.

That dusk Mother's hugs were tighter than usual and she said nothing. I could sense she wanted to but the words wouldn't come. Her eyes glistened but she didn't cry and I steeled myself not to shed a tear. Aunt Ció clasped me to her and said: "Come on, there's nothing to worry about. You'll see each other all the time."

Mother only said: "It's what his father would have wanted."

I made an effort not to look back when we went our different ways. Nevertheless, I wasn't sure about my new role as an adult, as an orphan abandoned to his own devices, and knew I couldn't let myself be swayed by nostalgia or melancholy. Growing up was all about that: breaking with the past and moving forward pitilessly, forcefully, and not looking back, as Quirze used to say, brutally if needs be, because that new world was harsh and only accepted the bravest, the most intelligent or wealthiest.

A few days later Mr. and Mrs. Manubens drove up in a black car. They greeted me with an "Are you ready to go now?" that stunned me, but then they rushed upstairs and went into a conclave with my uncle, aunt and grandmother and said nothing else to me. I was free for the whole day, and Cry-Baby and I ran to the threshing floor, the pond and hazel tree spinney, but we didn't burrow into our little den because we were both rather apprehensive and weren't sure what was going to become of us and we went straight to the wall around the heartsease garden and looked over at the meadow but nobody was there, perhaps it was too early or too late, though the green grass gleamed brightly, like a field of alfalfa that nobody has trampled over, and the trees' shade was pointless because there were no sick boys protecting their heads or bellies and the stunted, dried-out elm tree of my naked young man seemed ugly and flaky without his body beside it, a solitary, old tree with cracked branches and a hollow trunk, practically leafless, a moribund tree of no use to anyone.

I felt as if I'd been stabbed in the chest, as if my heart was warning me I'd been infected with a sickness, a mortal infection. We stayed there a while, our heads looking over the wall, our eyes staring at the empty meadow as if we couldn't come to terms with the fact that the sickly boys had abandoned us. It was the becalmed silence of a cemetery.

Cry-Baby said nothing, I was sure she was waiting for me to tire of that panorama and start our retreat. She always acted like an appendix to my desires. But I struggled to give up that vista, as if I could fill that desolate space with the memories and images I carried within me. I felt cheated, betrayed, as if the TB patients in the Saint Camillus infirmary had sworn an oath to dupe me. An act of infidelity. I'd never desired anything so vehemently as to gaze yet again at the naked youth lying in the shade from the elm tree. It was a new desire, like the rage I had discovered slumbering within me, a hazy, delicious desire, more languid and remote than any of the urgent desires I'd felt hitherto, a longing for something infinite and immeasurable, that swathed my whole body from the roots of the hairs on my head to my toes, and I was terrified I would lose it far from the contemplation of that pale, slender body, marked by a sinister fate that lent it urgency, an intensity healthy bodies didn't possess. And a moment came when I felt a stab of pain that brought a bittersweet taste, like the handful of saffron Aunt Ció threw into the rice to tinge it yellow, or the mixture of quince and cream cheese that brought a delicious bitterness to the plate and left a dry, tart taste on the palate that lasted long after the food was gone from the mouth. Cry-Baby's mute presence at my side, pursuing with her eyes the paths mine were tracing, had just shown me in a diffuse, unconscious way that only sacrifice can dignify that feeling of pleasure, that the mixture of desire and rejection, of desertion and acceptance, of annihilation and vitality, was the secret formula provoking that supreme pleasuring. That was the only way to explain the no-show by the sickly youths that afternoon, the sickly retinue of my adolescent prince and his mantle of a white, blood stained sheet, like the immaculate habits of the Saint Camillus order stained by the red cross, because his refusal to display himself to me for that one last time was the unambiguous mark of the longing he left in my memory, the thrust of the spear that would always remind me of his existence, the indelible memory that would live on within me, an absence hallowed by inner contemplation. It was nothingness, was Cry-Baby demanding nothing beneath the hazel trees; it was my mother's conversations with Aunt Ció in those long twilight farewells that only made any sense as an evocation of absences, as endless litanies for a stubborn, faithful advocacy that was terrible in its despairing, in its devotion.

We left the hazel tree spinney without doing or saying anything. The emptiness of the monastery garden seemed to have infected me. We returned to the farmhouse listless and aimless as if our legs were powering us, our minds a blank. Cry-Baby followed on behind but I couldn't feel her presence as on previous occasions. She was like a shadow at my side, without strength or will.

By the time we reached the gallery, Mr. and Mrs. Manubens were already on their feet and ready to go. Aunt Ció had prepared a bundle of my folded clothes. Grandmother rubbed her eyes and spectacles with a handkerchief.

"We'll come back for anything he's forgotten," said Mrs. Manubens. "Nothing at all for you to worry about."

As sullen as ever, Dad Quirze silently paced from one end to the other of the gallery. Now and then he looked me up and down, because you couldn't exactly say he looked *at* me, he ran his eyes over me, registering my presence in a kind of furtive glance, as if he was afraid of being trapped, and he said nothing. Then Mr. Manubens and Dad Quirze started to go downstairs ahead of the others, talking about the farm, the animals, the harvests, the market... Mrs. Manubens walked next to Aunt Ció with the bundle of clothes and my aunt told her what I liked to eat and what I hated, like beans, fresh cheese and the apron of cream on milk that's just been milked, but she assured her I would eat anything, that I had a good appetite and was very responsive. Before going downstairs with Cry-Baby, I went over to Grandmother, hugged her and kissed her on the cheek. She smiled and whispered: "The four bigwigs..."

I didn't know what to say and she pushed away me with her hand: "Off you go now, don't keep these people waiting. You've got to fly the flag, those people don't wait even for the king."

When the car, driven extremely cautiously by Mr. Manubens, juddered off, I looked through the window at the group on the edge of the track, my aunt and uncle and cousins all together, looking at us with that same expression we'd adopt on at school when the photographer came to take a class photo, with the teacher amidst the toddlers, eyes open wide and faces all expectant, waiting for the gadget to click so we could go back to our normal gestures, wanting all that to be immortalized in someone's memory, in my memory, the memory that freezes us in a few seconds at an exact given time, on a byway of existence, in an ordinary context that only a photo or memory can transform into something exceptional.

40

I lived those first days in Mr. and Mrs. Manubens' bungalow on the outskirts of Igualada that locals dubbed a "mansion," by the road heading to Santa Margarida de Montbui,
in a passive state, as if they had anaesthetized me.

I tried not to think, feel or be surprised by anything. Even
so, I took note of every detail, I registered every change,
observed each new feature, storing them in my mind so
I would behave in an appropriate fashion. The bungalow
had one maid who lived in and another who came on every
working day to help her, and a chauffeur who acted as gar-
dener and general handyman. Mrs. Manubens rarely left
home, to be driven to mass, in the Holy Christ's church at
the entrance to town, or buy the odd thing from the shops
on the main street, never in the market; Mr. Manubens
spent the entire day out, in the new factory or visiting his
farms.

I was allotted a clean and spacious bedroom, some
way from the main sitting room, with a balcony overlooking the garden and an adjacent lavatory with a bath, and
it all seemed luxurious and too big for just me. Later on I
heard comments on the fashion among the district's *nouveaux riches*, also called the *arrivistes*—a rich man wasn't
the same as an *arriviste* or a plutocrat that was the highest
level of *arriviste* or *nouveau riche* with a touch of the black-
marketeer—who liked to compare the quantity and quality
of the bathrooms they installed in their newly built bunga-
lows, mansions or flats—which they were beginning to call
their "residences"—as one indicator of their wealth and standard of living: social success depended on their bathrooms

and the fixtures they contained, porcelain bidets, Venetian mirrors, small cabinets with medicine chests and expensive perfumes, baths with a range of taps made of chrome, stainless steel, gold... The first thing farmers of the locality did when luck began to shine on them was to multiply the number of their bathrooms and buy large Seat cars. Mr. and Mrs. Manubens sometimes commented on such behaviour over lunch and had quite a laugh, because they considered themselves to be a longstanding wealthy family and were amused by a competitive hygiene they viewed with highly patronizing disdain. They, or so they claimed, never talked about bathrooms or politics. To talk about such things was to show a lack of breeding, or so they said.

I liked the dry climate and the surrounding wild, but attractive, landscape. The winter sun was warmer and shone for longer than on the plain. The light was more diaphanous. People, when I got to know a few, were more cheerful and gregarious and spoke with a slight emphasis on their vowels that showed how close we were to the territory of Lleida.

The school was in the Escolapian monastery, the same order that owned the church of Holy Christ of which my sponsor was a parishioner, a huge, ramshackle building on the road out of the city, at once dingy and disconcerting, with neo-Gothic pretentions local architects had invented to ennoble the sudden wealth of local landowners. They made a subtle distinction between landowners and small farmers in the conversations that Mr. and Mrs. Manubens allowed me to be present at, the small farmers were a sub-species of *nouveaux riches*, however much they might have become agricultural entrepreneurs, and the landowners, sometimes described as property owners, who were property owners in their own right—conventions promoted by the religious orders that had spread across the country to reinforce the faith and influence society, starting at the top, with future leaders, in the belief that those on high, the upper class and upper middle class, would project their behaviour and faith over ordinary people.

My classmates accepted me straightforwardly. The Escolapian in charge of the year, the one they called Father Prefect, let it be known, without any prior warning to me, that I was Mr. and Mrs. Manubens' nephew, and that my father had been killed in the war. He didn't mention my mother and nobody asked me anything else about my past ever. Most of the pupils were boys from well-off or well-to-do families—that were sometimes dubbed as the comfortably off or moneyed—I never did find out whether the second was a riff on the first: other subtle distinctions existed between a well-off or well-to-do household, a good household and one of high standing, the former were merely acceptable, met the minimum standard to warrant rubbing shoulders, a good household was a notch higher in the pecking order as a result of wealth or tradition, was one that deserved respect and could be treated on equal terms, and a family of high standing was at the pinnacle of the social ladder, the three or four families that weren't simply good but shared out the chief responsibilities and sinecures in the municipality, be it the Town Hall, the Patronage of the Holy Christ church, the ownership of the small provincial bank or the couple of industries that had been re-established after the war. They were the people who moulded the city's identity and shaped its future, who had splendid links with the powers-that-be in Barcelona, and, above all, in Madrid; some classmates came from good households but almost none from high-standing families because as soon as the latter—the boys and exceptionally a girl—were ready for secondary school at the age of ten or eleven, they were sent to board with the Escolapians in Sarrià or the Jesuits, some even boarded in La Molina or in Puigcerdà so they could spend their weekends skiing, hoity-toity ladies at their soirées would say they practised white sports to friends hanging on their arms. There were also scholarship holders from small farming communities, but they were older and acted as monitors or *ayos*—everything was in Spanish and we called them *iaios*—who watched over us even in the lavatories and timed how long we stayed in a stall, if we dallied, they rudely rapped on the door to warn us we'd been inside too long, because it wasn't good for us to spend that amount of time on our bodily needs, unless we were ill, and if that was the case, they informed us with a formula the prefect had taught them, it behoved us to pay the doctor a visit.

I immediately befriended a lad of my age in my year who came daily from a nearby village; he lived in a big farmhouse and initially was as reserved and silent as I was. The fact he was from a farm and the way his large, purple eyes bulged when he looked at anyone predisposed me to find him nice and friendly. He spoke sincerely, never spitefully, and described his father as an almighty god of thunder who forced his family to jump to his orders and allowed nobody to answer back. He forced him to study and prescribed the grades he must get. I realized that he lived in fear of his father and that was why he delayed going home as long as he could. Later on in the school year I invited him to the bungalow for a snack and so we could study together, but after two or three visits Mr. and Mrs. Manubens insinuated indirectly during supper, when often the three of us were round the table, that the boy had a long way to walk back to his house and perhaps his family wouldn't appreciate him staying back with me so often, he seemed a nice enough boy though he was rather slow on the uptake and possibly not as intelligent as he ought to be, and I should be making lots of friends, not just one, and you could be sure there were lots of boys from good households who could help me later on, who knows, life takes many twists and turns, one knows only too well, they become contacts, friendships, relationships, connections, acquaintances, allies, helping hands, old boys' networks…whatever, because you could never tell what might help in the future, and you never forget your childhood friends.

From my contact with Quim, his deference towards his father, and his life terrorized by the terrible shadow he threw over the farmhouse, I concluded I'd been very lucky with my own father, who was never angry with me, never forced me to do anything and always taught me to be completely free, even of clingy, emotional ties and viscous tears and laments. In this respect, his death was yet more proof of his generosity, of the way he opened up a road to freedom for me, without imposing the least obstacle or hindrance. I wondered how poor Quim would feel if he were ever freed from his father's powerful grip. I now lived under the shadow of Mr. and Mrs. Manubens, but with every day that passed I understood ever more clearly that when I became tired of them, I would leave, as soon as I felt adult and strong enough to stand on my own two feet.

Quim's life also affirmed the value of sacrifice, my father's in the first place, now he'd been transformed into a likable, distant memory I could summon when it suited me. I carried an equally light burden of the faces of Cry-Baby and of Grandmother Mercè when she said, "I'm on my way out now, but you two are still young and have a long way to go," a pleasant farewell that involved no recriminations or paralyzing promises, or the naked youth with TB in his silent struggle against death who had no idea of the energy he radiated, and besides that he carried in his baggage pain, sacrifice, illness and remoteness, all these acts preached and exalted by the church meant their figures were hooked even more powerfully into my memory, as if blood congealed their influence to us, enabling me to find them at will and seek refuge in the images they projected and to go my way convinced they would accompany us for ever more, that they formed part of us.

During those early days I summoned these idols to the solitude of my huge, austere room, and that made it easier for me to accept the change, the nostalgia, the new routines, and they always appeared against a backcloth of woods, a dark, enclosed wood, a deep, deep green, silent still wood that cloaked every mystery. A mystery needed a signal before it showed itself, and the woods masked the mystery that had to be unmasked.

We knew about these mysteries because of the traces they left, without those telltale signs only nothingness would exist, or so I thought. The woods, that in my imagination included the hazel tree spinney and the heartsease garden with the TB patients and their white sheets, was the shrine that hid and safeguarded the mystery of my entire future, everything that had to happen, everything that awaited me that I still found unfamiliar. The woods were a hideout and salvation that at once revealed and hid itself, that was simultaneously manifest and secret, within the same vision it displayed and camouflaged, enclosing and opening up paths..., like a promise it does and doesn't exhibit, like a small chest whose contents are unknown but whose mere presence implies secrecy and heralds mystery. Like the crust on black bread, on the desolate altar of the poor, its reality alone pointed to the whole ritual of sacrifice and pain that it nourished.

Near the bungalow and small city, there were no woods like mine, the one I felt to be my own, the landscape was all hillocks, sandy soil, clumps of pine trees and brush, and broad, bright, gently undulating hills. My mind was full of ravines, dark, inaccessible valleys, deep, damp arbours, dangerous gorges, abysses and escarpments, precipices... woods that were wild and enticing, that contained everything, where anything might happen, where one could get hopelessly lost, endless, infinite woods leading to France, to the end of the world, to freedom...

Mr. and Mrs. Manubens acted kindly and on Sundays they didn't wake me up to go to first mass, but mid-morning, to go to solemn mass, sometimes with Mr.

Manubens, sometimes by myself. They didn't tell rosary beads in the evening, but listened to the radio or put records on a small, hand-wound gramophone and they listened to their music in silent rapture, music I thought sounded like the litanies and dirges of the friars in their monastery; they often invited friends and the odd priest and chattered away, drank coffee and ate sweets, wafers and small pastries. They always summoned me to these conversations in the main sitting room and introduced me to their guests, who all shook my hand and gave me intrigued glances and I'd sit there for a few minutes, depending on what they were talking about, and soon after I'd stand up and say my good-byes using the excuse that I had to study or do homework. An old pharmacist who took a shine to me early on always put his hand on my waist and sometimes even pinched my legs or shoulder, joking: "Here's the heir!" or else: "So what's the heir of the house got to say for himself?"

I found the old pharmacist amusing, he'd flatter me though at the same time I found him rather disturbing. Occasionally, for no apparent reason, perhaps presentiments that arose from somewhere deep inside me, he reminded me of the figure of Mr. Madern, the teacher, and then, when I thought about it, on my way back to my room, I had experienced a new kind of fascination and excitement.

I could hear echoes of the conversations half-muffled by the walls in the passage, which I ignored, but sometimes, though not very often, if a word or sentence intrigued me, I'd listen and tiptoe to the door to catch what they were saying. But I never understood much and only grasped that they flitted easily enough from one topic to another, one minute they talked about the missions the bishopric was organizing in local villages to convert the world of labour—they talked a lot about the world of labour, never about the world of the working class my father used to talk about—and the Catholic Centres that had to welcome and set aright this world that had gone off the rails, and then it was the struggle against the Maquis and the lack of understanding shown by putrefying democratic states, then the different branches of Catholic Action, or whether it was or wasn't time for a change in the Town Hall and how they would balance their own candidates with the ones suggested by the Administration in Barcelona and the government in Madrid. The topics I found most amusing and accessible were the ones broached by Mrs. Manubens and her friends, who were fanatical about morality, that's what they called it "morality," as if it were an institution and above individuals, and they would argue about whether the bishop should ban once and for all couples dancing cheek to cheek, what they also described as modern dancing, that the authorities tolerated, or the way women dressed—here lay another subtle difference between women and ladies, women belonged to the common people and they and their friends were upper-class ladies—who couldn't wear skirts above the knee or sleeves above the elbow, and low necklines were completely banned, distinctions I found all the more amusing because I could never have imagined anyone bothering their heads about such trivia.

I began to feel better and better in that household with those people who lived so differently to the way of life I'd known with my family, at home or on the farm. These were people who never raised their voices, who never went in for melodramatic gestures, who never went out looking a mess or wanted to spend more money than they had, who couldn't bear to hear or see anything offensive to the eye or the ear, who always had someone in tow so they didn't have to stoop down if they dropped something on the ground, who seemed to live on fresh air, without doing a stroke or ever "getting their hands dirty" as women textile workers would say, who were never so hungry they couldn't defer until they found exactly the right delicacy to appeal to their palate, who knew how to behave properly towards everyone with the requisite

pleasantry on their lips from their repertoire of polite commonplaces and courteous smiles, that were never expressions of genuine joy, who lived their lives as if they were gods
because they knew their interests were eternal and would
pass from heir to heir across the generations, who possessed
so many qualities and opportunities it was impossible not to
be touched by their allure, their magnetism and their energy.

The event that marked my definitive break with the past
and my complete acceptance of the new world I was being
offered was my mother's visit. Mr. and Mrs. Manubens had
announced that my mother would come to see me any day
now, though they didn't know which. And one cold wintry
morning, with a freezing bite that reminded me of the icy
roads and frosted fields of the plain, the prefect interrupted
our class to tell me I had a visitor. Someone was waiting
for me, or so he said, in the visitors' room in the lobby. I
walked warily downstairs, trying to keep my mind blank,
acting under that total anaesthesia I'd committed myself to
that was bringing such good results. The second I opened
the frosted glass door to the small room, I found myself
face to face with my mother, standing in the centre, looking at me with bright, shiny eyes.

Mother was wearing a simple black dress, a dark, nondescript headscarf and ash-coloured stockings. Her hair was
gathered at the back of her head backwards with the curls
of an ancient perm bunched on the nape of her neck, the
only visible flourish, the remains of a grace that had been
ravaged. I thought she looked thinner and her cheeks and
forehead were lined with what seemed to be huge scars.
She was holding a cheap, lurid patent leather bag. I wore
my loose-fitting blue-striped uniform, a good size ten, as
Grandmother would have said.

We hugged each other silently, and I shut my eyes, my
face pressed against her chest.

I remembered that oily factory smell, mixed with the dry-
ness of the flock and the roughness of the skeins of raw cotton,

all tinged with a cheap cologne that smelled of medicine or pure alcohol, making my nose itch and me quite queasy.

"Are you all right?" she asked in a wispy voice.

I nodded.

"Do you need anything?"

"No…," I replied.

She didn't want to sit down. She said she'd first gone to the mansion but as she couldn't wait for me there because the only train to get back to Vic in the evening left at midday, they'd told her she would find me at school, on the road out of the town, that she couldn't miss it. She said she'd had to catch the first train from Puigcerdà when it was still dark and then change stations in Barcelona. That Tuites, a workmate of hers, was working two shifts in a row so she could leave the factory for a day with the boss's permission and tomorrow she would do the same for her.

"You know what they're like…" she commented as if she was talking about foreigners in exotic garb.

I didn't want to imagine what those people were like, what that distant world was like, or what anything I'd left behind was like, I strained not to think of that difficult journey and the futile—futile?—efforts made by Mother to come and see me. My heart beat painfully as I imagined her nibbling the bread and cheese or fried sausage she no doubt had carried in her bag so she could have lunch by herself in a forlorn corner of the train station. Something inside me cried out against the invasion of my new world by that skinny, frail, aged, lonely woman who was completely at a loss. An impulse that didn't surface because it was drowned by a wave of tenderness, warmth, sympathy, affection and melancholy that disappeared in an inner sea of tears. However, those tears wouldn't come, I refused to let them, I fought to repress and dilute them with that impulse that sustained my quiet, polite, formal behaviour, formal manners that could never be breached in my new universe in that lean and sunny land.

Mother kept repeating: "Are they treating you well?"

"Do you miss us?"

"Do you eat everything up?"

"Do you sleep...?"

Or recommendations like: "Be good..."

"Don't give them any reason to complain about you..."

"Make the most of everything..."

"Let them see we brought you up properly, that you're a well-mannered..."

We said hardly anything else. We had *nothing* else to say. The visit was over in next to no time. I accompanied her to the door and we both walked past the reception counter, where an old Escolapian and a scholarship boy who were filling in forms glanced up and gave us strange looks. Out on the road we kissed on the cheeks and she said that at Christmas she'd ask an old workmate of my father who now drove a small truck taking small jobs from the leather factories in Vic to those in Igualada whether he wouldn't mind bringing me back to town for the holidays, that the train journey by myself would be too complicated and she wouldn't be able to come back. I nodded halfheartedly. When she walked off down the grey, sparsely populated road towards the station, I shut my eyes so as not to see her.

I can still see her looking forlorn and lonely in the Escolapians' cold little waiting room, a room with shabby, monastic furniture, like a waiting room in a hospital for incurable paupers, with her sad smile and that factory smell no washing powder could eradicate and her almost empty garish, tacky bag, I could see her staring at me, her eyes glued to me, her whole bony body without an ounce of fat turned anxiously towards me, waiting for me, hour after hour on wooden benches in third-class compartments just to spend a few minutes with me.

I was stunned for the rest of the day. The two forces my mother's visit had released within me were fighting a muffled, mute out-and-out war inside me.

When I reached the bungalow—it didn't take much for me to call and make it my home—Mrs. Manubens and the maid referred to it pleasantly enough, not expecting any reply, as if it had been a trivial run-of-the-mill event.

"Did you see your mother, boy?"

"I expect she was pleased to see you."

And that was all they said.

That evening the three of us had dinner together and I ate very little. My stomach felt knotted up, in an irritating though not painful way. Mere irritation. Mr. Manubens told us excitedly that the factory business was going full steam ahead, that we'd go to Barcelona next week to meet a big manufacturer, one of the most powerful in the province, who had good contacts and relationships with Madrid and so on...

That night, in bed, I heard nothing of the conversations with the visitors who dropped by for a coffee. I hid my head under my pillow and was on the verge of shedding tears but they wouldn't come, they were dissolved by that opposing energy unleashed by my rejection of everything I didn't want to let back into my life. Deep, deep down the light from images of Cry-Baby and the boy with TB lying on a sheet in the monastery garden glowed mournfully. I didn't know what to do with them. It was like my mother's visit, I didn't know how to react to their pull, to the danger posed by their mute cry, to the demands made by their irrational felicity.

The silent, resplendent woods, the backcloth to everything, kept questioning me, like a pledge that wouldn't fade away.

And then I rediscovered that source of support I'd found on my last day of class at the Novíssima, that deep, persistent, implacable rage unleashed against everything and everybody, and I felt I possessed the strength to stay where I was and root myself in that house and turn my back—albeit politely, ever so politely, their supreme virtue—on my whole previous world.

It was my life, my decision, my future, my road, my body, my feelings, my choice, my experience, my rejection, my desire, my acceptance, my studies, my dreams, my world as new as I could make it, and my books...mine, mine, mine!

As my raging thoughts raised me above everything else in a fascinating dream-like flight, and the woods remained down below, secret, still and inscrutable, intrigued by my transformation, with a mixture of vanity and trepidation, I recognized that I was beginning to change into a monster. Into the monster they had planned I should be. Into a monster able to unite in a single body, in a single life, two different natures, two contrary experiences. A monster I myself hadn't realized was living within me. A monster.

About the Author

Emili Teixidor was born in 1933 in Roda de Ter, a small town midway between Barcelona and the French border, where he set up a writers' group with poet Miquel Martí Pol. In 1959 he founded a progressive Catalan school in Barcelona and ten years later started writing children's literature in the belief that there was a need for good writing in Catalan. His historical novel *The Firebird* (1972) became a popular classic. His first book for adult readers was a short story collection, *Sic transit Gloria Swanson* (1979). He edited a French film magazine in Paris in 1976–77. Subsequently Teixidor returned to post-Franco Barcelona where he worked as a publisher, newspaper columnist and television and radio scriptwriter. At the age of 70 he published *Black Bread*, the first of three novels exploring life in rural Catalonia in the immediate postwar years. The novel met with critical acclaim, won four literary prizes, and was made into a successful film, the first Catalan film ever to be nominated by Spain for an Oscar. The novel is recognized as one of the major works of contemporary Catalan literature.

Emili Teixidor died in Barcelona in 2012.

About the Translator

Peter Bush is a freelance literary translator and scholar who lives in Oxford, England. He has translated novels from the Spanish by Carmen Boullosa, Juan Goytisolo, Juan Carlos Onetti and Leonardo Padura, among others. Since 2007 he has also translated fiction by leading Catalan authors including Najat el Hachmi, Quim Monzo, Josep Pla, Mercè Rodoreda, Joan Sales and his wife, Teresa Solana. His translation of Josep Pla's *The Gray Notebook* won the 2014 Ramon Llull Literary Translation Prize and his translation of Joan Sales's *Uncertain Glory* was named as one of *The Economist*'s ten best works of fiction for 2014. In 2015 he was awarded the Saint George's Cross by the Catalan government for his translation and promotion of Catalan literature.